The Money Maker

THE

Money Maker

John J. McNamara, Jr.

THOMAS Y. CROWELL COMPANY

New York, Established 1834

Designed by Abigail Moseley

Manufactured in the United States of America

L.C. Card 72–82859
ISBN 0–690–55377–3

1 2 3 4 5 6 7 8 9 10

To the girls who made this book

Prologue

The jet, racing over the North Atlantic, spewed a silver contrail into the blue May sky. Far below, the dark green of the ocean lay tranquil and cloudless in the afternoon sun. On the flight deck, the co-pilot was just completing his check with Shannon Flight Control. He leaned toward the dozing pilot.

"Want me to disturb the boss?"

"No, I'll do it."

In theory, this Boeing 707 was a corporate asset of the nineteen thousand shareholders of Steele Minerals. For reasons leaked or gleaned by a powerful few, their shares that day were the most actively traded on the American Stock Exchange in New York. In reality, the Boeing 707 was the personal air yacht of the Chairman of the Board of Steele Minerals Company. His name was Jason Steele.

Jason Steele was awakened by a soft buzzing from the intercom near his head. He stretched across the well-tanned buttocks between him and the phone, giving them a light slap.

"Marty, get your ass up."

Marty replied with an awakening "Ooh" and curled up her long limbs. Steele propped a pillow against the bulkhead in the double bunk and picked up the receiver. "Yes."

"Mr. Steele. We'll be crossing the Irish coast in another four minutes. Air Traffic Control is expecting no delays. We'll be starting our descent in another hour and be on the ground, Geneva, right on schedule, five o'clock local."

"Very good." Steele replaced the call director, and by watching the panel lights knew the pilot was repeating his message to the other members of his party in the main lounge.

"Marty, you better get up to your cabin. Mrs. Wales will be by to wake you up as soon as the pilot finishes that announcement."

"Oh, very well." To get to her own cabin, Marty had to crawl over the naked Jason Steele. As she did, he cupped both of her breasts and gave them a firm squeeze. "Draw our bath as you go through."

"Yes, Mr. Steele, will that be all, Mr. Steele?"

"Impertinent bitch, I'll deal with you later."

Marty opened the door in the forward bulkhead to reveal a fully appointed bathroom. She turned on the water, tested the temperature and then slid aside the full-length mirror by pressing one of the attaching rosettes. This took her on into her own cabin. She silently slid the mirror back into place to face another full-length image of herself. As she was slipping on a negligee, there was a gentle knocking on her door. She opened it without pause. Marty faced Elizabeth Wales, Jason Steele's svelte, middle-aged executive secretary.

"Marty, the pilot has told us that we can expect to be in Geneva on schedule. We are over Ireland now. Sorry to break in on your nap. I wondered if you would join me in the secretarial cabin in a half hour. I'd like to run a final check on the deposit statements and our list of World Equities shareholders."

"I'd be glad to, Elizabeth. It will take me a few minutes to get put together."

"Take your time. I thought I'd go on up to my cabin and freshen up. Say in half an hour?"

"Yes, I'll be there." Marty closed the door and drew the locking bolt. As she hurriedly disrobed again, she mused, "How did a nice girl like you, Marty Darnley, ever get mixed up in a job like this, and with an operator like Jason Steele?

4

He's really something else . . . hidden sliding doors built into his bathroom, just so people won't know he's sleeping with his secretary . . ."

She again released the hidden catch, and slipped into the bathroom. The bath was two-thirds drawn and the temperature just right. She went on into Steele's cabin. He had dozed off, so she studied the body before her.

Jason Steele, Captain of Finance. Big enough bastard. The better part of six four. The face was a strong face with deep-set blue eyes and heavy, darkened jowls. When he smiled, he could be kind, but then again Jason Steele wasted little time smiling. In the Steele Company he was rude, overbearing, impatient, egotistical. In his sleep, he didn't look that way. His hair had thinned on top, but around the edges it was still black and thick. Marty thought back over the past year's change. Ever since the company had started business with these people in Switzerland, Jason had let his sideburns steal down the flanks of his jowls until now, this afternoon, he looked quite mod and rakish. This now showed in his latest wardrobe from London. Marty recalled the buying spree on their way to Africa last fall.

Perhaps it was his style that Marty admired most. He did things big, everything big—the planes, the limousines, the offices, the ranch, everything, including the women.

Marty smiled to herself. "Three hundred a week from the company, trinkets on the side, and trips all over the world . . . now what's wrong with that for a twenty-year-old. So I have to sleep with the boss every so often . . ." She shrugged to herself, and went back to her study of the dozing man. "Too bad he eats so much. He'd be a good-looking man if he didn't."

"Your bath is drawn, my lord."

Jason reached up and pulled her over him so that her nipples were just above his face. She felt his hand, that had been around her back, slide down between her legs.

"Your bath, Mr. Steele." Marty stepped around him and gracefully eased into the warm water.

When Jason slid in after her, his bulk forced the water over the edge of the large tub. He took up a face cloth and

5

lathered her bosom and armpits. Wriggling with the tingle of
the warm waters and the coarse cloth, Marty was the first to
come back to the reality of their flight.

"Come on, Jason, I've got work to do."

"Who says?" Jason was in no hurry.

"Elizabeth Wales."

"Damn that woman. She will not run my sex life, too."

An hour later, Jason Steele joined his staff in the main
lounge. The motif of this area was that of a gentleman's club
at the turn of the century, as interpreted by the Steele Company
interior decorators. There were deep, dark leather armchairs
set about in an informal quadrangle, each with its own footrest
and side table. Along the starboard side, there was a built-in
oaken bar from which hung a spot-lit Remington painting of
a wagon train of settlers struggling west in the teeth of a
blizzard.

As Jason entered the lounge, he met the thunderous snores
of Augustus Codman Emery. That was to be expected, for
Augustus Codman Emery drank too much. He was President of
Western Investors Company, a personal holding of Jason's, and
not the shareholders of Steele Minerals. Far too few had ever
read the fine print of the many prospectuses and segregated
that which was Jason's from that of his public shareholders.
Jason liked it that way, and in many speeches used the phrase
"The Steele Complex" as often as possible to create further fog.

Western Investors had offices all over the United States,
overstuffed with tailored and loquacious Ivy Leaguers. These
men touted the virtues of the several Steele Investment Funds
to the financial community, who in turn, for an 8 percent commission, sold the funds to the investing public. The fund companies were also owned by Jason Steele. Augustus Codman
Emery commanded these selling legions quite effectively when
sober. They called him "the Ace." With almost seven hours in
the air and an open bar, Jason could hardly have expected the
Ace to be sober. Thank God he was sleeping it off and there
was another half hour until Geneva. He could recuperate like
no man Jason had ever met.

Across from Emery on a leather couch slept Jason Steele's attorney and father confessor of the past ten years, the distinguished Boston attorney Elliot N. Hall. Jason decided it opportune to have a few quiet words with Hall before the rest of the party assembled for the landing. He tapped him on the sole of his shoe, and as the man yawned himself into wakefulness, Jason went over to the icebox beneath the bar. He took from it a fresh gouda cheese, and with a paring knife and box of crackers in hand, returned to an armchair beside Hall. When bothered, Jason ate.

"Elliot, you think we can trust the schmuck?"

"Are you referring to the celebrated Commissioner of the Securities and Exchange Commission?"

"I am." There was an air of exasperation in his answer. Jason knew that fifty-odd million of his own cash and perhaps his career and whole fortune rode on the outcome of this flight. He was aware of a nervousness within him that he could not set aside, but he wouldn't admit it, even to himself. Jason Steele never considered defeat. He had never a thought for the possible wreckage of the jobs, the life styles and the dreams of those enmeshed in the Steele empire.

Hall droned on in measured tones.

"Jason, the way I heard the conversation, Bernstein said virtually nothing. He in no way committed the Commission to any course of action."

"Well, if we make this play, what do you think they'll do?"

"I'm not sure. You did most of the talking and Bernstein did most of the listening. The one clue might be his using the phrase out of the American sales ban."

"Which phrase?"

"Remember when he used the words 'or associates'?"

"Yes, so what?"

"That's verbatim out of the S.E.C. decree regarding geographical restriction that World Equities signed two years ago. No associates of World Equities can do business within the jurisdiction of the S.E.C. either."

"Let's not play games. What are you getting at?"

"I think what could be in Bernstein's mind is, that if you

make this play, even if you do it by loans to World Equities Ltd., rather than taking over the shares, then by barring of the association, they might block you, if they so choose."

"What do you mean, if they so choose? If they push me too far, I'll take the thing right over their heads so fast . . ."

"Do you mean to the President?"

"Of course. Why the hell do you think we gave them half a million the last campaign?"

Elliot Hall rose to his feet, removed his half-rim glasses, and slowly rubbed the bridge of his nose. "I just don't know, Jason. It might be too big or too delicate for him to interfere. Balance of payments, political favoritism and that kind of thing. Remember Bernstein is a holdover from the previous administration and terribly outspoken."

Jason stomped to his feet and got to ". . . of course it's big. What the hell do you think . . ." when the buzz of the intercom distracted him. He reached for the phone.

"Steele here."

"Mr. Steele, we're cleared down to twelve. Expect clearance for an I.L.S. approach in another six minutes. Landing to the northeast. You may expect to see some of Geneva come up under the starboard wing."

Jason snapped the receiver into its notch and gazed pensively at the unchanging Swiss peaks, now rushing by even with the wing tips.

The 707 came to a whining halt by a waiting ramp in the general aviation area. Jason Steele could see the World Equities people had really laid things on. They had borrowed a debarking ramp from Swissair and from the officialdom standing about the waiting ramp, it seemed the Customs and Immigration authorities were being helpful. The five large Mercedes limousines were the final touch. No, there was something else that he had missed at first glance. There was a cluster of men waiting behind the glass doors of the aviation building. It would appear that they had been locked from the open aircraft area. They had to be the press.

8

Jason mused to himself. Well, that lets the cat out of the bag. The crimson trim of his private 707 was now well known. A recent *Forbes Magazine* cover had shown Steele with the plane in the background. If that didn't do it, they could certainly figure it out from the big red "S" on the stabilizer. He grimaced for an instant . . . shit, I needed a little more time . . . and then barked, "Where's Clayman?"

A now awakened Augustus Codman Emery replied. "When last I spoke with him, he was planning to do some work in the secretarial cabin."

"Get him."

Sol Clayman was Jason Steele's legal specialist in matters dealing with the United States Securities and Exchange Commission. He was an expert on what could or could not be said in print without violating their laws. He should have been, for the S.E.C. had been his employer for six years. Clayman now appeared in the main lounge, a tall, thin, very intense young man, rather baggy in his dress and with bushy hair that sprang up about a balding center.

"Yes, Mr. Steele."

"Sol, see the group there behind that glass door? It's the press, I'm sure. Damned if I know how they got wind of this. Possibly that Bernstein bastard. Now, can we say anything?"

Clayman thought for a moment.

"Hmm, no, I don't think it was Bernstein. Remember, they trailed us from the S.E.C. Building out to Washington National. Our pilots had to file a flight plan. I'm sure that's how it was done. Public document, you know."

"Jesus Christ, that's not what I asked you!" Jason Steele rose to his feet and glared at the ever logical Clayman. "Can I say anything about my taking over World Equities?"

Clayman stared at his chief in disbelief.

"Absolutely not! They might construe it as a tout. Too premature."

The next morning, the financial page of *The New York Times* featured a photograph of Jason Steele striding away from the big jet and the following story:

9

MINERALS MAGNATE
TO RESCUE TROUBLED WORLD EQUITIES?

"(Lausanne)   Jason Steele, Board Chairman of Steele Minerals Company of Houston, Texas, arrived at Geneva International Airport this afternoon aboard his personal jet. He was driven immediately to Lausanne, site of the corporate headquarters of financially troubled World Equities Limited, the largest money management firm in the world. Steele took residence in the penthouse suite of the Beau Rivage Hotel, and because of the security precautions surrounding his arrival, it was impossible to determine the exact purpose of his visit. It is rumored that Steele has come to Lausanne to offer financial assistance to World Equities.

"Meanwhile, in Lausanne, the members of the World Equities Board of Directors again met behind closed doors. There was another new arrival on the World Equities scene at the morning meeting of the Board. The Baron Edouard de Fonderville, President of the famous French banking firm, the House of de Fonderville, was seen entering the W.E.L. Headquarters Building at the time of the morning meeting. Baron de Fonderville led the underwriting group that first brought the stock of World Equities Management Company into public ownership. The Baron left the massive building just after one in the afternoon. The public relations staff of World Equities declined any comment on the presence of either the Baron de Fonderville or Jason Steele in Lausanne.

"For almost two months, the Board of World Equities has been in virtually continuous session. In that same two months, the value of World Equities Management stock has fallen to less than one-third of the initial public offering price. It is rumored that there are serious financial difficulties within the company, yet to this date, the management of World Equities has declined any and all comment. It is known that with the recent fall of securities prices on the world markets, World Equities has faced heavy redemptions of its publicly held mutual funds. It is further known that all these redemptions

10

have been met to date, although the full extent of these redemptions have not yet been published. The annual audited report of World Equities Management Company is over two months late in its release. It is rumored that there is a serious controversy amongst the Board members as well as the independent auditors. The controversy supposedly centers on the recent activities of Emanuel (Manny) Kellermann, 43, the colorful Chairman of the World Equities Board.

" 'Manny' Kellermann has been described in various publications as the 'World's most successful, swinging bachelor.' When Kellermann was first released from the American Army upon cessation of the Second World War, he settled in Paris and concentrated on the sale of American mutual funds to armed forces personnel stationed in Europe. Over the intervening years, he has built his sales force to a personal army in excess of twenty thousand, scattered through every nation where his funds can be sold. In the past ten years, under the banner of World Equities Limited, he has started his own mutual funds. In accomplishing this, Kellermann and his companies have been continuously at odds with the more established European financial institutions and have several times been embroiled in litigation with national securities regulatory agencies as to sales practices. Despite these difficulties, Kellermann has managed to amass over three billions of the public monies in the mutual funds of his World Equities.

"The arrival of Jason Steele in Lausanne offers some clue as to the center of the controversy on the World Equities Board. Steele, and his natural resources development company, Steele Minerals Company, has been Kellermann's American counterpart in meteoric success. In the past ten years, Steele has built his company from humble beginnings to one of the largest independent producers of natural resources.

"How Jason Steele can be of assistance in sorting out the difficulties of World Equities is a matter of some conjecture. [In Houston, a Steele Minerals spokesman stated that Mr. Steele was not available for comment, was not in the city, and that the company was not prepared to make any comment on his trip to Lausanne or his activities at this time.]"

At the Geneva International Airport, when Jason Steele reached the bottom of the aircraft ramp, he was greeted by, "Ah, Monsieur Steele, Monsieur Leibowitz awaits you in the first Mercedes."

Jason strode on, though his instincts were to turn for another view of the French girl as she directed the rest of his party into the cortege of Mercedes. As he approached the car, he saw the rear windows were covered by drawn curtains. The door was opened by a waiting chauffeur. Jason stepped in, and the car squealed into motion, headed for the Lausanne autobahn.

"Jason, good to see you. How did it go in Washington?" A smiling Edward Leibowitz, Executive Vice-President of World Equities, shook his hand.

"Ted, you're looking well. As to Washington, I don't think we have a problem." There wasn't the glimmer of a crack in Steele's confidence as he went on. "Of course, Bernstein wouldn't commit himself, but you should have seen his face when I told him I planned to can Kellermann after the reorganization."

"So it's no problem?"

"I don't think so. If it becomes one, I'm sure I can fix Bernstein's wagon. Now, how are things going over here?"

"Well, the shit's hit the fan. The auditors definitely won't sign off the annual report unless they get a look at those documents on the Greenland sale. The English and German factions are still looking for Kellermann's head, and mine for that matter. I figure we can do better with the Limeys. They're better people in a compromise. Not so stiff-necked. Timing? I don't know. Can we do it? I'm as sure as I was last month with you in Houston."

"Are you sure you've got to go when Kellermann does?"

"Oh, why not. It will look better. New broom sweeps clean and that rot. I have no illusions about corporate titles. It's control and bucks that count. To hell with the rest of it. As to bucks, you got that matter handled in the Curaçao bank?"

"It's handled, but it wasn't easy. Hey, who was the broad at the ramp?"

"Oh, that, one of Manny's latest secretaries."

Book One

1

The wind shrilled from the nor'west for three bitter dawns. The boat shed thermometer, shuddering at ten above, belied the marrow-cutting chill of the crystal Arctic air. The slate-green ocean writhed under this assault and gave up its sun-laden heat of summer in a blanket of swirling steam.

Benjamin Steele gave small thought to the cutting cold as he rowed his squat dinghy with short jabs on the oars to his fishing boat, the *Agnes T*. Benjamin Steele was the fourth generation of Steeles to wrest his living from the waters of Massachusetts Bay. The cold was part of his life.

The fifth generation of Steeles, Jason, a strapping lad of nineteen, huddled shivering on the stern thwart of the dinghy. Jason had finished Manchester High in June, and signed on with his father as a net puller for the summer run of mackerel. They were now working the winter cod. It was this row to work each morning that gave Jason Steele a growing regret, for he detested the cold New England winter, and the whining wind made him wish he had more definite plans for his future. Occasional chunks of harbor ice clumped against the bow.

Benjamin eased the dinghy alongside the boat with a quick jab. In one motion, he had the oars in, stowed, a hand on the rail, and stood waiting on his son. The thump, as the hulls met, stirred Jason from his yearning for the warmth of bed. He climbed stiffly, yet carefully, over the ice-glazed gunwale, and he took the painter from his father. The elder Steele hauled himself aboard the cockpit of the *Agnes T.*, groped for a moment with the companionway lock, and disappeared into the engine room.

Jason set about his chores. He stirred up the coal stove, banked and smoldering from the previous day, and put on the kettle. He swept away the night's snow and scattered salt and ashes about the deck for traction. Clumsily, he dropped back into the dinghy and fetched the Swampscott dories from their own moorings. After they were lashed alongside, Jason scuttled back to the warmth of the cabin. The throaty throb of the big diesels had now joined the din of the morning.

As the Steeles finished their preparations, the first gray streaks were now full grown to the flat white of a winter dawn. Jason stoked and coaxed the coals of the iron stove to a glow, and when the kettle came to a happy chirp, he made coffee. There were no words as both Steeles replaced their shoreside clothing with scale-specked aprons, rubber gloves, and lined sea boots. The engines had settled to a warm low burble, as Ben Steele slid the dip stick of the port engine back into place. As he got to his feet. he grunted to his son, "Time to git goin'."

Jason gave him a grudging "ayuh" as he took a final gulp and headed aft for the dinghy. With the painter in hand, he cautiously eased himself out on the foredeck. The water temperature was in the thirties. It was no time for a swim. A man could last in that water a couple of minutes at best. Jason made the dinghy fast to the mooring pennant and looked aft to his father. Ben nodded his readiness. Jason cast off the pennant and bellowed into the wind, "Mooring away."

As the *Agnes T.* settled down to Ben's course, Jason checked about to see that all was as it should be aboard. Checking about was what makes for old fishermen; his father had taught him that young. Jason payed out the tow lines of the big dories on each quarter. Ben was checking too. Everything seemed okay. Maybe the kid would learn yet. Nope . . .

there was something missing. To a man of the sea, a boat is the sum of its sounds. Something missing . . . ayup . . . the radio phone. The kid hadn't turned on the radio phone. Ben reached over and clicked it on.

"Dammit, Jason. You forgot it agin, the radio." His tone was fatherly, yet firm.

"Sorry, Dad." The big youth avoided his father's eyes as he sought the shelter of the windshield.

"Some day, you won't have time to be sorry. Thank the Lord we've never had need of it yet. Don't carry the damn thing for entertainment. It's only here for that one day we need the Coast Guard. When we do, boy, it better be warmed and ready."

"Yes, Dad."

Ben Steele nodded to the steaming sea.

"She don't wait."

"Yes, Dad."

The *Agnes T.* took on a roll in the open roadstead of Salem Bay. As she cleared the mouth of Manchester Harbor, Ben's mind drifted between his boat and his son.

Man had to give a lot of thought to his gear if he was going to make it on the sea. Specially onshore fishing. He tried to say this to Jason a dozen different ways. Lad didn't seem to listen. Mostly cared about money. Lot like his mother. Only time he noticed a real perk-up on Jason's part was coming out of the Shawmut Bank by the Fish Pier down in Boston. The lad was right good on checking Noonan and Company's balance against the Steele records. The Noonan family were the commission men that bought and distributed his fish. Nice people. His father before him had dealt with them. Made mistakes though. Jason had caught a couple.

The boy took after his mother. Always wanting something newer or better, that woman. Kid, the same way. Cars and clothes, for the most part. 'Course, the kid worked hard for his cars and traded right shrewd. The cars always gleamed, waitin' out front for a shiny neat Jason, with the room behind him a shit heap. Agnes and Jason were a pair, her with her parlor and him with his cars. Woman would never forget her old man was a

17

branch manager in the Tedesco Trust Company. Always the latest, with ne'er a thought to their wake.

Ben mused on, of his own ways as well as his son's. Kid had little sea sense. Never put things back, nor stowed 'em proper. This never set well. On the *Agnes T.* everything had its place and its time to be tended. Now take engines. Most people run 'em till they give 'em trouble. Not Benjamin Steele. The *Agnes T.* spent half of September and a goodly part of October up on the town ramp by the boat shed. Indian summer to some. For him, the time for painting and going over the engines. September was hurricane season, and for that matter, the mackerel started to thin out, and it was too early for good haddock. His father had taught him this time-to-haul and time-to-mend view. And now, he tried to teach this life on the sea to his son.

2

As the *Agnes T.* steadied down on the last two miles for Middle Breakers Ledge, Jason, in the far corner of the windbreak from his father, glanced at his watch. "Ten of seven," he said to himself. His deep blue eyes took in the Christmas card scenery of Gale's Point and Bakers Island Light. The Nor'wester had taken every cloud from the sky and marched them off to Nova Scotia. What was left was a bright glare of white washed down with just a bit of blue.

Out on the open water, the swirling carpet of steam was now broken into rolling foothills. The sea took on a goodly roll, out from the shelter of the land, and the steam tumbled with it. The slate green broke through the swirls in the troughs. As the *Agnes T.* plowed across the Bakers Island Passage, the icy mass of the island and the tall tower of the lighthouse loomed high above her close on the port hand.

Jason squinted through the salt-streaked glass at a large

brick mansion on the near headland. He knew it like his father knew the *Agnes T.* It was the Carter place, and his eyes were riveted to the upper left hand window, for that was Janice's room. Janice Carter was Jason's girl. She was seventeen and in her last year at Foxcroft School in Virginia. She would be home for the Christmas holidays this coming Thursday, so her latest perfumed letter said.

The Carters lived in the same, yet a different, world from Jason Steele. Janice's father, Lawrence Carter, was the President and principal stockholder of the Prescott Management Company in Boston. Had Jason chosen to look west that day, to the mass of Boston buildings dancing crazily on the rolling carpet of the sea, the tallest shaft of them all would have been the Prescott Company Tower.

Jason had as yet no interest in the Tower, nor the funds that were sold there. The girl and what she could mean, that was another matter. They had met at a party given by her cousin in June, and had grown inseparable since. This was Wednesday, and just the thought of Thursday night brought a painful rigidity beneath Jason's fish-flecked rubber skirt. He stirred uncomfortably.

Ben Steele cut back on the big diesels as the *Agnes T.* drew nigh of Middle Breakers Ledge. The startling quiet brought Jason back to the reality of his morning at the nets. Middle Breakers Ledge was Back Breaker Ledge, cold, and cuts that never healed, and the sea, ever waiting for a tumbled dory. This Jason knew and detested. He would find an easier way.

The Steeles had maintained fish weirs or gill nets in the more quiet waters between Outer and Middle Breakers for forty years or more. These net locations along the New England coast were passed on in fishing families like fiefs in the Highlands. In the mid-twentieth century, such a weir might seem an economic anachronism, were it not for the City of Boston. Boston meant a delicate filet, butter-laden, at Locke-Obers Café on any day, and also the hellfire ferocity of His Eminence rushing about mending the seams of Mother Church and defending the ancient battlements of birth control and Friday night codfish cakes. To most of Boston, meat on Friday was an iniquity on par with voting Republican. At this time of Jason Steele's life, Boston was a good fish town.

The Steele family, with but two pairs of hands and a thirty-eight-foot vessel, had no swelled ambition to serve the mass market. They left that to the other members of the fishing fraternity that dragged the banks far out beyond Cape Cod. There was no way the Steeles could compete with the massive gear and large trawls the offshore brotherhood brought in under ice every ten days or so. Conversely, those ten days were the vulnerability of the offshore operations and it was in the freshness of catch that the Steeles competed most effectively.

The fish dragged aboard the Steele dories by eight in the morning were usually gutted and under refrigeration in their truck by ten. Within the hour, they were in the locker of the commission men, and soon were redistributed to the specialty buyers such as the Ritz Carlton or Josephs or Durgin Park. These buyers were the market whose palates would brook no tolerance of the sometime variable quality in the catch of the deep water draggers. They boasted customers who claimed to differentiate the freshness of their fish in terms of hours, and were willing to pay well for their vanity.

This was Ben Steele's market. He worked hard to hold it and served it well. It called for an absurd way of life geared to the flood of the tide and weather reports and winds. There was little time for home life, with the result that the *Agnes T.* under his feet and the one which shared his bed were almost equally wooden. This was just part of the price Ben Steele paid for his livelihood, and for a man of his education, it was an excellent livelihood. In most years, he took home fifteen thousand dollars after maintenance, gear replacement, and his own insurance reserve. He didn't have much time to spend it either, though his Agnes of the beach helped out in that department.

One might have thought the hardness of his life would have made Benjamin Steele as cold as his cod. This was not the case. He was a quiet man, from years of fishing all alone. His skin was leather and tanned as good as the best of the Peabody tanneries. Hard, he certainly was. His shoulders were broad and his arms sinewy from years of net hauling. Coming through his forty-second year, he was putting on a bit of belly, not yet too noticeable on his six-foot frame. It probably would go away if he cut back on the rye and water at night, but a man had to have some pleasures. Quiet and hard, yes, protective and generous too. He was very attentive to the needs and wants of his wife and son.

If the appearance of Ben Steele had any prepossessing characteristics, they were the calm and clearness of his eyes, set off by countless wrinkles and crow's-feet. These were hallmarks of his trade, garnered from years of squinting up sun or weeping into winter gales. Ben Steele was a man at peace with his lot in life.

This could not be said of his son. In physical things, much of Benjamin had flowed on into Jason. With slight variation, they shared the deep-set blue eyes. If a stranger were to look at the two, the paternity would never be questioned, yet where he might have called Ben's eyes calm, he might have used the words "cold" or "intent" of Jason. They shared the same thick black hair, though Ben's had gone to a bit of gray at the temples and thinned to a memory on the forepeak. Jason, though a good four inches taller than his father, was not as powerful through the shoulders or chest, but then, he hadn't hauled nets for twenty years. Jason had better than two hundred pounds scattered over his frame. It was not knit to the hardness of his father, but it was good enough to put him on the first team as right end for Manchester High the past two seasons. All in all, Jason Steele was a big, handsome youth.

The two Steeles were farthest separated in their temperaments. Ben Steele was known for his generosity along the waterfront. A new fellow, just starting out fishing, could go to Ben and get it straight on what he should do. Where Jason's interests were involved, however, Jason came first. If a fellow had a request and it didn't interfere with his own plans, he might lend a hand, but one couldn't count on it. Jason was an only child, and what he had wanted, Agnes Steele had pretty much given him. There were few of his classmates at Manchester High who had any nicer clothes and possessions.

Ben Steele never forgot the row he got in with his wife

the day she and Jason came home with a Studebaker sedan but two weeks after his son got his driver's learning permit. It was true that most of the five hundred dollars were Jason's summer savings, but not all. Ben didn't begrudge the boy the car by any means. He just didn't think the time was right.

Ben Steele would be the first to say, two years later, that it hadn't been a bad move. Jason took good care of his cars; fixed them up with his own time and paint where he could and traded hard with his friends. He saved every nickel, and now talked of a car repair shop or dealership or some such thing. The trouble with Jason, as Ben saw it, was that he never was satisfied. He had talked to his son of reaching too fast, of taking things as they were. But Jason always wanted something newer and better and bigger, and once he set his mind on a goal, he would let little stand in his way.

Ben brought the *Agnes T.* head to the downwind corner of the weir. As she nosed into the sea, the waters inside the netting broke into a frenzied froth of panicked fish. Just the underwater noise of the diesel was enough to spook them. Ben could tell from the size of the froth that this was one of their best days.

Jason broke the silence between the two. "Gee, Dad! Will you look at that." The astonishment was wide in his face.

"Ayup. Let's get at it, couple of hours work there."

Ben nosed the *Agnes T.* up on the corner mooring buoy. The term "mooring buoy" was a bit of a misnomer. The buoys of the weir were really Narragansett beer kegs. Ben Steele didn't spend a dollar that he didn't have to. Jason picked up the mooring pennant with a boat hook and the *Agnes T.* was made fast.

The elder Steele left the diesels ticking over in idle, poked his head below to check the coal stove and give it a bit of stoking. They'd need that heat later on. He added a bit more water to the kettle and closed off the cabin. He then joined Jason on the port quarter and lent a hand as they drew the towed dories alongside.

They each eased into a dory. After pumping off what water the boats had picked up on the tow, they got out their oars and made for the downwind nets of the weir. They started

22

to haul back on the nets, gaffing and grabbing as they went. The flopping haddock filled up over their feet. Despite their lined gloves, their hands were numb in a few minutes. The wind tore at the corners of their eyes, drawing salty tears. Foot by heavy foot, the Steeles hauled the weir into their dories, spewing a wriggling tapestry of brown and silver haddock, running three feet or more, and some hefty cod.

In less than a half hour, Jason's load of fish were well up on his booted thighs. With the fish came sea water. He hollered over the wind, "Jesus, Dad. I'm cold."

Ben did not reply. He was wrestling with this quandary of success. There were more fish than he, Jason, and the two dories could ever handle on the calmest day. He had a couple of choices. They could unlash the unworked half of the seine, tie it back on itself, and come back later, after they got what they had underway to the market. This was probably the most sensible course, but Ben didn't like it much. They'd be sure to lose most of the bigger cod on the turn of the tide. And by the time they got this catch gutted and on its way, there wouldn't be much daylight to get back out.

The other choice was to work the remaining half of the net from the *Agnes T*. This wasn't so easy, for if there was a mistake, and the net got onto the props, he knew they'd have one hell of a time clearing it in this sea. And help wouldn't be fast coming, either. Ben weighed the choices, then shouted to his son, "Jason, we're going back to the *Agnes*."

Jason hastily rowed his wallowing dory back to the bigger vessel, happy to call it a day. As they clumped into the cabin, Ben said, "We'll tie off the dories and take the big boat back onto it."

The words shattered Jason's smile as he half-whined, "Shit, Dad. I've never been so cold. We got enough for a week."

"Got to get it while we can. Prices right good this week."

"My hands are falling off."

"Fix you up right quick with a hot cup of coffee. Come on." In the close confines of the snug cabin, the father silently filled the mugs. As he passed one over to his son, now huddled close by the stove, Jason answered,

"I need more'n a cup of coffee. Let's call it quits."

23

"Nope." Ben Steele was peeling off his rubber clothing as he answered.

"Gawd, Dad. Can't take any more of this. My hands hurt something awful." The returning blood brought a sharp tingling pain.

"You got to get used to it, son. Take off your gear for a bit, but can't stay long, either. Be worse when we git back outside." The kindness was in Ben's face, if not in his words.

"Dad, we got enough fish for every fancy restaurant in Boston."

"Jason, you gotta learn in this business you take it while you can. Tomorrow can be nothing. You never know. We can sell the surplus to the supermarkets."

"There's no tomorrow for me in this damn business. I've had it." Jason glared up from the stove at his father as he spoke.

"Now, Jason. You only been at it a couple of months and you're ready to quit. That ain't the way. Where else a lad of your years make a hundred or more in a week. You stick to it and you'll harden up. That, or go back to school."

"Harden up! Shit! I'm ice already. There's got to be easier ways to make it than this."

"Well, I tried to tell you to stick with your schoolin', but you wouldn't pay me no mind."

The tingling pain came back to Jason's toes. As it did, Ben Steele drew himself up, placed his mug on the rack, and put on his windbreaker and fish skirt. As he edged aft, toward the companionway doors, he laid a hand on his son's shoulder.

"Now mind you, lad. We gotta be Keerist awful careful. We get that net about these props and we'll be out here forever."

"I've had it, Dad. I'm through."

"Ah, come on, lad, it won't git any easier and it's got to git done."

"I'm through, I tell you. Through, through, through."

"Jeeses, son, I lay off old Bill to take you on. Now here you are, the first rough one comes along and you're ready to quit. I'll split what we net, that'll give you a start." Ben stomped out of the cabin, disgusted with his son, himself, and his bribe.

24

Jason watched the set of his father's jaw as he spoke, and he knew, just this once, he had to go back out in that wind. There was no other way. But this trip was his last.

By ten that morning, they had all they could net and still make Manchester Harbor with any degree of safety. They cast off the mooring, picked up their dories and headed back. In little time, the trailing cortege had a whirling halo of herring gulls, diving into the laden dories to exact their tribute. The scaw of the gulls heralded their success of the morning.

3

Jason Steele had first met Janice Carter at a post-race party given by her cousin, Peter Pickering, the previous June. It was a party that Janice didn't want to go to and was late getting to, for though she was very close to her cousin, Pete, parties in general and sailboat parties in particular made her uncomfortable. That afternoon, she had expended her reluctance in the most meticulous grooming her mare had ever received. It was well past six when she returned in her riding jeans to the Carter mansion, where Catharine Carter brushed aside her daughter's feigned forgetfulness with no-nonsense orders to get up the stairs and into a bath. With this for a prelude, Janice found herself walking at a very measured pace up the raked gravel drive to the white colonial expanse of the Pickering home to see a solid rank of parked cars. The pink twilight was that of a warm June day and the stillness was broken only by the gentle stirring of a night wind high in the new green of the marshaled oaks, and the measured crunch of her feet. There was more to her reluctance than her discomfort with the sailing crowd. Janice Carter was very unsure of her appearance. She had just returned from boarding school and was annoyed at her mother's insistence at getting into the summer swing of parties on the shore. Janice was a serious girl and this showed in the level gaze of her deep green eyes, eyes that considered and measured every word spoken to her. The giggling frivolity of many of her friends did not come easily, and she asked serious questions that made boys uncomfortable. Janice knew this and had concluded parties were not for her. What she did not take into account was how much she had changed in looks during the spring term. She thought of herself as a tall, spindly stick. Tall she was, yet somehow the flush of a day of riding, a bright green dress, the demure pageboy cut of her thick brown hair combined with the new maturity of her slender figure and her serious green eyes had all melded together to make her a very pretty young lady.

The bustle of the party flowing about the house from the far lawn began to make her stomach tighten. She decided not to face Aunt Harriet, her mother's sister, whose distinct whinny she heard through the now lit foyer, but slipped around the house through the rose garden to join the party as unobtrusively as possible. This gave her an opportunity to observe the crowd. Almost all were familiar faces from day school and dances, assemblies, and parties. The boys were drawn into raveling and unraveling knots, buzzing and chattering about the bar, teasing the pretty girls. Her fears were confirmed. She had known all the boys too long and there was nothing new to say. For a second, she thought of turning back to her car and home. She would have, had not her cousin's back been so close at hand. Pete Pickering was giving a detailed description of a jibing duel to an enrapted blonde whom Janice vaguely knew and to a tall boy who was a stranger to her. Janice slipped up behind her cousin and gave his motioning elbow a shy tug. Pete turned around in surprise. "Hi, Jannie, glad you're here, let me get you a drink, this is Deirdre Singleton and this is my crew mate, Jason Steele." It rolled out in one long burst and Pete was off to the bar, leaving Janice to exchange pleasantries with Deirdre and shake hands somewhat awkwardly with Jason Steele.

Deirdre launched off on an ecstatic description of her spring term at Concord Academy. Janice interjected the appropriate "oh's" but for the most part, her attention was on the tall young man at her elbow. She, who had always considered herself too tall at five nine, was drawn to his six three or more. He had very dark black hair and a strong face and was deeply tanned. Janice thought he looked very hard and powerful. She wondered if Deirdre was his date. Pete was soon back with her gin and tonic, and as he quickly drifted off again into the kaleidoscope of couples with Deirdre in tow, her question was answered. Janice nervously took a large gulp of her drink. Almost choking on the free-handedness of the bartender, she attempted a bright "Well, how'd it go today?"

Jason was slow to reply and when he did, it was in a level voice with a tinge of salt. "Well let's see, we were third around the weather mark, goin' good uphill, but played it to the west and two guys fetched out from under us. Got lucky tackin' downwind. Bagged old Fallon with a hundred yards left and got the gun." It was very nonchalant and factual.

Janice suspected he saw through her discomfort, but she enthused, "Oh great! Congratulations!"

"Thanks, but save it for Pete. He was driving. You sail?"

"Yes, yes a bit. Cruising mostly. Maine a lot."

"Oh?" Jason grew more interested. "What do you sail?"

"Well, Dad's got a sloop, *Capella*. She's moored right off . . ."

"Hell, I know *Capella*!" His interest was written in his smile. "Why she's the prettiest thing in the harbor. Old Herreshoff design. That's yours, huh?"

"Well, it's really Father's. My brother and sister and I take her out every so often." Janice was pleased with his interest, even if it centered around her father's sloop.

"Hmm." Jason was mulling over her answer. "Must be fifty feet. A lot of boat for three kids."

Janice flushed for an instant, annoyed at his tactlessness. There was a cool edge in her answer. "Oh, I don't know. Larry, that's my older brother, he's nineteen, plays freshman hockey for Harvard. Jean and I, well we've been sailing *Capella* just about all our lives. Of course," she added, with a trace of haughtiness, "we just stick with the working sails, no genoas

27

or spinnakers and there's always the captain." As she finished, she looked into Jason's eyes and knew she was being teased, and for once she liked it.

"I'd forgotten *Capella* had a paid captain." His voice trailed off, yet his manner stayed as friendly. Janice tried to draw him out, asking about his interests and got a very nonchalant "Oh I play a bit of football and basketball." He then turned the conversation back to her and what she liked—a new experience for her. They talked of her afternoon ride and her mare and riding to hounds. It was soon apparent to him that horses were her great love. Jason knew little about horses, but he was an attentive listener when he wanted to be. He liked her earnestness, and the small things in her manner that made her seem different from the girls he knew at Manchester High.

For her part, Janice was feeling very pleased with herself. She was having an easy conversation with a handsome boy. Not only was he good-looking, but he seemed interested in her. In her seventeen years, Janice Carter had never really been comfortable with boys. Through all her past school holidays, her dance partners had usually been either arranged by her mother or her mother's friends. When the boys she thought attractive cut in, she was suspicious they were simply doing their duty. She became either tongue-tied or overly enthusiastic, sometimes so enthusiastic she found herself leading her partners. Until this twilight night on the Pickering lawn, Janice was certain of herself in but a few areas. Skis and horses and books were the pillars of her world. Now, talking to Jason Steele, a new world was suddenly opening up.

When she asked Jason of his plans for fall, expecting talk of Yale or Dartmouth, she was surprised when he said he would fish with his father while he looked around for his own business opportunity. He said he planned to make it, and make it big in his own way. She knew he was what her parents would call a rough diamond, and she found this intriguing.

Three nights later, Jason called, and they went to a movie in Salem. Within two weeks, and on their third date, they found themselves in a wind-rustled pine grove, a turn-off from a rutted lovers' lane by the edge of Chebacco Lake, over by the Hamilton border.

Jason was gentle and kind from the outset and their game of "kissy face" matured from boy-girl gropings with each night of early summer. By mid-July, Catharine Carter suspected the very physical nature of the relationship. She and her daughter had always had an easy rapport, but for the first time, this was gone when she tried to draw Janice out on the topic of Jason. Mrs. Carter saw the danger signals and swung into a desperate rear-guard action.

In less than a week, Janice had a letter from her cousin, Lillian Clarke, in Wyoming, asking her to join them for a pack trip up into Yellowstone National Park. Janice had spent the whole summer, two years ago, on the Clarkes' beautiful dude ranch north of Jackson Hole. That summer, the world of Janice Carter was complete with tall trees, snow-capped mountains, clear, cold water and horses—horses most of all. Under any other circumstances, an invitation from the Clarkes would have been the happiest of events. But now it meant leaving Jason. Janice ignored the problem by burying Lillian's letter in her kerchief drawer.

The letter would not stay buried. Within the week, while driving back from a skirt fitting at Appleseed's Store, Mrs. Carter casually opened the conversation. She was a handsome woman in her early forties. Her hair was long and rich brown, and her figure reflected an active life of walking and skiing and tennis. She had a gracious way about her that many found charming, yet there could be a strong streak of no-nonsense firmness when it came to matters of her family. Janice recognized the latter as her mother spoke.

"Janice dear, I had a call last night from Aunt Helen!"

Janice flushed and concentrated on the road as she tried for an equally casual response.

"Oh, how is Aunt Helen?"

"Well, dear, she's fine but a bit disturbed. She was trying to make final plans for guests and their cabins in August . . . said that Lillian had asked you out . . . you never mentioned it to me. . . . You were out rather late last night so I told Helen that we'd call her back tonight."

"I just got the letter . . . must have forgotten to mention it . . . I sure would love to see Jackson Hole again, but you know how Dad's been lately about the stock market and things. I just didn't think it was the time to ask for any money for Wyoming."

Catharine Carter smiled, amused at her daughter's excuse.

"That was very thoughtful of you, dear, but don't you mind about the money. If that's your only concern, then the matter is settled. We'll call Helen tonight and accept."

"Yes, Mother." A crestfallen Janice had built her own box.

Eight days later Janice Carter was on a United flight to Denver with connections to Sheridan, Wyoming. The Clarkes sent a car down to meet her. Janice found herself in her favorite place in the world and was miserable.

The miles did not stop the mails. Janice wrote faithfully, twice a week. Jason learned of rodeo week, preparations for a pack trip, Lil Clarke's romance with a rancher's son, and how desperately Janice missed him. Jason was neither as facile nor as frequent in the use of his pen. He did get across that Manchester in August was hot, the mackerel were running fair for his father, that he spent most of his free time tinkering with his car, that he'd been crewing on weekends for her cousin Pete in his sloop, that they were winning their share of races, that he hoped Labor Day would be coming soon, and that he missed her. It took four letters to say all that.

Catharine Carter fought with determination but against the hard odds of the young in love. In mid-August, she set about organizing her defenses for the seven free days Janice would have after the ranch and before she returned to her final year at school. By late August, she had her daughter's time committed for almost every waking moment, with doctor, dentist, and dressmaker appointments and with parties. She kept Janice informed of her progress in gushing letters. If Janice had not been her father's daughter, Catharine would have won hands down. When Catharine Carter phoned Wyoming to announce that Janice was going to the Labor Day Country Club

Dance with that attractive English student that the Winthrops had over for the summer, Janice dug in her heels and said a flat "no." Thus on her return, Janice and Jason found themselves with two nights to themselves.

Janice was due in Boston at noon on an American flight from Chicago and Jason had planned for a month to meet her. Two days before her arrival, he received a telegram: DAD IS MEETING ME. COME FRIDAY AT SIX. LOVE JANICE.

Jason recognized the hand of Mrs. Carter and realized he and Janice were just going to have to work around her. He was already shrewd enough to pick his time and his ground.

Jason arrived at the Carter place at precisely six that Friday night of Labor Day weekend. He was scrubbed and slicked and, in his black tie and white linen jacket, knew he was as presentable as any "Preppie" on the North Shore. He had shined the paint off his Buick in the afternoon and the top was down and the chrome gleaming.

Mr. Carter must have heard the Buick on the gravel of the long drive, for he was standing in the doorway as Jason got out of his car.

"Ah, Jason. Good to see you. Have a good summer?"

Lawrence Carter swung open the screen door and offered Jason a firm handshake and a hearty smile.

Jason, who liked Mr. Carter, responded with a "Good evening, sir. Yes sir, I did," and stepped into the foyer.

"Good. Jan will be down in a moment. These women and their dressing, you know. Come on out on the terrace."

"Yes, sir."

Jason fell in behind him as he led the way to the tall glass doors at the end of the hall. Lawrence Carter's most remarkable physical features were his solid width and the silver whiteness of his full head of hair. The whiteness belied his forty-four years, but the trim solidity of his torso spoke well of his many hours at court tennis and handball. Jason could readily see how "Bullet" Carter had been one of Harvard's more famous halfbacks before the war. Jason might have been surprised to know that Lawrence Carter's mane was less than white without the weekly ministrations of the Ritz Barber Shop. Lawrence Carter had learned early the value of solid appearances in old Boston. His conservative clothes were meticulously tailored. This image and his dependable manner led to trusteeships and board appointments. Inheriting the controlling shares of the Prescott Management Company and a fortunate marriage had not hurt either.

Now he graciously held the patio door open for Jason. With a nod of his head, he indicated a rattan armchair.

Dealing with this age group was always a problem for Lawrence Carter, though young Steele seemed very self-assured for his years, he thought. Indicating the nearby bar, he casually offered, "Something to drink?"

"No thank you, sir."

"Are you sure? Coke, beer, ginger ale? They're all right here." Carter set about making himself a gin and tonic.

Jason shook his head with an easy smile and turned to study the view from the Carter terrace. In the soft light of a late summer day, it was at its very best. The terrace sat high on the granite ledges above the waters of the Bay and was sheltered from the wind by the seaward-reaching wings of the Georgian mansion. The white tower of Bakers Island Light was just across the channel on a matching headland. Below them, several sloops were slowly beating back to Marblehead in the fading breeze. Down from the terrace stretched a set of formal gardens that led to a swimming pool blasted from the granite. The Carter place was the highlight of the annual Manchester Garden Club tour.

That night, Jason formed the resolve that someday he would have a home like this, or bigger and better. He would have *his* place on *his* hill with the working world beneath him. How he would get there was another question, still vague in his mind; yet he was certain of one thing and that was that Lawrence Carter's daughter was the first step up the hill. Carter came back from the bar.

"Jason, Mrs. Carter and I thought it wise that we have a few words, before you all went off for the evening."

32

"Yes, sir." Jason thought to himself, "Oh God, here it comes."

"As you know, Jan has been up traveling the last two days . . . had that long drive down to Sheridan to catch her plane . . . probably quite tired, though she'll never admit it. We'd be very grateful if you two would call it a night at a sensible hour, this evening . . ."

"Oh sure, Mr. Carter, that would be fine with me." Jason nodded with certainty as he spoke.

The screen door opened behind them, and Janice stepped onto the terrace. Mrs. Carter was close behind her, but Jason took no notice. He thought Janice had never looked lovelier. The thin air and hard light of the high country had darkened her skin to a golden mahogany. This same light danced in the strands of her hair. The darkness of her skin set off the even whiteness of her teeth and the greenness of her smiling eyes. Her greeting was demure and very ladylike. "Hello, Jason." Janice lightly shook hands and dropped gracefully into one of the tall rattan seats.

"Hi, Jan. . . . Oh, good evening, Mrs. Carter."

"Good evening, Jason." There was an awkward moment, and then Mrs. Carter went on, "Have you had a good summer?" She took the nearby sofa.

"Yes, ma'am." Jason didn't know just what to say to the cool lady before him whom he knew wanted no part of this town boy messing about with her daughter. Here was the dragon before the gate of his princess. But she couldn't burn him for what he didn't say, so he said little.

Lawrence Carter, still on his feet, interjected, "Kit, a mart or a G and T?"

Catharine Carter frowned for an instant. "A gin and tonic, dear."

He turned to Janice. "I've already tried Jason. What about you, Jan?"

Janice was on her feet before he had finished the question. "Oh, Daddy, thank you so much, I don't think so. We'd better be going or we'll be late for the dinner dance."

This was not quite true, but Jason was on his feet on the

instant and the young pair were through the screen door and out on the front drive before Catharine Carter could voice a word of restraint. Lawrence Carter chuckled at her consternation as he sliced the lime. Jan might have done worse for her first beau, he thought. He brought the glass over to his wife with a smile.

They said not a word until Jason stopped at the foot of the drive to let an oncoming car pass. "Gee Jan, you look terrific." He reached for her hand.

She replied with her first-team smile, "I've missed you too."

While waiting for the traffic, Jason turned to look at her. He took note of the fullness of her breasts and of her bare shapely legs. One wouldn't say that her Lanz print put an emphasis on her sexiness, nor, on the other hand, would it be accused of understatement. The scoop neck, cap sleeves, and snug bodice brought full attention to her even tan. Jason thought for a moment of how she probably got it up in the high country.

"Jan, your mother knows damn well the dinner dance doesn't start until seven. We're a good half hour early before we're due down at Essex."

"I know, silly, but you didn't want to sit around through a whole bunch of Mother's questions, did you?" Her tone was that of a patient older sister.

"No," Jason sheepishly said with a smile half apology and half pleasure.

"Besides, I wanted to be with you." She slid over close after the traffic passed.

"Well, what do you want to do for a while?"

"We could go down to Singing Beach for a barefoot walk. It seems like forever since I felt sand between my toes."

Jason turned the open car toward the beach.

At the dance, it was quite obvious that Janice was no longer in the wall flower class. Every boy in the place wanted to dance with her. At least, that is how it seemed to Jason.

He was forever being cut in on and finally, by ten-thirty, frustrated, and bored with the other girls, and thoroughly aroused by Janice's flirtatious behavior towards him, he had had enough. He strode purposely into the middle of the dance floor, tapped her partner on the shoulder, and immediately steered Janice towards the door. "Let's get out of here Jan," he said.

"What will we say to the chaperones? Mrs. Amory is a terribly good friend of Mother's." Janice looked toward two middle-aged couples in deep conversation around the corner table at the far end of the dance floor.

"Screw 'em," Jason whispered, far too impatient to have Janice by himself to be concerned with such niceties. "You go to the powder room and slip out the back door by the tennis dressing room. I'll get my car around behind the volley board and we'll go out the back drive. No one will miss us in this madhouse. It's almost eleven and you have to be home by twelve-thirty. Now git."

Janice put up no argument, and in another five minutes they met behind the volley board. Because the night had a slight chill, and for privacy, Jason put up the convertible roof. Driving through the back roads towards the lover's lane of Lake Chebacco, he put his free arm around Janice's waist and drew her as close as he could and still keep the car on the road. He groped the light but voluminous material of her skirt into a heap on her lap, until finally he had the hem high enough to get his hand between her legs. Janice had on the thinnest of panties, and she was already moist.

By then they were on the bumpy dirt road into the lake, and in a few more moments they had found their own private grove of pines. From the occasional beep of horns or the low rumble of starting engines, they knew the lake was not theirs alone that night. They did not care. They were lost in a throat-searching exchange of tongues.

Jason remembered the Labor Day dance very well. He remembered the difficulty he had with the covered buttons of her fitted bodice. He remembered his flush of embarrassment when she had to reach behind and help him. He remembered with surprise how quickly and deftly she had fondled and

35

stroked him into hardness. It was an outpouring of the pent-up needs of healthy young animals. But Janice insisted on one ground rule. She would not let him inside her. That ground rule held through the remainder of her vacation.

Catharine Carter might have blocked off most of Janice's time but there was some time that they had together that she could do little about. Janice and Jason went off for an afternoon's sail in the family sloop and got becalmed on the far side of Bakers Island. That had even happened to Catharine Carter twenty years earlier.

Mrs. Carter breathed a sigh of relief as she placed Janice on the Washington plane for the fall term of her senior year at Foxcroft. She rationalized that Janice had been bound to discover boys, that Jason seemed a nice boy, that her Janice was certainly a nice girl, and that Janice would meet many other nice boys during her coming debutante season.

Janice came home for the Thanksgiving holidays to a string of family affairs that she couldn't get out of. When she explained her predicament to Jason, he was surprisingly understanding. They had plenty of time, he said. For his part, Jason knew that he was in love with Janice, although he had never told her so. He was sure she felt the same way and he could afford to wait.

Upon her return to school in September, Janice had thought of little else but Jason and her desire for him. He had been very patient and had never overstepped the bounds she set. For that, she was grateful, but also rather annoyed. She had no illusions that she was his first girl, and one side of her was a little hurt that he hadn't been more aggressive no matter what rules she had laid down. But she was convinced that there was now no other girl and that was all that mattered. She was in love with him and she was determined to make him wholly hers soon, for she knew he would not be patient forever. This feeling grew so strong that it overcame her fear and natural reluctance of taking that final step, a step that would brush aside years of strict and proper upbringing.

36

When Janice came home for the Christmas vacation, she had a date with Jason for the second night. She had resolved this would be her last night of virginity and had intimated as much to him in her last letter. That night in the driveway of the Carter home, Jason was assured of her resolve. When he got behind the wheel after closing her door and, despite the brightness of the entryway lights, had leaned over for a hurried kiss, he asked, "Where we heading, Jan?"

"The Hamilton woods," was her answer.

When they found their quiet place in the woods, Janice was neither shy nor scared. They kissed and in a few moments Jason had her free of coat and sweater. If either had an element of fear, it was Jason. The thought that this was Catharine Carter's daughter kept coming back as he fumbled clumsily with her bra clasp. Janice had no such thoughts. She had made her decision and drew back from him for a moment, then with a shrug had her slip straps clear of her shoulders and her bra unhooked. Taking his cues from her, Jason hurriedly unbuckled his belt and shoved his pants and shorts down about his knees. His last visions of Catharine Carter disappeared.

When he produced from his pocket a tinfoil packet, Janice giggled. "Well, aren't you the boy scout."

Jason's reply was a grunt, since he was opening the packet with his teeth. Despite her remark, he could sense that she was relieved. "I love you too much to take any chances, Jan," he murmured in her ear as his hands began to move over her body, caressing her.

Janice wriggled out of her panties and pulled her skirt up around her waist. Jason drew her astride him with a quick movement. As she felt him enter her, she buried her face in his neck and began to repeat "I love you, I love you," over and over. Jason could feel her every throb throughout his length. She began to writhe and when the writhing quickened into sharp thrusts, he said, "Janice, I'm coming, I'm coming. I'm sorry, I wanted to wait."

She whispered, "That's all right, that's all right. Give it to me." And she drove down and met him and took him full sheath as he came.

37

4

On New Year's morning, Catharine and Lawrence Carter knew they had a problem on their hands. Catharine Carter had spotted all the danger signals. When she pointed them out to her husband, they faced the facts as a team. They had done this from the beginning of their marriage twenty-two years ago. As with other crises, they faced the Jason Steele problem with calmness and deliberation. Catharine proposed a walk down to Singing Beach before lunch.

The day was bright and windless, a fine day for a walk, though the mercury hovered at twenty-six, and there was little warmth from the low winter sun.

As they crunched down the drive with matching strides, Catharine was her usual direct, modulated Yankee self.

"Larry, I am certain that Janice is sleeping with Jason."

"Oh Kit, that's nonsense . . . puppy love at best . . . Why, she's only seventeen."

"Well, last night was the third night in a row that she came in around two o'clock. They were over at a record hop at the Stocktons'. I just happened to be talking with Ann Stockton this morning, you know, about whether they are going to join us in Franconia next weekend. I asked how Joan's party went. Ann said it went fine, very quiet, everybody seemed to have a good time and were on their way home just after midnight. Well, you know as well as I do that it's no more than five minutes from here to the Stocktons'."

Lawrence Carter couldn't keep back a wry smile.

"Kit, you just happened to be talking to Ann Stockton. Why, you've been stewing for an excuse to talk with her since midnight."

"That might be, but what about the five-minute drive from here?"

"I can't argue with you about that. But may I remind you

that only two years ago, when Larry was home on holiday from Saint Paul's, he never seemed to get home before three or four and you weren't all riled up about it."

"Oh Larry, that's not my point. That was different. He's a boy."

"How so?"

"Now don't be difficult."

"No, Kit, I'm serious. Our Larry was obviously out with girls who had parents. We now have to look at it from both sides, the boy's and girl's, the best interests of both Jason and Janice. If we don't go at it that way, if we try and break them up now, just remember, this seems to be Janice's first real beau. I think he's brought her an awful lot of confidence. Why, hell, we just got her off a horse last year, and if my memory is at all accurate, she was still wearing braces on her teeth two Christmases ago. If we try and drive a wedge in on her very first boy, we'll lose all ability to communicate."

Ignoring the lapping waves and the beauty of the ice-strewn beach, the Carters strode on in silence. When they came on the high ledges, they turned back and Catharine again spoke.

"Then Larry, the way you see it, we shouldn't make any move to break off this affair, right here and now, today."

"That's right."

"But why not? Maybe it would be easier on both. He's the son of a fisherman. It can't go anywhere."

"It's remarks like that, Catharine, that from time to time make me want to paddle your ass pink. Jesus H. Christ was a fisherman and most of our Chilton and Somerset Club friends are the descendants of fishermen, whether they like it or not. I think there's more substance to this Jason lad than the few others I've seen come around. I'd rather that he go on with his education, but then, maybe that isn't always so important."

"You can't be serious, Larry. Jan's only seventeen. Why, she hasn't even come out yet."

"I don't say that we marry her off this afternoon. I don't say break it off either."

39

Catharine Carter's features pursed into a long frown and then slowly broadened into a wide, feline smile.

"I know you too well, Larry Carter; you mean to kill it with kindness."

"Not necessarily, but if that's what kindness does, so be it. You may recollect, your mother was terribly strong on that Yalie oarsman—Reid, wasn't it?—when you came out. Look what kindness did to that affair."

"Larry, that was not an affair. Besides, we were talking of Jason and Janice."

"Yes, I know, and I think we can help him out."

Once they had agreed upon a course of action, the Lawrence Carters settled upon their battle plan in the remainder of their morning walk. On their return from the beach, they met Janice in the entrance hall.

"Janice dear," Catharine Carter said. "Your father and I wondered if you would have tea with us this afternoon?"

Janice, expecting an upbraiding for her late hours, was taken off guard and cast about in her head for alternatives. She came up with nothing but a reluctant "Yes, Mother, I'd love to."

Their tea was served in the paneled library of the west wing. This room was at its best in the late afternoon. The flat, pink light of a winter sunset filtered softly through the tall glass doors. There were heaps of wind-blown snow over the lower panels. Lawrence Carter had a crackling fire underway in the fieldstone fireplace and the best Canton China service was set on the coffee table. Janice recognized all the storm signals the instant that she entered. Her mother never used that service on anything but the most special family occasions. It had been brought around the Cape of Good Hope in the hold of one of her Haskett ancestors' ships ten years before the War of 1812. As her mother set about pouring, Janice recalled the afternoon several winters past when her uncle had come over for tea. He was curator of a museum in Salem and was on a fund raising tour and he and Mrs. Carter got into a long discussion of Salem and the Canton trade. Janice had listened with great interest, for it was obvious from that conversation that the Haskett family wealth was far older than her father's family's was.

Her uncle had said the Canton service was the finest he'd ever seen, as he put out the broadest of hints that it warranted a very special place in a museum with remarkable tax consequences to the donor. Her father had started to get interested when her brother Larry stepped into the conversation with both feet.

"Hey, Uncle Pete, if what I learned in school is right, wasn't opium smuggling the real reason the Salem merchants got so interested in the China trade?"

Janice remembered her mother almost choked on her tea.

The other lovely amenities of the library, the gumwood paneling, the Cozzens watercolors, the smell of leatherbound books, even the fading filtering light; all of these things escaped her. Her stomach was a little ball in her throat. Janice felt the setting would have been better at dawn by the wall of a prison yard with the squad commander offering her a cigarette and a blindfold.

Janice spent the next hour walking on a mental tightrope. Her father opened the conversation with a polite inquiry as to her progress at school. She was on firm ground here for she had led her class for the past three years. And she knew that her term report, a good one, had arrived several days earlier. She had seen the envelope on the silver plate in the front hall. Her father brought this up and said he thought her efforts merited a raise in her allowance of five dollars a week. All of the Carter children were on allowances that included schooling and clothes. They had been taught the reach of a dollar very young. The conversation went on to her preparations for the second round of College Entrance examinations, and was she still interested in Sarah Lawrence and Radcliffe? And would she join her mother for a shopping session on Newbury Street Tuesday morning. Mrs. Carter had seen a lovely white dress at Fredley's that Janice might consider for her coming out party in June and had asked to have the dress set aside.

Before the last of the pink was gone from the western sky, Janice was completely bewildered. She had been worked on by

41

experts and never even felt the nick of the Novacain. As Catharine Carter drew together the tea things, she asked if Janice might like to have Jason come for dinner on Wednesday, her last night before school.

As the young couple drove off to a movie later that night, Janice summed up her afternoon:

"Jason, they were terrific. That's all there was to it. I just couldn't believe it!"

5

Two mornings later, the company limousine picked Lawrence Carter up at 8:10. Carter nodded to the chauffeur in a friendly fashion, sank back into the plush upholstery, and picked up a crisp copy of the *Wall Street Journal*. He glanced absentmindedly at the front page for a few moments as the car started down the drive. He soon set the paper down, for today was Wednesday, Janice's last day of vacation, and Jason Steele was due for dinner. Carter had a problem that he wanted to solve by dinner time. He kept asking himself, "What do I do with a big nineteen-year-old who has no trade, wants no part of school, I am told is ambitious, and might be my son-in-law?"

Lawrence Carter had pondered this question since his weekend walk with his wife. He had considered starting him out with a clerkship in the Prescott Company, and concluded that it was out of the question. The probabilities were very high that the young infatuation would cool by June, and Jason would probably have wasted half a year. He would be starting at the bottom of the heap with many better educated lads piling in on top of him all the time. That wouldn't be fair to Jason, and having him that close to the family might prove awkward, should any of his supervisors conclude his services were not satisfactory.

Carter was certain that Jason was done with fishing. That rather disappointed him, for the elder Steele appealed to his romantic side. Both men had served on a special committee set up by the Selectmen of the town to deal with harbor problems. Lawrence Carter was the representative of the yacht club, and Benjamin Steele spoke for the fishermen's association. Their acquaintance had never really ripened into friendship, yet it did have warmth and respect, especially on Carter's part. Over the years, Carter had become familiar with the bottle-green shape of the *Agnes T.* Most mornings, as Carter was stepping from his shower, the *Agnes T.* was passing under the window, heading out for the ledges of Bakers Island. Carter had vast admiration for a man who could meet life on such raw terms.

As the limousine moved on toward the city, Lawrence Carter still faced the job placement problem for the son of Benjamin Steele. This should not have been hard for a man whose telephone moved an army of salesmen, clerks, analysts, and typists. But Carter was considering every possible outcome of the infatuation. He had no way to judge the accuracy of his wife's concern that Janice and Jason were already sleeping together. He had no background for such a judgment. Catharine Haskett had come to their wedding bed a well-rubbed virgin only two days after the Harvard-Yale baseball game in June of his graduating year. It was the year after her debut, and Lawrence Carter had looked at no other girl in his last three years at Harvard College. The actions of this new generation were beyond his experience, for he had never "fooled around."

The business head of Lawrence Carter was certain this young flame would sputter out by spring. But his knowledge of his daughter was really what disturbed him. He had seen her schuss the toughest trails at Saint Anton when she was twelve, and it wasn't many years ago he had watched her pick herself out of the mud of the Myopia riding ring three times. On the third time, she sat that horse for the rest of her morning lesson, and he was a mean one. Janice had grit and a strong will when she wanted.

This made Carter's problem bigger than just a boy named Jason and a job. There was a way of living for his Janice to consider and there could be Carter grandchildren that would come under the family trust. Lawrence Carter was well aware of the price of a life style. It had not all come easy, even to him.

43

He remembered the lean years of the Prescott Company. The depression had come on the company like a cold March rain that went on and on. It started two years after Lawrence's graduation, and there were few signs of an economic spring until Adolf Hitler marched into the Sudetenland. Carter remembered how desperately his father, Edward, had struggled to hold the Prescott Company together.

Edward Carter had fought the long fight of the lean years well. And then came the war. The war shook the very roots of his son's genteel view of things. The younger Carter had put in three hard years on the G-2 staff of General George S. Patton in his race across Africa and Europe. In the mental pantheon of Lawrence Carter, there was none to equal General Patton. Mrs. Patton had come from a neighboring town. For that matter, the Carter sloop, *Capella,* was moored just a bit inshore of the Patton schooner, *When and If.* The proudest trophy that Lawrence Carter owned was the Patton Memorial Bowl that he had won off Gloucester, three summers before. He chuckled to himself for a moment. That Jason might make a fine foredeck man was at least one plus.

As the big car crossed the Mystic Bridge, Carter was no closer to an answer for Jason Steele. His thoughts went back again to the time when he came home from Europe and the Prescott Company funds were growing very fast. He had been assigned to build new sales in the California and southwestern markets. It had meant a lot of traveling, away from his family, which he hadn't liked. As Vice-President in charge of sales, there was no other way.

Lawrence Carter had been fascinated by the big-sky openness of the region, the endless miles of flatness and opportunity. He had witnessed the glass slabs of Houston bursting from the flatness in the years after the war. He had more problems getting the Prescott licensed for sales in Texas than all the other western states rolled together. Those Texans were hardheaded but had proved worth the fight. The fund sales were huge and subsidiary investments in the mortgages and land by the Prescott Company around Houston and Dallas were the biggest winners in the company's many investment portfolios.

Carter's time in Texas had led him into oil. There was no

44

way around it in that country. The company had never drilled on its own, but it did a booming business in equipment mortgages and, later, leasing. Some of the directors had done some drilling for tax shelter through Prescott Company contacts. One would never have described this as a major activity of the company, for the Board were Bostonians, and they liked to see or touch what they owned, or at least quote it on any business day in the *Journal*. The Carters had set up a small personal investment company in Texas, Southwestern National Ventures. This company specialized in leasing of tanks and pipelines and tank ships, and had prospered mightily.

Perhaps, he mused, the Southwest was the answer for Jason Steele—nineteen years old, big and strong, sort of a throwback to older days. Definitely not in a Carter company. That might smack of nepotism. Yet, the Southwest . . . the big country . . . and a lot of miles from Boston. That would please Kit.

The limousine drew up to the Back Bay curbstone. The chauffeur came around and opened the door as the chimes of Trinity Church struck nine. Lawrence Carter went into his tower.

"Bullet" Carter made up his mind in the executive elevator. He would try Jason in Louisiana or Texas. He strode into his offices with a smile for the young receptionist. In the middle office, his personal secretary, Miss Bernice Lovejoy, rose as he entered and trailed him into his glassed corner office.

"Good morning, Mr. Carter."

She had said this to two generations of Carters since Lawrence's father had come back from France at the end of the First World War. Miss Lovejoy was nineteen then. Now she was in her mid-fifties and a distinguished, silver-haired woman, well-tailored in colorful tweeds. Bernice Lovejoy was far more than a secretary. She was an adopted aunt to the Carter children, overseer of the smallest Carter detail, and the unflinching guardian of the Carter family interests.

As Carter shrugged off his overcoat, he turned to greet her.

"Good morning, Miss Lovejoy. Could you please get me Mr. Fergusson in New Orleans?"

"Yes sir, Mr. Glenn Fergusson, Fergusson Drilling, New

45

Orleans." She picked up his coat and left for her desk, closing his door behind her.

Carter started to pace the vast office, absentmindedly studying the familiar snow-strewn panorama of Greater Boston that lay about him thirty stories below. The Prescott Tower dominated the Boston skyline and Carter had an excellent view of the harbor to the east and the ice-packed Charles River to the north. There was a good-sized tanker laying in the lower anchorage out beyond the airport. Otherwise, the harbor was quiet. To the north, a sharp west wind herded low cumulus clouds to the sea. The broken shafts of sunlight caught the gilded towers of the Harvard Houses further up the frozen Charles. This was a far cry and a distant place from the first day "Bullet" Carter met Glenn Fergusson.

That was nine years back, in the fall of 1944. Eisenhower had just turned Patton loose. His Third Army was in a hell-bent race with Montgomery's for first across the Rhine, but his scout elements were hung on the Meuse. Patton didn't know how to lose, and yet, at the dawn briefing, there was this cluster of pins on the status map around the town of Commercy. The general started to rant and wanted a complete report. He couldn't get it by radio. Major Carter was sent up in a half-track to get things going.

For two miles west of the town, the road was cluttered with Sherman tanks and half-tracks. The lack of dispersal reflected the Third Army's contempt for the remains of the Luftwaffe and seriously hampered Carter's progress. After several hours of threats, shouting, and detours through ditches, Carter came on the bridgehead to be met by a weary captain of Engineers. The captain greeted Carter's fig leaves with the sorriest of salutes. Carter asked for a report.

In two hours, and with commandeered work parties of the waiting tank men, the polished staff officer and the dusty engineer had a pontoon bridge thrown across the river. The Third Army was off and rolling.

After Carter reported this to his general, he invited the captain to share the shade by his half-track and a liberated bottle of Cognac. They spent a pleasant afternoon watching the Shermans lumber over the captain's boat bridge and be-

46

came firm and lasting friends. Glenn Fergusson was a man who got things done. He was the first man that Lawrence Carter visited when the Prescott Company had financed much of the new equipment needs of Fergusson's expanding drilling company. Two years ago, Glenn had been invited to a Board membership on one of the larger Prescott Funds.

The flash of the intercom brought Carter back to the reality of his office.

"Mr. Fergusson on line three, Mr. Carter."

"Thank you, Miss Lovejoy." Carter hung up and picked up a second phone.

"Glenn! How are you? . . . and how's Joan?"

"That's wonderful . . . No . . . You're right though, I'm always interested in the growth of the Fergusson clan as well as the Fergusson Company . . . Glenn, I have a special problem. There is this young lad up here in our town, good background, good family . . . well, he had his fill of school, only nineteen, but a big fellow, knows quite a bit about boats and engines. The thought occurred to me that this fellow just might find his place in the oil business or maybe in the off-shore service business. That's very kind of you. Now, I don't want any special treatment. No, we're not running him out of town . . . a friend of my daughter Janice. I would like to learn what he's made of. He's a good boy, and his father and I know each other . . . Glenn, that's wonderful. See you next week at the Director's meeting . . . Oh, his name? . . . Jason Steele . . . Good, then I'll hear from you this afternoon. Thanks, Glenn."

The Wednesday dinner was strained at the outset. The Carters worked hard at building a bridge to the young, but a conversation can only go so far with polite "Yes, sirs" and "No, sirs" in response. Lawrence Carter plugged on, and asked Jason of his future plans. There was a pause as Jason studied his plate for a moment, and then he started in. He first spoke of his draft obligation, for America was then in the final throes of withdrawal from Korea, and it was on the front page each day. As Jason went along, he gained his ease. Mr. Carter was pleased to find that the lad could talk as an equal and reason well.

Jason said he had been recently checked over by Dr. Drake, the general practitioner in the town, who was certain that Jason's bronchial problem was ample ground for a medical deferment from the draft. If that didn't do it, then his childhood bout with rheumatic fever would.

He had already told his father he couldn't see fishing for a lifetime. It was only a help while he was looking around. He had hopes for a specialty-car shop fitting out dune racing buggies and he figured he had enough saved to get this going. He said that he knew the car business was well established and very competitive, but he felt he was good at things mechanical and he wanted to try a business on his own.

Lawrence Carter listened with patience, for he well knew the long odds against the success of a start-up operation. When Jason had finished, Carter started to spin his own web of past experience. Janice was surprised for seldom were the business activities of her father ever discussed at the dinner table.

Carter began with the story of his company sending him down to the Southwest just after the war to build fund sales. He went on into the far-reaching relations of the oil business. He started with Jason filling his Buick down at Slattery's station. He then worked the oil chain backward through trucks and terminals, tank ships, refineries, and pipelines. He explained the difference between major integrated companies and the smaller independents and how and where they competed against each other. He went even further on back into field production and well-head pumps.

Carter said that he and several of the Prescott board members had drilled successful wells down in Texas with the Fergusson Drilling Company. He touched on the fact that it was very advantageous from an income tax aspect and then went on with his views on the future potential for petroleum. Jason listened intently as did Janice. From the annual reports of the Prescott which she received from some of her own trust holdings, Janice had some idea of the many shares of the Standard Oil Companies and Socony Mobil and the Texas Company that they held. Until this night's dinner, however, they had

48

been just names. She never even saw the dividend checks. Miss Lovejoy took care of those things.

With Yankee forthrightness, Carter summarized the alternatives for Jason. Why not keep his own savings in the bank for a bit longer, see some other parts of the country and get paid while learning? Jason nodded that this made some sense. Carter said he had a friend from Louisiana in the offshore drilling business who would be in Boston the next week who might have a place for him. He offered to set up a meeting if Jason was interested. Jason was more than interested.

6

The steady drone of the big Lockheed had finally lulled Jason into a fitful sleep. A slight pain in his ear from the lowering altitude and a change in the pitch of the propellers brought him back to wakefulness. The stewardess was saying something on the P.A. system about seat belts and final approach. Jason cinched up his belt and turned back to the window. The week past was as much of a blur as the morning clouds racing under the wings.

In the week since Janice returned to school, Jason had not had time to feel lonely. He had gone right from seeing her off to a luncheon meeting with Lawrence Carter and Glenn Fergusson at a club on Beacon Hill. At lunch, Fergusson offered him a job and Jason accepted. Three days later, he received a detailed itinerary in the mail.

Jason made arrangements for a transfer with his draft board and worked out a cash sale of his Buick to a man in Gloucester. He came out of the deal almost one hundred and fifty dollars ahead. After he had arranged all his affairs, Jason left Manchester in his nineteenth year with better than two thousand dollars in the bank. He carried a duffel full of clean clothing and a head full of unfocused dreams.

Benjamin Steele drove his son to Logan Airport that last

night. Agnes Steele thought she was coming down with a cold and decided it best she stay inside. Jason was glad of this decision; her tears and cautions at the back door were enough emotion for one day. There was little said on the drive to the airport. When they got there and found a parking space for the pickup truck, there remained an hour until the eleven o'clock departure. Ben Steele shouldered the duffel over Jason's objections, and they headed for the Eastern ticket counter. The elder Steel paid cash for the ticket. This matter had been settled earlier in the week, for Jason Steele had wanted to pay from his own savings but Ben Steele would have no part of it. He had a right to give his son a start in life.

There was still three quarters of an hour until flight time. Knowing that his father would be up and about again at four-thirty, and that he faced the drive back, Jason suggested that he go along. But Ben stubbornly insisted on staying and they silently waited until flight time.

7

The Constellation was on long final, letting down gradually over the dark waters of Lake Pontchartrain. It was 7:15 on a hazy morning. Jason could see nothing in the morning mist.

As he stepped down the ramp, the heat and moisture hit him. For a New Englander, it was summer in January. The southern air was heavy, and it hung, like a windless August afternoon at Manchester with a thunderstorm coming down the Salem channel. Jason fetched his duffel and took a bus into the city. At the bus depot he asked directions, and decided to do the half mile on foot. His walk took him through some of the oldest and loveliest quarters of New Orleans but the delicate balustrades and wrought iron tracery passed right over his head. Buildings were buildings as he strode down to the waterfront.

Jason sensed tidewater close at hand from the long horn of a vessel backing from her slip into the stream. When he turned the last corner, he came onto the cobbled stones of the waterfront, and two more blocks to the south he found a five-story warehouse sort of building, set at the head of a long wide wharf. The wharf looked more like the bustling yard of a building contractor back home than that of a marine enterprise. It was heaped with piles of piping and cranes and gantries and all kinds of heavy equipment.

The gold and black sign over the door read, "Fergusson Drilling Company." As he got closer, there were other signs off to the side of the door: Fergusson Barge Company, Fergusson Tow Boat Company, and the Fergusson Offshore Company. The multiplicity of enterprises within this medium-size building impressed Jason.

He entered to meet a matronly receptionist at a small switchboard.

"May I help you, young man?"

"Yes, ma'am. My name is Jason Steele, and I'm looking for the office of the Fergusson Tow Boat Company."

" 'Round here, they're all one and the same. Are you expected?"

"Yes, ma'am."

"Well, if you'll please take a seat over there, I'm sure the personnel people will see you right away." She indicated a lounge area as her board started to buzz. She quickly had it plugged and spoke into her own receiver.

"Gertrude, ah got me a big handsome Yankee down heah, by the name of Jason Steele. Says he's lookin' for the employment offices of the Fergusson Tow Boat Company. . . . All right, I'll send him right up."

The telephone operator unplugged her board, turned to Jason, and gave him directions to the elevator and the third floor personnel offices. When he got there, he was greeted by a gray old lady, almost hidden behind a high clerk's desk. She reminded Jason of his English teacher last spring, but she was far more friendly. He was pleased that they already had a labeled personnel folder for him.

Jason filled out the forms and learned the terms of his

employment. He was to start at two dollars per hour. The old lady thought he might be working on one of the tugs or launches, but that was up to the dispatcher. He would be working an eight-hour day, time and a half thereafter. He was entitled to a week off with pay for every three weeks he either spent out on a rig in the bayous or at sea. If he didn't want to take the week off, he was entitled to get paid for it anyway, and could work right on through. When asked about savings accounts, she said the company would put whatever he wanted in a savings account. Jason thought for a moment and decided to bank 75 percent of his earnings. He was then sent out for a hurried physical exam and told to report to the dispatcher's office at one.

Jason wandered the waterfront for a time and was back at the Fergusson Operations office at the stroke of one. He knocked several times quite loudly, for he could hear voices inside. There was no response, so he entered. The room reminded Jason of the police radio rooms he had seen on television shows. The principal difference was the maps. The walls were lined with marine maps of the Gulf Coast from Corpus Christi, Texas, over to Tampa, Florida, and of the entire Mississippi River system on up to the north of St. Louis. There were printed names and metal hooks all over them. On many of the hooks, there were small blackboards, maybe a foot square, with what looked like the names of boats painted across the top and numbers in chalk that were unintelligible to Jason.

In the center of the room, a chunk of a man squatted at a desk. Behind the bull neck and sloping shoulders, Jason could see a microphone and radio console. A speaker was mounted in a wall over the center map. Jason could hear both sides of the conversation.

Bull neck to the microphone—"Bill, just to be sure now, you're saying to me that you want to revise the E.T.A. of the *Clovis W.* arriving Natchez, zero two hundred hours tomorrow. Is that correct, ovah."

Speaker on the wall—"That is correct, Herman, that is correct. This is the *Clovis W. Fergusson,* Whiskey Julliett 6752, off and clear with base. See yah, Herman."

"Base off and clear with the *Clovis W. Fergusson*—Come

52

in, son, come in." The bull neck didn't even turn to Jason. He was scribbling something on one of the little blackboards in chalk. When finished, he extended a chalky paw. He didn't rise, for he was a very fat man.

"Son, you can do me a favor afore we get to chatting. This heah blackboard. Ya see that hook there, way up above Vicksburg, yah, that's right, Fitler, Fitler, Mississippi, you're right there. Well now, I thank ya. You must be Jason Steele, and I'm Herman Swetser."

"Yes, sir, I am." Herman Swetser reminded Jason of a calm old frog with glasses.

"No sirs around here. There ain't enough of us. I'm Herman to everybody."

"Yes, Herman."

"Well, now. This paper heah, it says you know something about boats, or it says that Mr. Glenn thinks you know something about boats and engines."

Jason flushed as he replied, "Been around 'em all my life, Herman, and my dad before me."

"We'll soon see. Gotta tow goin' west outta New Orleans, 1600, this afternoon. Tug *William V. Fergusson* and the M-36 barge. They're takin' some pipe and mud on over to that Humble hole we got working, over in Vermillion Parish. I got ya down for that tow."

"Fine with me, sooner the better, Herman."

"Well, good, ya seem right anxious. You oughta get there 'bout 2200 tomorrow night. You'll report to Jasper Moffett, he's the drilling boss on *Discoverer Six*."

"What's the *Discoverer Six*?"

"She's a bayou drilling barge, not the biggest, but big enough. She can cut close to eighteen thousand foot of hole without much sweat."

The speaker started to crackle, and Herman handled another check-in. The interruption gave Jason another chance to study the walls. A quick count indicated there were over seventy-five little blackboards on the walls; a lot of gear, Jason thought to himself, yet a neat simple way to keep track of it. Swetser again came back to him.

"Well, anyway, when ya get out there, you see old Jasper,

53

give him this heah envelope." Herman handed Jason a sealed manila envelope.

"What am I going to be doing out there?"

"We got a little forty-foot crew launch on that job. A high-speed diesel. Use it to fetch out drilling crews from a little town across Vermillion Bay on up to the drill site. We thought to start you on her."

"Sounds great to me." It was right down his alley, and Jason knew it.

8

As Jason came down the dock, a crane crew was still swinging racks of drill pipe aboard the barge M-36. His early arrival gave him the time to inspect the trim tug as she lay outboard of the leading barge. The first man to greet him when he had worked his way over and around the steel and mud sacks of the barge was the tug's skipper, Jack Broussard. "Well, I'll be. Old Herman told us we'd have a Yankee lad this trip. We all thought he was joshing. Come on aboard, son."

Jack Broussard was tall, leathery, and very thin. He was a man in his early fifties, and his years in the sunlight had dyed his skin a light walnut. He took Jason to a cabin neatly fitted with shower and toilet and two tightly made bunks.

"You got this to yourself, this trip. Come on, we'll go back to the kitchen and get some coffee."

At 1600, as the ship's clock struck eight bells in the wheel house, he had been asked up to the bridge, probably as much to keep out from under the deck crew as to have an excellent view of the whole operation. Jason guessed that the *William V.* ran a good eighty-five feet. He was surprised what good shape she was in, for the commercial craft he had been aboard were rusty and run down. The *William V.*'s black hull was without a rust streak, and the soft tan of her superstructure was neatly set off with dark red trim. She had a tall funnel done in gleaming black enamel with a crimson "F" set on a wide white stripe. Jason found it a trim craft, even by his father's standards.

What first set him aback was the manner of these rivermen's speech. As the non-nautical phrases slid off Broussard's tongue in a thick bayou drawl, Jason suspected he was getting his leg pulled. He'd been about boats all his life, and port from starboard came easier than left from right. To his amazement, he found the whole crew spoke the same way. These rivermen went to great lengths to avoid a nautical phrase.

Their lack of "salt talk" had no effect on their boat handling skill, though. Broussard eased the tug into the flow of the Mississippi and swung a tight circle. He came back at the M-36 barge and gently nudged the rubber covered snout of the tug into the pushing notch cut into the barge's broad stern. It was as neat a piece of boat handling as Jason had ever watched. Captain Broussard had the whole rig clear of the deck and underway upstream to the Intracoastal Waterway cut in less than ten minutes.

New Orleans was a hustling port but it wasn't the size or number of the ships that were impressive. It was the huge lash-ups of barges and tugs. Just before the Gretna Cut, they came on a thirty-barge train pushed by two tugs. It looked longer than the *Queen Elizabeth*. Broussard said there were some new boats being built to shove forty barges at a crack. As the tug swung west into the waterway, they were soon lost in the lushness of the bayous in the fading twilight. Broussard broke the crew into three watches of men. The engineer and cook didn't stand a watch. On the watch bill, Jason was paired with the captain, which pleased him. They stood four hours on and eight off. These hours gave him both sunset and dawn on deck in this strange new country.

He was beginning to realize just how strange and unique was this land of the bayous. The heavy heat and vegetation told him how very far he was from New England's rock-ribbed coast. But his senses could not tell him how, for eons, the mighty river had drained the continental heartland of its topsoil and carried it to the Delta to make a land of its own, a

55

sleepy land clothed in marshes and prairies and occasional clusters of cypress; or how, layer by layer, far beneath, the river built one of the great powder kegs of resources in all the world, of oil and gas and sulphur. This Jason would soon learn in his time working about the drilling rigs of the Delta.

The Intracoastal Waterway was a happy meeting of the Lord of Genesis and the United States Army Corps of Engineers. There were man-made cuts and embankments as were necessary, but for the most part, the engineers had followed the Way of the Lord, with a few lighted markers to define the channel.

Captain Broussard occasionally broke in as Jason watched with fascination the banks of tall oaks, swaying festoons of Spanish moss, and muddy brown water.

"Jason, ya see those logs up ahead there on the right?"

"Yes, sir, sure do; better go to port a bit."

"Port a bit, bullshit, left and right boy, but those ain't logs, they'll be gators." Jason tried to make them out in the fading light as Broussard drawled on.

"Gators and cottonmouths. Those the things ya keep your eye out for 'round this country."

The logs disappeared in a swirl as the tug chugged on into the darkness, matching the heavy chug of her diesel to the croaks, snorts, and snuffles of night in the bayous.

When the dispatcher told Jason he would next work out of a small town, he did not exaggerate.

Orchila had slumbered for a century. The town consisted of four dilapidated houses, an unpainted Baptist church, a restaurant, and a fueling dock on the Intracoastal Waterway. It was the last fueling place before crossing Vermillion Bay.

People said that Orchila had been something a hundred years ago; what remained was once the tidewater landing for the Orchila Plantation. Edward Orchila, the last male of the family, went off as a captain of Louisiana militia in the Civil War, and was killed in action. His plantation was soon a shrine of crumbling porticoes and teetering pillars to the dream that died at Appomattox Court House.

56

Then after ninety years, the sleep of Orchila was shattered by the explosions of seismic crews working the Delta country. Then came the work boats and drilling barges, the roustabouts and engineers. These people needed a place to stay. The Landry family, that had bought up most of the old Orchila place, decided that beds, fuel, food, and beer were better business than tilling soybeans. They fixed up a couple of the old houses as bunk rooms for the drilling crews. They built a long fueling dock for the tugs along the levee and added a diner alongside the dock. They called it the "Blue Heron" and made money from the day they hung up the sign. That was ten years ago. The drilling rigs were still working the neighborhood as hard as ever. They kept going deeper each year. Along the Canal, a couple of hours at the Blue Heron had grown to be an unspoken work right of every tow crew running the waterway from Port Arthur to New Orleans.

On this morning in March, Jason found himself edging the launch *By-Stander* alongside the fueling dock of the Blue Heron. Coleman, the skinny black lad who handled the docking lines, was there to greet him. Jason came over to fetch or deliver something at least four times a day, and he and Coleman had become friends.

Jason nudged the *By-Stander* into the piling, slipped her into neutral, and heaved bow and after spring lines up to Coleman.

"Mornin', Coleman."

"Mornin', Cap'n Jason." The dockman's face was a sunburst of teeth.

"You seen anything of a man in a Baroid car, the mud guy? He's supposed to be driving down here from New Iberia. Jasper sent me in to fetch him."

"No, suh. He ain't showed up heah yet. I'd a noticed."

"Well, make up on these other lines and come on down here and cool your black ass if you like."

Jason indicated the glassed main cabin of *By-Stander*. The launch was laid out like a floating bus, with Jason's driving cab perched way up on the bow, then the air-conditioned main cabin, with settees and a coffee galley, and back aft, a flat, open deck out by the transom where they hauled mud sacks and

57

light supplies. The hull was of steel, shaped in a wide flat V. She drew a bit less than two feet of water, and with her two big GM 6–71's she could really fly. When Jason first wrote home to his father, he told him how proud he was of his *By-Stander* but confessed that he didn't think she'd be worth much in a winter westerly off Manchester.

Coleman followed Jason into the passenger cabin, accepted his offer of a cup of coffee, and flopped out on one of the settees. The chilled dryness of the cabin was a comfortable contrast to the heavy steaminess of the Delta country air.

"Coleman," Jason said. "How long's it been since you been with a girl?"

"Hey, man! Not since last night."

"Well, for me, it's coming on three months, and I know it. You know any girls?"

While the drilling crews had regularly rotated back to New Orleans, Jason had put away eight hundred dollars in his New Orleans savings account, by staying out on the *Discoverer Six* through three full cycles. Now he'd had enough of a monastic life. Janice's longing letters only increased his need for a woman.

"It's gotta be black, Cap'n Jason."

"Coleman, at this point, I don't give a shit if it's purple."

"I'll talk to Sue Ann. She's the tall one with the big tits, works on the grill most of the time. Might cost you, though."

"About how much?"

"Maybe three bucks, and maybe a tip, if ya like her."

"She's got a deal."

Their conversation was broken off by the clunk of the missing Baroid technician struggling down the ramp with a large suitcase in each hand.

As Jason hauled in the docking lines, he shouted up to Coleman.

"Be back for those crates 'round dinner. Gonna need some fuel too."

"I'll take care of it, Cap'n."

58

9

On the forty-minute run to the rig, the Baroid technician stuck his head in the steering cabin door. "Want some company?"

"Why, sure, come on in and close the door." Jason indicated a tall oak stool by the port window.

He was a good-looking fellow, no more than three or four years older than Jason, of slender build, medium height, with wide brown eyes, curly blond hair, and an easy smile. He reached over and extended his hand to Jason. "Hi, I'm Dan Bacon."

In the course of their conversation, Jason learned that Bacon, a Rice graduate, had done a year of graduate geology work toward a master's at M.I.T. He had dropped out for a couple of years "to pile up some scratch," but still had hopes of getting back to Cambridge and finishing up. Since Bacon had spent quite a bit of time up on the North Shore of Massachusetts Bay around the Crane's Beach area, this gave them some common ground.

The conversation drifted back to the kind of work Bacon was doing. He explained how the "mud" he sold wasn't really mud as most people knew it. He told Jason of how these mud or chemical mixtures were forced down the drill pipe and acted as a lubricant on the bottom as the drilling bit twisted deeper into the earth. There were different mixtures of mud for drilling through different types of rock, and the little flecks of cuttings that came back up the hole as the mud was recirculated were the best indicators to the driller and the geologist of what they were cutting into. He had a simple way of explaining technical details and Jason listened attentively to his lecture on mud and its virtues. It was his first sight of an enthusiastic salesman at work.

By-Stander tore across the bay, flat out, and was soon pushing up to the clanking bulk of *Discoverer Six*. There was nothing fancy about *Discoverer*. She was a big steel spindle tower, just like any one might see about the older fields of Texas or Oklahoma. The tower and drilling platform were mounted on a huge rusty barge with a drill hole cut right through its bottom. Except for the barge, it wasn't much different than drilling on land.

Jason got his lines to the gangway bollards as Bacon gathered up his gear for a climb up to the mud tanks. "Professor, thanks for the lecture. You spending the night at Orchila?"

"Gawd, I hope not. All depends on these tests."

"Well, if you have to, I'll be takin' you in. Maybe we can have a beer and a bite of dinner."

"That would be just fine with me."

Bacon disappeared over the rail cap with a smile.

As matters turned out, Dan Bacon did spend a reluctant night at Orchila. The mud returns showed they were cutting a more porous limestone formation than had been encountered at this same depth in the offsetting wells to the east and north. This called for a change to a heavier mud, which would be down on a barge first thing in the morning. Moffett, the rig boss, decided to haul back on the drill string and change bits while waiting. Since Bacon was a young salesman and Humble his biggest customer, he thought it best to stick around and see that his end of the deal went right.

Dan and Jason had dinner and many beers that night although the ratio of liquid consumed favored Bacon over Steele two to one. Jason had never been much of a drinker, especially when there were things he wanted to learn. They were the last customers out of the Blue Heron. It was close to eleven when Bacon headed for his hotel bunk and Jason for the *By-Stander*.

He carefully checked the docking lines and the shoreside connection for the electricity. The air conditioner didn't work without it. It was that or turn on the generator, and that was too noisy.

As he was getting out of the shower and into a clean pair of shorts, he heard steps and laughter on the dock ladder. There

60

was a knock on the main cabin door. When Jason got aft, he met the grinning face of Coleman and waved him in. Coleman had two girls in his wake.

"Cap'n Jason, this is my friend Sue Ann. Sue Ann, this Cap'n Jason. He runs this heah vessel. Now, Sue Ann was 'fraid she might get lonesome so she asked me to bring along mah friend Betty. Betty, this is Cap'n Jason."

The girls dutifully shook Jason's hand, exchanged shy "Hi you-alls" and started to giggle at the white man standing about in his shorts. In the dim light of the cabin, it was difficult for Jason to distinguish their features clearly. He had no wish to turn on any more light, yet he could see they still wore their white waitress uniforms from the diner. Sue Ann was the big girl he had watched that evening at dinner. She was tall, close to six feet, with wide, even features, huge breasts, and a big rear on a slim wiry body.

Coleman spoke up. "Cap'n Jason, you got some gin or maybe scotch aboard?"

Jason said that he did and went forward to fetch a half bottle of gin from under his bunk. He set that and some plastic cups on the galley counter and got out some ice from the box below. He poured three stiff gin and gingers and a weak one for himself.

After the second round of drinks, Jason announced that he had to use the head. A few moments later, he smelled her. The heavy muskiness of her body smell, and the dried sweat of her night over the grill, all of these in the close quarters of the head started his body to pulse and to swell. Before he could turn, he felt her breasts rubbing into the bare blades of his shoulders.

"Coleman tells me you wanta fuck a nigah girl." Sue Ann's voice was husky.

Jason Steele whirled and grabbed her. "Coleman is telling you right, girl." She was naked and his hands were all over her, as he pushed her back, across the companionway and into his bunk in the adjacent cabin. He drove into her at once with his full weight. There were no niceties to their mating. It was animal need and she was as ready and wet as he was hard.

Sue Ann had buttocks and thighs of spring steel. She locked

61

her legs about him and lifted him clear of the bunk. Jason
Steele never forgot Sue Ann of the Blue Heron. She had made
him stand again a second time without ever pulling out, all
with wriggles and muscle twitches while her legs were still
locked about him.

10

By May, Jason had rotated through the various jobs
on *Discoverer Six*. He held his own through all of them and
won the grudging respect of his Cajun co-workers. They never
really understood the presence of this young Yankee, and Jason,
for his part, was quiet and self-contained. He made neither
lasting friends nor enemies. When it came to work, he pitched
in and sweated just as hard as the rest. His first job, as launch
driver, was his favorite, for it gave him freedom, his own cabin,
air conditioning, and time with Sue Ann. However, rig work,
his next assignment, paid better. He was now up to $2.50 per
hour, and as he continued to refuse his week of rotation back
to the city, he had piled up over sixteen hundred in savings.

That wasn't to say that Jason became a working monk
when he moved from the launch to the drilling barge. Even
then, bushed as he was from days in the sun, working the mon-
key job high on the drilling rig, stacking and racking ninety-
foot stands of drill pipe, Jason still managed to work a trade
off with the new launch driver to seek his pleasure with reasonable regularity.

Jason never thought of Sue Ann in relation to Janice.
Janice Carter was a pretty white girl with a beautiful white
body, who went to an all-white school that was a good thousand
miles away. Janice Carter was a way of life that Jason had determined to have. As he listened to the bunkhouse chatter of
the roughnecks, he mused on their contentment in their sweat.
They never resented their productivity going on to the purses
of tailored trustees and sunbaked widows in far-off places. He

was not so accepting. He aimed for the other end of the pipeline. Though just in his twentieth year, Jason saw the larger picture. He knew that life with Janice would take money and would mean money. He understood what the Carter name could do for him, and he knew he would need a grub stake to get on any kind of a workable footing, and move up that pipeline.

If Jason didn't think about faithfulness, Janice, for her part, safely walled in a girl's boarding school, didn't have any workable alternatives. Her letters continued their weekly deluge of her hopes and wants and needs. She talked of time and how it would fly and how their summer would be. She artfully drew him out on what he was doing each day. She followed the drilling of that first Humble well foot by foot through his pen, and was almost as pleased as he was when it came in as a dual producer. Jason sent her a small clipping from the New Iberia *Picayune* that told the technical details. Janice proudly sent it along to her father.

Her barrage of mail continued. She asked if he would come up to her graduation from Foxcroft. Before Jason could reply, Janice had decided for both of them. She had called the airlines and discovered it would cost close to $175. Janice concluded rather sensibly, "I think we should save the money, because I'm going to be surrounded with relatives and there just won't be time for us, and I don't want that." Jason agreed with the second letter and congratulated her on her acceptance by both Radcliffe and Sarah Lawrence. He preferred Radcliffe; it was closer to transportation. On receipt of his letter, Janice picked up her pen and completed her Radcliffe commitment.

Toward the end of May, just before Jason was pulled back to New Orleans with a promotion to a second mate's job on one of the waterway tugs, Janice wrote that she had wrangled with her mother for a month about canceling her debut and had won. But her mother had arranged for a graduation present tour by Janice and her cousin, Lillian Clarke, to Scotland and Ireland. Could Jason plan to take two weeks of vacation in June before she set off on her trip? Jason promised that he would.

Jason, having already purchased his airplane tickets, was

heading out for a movie one night with his new apartment mate, Dan Bacon, when the phone rang. It was Herman Swetser, the dispatcher at the Fergusson Company. Herman had a long tale of woe about the second mate on the seagoing tug *Julie S. Fergusson*. The man had just come down with a bleeding ulcer that afternoon and was in the Mariner's Hospital for at least a week, maybe two. The *Julie S.* was under contract to Creole Petroleum for the tow of a new production platform to Lake Maracaibo, Venezuela. Jason was needed to fill in as second mate.

The request caught Jason by surprise. His plans were made and he wanted very much to see Janice, but he quickly saw the opportunity. Feigning indignation, he answered, "Hey, I've got a vacation this Friday and a promise."

"Hell, boy, a lad like you can cash in a promise any time he wants."

"This is a special promise. I might even marry her."

There were a few seconds of silence on the wire, and then Herman blathered on, "Jason, you're sick, my boy. What you need is a long trip in the sea air. Come back with a clear head."

"What's in it for me?"

'You got me by the short ones, boy. I need you. We'll pay you first mate's wages for this trip. You're not worth it, mind."

Knowing the problem this was going to cause in Manchester and what Manchester could mean to him, Jason decided to trade.

"What's that come out to, Herman?"

"Now let me see, $3.75 for eight, time and a half till twelve. Double time thereafter. One day off for every two at sea."

"How long am I gone?"

"This trip ticket, it was worked out on one thousand, six hundred and ninety-three miles, down through the Yucatán Channel."

Jason's mind raced through the numbers. "Jesus Christ, Herman. At three knots dragging that big platform, that's about, hell, that's over five hundred and sixty hours. Twenty-three days, just one way."

"That sounds about right, but I really need you, lad, and you'd be back with money in your pocket."

"Throw in an extra week of vacation, full pay as a first mate, and you got a deal."

"You're on and I thank you, Jason."

After hanging up, Jason worked the deal out on a scrap of paper. At nine knots back to New Orleans, there were more than thirty-two sea days, and without any overtime or double watches, he would come home with another fifteen hundred dollars. He then tried to anticipate Janice's reaction. She'll be mad as hell, that's sure. But there's not much I can do about her for a while anyway with all Mrs. Carter's plans, he thought. Mrs. Carter's talk about time was still a burr. That Mr. Carter might think his a sensible decision, Jason also considered. He concluded that Janice would be there when he came back. He was confident of his hold.

When he phoned Manchester, Janice was first heartbroken and then furious and then in tears. She finally slammed down the phone, saying she never wanted to see him again. When she related what had happened, Catharine Carter was sympathetic and secretly pleased. Lawrence Carter barely put down his *Evening Traveler*. Behind the newspaper, he was quietly impressed with the good sense of Jason Steele. Neither parent again mentioned the incident.

Jason made the long voyage down to Venezuela. It was a good trip without a hitch. The tug had just been launched and was the pride of the Fergusson fleet; 115 feet, five thousand throbbing horses, and air-conditioned comfort throughout. Captain LeClerq, her skipper, was the martinet of the Fergusson fleet. He took a liking to the sober young Yankee and taught him the use of the sextant and how to find his way by the stars.

If there had been letters, Jason would not have received them until his return to New Orleans in August. There were no letters.

Janice spent most of August on a tall Irish hunter near Connemara in the west of Ireland. She and her cousin were guests of a friend of Mr. Carter's. By that time, her anger and bitterness with Jason had eroded to remorse. Janice was still young in her ways about men and her cousin Lillian was of little help. Janice was confident Jason would write, for he was in the wrong. The thought that she might pick up her own pen got mixed in a miasma of Carter pride and girlish uncertainty. Each letterless day, Janice rode that much harder. If there had been boys about Connemara, perhaps things might have been different. But the only boys were from the village. Their paths never crossed.

To do something different, the girls took the *Queen Elizabeth* back to New York in the first week of September. They had a large first-class cabin to themselves for the first night out. Lillian soon snagged a blond Dutch student on the shuffleboard court. In the pool on the second morning, Janice met an English youth, Anthony V. S. Ormsby, on his way to a year as an exchange student at Yale. Janice soon found herself groping about in her bunk with her new English beau and life became very confused. She was pleased that other young men besides Jason were drawn to her, yet despite a hardy summer of Irish horses, she found unloving love impossible for her. No matter how hard she tried, when she kissed Tony, she found Jason. Tony worked desperately through the nights, but never in Jason's ultimate preserve. As the harbor pilot boarded the *Queen* for the final run into Manhattan, Janice was more confused than ever. She hurried home to Manchester to a loving family and was hurt anew to find no letters.

The heady whirl of her freshman year at Radcliffe burst upon her—a time of tea dances and football games and new boys, but she still thought often of Jason. Her studies deteriorated to a degree, but by mid-term hour exams she had crammed herself back to a B average.

Tony Ormsby, the boy from the boat, asked her down for the Harvard-Yale weekend. Janice was torn, for her friends were going, and it was "The Game" in the Bowl. She also knew what to expect. She spent the night in a Darien motel with Tony, but it was not a success. Janice grew angry with herself, for she found Tony attractive. She returned his invitation, and he came up for a December weekend at Manchester. Mrs. Carter

66

was impressed that Tony's father was a belted knight. Mr. Carter was intrigued that Tony's father held a seat in Lloyds. Janice Carter was bored with Tony. The weekend at Manchester put the lid on that.

The Christmas holidays were soon upon Janice, a time of mistletoe, merriment, and the anniversary of her lost virginity. It was a time of good will to all. Janice decided to send Jason a Christmas card.

Jason replied, and in a scribbled note made mention of a visit to his family at Manchester some time in February. Several weeks later, Janice very casually wrote again and said she would like to see him when he was home if they could find the time; that she had a week of vacation coming up over Washington's Birthday weekend. Her present plan was to go up to Franconia to the family winter place and ski. She hoped that she would not miss his visit.

Jason, who had never doubted throughout the fall that Janice would eventually make the first move toward reconciliation, rearranged his vacation and replied to her note.

11

One night in February Janice made a brief phone call to New Orleans to ask Jason if he needed a ride from the airport down to the shore. He said he did.

On the morning of his Boston arrival and as the Constellation wheeled toward the passenger gate, Janice, to her consternation, found her heart matching the high throb of the props. For weeks, she had told herself she was only curious as to how the maverick Jason might have changed. She planned to be composed and friendly, yet, as the props wound down and the cabin door opened with a thump, there was a catch in her throat. He looked older, older and more worldly than his contemporaries about Cambridge. She liked that.

Jason first caught sight of Janice through the glass by the

gate. He gave a wave and a smile, controlled yet friendly. Once inside he ducked under the barrier and held open his arms. She flung herself into them. They kissed, a long kiss, and he whispered "Hi, Jan" in her ear. In that instant, their summer of silence was gone.

They waited quietly for his luggage; the bustling lobby was no place to talk. In the parking lot, Janice offered the keys to her station wagon, a hand-me-down from her mother, to Jason as he opened her door, but he declined.

"No, I'd rather look at you."

They started up Route 1 and, at Jason's suggestion, stopped for a drink in a dim bar. When the waitress had gone back to her television, Jason spoke.

"I've missed you very much, Jan." He reached across the table for her hand.

Tears almost welled forth. "Oh, Jason, I've missed you too. I wish I hadn't been such a hot-headed little bitch last summer."

"Don't worry about it. I think I understood. Besides, it's all behind us now."

"Did you understand, really? I wanted to see you so very, very much before I went away."

Jason looked at her steadily and answered solemnly, "Yes, I had a lot of time at sea to think—to think about you and us. I love you." That turned loose a torrent of tears. Jason patted her hand and went on. "I had to be sure of myself and to sort out what I am and what I want to be and where I'm going. God knows I've never been much for books and I know the way you've been brought up. Jan, we're young, and if I didn't settle down very early, I could never give you the things you're used to, plain and simple every day used to. I have to do that or nothing will work. That was the only reason I took that job to Venezuela, nothing else. I wanted to come home to you." Jason's sincerity carried across in his every word.

"Oh Jason, I was so selfish," she blurted. "I just wanted you there, that week, that day, that night. It would have been so perfect, and now, we've wasted . . ." She looked down to search about in her bag for a handkerchief.

"Jan, it's not wasted. We both know that. You've got to

68

put yourself in my shoes, too. Look, I had to prove I could do something. I want to marry you, but my way . . . that includes standing on my own. Look, I'm not ashamed of it. These guys down on the shore, the ones that went off to fancy schools, they're all going one way and I'm going another but I want you with me. Hard knocks versus Harvard. It's one hell of a game, and I'm going to win it."

On the drive to Manchester, they agreed that it might be best if her parents did not know he was back. Janice said her mother had been terribly touchy of late, and she had an idea it might be something to do with an early change of life. She wondered if there might not be some casual and natural way that Jason might meet them again. That would be far easier all around. Until the opportunity appeared, Janice would say nothing, and she would pick him up at his home that night.

After dinner in their respective homes, they set off for a movie in Peabody. Janice nestled close by Jason as he drove. At a red light in Salem, they found themselves in a long kiss broken only by the irate blare of a horn from behind. Jason turned back to the wheel as he growled. "To hell with a movie." Janice nuzzled that much closer.

The station wagon responded to the weight of his foot, and after a hurried stop at a liquor store, Jason drew up before the gaudiest motel on Route 1. Janice remained in the car as Jason made his arrangements with the night clerk. The old man never glanced at the signed register. He was solely interested in cash in advance from early risers.

Janice preceded Jason into the motel room. As he struggled for a moment with the drawn bolt, he couldn't miss the wrinkling of her nose as she took in the commercial sterility of her surroundings. Jason set down his bottle, and drawing her to him said, "Jan, honey, I took the one where no one from Manchester would ever . . ." She looked up with a quick nod and his words were lost in their kiss.

Later on, Jason slid from beneath the rumpled sheets and strode across the room. "This calls for a celebration." Janice watched as he twisted off the wires of the bottle. She was contentedly propped on her elbow, revealing the rich fullness of her figure.

69

Jason was quickly back beside her, having set thick tumblers down on the night table. He now had the bottle wrapped in a towel as he wrestled with the cork. A muffled pop signaled his success. He slid down beside her, and attempted to hug her and neatly fill her tumbler at the same time. Amidst his jostling and her giggling, much of her champagne dribbled down her chin. Jason was more successful in stanching these racing rivulets in the valley of her breasts with his tongue. Their tumblers empty on the carpet, they made love for a less hurried second time.

The next morning, Janice set about to convince Jason he should go skiing with her, but he was reluctant; he had never skied. However, she had her way and he agreed to give several days in Franconia a try. As long as she was committed to going with her family, it was the only way they could be together.

At home, Janice volunteered to go up to New Hampshire three days ahead of the family to see that everything at the house was ready. She told her mother that she had a term paper to finish and she thought Franconia was a nice quiet place to get it done. Later that same day, she started north and on her way through town, she picked up Jason.

When they got to Franconia, Janice stopped by Lovetts' Inn, where her family had stayed for years before they built their own place. With every cajolery and wile of which she was capable, she found a single bed in the boys' dormitory two nights hence. With that chore attended to, Janice and Jason disappeared into the Carter place.

Two years earlier, when Lawrence Carter came into control of the Prescott Company, he had commissioned an architect friend to do a contemporary winter home on the crown of Sugar Hill up beyond Franconia Notch. It was a beautiful place of weathered planks and picture windows with prospects of all the pine-capped peaks. Octagon in shape, it was built around a huge fieldstone fireplace. For two days, the surrounding circle of soft lounges were used for a purpose Lawrence Carter had never intended.

On the eve of the family's arrival, Janice and Jason went out for the first time to the beginner's slope on Cannon Mountain. Jason had never been on skis and Janice worked hard at

70

suppressing her superiority. She patiently took him through the snow plow and taught him how to use his poles and even how to pick himself up after a fall. Jason's bulk was happy prey to gravity. He couldn't master the principle of weight on the downhill ski. In the years to come, he would studiously avoid skiing. Jason Steele would never take on that at which he couldn't excel.

As an entourage of Carters unloaded their ski gear at Sugar Hill, they found a studious Janice deep in her books, a snapping fire on the center hearth, a full ice box, and a cheery kettle warming water for late tea.

The next morning, Lawrence Carter, his son and daughter were the first passengers at the tramway gate and made the trip to the summit with the milk cans for the upper restaurant.

There had been a light fall of snow through the night, no more than three inches but enough to create the illusion of virginity on the expert trails. This can be the most treacherous of conditions on the tree-lined mountain trails of New England, for the icy ruts of the previous days are still there, hidden. It held no fear for the Carters. They had skied for many years. Lawrence Carter, whose age paralleled the explosion of skiing in America, learned three different systems of skiing. He had learned them all well, but on the rare occasion that he caught an edge and was in trouble, the composite nature of his ski knowledge came out in flailing arms and uphill stem checks. This was not so of Larry and Janice. They had been brought to the hills when the Austrian and French instructors came to a peace treaty, and the ski schools of the world started to teach the tight parallel that later merged into wedelin.

The younger Carters could take any trail at Franconia full bore. They could wedle the moguls of Polly's Folly or nose into the pitch of the Zoomer with suppleness and fluidity. Lawrence Carter was justly proud of his children and spent all of his day trying to stay out ahead of them. The young tolerated his vanity and heel checked just often enough to keep him happy.

By noon, the threesome had had six full runs on the toughest trails on Cannon Mountain. At the tram station at the base, the length of the waiting line was discouraging. Janice, flushed with the cold and her concealed happiness, casually said, "Hey, you guys, what about lunch? I'm starved."

Having spent enough time at Franconia to know that an early lunch was a smart move, the other two agreed. After stashing their skis in a snow bank, they joined the food line in the cafeteria.

Lawrence Carter took the lead in the tray line. Somewhere between the apple juice and cocoa, he turned to Janice.

"Hey, Jan, you see who's over there?"

"Who? Where?" Janice looked about, wide-eyed, the picture of innocence.

"Second table beyond the water fountain."

"Oh, my god, it's Jason Steele. What's he doing here?"

"I certainly don't know. Let's join him and find out." An opportunity to tease his daughter seldom escaped him.

"Oh, Daddy, let's forget it."

"No, come on. You can at least be civil."

And so the Carters joined Jason Steele for lunch. He and Janice exchanged barely a glance as they shook hands. Lawrence Carter settled into his most affable mood and asked Jason to tell him all about what he had been doing. Jason gave him chapter and verse about the business with poise and self-assurance. He talked easily and charmingly. Toward the end of lunch, Carter switched topics.

"How about skiing with us for the afternoon, Jason?"

"No thank you, Mr. Carter, I'm just a beginner." Jason's reluctance was obvious, and Lawrence Carter had no wish to embarrass him.

"Well, what are you doing later on?"

"I thought I might go back to Lovetts' and see what was up. I really don't have any plans."

"We've got this place over on Sugar Hill. How about coming by for a drink? Maybe Janice and Larry and their friends can find another plate for dinner."

"Well, Mr. Carter, that's very kind, but . . ." Janice and Larry assured Jason that he was most welcome.

And so Lawrence Carter brought Jason Steele back into his daughter's life. He later had some difficulty explaining the whole thing to his wife.

72

There was little time in the whirl of the family weekend for Janice and Jason to talk, but it didn't matter. Looks said all that was necessary. On the long drive back to Manchester, Jason asked, "Jan, where do we go from here?"

Janice studied the whirling trees through the steamed side pane for a long time and then said in a small even voice, "I'm in love with you, Jason, and I really don't know where we go. It's sort of up to you."

"You remember last year when your mother talked of time; she sort of hinted that if we were right for each other after a year or two . . . you remember that?"

"Of course I remember, you big ape. How could I forget?"

"Well this is February, and June isn't that far. Will you marry me?"

Janice snuggled close beside him and whispered in his ear. "Yes, I will, Jason, yes I will."

"Then when?"

"This summer."

12

Jason Steele married Janice Carter in Saint George's Chapel at Manchester on the second Saturday of July. Their marriage was one of the high spots of the season on the North Shore. Catharine Carter looked, and was, the personification of a gracious hostess, the happy mother of the bride. Her smiles and kisses seemed so effusive and so real, the most discerning person could never have told how hard she had initially fought this marriage. Her words of waiting of the previous year had been brought back to haunt her. What really exasperated her was the apparent neutrality or even acquiescence of her husband.

When Catharine Carter realized Janice was serious, and the choice narrowed to her kind of marriage or an elopement, she was forced to capitulate. Janice was nineteen in May and with Jason now twenty-one, they could marry, with or without the Carters' consent. It was this set of alternatives that had led to the pink-striped tents over all the terraces, the dance floors by the cliff and the pool, the champagne and orchestras.

Perhaps Catharine Carter's real objection was that it had happened too quickly for her. She even tried that argument once or twice to little effect. Janice pointed out that she had known Jason for almost two years. Janice also pointed out that she was one year older than her mother was when she had married.

Catharine Carter's next line of attack was that Jason didn't have a good enough job to support a wife nor the means to set up a home. This argument, too, didn't get very far, for Jason had saved over $14,000 and was earning, with overtime, $15,000 a year. Even Lawrence Carter's cash position on his wedding day couldn't match that.

And so when there was no other choice, Catharine Carter gave her daughter the biggest of hugs and produced one of the more gracious weddings that Manchester had seen in many a year.

By measurement of the circles of friends that the Carters might have invited, it was a very small wedding. There were only two hundred and fifty guests, and just about all of them were from the town of Manchester. In the receiving line, Ben Steele introduced Catharine Carter to the fire chief and the town clerk and some of his fishing and lobstering pals. The obvious happiness of Janice and Jason, the music, the wine, and the sun-drenched afternoon all contributed to the general feeling among the guests that this would be a good marriage.

The bridal couple left the wedding reception just after sunset. Larry Carter, the best man, whisked them down the drive amidst showers of rice and confetti and tears. Beyond the village, they switched to Jason's new convertible and drove on into Boston. Their bridal night was spent in a comfortable suite of the Ritz-Carleton Hotel.

The next morning, the Jason Steeles took the ten o'clock Pan American flight to Bermuda and spent a week at the Coral Beach Club. They were seldom seen out of their suite.

74

Book Two

1

The newly married Steeles returned from their honeymoon to a tiny apartment on the narrowest street of Beacon Hill. Acorn Street was a charming cobblestoned, gaslit page from the century past. Its red brick buildings precariously piled on each other on the steep west flank of Beacon Hill had metamorphosed with time from the houses of coachmen to the homes of Boston's first families, Catharine Carter had friends on Acorn Street, the Amorys, who had a tiny apartment in their cellar. Its size and cost neatly fitted the needs of the young couple.

When Janice won the battle of the wedding in May, her father offered his future son-in-law a job. It was not exactly a spontaneous offer. With normal Boston prudence, Lawrence Carter checked with Glenn Fergusson on Jason's performance in New Orleans. Fergusson's report was complimentary; his superiors had described him as willing to work, ambitious, honest, and a quick learner. This had also been Carter's impression from his several meetings, and so the offer was made: a trainee in the Prescott Sales Company. Jason left the Gulf Coast with a certain reluctance. He liked his life in oil, yet he knew with shrewd certainty that his horizons in Boston were far broader.

For reasons of federal and industry regulations, the sales efforts of the Prescott Funds were segregated to a separate company, Prescott Sales. This was a wholly owned subsidiary of Prescott Management Company. Every endeavor was made to run Prescott Sales on a covering of costs basis, but the prime effort was always to expose the investing public to professional money management in the Prescott Funds, where the repeatable profit lay.

The sales technique was the antithesis of high pressure; the wholesaling staff visited brokerage offices scattered across the land and politely extolled their funds performance. They never preached a doctrine of mutual funds for all. They knew better, for the more sophisticated brokers had no desire to see their customers' dollars go into a fund, once and forever. The firms knew their bread was buttered by trading stocks as often as sensibly possible. And so, the Prescott wholesalers based their pitch to the brokers on using mutual funds for only certain customers: the small, the timid, the time consumers, and those with special investment objectives and too few dollars to buy a broad sheaf of stocks on their own. For the brokers who did well by the Prescott, there was always the seldom discussed additional commissions through fund transactions on the several exchanges as a second incentive. Jason would come to learn this type of selling well.

There were other funds, not based in Boston, that were sold in a far more aggressive fashion. That was not for the Carters. They had close to four billion dollars under direct management and kept the performance among the top five in the nation, year in and year out. They dealt only in the best of securities.

Jason was started on the very bottom rung. His boss was the director of sales, a capable man named Thornton Fisher and an old classmate of Lawrence Carter's at Harvard. Jason saw Mr. Fisher only once in his first two months. He spent the first month as a mail boy visiting all departments of the company on his rounds. He never saw his father-in-law. His immediate superiors had been briefed. Jason was to make his own way.

At seven-thirty each morning, Jason set off from his apartment for a pleasant walk across the Common to the Prescott Company Tower. Janice was up and about well ahead of him, working attentively at her new role of wife. The three small rooms and kitchenette that made up their world could be attended to in an hour. In the first month after their honeymoon trip, she dutifully chopped away at her thank-you list for the wedding presents. That still left much time in the day, for Jason was not free until four-thirty in the afternoon. She thought of a summer course in Cambridge, but the summer was too far along by that time. The apartment had no air-conditioning, and Janice, long used to the cool freedom of Maine or Manchester, was miserable in the steaming stillness. So she escaped from the city to Manchester, and whiled away August and early September on horses or tennis courts or sailboats.

Usually, Janice would drive back to the city in the afternoon to fetch Jason, always careful to meet him a block away from the Tower. They would often go down to the Carter place in Manchester for a twilight cookout by the pool. Janice's parents and her younger sister spent August in Maine, but Lawrence Carter was occasionally in Boston for investment committee meetings and would join them for dinner.

Jason and his father-in-law got on well. Most often their conversation centered on boats. Carter had taken his sloop *Capella* north to Maine and invited Janice and Jason to race with him in the weekend race to Monheghan Island. Jason did yeoman service on the foredeck and was pleased to see his new bride had a light, steady touch on the wheel. *Capella* came in second in Class B and fifth in the sixty-boat racing fleet. This was far better than they had done in the past two years. Lawrence Carter was heard to grumble of the handicap and the bastards with rule-beating boats. Jason took it as it was said, for his father-in-law could buy any boat in the fleet or build a better one. That he chose to race a pre-war Alden sloop against the latest of these racing machines was his own choice. Jason

79

couldn't understand this Boston view of making do with what one had. He felt that if Lawrence Carter really wanted to race, he should quickly brush aside the fish hooks on his purse. Jason's creed was, if you're going to play at all, play to win. He had no sympathy with his father-in-law's elaborate Yankeeness. He almost told him so, but thought better of it. The *Capella* crew went to the prize-giving and got pleasantly tight before going their several ways—the Carters to a leisurely cruise back to North Haven, and the young Steeles to the hot city.

In September, Janice returned to Radcliffe and Jason spent longer days in the Prescott Tower. After a month in the mail room bundling and wrapping prospectuses and sales brochures for shipment, he was moved to the research library where reports and clippings on any company of consequence were filed and cross-indexed for easy retrieval. With the multiplicity of companies that the Prescott Fund kept track of, the work load was always ahead of the library staff. In a later time, microfilm and automated filing would make this task easier. In the time of Jason's apprenticeship, it was still done with scissors and eyeballs. He started taking some of the more colorful reports home for a night's reading while Janice was at her studies. He found most interesting the files that contained the fund analysts' personal comments on the ethics and executives within these companies.

If there was a lack in their first year of marriage, it was that of close friends. The girls Janice knew were off at college and single, while Jason's friends from Manchester were either in the service or else had drifted away. Jason's younger associates in the Prescott, for the most part, lived in the suburbs and took their social lives back with them on the commuter trains. The couple they saw most often was Janice's cousin, Pete Pickering, and his new bride, who lived in Marblehead. Pete was starting a nautical gift shop for want of more pressing ambition. His father was now gone and Pete had inherited a very sizable income. Jason and Pete got on well.

The young Steeles lived on a tight budget. Jason's gross salary was only $125 a week. Her son-in-law's salary was the first and only intervention of Catharine Carter in the affairs of the Prescott Company. In the week before the wedding, and with her characteristic thoroughness, she asked her husband of his plans in starting Jason off. She was appalled to learn that he was to begin at the regular trainee level of $85 a week, and she pointed out the comedown from Jason's Gulf Coast income. Lawrence Carter defended himself on grounds of company policy. But while the young couple was off in Bermuda, he discreetly moved the starting level to $125, and his wife raised Janice's allowance $100 a month over tuition and clothing. Even then, there was little left over from their combined incomes at the end of the month.

Sex was still their principal preoccupation, although, for the most part, the weekdays were too hectic and regimented. The weekends were another matter. There were many days when they never got out of bed. If they had a fear, it was of pregnancy. Janice had been carefully fitted to a diaphragm by the leading specialist at the Boston Lying-In, but there were some mornings when she would forget, or there wasn't time.

2

On their first anniversary, the Steeles still lived in their apartment on the Hill. Other facets of their lives had moved ahead more rapidly. Jason served his apprenticeship with honors and flew all over the country in his second year as an aide to Thornton Fisher in his inspection rounds of the sales offices. Despite her double duties as student and wife, Janice held a B average through her sophomore year.

Their immediate family finances had improved. Jason's salary was increased with six months service to $150 per week and at the end of the year to $175. Jason was never told, but this was the first time that the suggested raise of a trainee was forwarded to the President's office for final approval. The recommendations were based on merit, for Jason had done well in every department. Thornton Fisher, in his constant travel with the young man, grew impressed with his sharpness and his quick ability to size up selling brokers and sell each according to his makeup. Jason, when given a chance, also showed promise as a public speaker. This was the key to success in the fund-raising business, where control and presentation of a meeting are vital. Jason found the average broker a harried man with little time to turn a new sales pitch into dollars unless it came easily. He learned to keep his pitch quick and simple.

There was a second factor in the improvement of Jason's financial affairs. As he visited the many firms within the financial canyons, he struck up friendships with several young brokers. These were young men with bright ideas just starting out. Two of them knew quite a bit about the emerging fields of electronics and optics. Jason took several of these ideas home for discussion with Janice. They decided to take one-half of his $12,000 in savings, the remaining balance after a new car and furniture, and speculate with it. This was a lucky decision. The money was principally invested in Texas Instruments, Polaroid, and Itek and in two years, the $6,000 was worth over $22,000. This was not to say that Jason caught stock speculation fever; he had too little time. Yet he did have the freedom to speculate, and being in the sales subsidiary, he could move in and out of the stock market far more freely than the men in the analysts section of the management company who recommended or tracked the holdings or proposed holdings of the funds. They were severely restricted from any investment where the Prescott might have an interest. The Prescott management were very conscious of conflicts of interest and worked hard to avoid even the shadow of a doubt.

In March of their second year, Janice was forgetful once too often. In April, the family obstetrician who had brought her into the world confirmed that she was indeed pregnant. Janice finished her junior year and left Radcliffe. In early December, Catharine Agnes Steele was born at the Boston Lying-In Hospital, a squalling healthy seven-pounder. The grandparents seemed more pleased than the parents. The infant was soon called Cas, and she happily bellowed the young Steeles out of their small apartment and off Beacon Hill.

Through the ensuing spring, their second home was the

major topic of debate. Jason wanted to live by the sea but water frontage in the closer towns of Marblehead or Beverly Farms or Manchester was impossible on any young budget. Janice wanted room and fields and perhaps a place for a horse. After much searching, they found a compromise in an old farm house on a rolling hill that overlooked the tidal marshes in the town of Essex. Their new monthly mortgage was three times their city rent, but Jason had been advanced once again. The farm had its problems; the heating system was rudimentary, and the walls had been a long time away from a paint brush. They moved in May, and Jason joined the briefcased ranks of those who read their way to the city for a jolting hour. The Steeles worked at the farm each free moment of the long summer twilights and all of the weekends. By early fall they had a trim snug nest.

The housewarming they gave for their friends and neighbors was a noisy, joyous success. Jason, circulating among the crowd and visiting with everyone, was the perfect host. His business training with Prescott Sales was starting to show. He talked for some time with Francis McCaffrey, a bubbling, heavy-set man in his late forties, and their closest neighbor. He was in insurance and in real estate, a selectman and a Republican, despite his Irish name. He was slightly tight before he arrived, and garrulous in his joy that the old Tyler place had come into such good hands. He told Jason that he hoped he would take an interest in the town. Few of the young people did, and yet, he said, they were the loudest to bitch about taxes at town meetings. Jason assured him that he intended to take an active part as soon as he was settled in.

Later in the evening, Jason approached Pete Pickering, his cousin-in-law. Pickering was a tall, slender man of twenty-eight, meticulous in his dress and speech, though three or more bourbons took their toll too often. He was swaying somewhat uncertainly through a conversation with a serious Vassar senior. After an exchange of pleasantries, she drifted back to her date and Jason slapped Pickering on the back.

"Pete, sorry we haven't had a chance to talk earlier."

"Quite all right. Nice party. Like your house." Pete was

concentrating on a blonde with her back to them both. "Pretty girls, good booze, what else?"

"Why, you dirty old man!" Jason laughed. "You're married, remember?"

Pickering had no inclination to remember, although he got on well enough with Susannah, his Virginia belle. For that matter, Pete got on with everyone. Jason had never heard an ill word about him from anyone. Perhaps it was because he was so detached and easygoing. Nothing bothered him for more than a moment. Nothing mattered very much. There was always his mother's Haskett wealth, old and vast, as well as money on the Pickering side. That left little for Pete to do. He had tried a number of things, including selling small planes and the wholesale lobster business. Now his nautical gift shop gave him a place to go every day.

His eyes came back from the blonde. "Say, Jason, I came across something the other day." His tongue was thick with his fifth bourbon, and Jason had to lean close to hear. "Well, anyway, it made me think of you. There's this . . ." The blonde had turned in profile across their mutual field of vision and her thirty-six-inch bust was too obvious a distraction for Pete. His voice trailed away.

Jason loudly cleared his throat. "You were saying, Pete?"

"There's this, ah, a small little oil dealer over there in Marblehead. He's built up a pretty good business. His wife wants to move to Florida, just can't take these winters. Thought of you."

It wasn't a very coherent explanation, yet Jason knew Pete well enough to translate what was left unsaid. Not one to let an opportunity slide by, Jason asked, "Well, what's its name?"

"North Atlantic Fuel." Pete wanted to get along to the blonde and was edging in that direction as Jason persisted, "Well, why did you think of me?"

"Oh, I just thought it might be interesting, that we could do something with it. Have the figures at home. Talk about it tomorrow." With that, Pete headed toward the blonde, unmindful of the glare from his wife on the far sofa.

84

3

The next afternoon, Jason went to the Pickerings' handsome home overhanging the sea on Marblehead Neck. Susannah Pickering, the first to greet him, was in fine fettle for a Sunday afternoon party. The makings of the noontime Bloody Marys stood about the bar. But Jason was more interested in the figures of North Atlantic Fuel. After polite pleasantries and the one drink that Pete insisted upon, Jason holed up in the den to study the numbers. His two recent months with the financial analysts of the Prescott were now helpful. After an hour, Jason concluded the fuel proprietor had been lax on collecting bills and had paid the banks too much interest for the time he was waiting. The cost of product seemed competitive, yet Jason left a question mark by that column. Were he in command, trading with his supplier would be his first area of attack.

Taxes were not Jason's strong point. He worked his numbers on a pre-tax basis, and concluded that if the collections were speeded up and more capital injected to cut the interest charges, there was an attractive profit potential. The degree of profit would hinge on the price of the company. Jason rejoined Pickering to discuss his findings. Pete thought the company could be bought for $75,000. Jason thought that far too much and said he wouldn't go a penny over forty. Pete didn't want to haggle. The fuel man had treated him well over the years and Pete was very loyal. They compromised on an offer of fifty.

When Jason said he had very little free capital, Pete offered to put up forty-five to Jason's five and give Jason two years to put up his twenty and buy even on the ownership. Jason knew that was generous, yet he let it pass without comment. Two weeks later Pickering and Steele were the proprietors of North Atlantic Fuel Company. It might have been done more quickly, had Pete's attorneys been less meticulous in verifying inventory. His old money was guarded by excellent lawyers.

The Pickering-Steele partnership brought a new approach to the mundane peddling of oil on the North Shore. Pete worked at it within his regular ten-to-four day with time out for long liquid luncheons. Jason went at it with every moment that he could steal from the Prescott or Janice and the farm. As with all new entrepreneurs, they started first with family friends. This was a broader social circle than most of their competitors could ever hope for and proved very successful. Few of their friends had any established rapport with their existing suppliers beyond their monthly bills. A friendly call on a personal basis worked wonders.

After two months of persistent doorbell pushing, Pete and Jason better than doubled the original homes under North Atlantic Fuel contract. Once they reached four hundred homes and firms under fuel contract, the young oilmen calculated they now had better than a $200,000 annual business. This required another truck and driver but held promise of a two-year payout on their original purchase of the company.

As Jason finished his third full year with Prescott that spring, Thornton Fisher assigned him a sales territory of his own, consisting of northern New England and upstate New York. His office was still in the Prescott Tower, for the company was ever watchful of overhead. Yet Jason spent most of his time in his car or around the kitchen table with the smaller broker dealers who ran their selling efforts from their homes. These men knew the Prescott, which was half the battle in New England. As Jason had replaced an elderly gentleman who had slowed down and then retired, he was making calls that hadn't been made in several years. The personal visit again proved productive, for no matter how respected the Prescott name, somebody had to keep the funds in the front of the salesmen's minds. Jason easily adapted his father's nasal twang in his speech to be more readily accepted by his customers. In his first year on the road, Jason increased the production of his territory by better than 50 percent.

His many week nights away from the Essex farm began to

86

be a sore point with Janice. Through the fourth summer of their marriage, she was again pregnant. James Carter Steele was born that October. Two infants and a farm and many lonely nights led to several family quarrels. Janice missed the ever absent Jason. It was this more than any resentment of the drudgery of her daily chores that prompted their squabbles. When first they took over the farm in Essex, Jason had insisted that she get a full-time housekeeper. This put a small strain on their budget, yet Janice was grateful for the woman who came in each day from the town. She was also aware how dearly Jason wanted his every penny for either North Atlantic Fuel or the stock market. With his complete dedication to success, Jason failed to notice the drain the second child made on Janice.

Catharine Carter, despite her many charitable activities, managed to visit the Essex farm three or four times a month. The grandchildren were a new delight in her life and they were showered with everything that a sensible doting grandmother could think of. Janice's strain and fatigue did not escape her mother. When she asked after Jason, Janice loyally said that he was working terribly hard.

The Carters had a family reunion over Christmas weekend. When the Steeles arrived that Christmas Eve with their bassinets and bottles and diaper bags, the whole Carter family was gathered for eggnog by a crackling fire in the library. The new baby made it loudly known that his six o'clock bottle was late. To the family's surprise, "Bullet" Carter insisted on personally administering the bottle. This had not happened in twenty years since the weaning of Janice's sister Jean, now a bosomy Wellesley junior. Lawrence Carter handled his grandson with awkward firmness and one way or another got most of the bottle's contents where they belonged.

The children were turned over to the upstairs maid, and the Carter family went in to dinner. After dinner, Mrs. Carter retired with her daughters for coffee in the library. Larry was called to the phone as his father was offering Jason brandy and cigars. After a ritual of snipping and dipping and a long draw, Lawrence Carter spoke.

"Jason, they tell me you've got your sales really perking."

Jason looked surprised. This was the first time that Mr. Carter had directly discussed company business with him. He answered with an air of assurance. "Yes, sir. Seem to be coming along."

Carter studied Jason for several contented exhales before he again spoke. "Well, I wanted to say that we're delighted, and hope that it continues. However, that's really not what I wanted to talk about with you tonight."

Jason gave him a questioning look.

"Yes. You're aware that your wife is rather well off?"

This caught Jason completely off guard. First a question of business, and now family finances. Jason was not sure which way to answer. However, the understatement within Mr. Carter's question prompted him to smile as he answered, "Ah, well, yes sir. I'm aware of that."

"Then you know of the Haskett Trust?"

"I know that Mrs. Carter and Mrs. Pickering are Hasketts, and they have some sort of trust over in the Tedesco Bank."

"Yes, well, they're the third generation. Here in the Commonwealth, one can put family money into three genera- tion trusts. That leaves Janice and Jean, Larry, and Pete Pick- ering as the remainder men. Now, of course, there will be no distribution of the principal until the last of the second genera- tion passes on." Carter poured himself a second splash of brandy. As he put down his snifter, he again spoke. "Within the trust, Kit has the right to pass along some of the income as she so chooses. She may 'sprinkle' it, so to speak. God knows, a lot of hers is going to the government right now, so it makes a certain amount of sense for our own tax purposes if she does pass some along. Larry is just coming out of law school, and Jeannie will turn twenty-one this spring. Mrs. Carter's Christ- mas present tomorrow is twenty-five thousand of income to each of our children.

"I wanted to discuss this with you before tomorrow morn- ing. You're the master of your own home, and I foresee that Janice having an independent income could cause problems. I went through it for a while with Kit in the years after col- lege. It can be awkward unless it's handled well. I also want to say that I'm very proud of you as my son-in-law, and neither Mrs. Carter nor I would ever wish to cause problems." Carter went back to his cigar for several contemplative puffs.

Pleased and surprised, Jason waited quietly. He knew there was more on his father-in-law's mind. Carter went on. "Well, I've thought about it, about Mrs. Carter and her wishes. I also know that a man has to wear the pants. I have concluded that there is one way to handle it." As he spoke, Carter reached into his breast pocket and took out an envelope, and laid it on the table. "This is my Christmas gift to you. No one is to know of it, and it will never be repeated. You can never come back to this well again and that must be clearly understood. Jason, I'm not being hard. All my children are out of my will. They have their grandfather Carter's trust coming to them and are the remainder men in the Haskett Trust. Your children and theirs will be my beneficiaries. Well, anyway, so much for speeches. My accountants have done the tax work, and the gift tax has been paid on this. If you handle it wisely, your income shold exceed Janice's for the foreseeable future." As he passed the envelope across to Jason, Carter concluded. "Just remember, this is it. Merry Christmas. Let's join the girls." He was up and out of the dining room before Jason could express his thanks.

Jason quickly ripped open the envelope and stared in the flickering candlelight at the check, "to the order of Jason Steele in the amount of $500,000."

4

The new affluence of the Steele marriage in its fifth year was by no means blatant. A cheerful young girl from Newfoundland now lived at the farm and took care of the children, giving Janice freedom to enjoy her horses and riding to the hounds in the fall. Jason put his money to work: one-third in high-grade bonds, one-third in triple A stocks, and one-third in electronic stocks. He also paid the outstanding balance to Pickering for his full half of North Atlantic Fuel.

One Monday in July, Jason went to the Prescott Tower for the bi-monthly wholesaler meeting. In his call box, he found a message from a Mr. Bacon, with a Cambridge telephone number. Upon dialing the number, he was greeted by Dan Bacon's Southern drawl. Dan was back at M.I.T. He explained he had hopes of finishing his master's in geology the following spring. Jason invited him out to Essex for the weekend.

That Friday, Dan came into the Tower to take the train out to the farm with Jason. He was a bit heavier than in his days on the road selling "mud." For that matter, so was Jason. His sedentary life in cars and at business luncheons was pushing him close to two hundred and forty. Janice had given up chiding Jason on his weight. There are only so many times a wife can say something, and she had used them up by the fifth year.

Janice had misgivings all week about having a "bachelor days" house guest, for by now she had no delusions as to Jason's monasticism in New Orleans. But when Dan arrived and made an immediate hit with the children, she changed her mind about the curly-haired, easygoing Texan.

The Pickerings and several other couples came over on Saturday night for a cookout. Once Janice had sized up Dan, she invited Sue Butler, a beautiful blonde classmate, as his partner—the same blonde, in fact, who had so mesmerized Pete Pickering at the housewarming a few years before. So it was that Dan found himself in a three-cornered conversation with Sue and Pete most of the night. Jason had not mentioned North Atlantic Fuel to him and it came as a surprise to learn through Pickering that his Yankee friend was moving over two million gallons of his beloved petroleum. He was impressed.

Dan Bacon came to the North Shore quite often that summer. Sue Butler had a swimming cabana down on the Ipswich dunes and the Essex road by the Steele place was one way to get there. Jamie and Cas Steele came to adore the handsome

Texan who toted them off to the beach when their mother or nurse would permit. Often Janice would join them, but Jason never seemed to find the time. Whether it was making good at the Prescott, or getting North Atlantic on its feet, or some new deal, he was always on the run. And this summer it was politics.

The Steeles had talked about this unceasing drive of Jason's on many occasions. Jason aways told Janice he was doing it for her and the children. In the first years, when things were tight, Janice shared his ambition. As he met with growth in his sales and success, she was proud of him and shared his enthusiasm. Jason was frank to say that he took his job at the Prescott as a time of learning, that he really wanted to get out and do things on his own. Janice understood this too. She privately hoped that he would decide to stay with the family company, for this had been the mooring of her early life, and with children and mortgages, her every instinct went toward something solid. But that Jason would want to do things on his own, she accepted. But now, with Jason's success with North Atlantic Fuel, with all their bills current, with money in the bank and having acquired most things any young couple could ever want, when there still was no sign of his letting up, she began to have some doubts as to what the future held for them. She began to wonder if she and Jason didn't have very different goals in life, and if this was so, to wonder if it would come between them.

A case in point was his decision the previous spring to keep his promise to his neighbor, Francis McCaffrey. After several long talks with McCaffrey, Jason was persuaded to run what looked like a token race for a seat in the state senate. McCaffrey held little hope of a victory, for the incumbent was a well-known and popular Democrat from Gloucester, the principal and heavily Democratic town in the district. McCaffrey's rationale was that Jason would get to know a lot of people and be in good standing for a town selectman's slot in another year. Jason knew that in politics lay the shortest road to power, yet he reserved any commitment until after he had spoken with his boss. To Jason's extreme surprise, Fisher thought a cam-

91

paign might be a fine idea, but he said he wanted to think it over. The truth was that he wanted to get Lawrence Carter's opinion. At their next meeting, Fisher told Jason to give it a run, and if he were by some miracle successful, they would find another slot in the Prescott that would afford him time for his legislative duties. And so with McCaffrey's backing, Jason received the Republican nomination unopposed. He spent the summer at every town fair and public gathering on the North Shore.

Jason had not undertaken this side journey into politics without a good deal of thought. He knew that his way in the Prescott was well-greased and his future advancement only a matter of time. With time, he would get very close to the top. But there was no challenge to it, and the prize wasn't big enough, and no matter what he did at the Prescott, he would forever be Lawrence Carter's son-in-law. The campaign for the Senate seat was his solo. Jason tried several times to explain politics as a sensible first flight to Janice, but got nowhere. Her upbringing had been such that she was convinced that Massachusetts politics were a hopeless morass and nothing in the world would ever change it. Still, it was his choice, and she wouldn't stand in his way.

Jason's campaign was shoe leather and handshakes. He had not evolved a political philosophy of his own, and stuck closely by the party line on matters of taxes and fiscal responsibility. This appealed to the close-fisted Yankee constituency in the smaller towns of his district. It carried little weight with the labor force of Gloucester where Jason was at his weakest. In one or two speeches there, when he mentioned that he was the son of a fisherman in the nearby town of Manchester, his wily Irish opponent threw that pitch right down his throat. He never let up on young Steele, the wet-behind-the-ears son-in-law of one of the richest men in the Commonwealth. "Folks, you don't have to take my word. Just take the Missus for a Sunday drive, and go see the Carter mansion up there at the end of the point." Jason swallowed the poor-boy ploy and went back to taxes and fiscal responsibility.

With all the activity and heat, Jason shed fifteen pounds,

and Janice returned from a cruise with her parents to find the solid young man of her honeymoon days. This side benefit of politics pleased her, and the third of their children was conceived that September.

As the first Tuesday of November drew close, there occurred one of those political explosions that often happen in Massachusetts. The incumbent governor, a two-term Democrat, had supposedly retired from his family cement business upon his election to office. Two weeks before election day, he was indicted by the federal government on a charge of fixing the bidding on a newly finished Veterans Hospital. Much of the concrete facing work gave way in the first serious windstorm. An investigation was precipitated that was impossible to sweep under a rug. The indictment spurred a special caucus of the party to map a disaster strategy. Jason's opponent attended the caucus and left very drunk, as was appropriate for such an affair. He mistook an embankment for a bridge in Beverly and was found in the bottom of the creek the next morning. There followed a somber high requiem mass, attended by all the state officials, including the indicted governor, and by an uncomfortable Jason Steele. Two Tuesdays later Jason Steele was elected to the State Senate of the Commonwealth, narrowly defeating the dead man.

5

In January, Jason was sworn in as a senator in the Great and General Court of the Commonwealth of Massachusetts. As with many things in Massachusetts, the title of the legislature is a holdover from Colonial days and is to be in no way confused with the upper levels of the judiciary system. On the Monday before the ceremony, Jason was called to Thornton Fisher's office in the Prescott Sales Company and told of his promotion to Director and Coordinator of Public Relations.

He was to oversee the production and distribution of sales literature and keep an eye on any federal or state legislation that might have an effect on the mutual fund industry. By Boston standards, this was quite a promotion for a twenty-eight year old. It carried a salary of twenty thousand and was a perfect job for the entrepreneur Jason aspired to be. A New York firm put together most of the financial literature and advertising for Prescott Sales, so most of his job was done for him. Jason now had the room he needed to wheel freely beneath the golden dome of the State House.

Jason took readily to his senatorial duties. Back slapping in the corridors and long Parker House luncheons with lobbyists filled much of his day. As one of the youngest members, his committee assignments were few and lowly. He was appointed to the Commission on the Metes and Bounds of the Commonwealth. It was considered the biggest "nowhere" assignment on the Hill. The principal duty was an annual tour of the boundary stones along the state borders.

Jason turned this lowly assignment to his advantage under curious circumstances. In the late spring, Dan Bacon came down to Essex for another weekend. He was about to complete his master's degree and he had an idea that he wanted to discuss with Jason and Pete Pickering. Dan proposed that North Atlantic Fuel create an exploratory arm that actually drilled oil wells. He pointed out that both of them had many wealthy friends and were in an ideal position to sponsor a partnership in oil drilling. The tax shelter afforded by oil drilling would be attractive to the investors, and if they came on oil, the profits could be tremendous. Surprisingly, Pete Pickering was more enthusiastic about this proposal than Jason.

After they had agreed to meet with the company lawyers, Jason, in an offhand manner said, "Dan, is there a chance of anything off this coast?"

"You don't mean little old rock-bound Massachusetts, do you, Jason?"

Jason answered nonchalantly, "I was just asking."

"Look, Jason, I know you too well by now. What's up?"

"Oh, I'm on this stuffy old boundaries commission, and I

94

just noticed that down there by Buzzard's Bay, the boundary into the Bay has never been settled with Rhode Island. I've been wondering who owned the bottom of the sea off Massachusetts. This offshore drilling thing seems to be getting pretty big nowadays."

"I don't think there's much out there from what little I know, but it's worth a shot. I'll do some checking. Think you can get a concession or an exploratory permit or something?"

"Don't you worry about that," Jason smiled. "That can be handled."

The following Wednesday, the young trio met in the reception room of Standish and Adams, Counselors at Law. Their offices comprised the top three stories of a very old, very solid building on upper Washington Street. This was Jason's first visit, and he was amused at the cracked leather of the deep couches, the prim spinster receptionist, the mustiness of the air, the library-like quiet, and the loud ticking of a grandfather clock. He was unawed by Standish and Adams.

Dan noticed Jason's reaction and couldn't let the opportunity slide by. He turned to him with a wide grin. "Well, now, ain't this somethin'. These the gentlemen that counsel the growin' North Atlantic Fuel Company?" Pete looked up without comprehension. Standish and Adams had counseled three generations of Pickerings. If the offices had been in any way different, he would have been concerned.

The exchange was interrupted by the arrival of Charles C. Standish III, a tall, serious young man in his early thirties, whose Brooks Brothers tweeds were badly in need of a press. Standish went directly to Pete and shook hands with an unexpected vigor. Pete, in turn, introduced the young lawyer to his partner and to Dan Bacon.

They were ushered down a long, hushed hallway to the offices of Charles C. Standish, Jr., who came from behind a massive old desk to greet them. He was of an identical cast to the son, thirty-odd years older and white about the temples. He smiled a very controlled smile through gold-rimmed glasses. After appropriate introductions, the visitors took comfortable armchairs along one side of the polished desk. The younger

95

Standish drew up to the other side, pulled out a writing extension and waited with pencil poised over a blank legal pad. Standish, Jr., asked Pickering, "Well, Peter, and how can we help today?"

Pete launched off into an enthusiastic, slightly garbled version of their idea for an oil-drilling partnership. He soon had matters hopelessly mixed up and turned to Jason and Dan for aid. As Jason's eyes were reviewing the marshaled legions of leather-bound tomes, Dan, in the middle seat, picked up the lost thread. For the next twenty minutes, he relayed to the attorneys an outline of what was wanted.

Throughout his outline, the elder Standish leaned back in his tall chair, his slender fingers cat-cradled across his chest as he steadily gazed at the ceiling. Jason had him pegged as another old Boston fossil and he didn't change his view when the elder Standish very quickly, in no-nonsense terms, summarized the requested partnership and then looked to Pete for confirmation. "Well, Peter, I think we have a good idea of what you want. Do we assume that you and Mr. Steele have agreed to North Atlantic Fuel becoming the general partner in this, ah, endeavor?" Both nodded their agreement. Standish went on. "An oil exploration partnership is not an everyday occurrence here in Boston. With your permission, of course, I happen to have a law classmate in what we might term a sister firm in Dallas. I'd like to confer with him to ensure that this partnership is couched in the proper parlance and practice of the industry. Now this may incur another thousand or so dollars of additional expense." Pete assured Mr. Standish that would be just fine. Jason said nothing. He had been unimpressed from the reception room onward and this latest turn cemented his convictions.

The conversation progressed to what North Atlantic would charge its partners for services. Dan thought five percent of the subscribed monies would cover selling costs and fifteen percent of any net profits after lifting costs was reasonable. The younger Standish dutifully took notes and then asked whether they were considering a security registration with either the state or federal authorities. Jason asked his recommendation. Father

and son conferred for a few moments. The father then concluded that the first pilot program could be best treated as a
"private placement with sophisticated knowledgeable investors"
within the bounds of the Commonwealth and thus would not
be subject to any registration. He said the firm would furnish
a brief on the details of how the offering could be legally made.

In late February a hefty manila envelope arrived in the
offices of North Atlantic Fuel. It contained eighty pages of
terms under which the North Atlantic Exploration Partners
had been formed. Attached to the last page was a hand-scrawled
note from the elder Standish to Peter Pickering expressing his
interest in subscribing $25,000 to the venture provided the
monies would be a tax deduction that year. Jason promptly
revalued his initial assessment of Charles C. Standish, Jr.

6

The formation of North Atlantic Exploration opened
a new chapter in the career of Jason Steele. For the first time,
he had a product of his own to sell and he set about its sale
with full enthusiasm. The final list of subscribing partners was
diverse in its makeup, and there were those in Boston who
would have been quite shocked to learn the full background
of several of their co-partners. For the most part, the $300,000
was subscribed by the old, monied investment banking fraternity that lived in the smaller towns of the North Shore and
commuted into the city. The minority of investors came from
Jason's new political activities on Beacon Hill. Jason now
circulated through all the social levels that had an interest in
the activities of the Great and General Court. Two of these
new acquaintances took down better than $100,000 of the ex-
ploration fund. One of them ran the largest dog track in New
England. The second had no visible means of support, yet was
ardently interested in any and all forms of tax shelter. He was

rumored to control the numbers activities in the Northeast. Jason was to draw on him for other services in times to come.

Dan Bacon completed his master's requirements that February and returned to Houston to open the exploration office of North Atlantic Fuel. Throughout March, Jason spent every free moment calling on Pete's wealthy friends. By the end of the month, the entire $300,000 was spoken for.

In his twenty-ninth year, Jason Steele had more than $100,000 a year from four sources. His Prescott salary had been raised to $25,000. His senatorial seat brought in another $12,000. Mr. Carter's Christmas gift had been sensibly invested and now yielded very close to $40,000 of repeatable dividends. North Atlantic Fuel had succeeded to the point where Jason and Pete were each taking out $25,000 a year.

The very success of their exploration fund sales first tested the friendship of the two men. In their first two years of peddling home heating oil, they had never had a squabble. Their initial money fight was over the sales commissions for the fund sales. Pete had opened most of the doors that Jason had knocked upon through the long March nights. One of Jason's few failures had been his father-in-law, who politely said that he was already committed for the year, but wanted to hear of the results. Maybe next year.

The fund agreement called for a five percent cash commission on the monies raised. Jason felt this was his as he had closed all the sales. Pete considered it a team effort and thought the monies should remain within North Atlantic to cover the cost of getting the fund into operation. He was so offhand and blasé in his manner that Jason was shamed into agreement. But he nursed a grudge that would break into the open in another year.

In Houston, Dan Bacon hired a three-man staff and set about investing the money. He was incredibly lucky at the outset. One of his Rice classmates was now an assistant district manager for one of the largest major oil companies. This major company had just brought in a lush discovery to the east of Midland, Texas. The classmate was crestfallen when his New York headquarters wouldn't grant him the necessary monies to drill the offsetting acreage block. This left him in the awkward situation of having a great discovery and no funds to follow up on it. Although not a common occurrence among the major oil companies, it does happen from time to time when the "slide rule boys" at headquarters have to make a decision between gas stations, refineries, boat bottoms, and wells. Great fortunes have been made from the crumbs that fall from major tables.

In this instance, Dan Bacon was the beneficiary. He met his classmate at a dinner party on the night that the latter had received his rejection. Dan quickly worked out a farm-out agreement that enabled his new fund to develop the offsetting locations. In his first six attempts, Dan brought in six producing wells. Three were even better than the discovery well. These six wells expended the initial $300,000 and left the fund in the curious position of having fourteen more promising locations and no money in the till to drill with. The investors had a real windfall for several reasons. They had been able to deduct the entire $300,000 from their taxes. The average of six wells had an open flow potential of eight hundred barrels per well per day. They were not allowed to produce this fast, for the Texas Railway Commission had the final say on how much could be produced per well. The proration slowed down their return on investment, yet the investors had no reason to complain. Dan Bacon had found a bank in Midland that was sufficiently impressed with the wells that it lent the partnership all the funds necessary to purchase the production pipe and equipment. The investors were able to deduct the interest to the bank as an additional expense, and also use the depreciation on the equipment.

Dan called Jason in mid-July to explain his need for further drilling money. When Jason fully grasped the potential within Dan's problem, he said that he'd be on the next flight to Dallas. It was up to him to make all the company decisions, for Pete had taken his family on a two-month cruise to Labrador. In promising to fly to Dallas, Jason gave but a fleeting thought to his commitment to spend the weekend at North Haven with Janice and the children. He would explain when there was time.

99

The following morning, Jason met Dan in Dallas, and they chartered a twin Bonanza for the next leg to Midland. Jason spent his weekend walking the offsetting acreage and reviewing the cash flow from the existing wells. Despite the overriding royalty to the major that had farmed them the acreage, it looked like the investors would be paid back in three years, or perhaps less, if the demand for crude oil increased through the winter months.

That night, Dan and Jason took adjacent hotel rooms and proceeded to work out their next moves. Once they had reduced their requirements and numbers to paper, Dan felt the potential called for a party. At an oilman's bottle club in midtown, one gin led to another, and with each, the bosomy blonde who brought their setups grew more attractive to Jason. As midnight passed and the club emptied, Jason negotiated with his blonde. Leaving Dan behind with a willowy singer, they went back to the motel and, one hundred dollars later, Jason was relieved of his more pressing needs.

7

On the night of his return from Texas, a triumphant Jason came into the farmhouse. Janice was reading on the screened porch. She acknowledged his arrival with a flip of a page and a grunt. Although Jason had conveniently forgotten his promise of a weekend at North Haven, Janice hadn't. Well, Jason thought, now's as good a time as any. Let's have it out. He sat down on her footstool, and leaning forward gave her a kiss that she shrugged aside. Undaunted, he said, "Jan, baby, we've got it made."

She set down her book and looked at him with a mixture of anger and pity. Jason Steele was not to be set down so easily. Beaming, he went on, "Yes, ma'am, we really hit it. We've got ourselves a major oil field."

Anger won out. "My God, Jason," Janice said. "I don't give a damn if you've found all the oil in the whole world. What I care about is us. I was waiting here with the station wagon packed and three fidgety kids. What do I get? A damn phone call from your secretary . . . you're on a plane for Dallas. Not a word from you." Janice got to her feet, deftly avoiding his open arms as she went to the glass table in the far corner for a cigarette.

Jason's face was a mask of hurt amazement. "But, Jan, I had to go. There were some decisions that could only be done down there. I did it for us."

Janice smashed down the lighter on the table. "Oh, bullshit, Jason. Three or four years ago, I would have believed you, but not now. You went for only one reason, and you won't admit it, even to yourself."

"Oh, Jan, come on. We've really got it made. I'm here. I love you and I need you."

There was the hint of a tear in her eyes as she answered. "Jason, that's what's so sad. You won't look at yourself, or us for that matter. You keep reaching for more and more, and what is that doing to us? We're losing each other."

Jason, about to answer back, thought better of it. It would be best if she got it all out.

She fumed on. "It's always what *you* want, what *you* need, and when *you* need it. What about me? You don't give one thought to what I feel. Jason, you just don't understand. It cuts both ways . . ."

Jason, watching her pace across the porch, assumed a posture of humility, repentance and sincerity. There was even an undercoat of success unappreciated.

As she wound down, he tentatively went on the offense. "Jan, I've finally got the big hit on my own. You know how important that is. We've talked about it countless times. Now it's here, and all you can do is make accusations. That's not fair."

"Fair!" The word lit a new fuse to an untapped magazine. "You've got a hell of a nerve. Fair! How fair is it of you to fly off to Texas without even the courtesy of a phone call?

Fair! Why, Mother and Dad were expecting all of us, not just me and the kids. What do they think? Damn it, we went all through this in your campaign last summer . . ."

Jason instantly saw his advantage and bounded to his feet in a counter-explosion of wrath. "Look, girl . . ." He grabbed her about the shoulders, shaking her as he shouted. "Your parents have nothing to do with us. They've got theirs. I haven't, but I will have. You can't seem to get it through your thick head. This is for us! Jason and Janice Steele! You think I enjoy being away all the time?" As he said it, he believed it. Janice dissolved in tears in his arms. Mentioning her parents had been a mistake, and she knew it. She had taken Jason Steele as her husband largely because of his ambition. The malignancy of its growth was what she had not anticipated, and now it seemed to be overwhelming her.

All through the droning flight from Dallas, in every twisting turn of the road down to Essex, even through most of his confrontation with Janice, the central strand of Jason's thoughts had been on the gigantic potential of the oil play in Midland. He couldn't set it aside, even with Janice now contentedly acquiescing to his fondling. Jason took her head in his hands and gently kissed away the tears. Finally, Janice smiled and they were soon locked in a long kiss. They laughed and kissed their way up the stairs to a peace treaty—their clothes were soon an intertwined heap at the foot of their bed.

As they moved on to the spent contentment of sleep, Jason's last thoughts were on how to handle the Midland development. Janice slept beside him in another world. Her final murmur was "I'm glad you've found what you want, Jason."

Jason was a dutiful husband and attentive father at breakfast. A happy thought had come to him in the shower which had crystallized to a plot while shaving. He left the farm to kisses and hugs and drove flat out to the Marblehead office of North Atlantic Fuel.

At the office Jason drafted a masterpiece of notification to the investors. The partnership agreement drafted by Standish and Adams had provision for just this situation. If a discovery were made, North Atlantic, as general partner, was to notify the individual partners of the offsetting potential and inform them what it might cost to drill the adjacent wells. The partners had fifteen days to agree to go along for additional money. If they chose not to, any of the partners, including North Atlantic, had the right to pick up the unsubscribed interests. Any who put down money on the unsubscribed portion were entitled to a return of three times on their risked monies, before the partners who "sat out" came back in for the cash from the entire field. This was a perfectly normal provision within the industry at that time, but it did require keeping up with one's mail.

Jason's notice carefully met all of the provisions of the partnership agreement. It stated the technical facts of what had been accomplished, put little emphasis on the potential return on investment and great stress on the estimated $800,000 of additional costs. It carefully pointed out that the investors did not have to go along unless they chose to, and ended with a recitation of the sit-out provisions of the agreement. This was neatly underlined in such a way that "sitting-out" on the development wells looked like a good idea to most of those who read the notice. Jason was content that this met all his obligations to his partners. If they didn't want to go along, that was their choice, not his.

Most of the fund's investors took off the month of August for vacations with their families. Jason was aware that many of them left standing instructions with their firms not to be bothered about business unless a major disaster occurred. By mid-August only $150,000 out of the $800,000 was taken up by the original partners. Jason had not wasted his time over the intervening weeks. He went to his father-in-law's bank, the United Bank of Boston, and negotiated a personal loan of $200,000, putting up his bonds as collateral.

His next step was to invite his numbers friend to dinner at a North End restaurant. The man's face was leaden with either incomprehension or impassivity as he listened to Jason spiel on about the dollar potential of the Midland acreage. He proposed a $450,000 pool to take up the unsubscribed interests in his own name, with twenty percent of the profits going to him after the pool monies were recovered. At the end of dinner, his friend said, "Ya gotta know by the sixteenth, right? Four-fifty's a lotta cabbage. I'll do some checkin', my way. Just be right, Jason."

On the night of the fifteenth, Janice, who had come down from North Haven for the midweek nights with her husband, took a phone call. There was a pause for a moment, and then a gravelly voice came on. "Ah, Mizzus Steele?"

"Yes."

"This is Jason's friend, Salvatore. Will ya tell him I'm go."

Janice's face was a portrait in consternation as she asked, "Could you give me your name again, please?"

"Just tell him Sal said go." The receiver went dead in her hand.

8

Pete Pickering sailed back into Marblehead in mid-September. It took him another week to put up his yacht, sort out his mail, and fully comprehend what had gone on in his absence. That his partner would have cut him out of such an obviously profitable venture came first as a shock that soon festered to hurt and then to total anger. As Jason was away on the West Coast for the Prescott Company, Pete angrily called a hurried meeting with Charles Standish, the elder. He was crestfallen to hear that, in Standish's opinion, Jason had acted right to the letter of the partnership terms. Standish had received his option notice in proper form and, for that matter, had added another fifty thousand to his initial commitment. When Pete said that Jason had taken down the entire unsub-scribed percentage for his own account, the old lawyer rocked back in his chair for quite a time before replying. "That was his privilege, Peter. From what I have either read or heard, he acted properly."

"But what of my friends? They were all away in August. What do I tell them?"

Standish answered in a fatherly tone of tried patience. "Peter, you have to stop worrying over what people might think. Most of them have staffs to look after their affairs. The fund was a business proposition, and Steele gave them the opportunity . . ."

"I still think it was sharp!" Pete sputtered.

Standish came around his desk. "Well, not according to the agreement." As he led Pete to the doorway, he had one last question. "Peter, just how much did Jason subscribe to this second round?"

"Oh, almost eighty percent . . . a little under six hundred and fifty thousand dollars."

The old lawyer's eyebrows arched perceptibly as he closed his door.

Pete let the development option go undiscussed throughout that fall. The drilling reports came in daily from Houston. Pete quietly read them and said nothing. By year end, Bacon brought in thirteen wet wells out of the fourteen drilled for the second-round subscribers. As Jason waxed more expansive, Pete took less of a day-to-day role in the affairs of the company. This also carried over to the relations between the two families.

Several days before Christmas, Janice stopped by the Pickering home in midafternoon. She and the children were on their Christmas present rounds. Janice was surprised to find her cousin home at that time of day. That he had been drinking came as an even greater shock.

His greeting offered no assurance. "Well, well, the oil tycoon's wife, as I live and breathe."

Susannah Pickering tried her best to hush her husband. Janice brushed the greeting aside and turned to round up her children, who had clomped off with the Pickering brood to the playroom. Pete was not to be hushed so easily. He went on. "I just don't see how you can live with that greedy bastard."

Janice strode across the large room to glare down at her cousin. "And just what does that mean?"

Pete reached for a brownish tumbler at his elbow as he answered. "Just what I said."

"Well, I think that's one hell of a thing to say about your own partner."

"Partner! That's a laugh."

"Come on, Pete, make sense. Just what's bothering you?"

"Well, you heard about that big Midland field, didn't you?"

"Yes, I did, and I thought you were all very happy about it."

"Jason is. I'm not." Pete Pickering then set forth on a long, somewhat incoherent tale of how Jason had taken advantage of his partners.

Janice listened in silence and then said, "But you say yourself that Mr. Standish thought it was all right and proper."

Grudgingly, Pete had to admit this was true. Janice was quiet and thoughtful as she drove back to the Essex farm. She never mentioned the conversation to Jason.

9

That same December afternoon, Jason Steele found a call slip from Bacon waiting on his desk in the Prescott Tower. He quickly returned the call—nothing but good news had been coming from Houston of late. After a brief exchange of pleasantries, Dan got down to business. "Say, Jason, you recollect askin' last year if there might be anything off that coastline up there?" Jason remembered very well, and Dan went on. "Well, one of my people came across a new paper published by those Woods Hole Oceanographic guys. Seems like it might be a right interesting play." He launched into the geologic details.

Jason soon brought him up short. "Hey, Dan, never mind the technicalities. What do we do about it?"

"I don't rightly know, Jason. Down here on the Gulf, the feds got their mitts on just about everything. Lot of it's still tied up in the courts. Now, you mentioned something 'bout the boundaries bein' a bit unsettled up there."

"That's right. Now, how far out do you think we gotta push these boundaries to be on anything meaningful?"

"Well, this Woods Hole report's okay as a regional study. We'd have to do some detailed shootin' to be positive. I'd say we can get on something worthwhile within sixty-odd miles of Nantucket."

Excited by this conversation, Jason phoned Pete to discuss tactics. Pete seemed very disinterested and said the fishermen and bird lovers and yachtsmen would never let it happen. Jason next called Standish and Adams. Charles Standish III took the call.

Jason quickly outlined his needs to extend the boundaries of the Commonwealth into the sea. The younger Standish grew enthusiastic as he listened and said there was one very eminent authority on tidal ownership within the Commonwealth, the senior partner of another large Boston firm. He would arrange a meeting.

The following afternoon, Jason Steele found himself in the cluttered office of Elliot N. Hall. As the younger Standish outlined the request, Jason studied Hall and liked what he saw. He was a huge man, very close to six-five and still lean, though forty years had passed since he'd stacked his oar as the celebrated stroke of an unbeaten Harvard eight. His specialty was now corporate law. His hobby was tracing the many colonial laws that make up the patchwork quilt of riparian ownership in the Commonwealth. Hall had recently published a learned treatise on his hobby.

Elliot Hall and Jason were drawn to each other from the outset. Hall was taken with the boldness of the younger man and amused by the problem that Jason's proposition posed. Over the past two decades, he had watched the federal government assert ownership of the sea bottom on the most tenuous of arguments. This grated on his conservative views towards real property. The federal people gunned down California and then Louisiana and Texas with political decisions in the

Supreme Court. But the older Commonwealth might be a harder nut to crack, for it existed before the federal government. Hall sketched out his argument for Jason, whose mind was whirling.

Three months and fifteen thousand dollars in legal bills later, North Atlantic was the best known fuel dealer in Massachusetts. Pete complained about the bills for a while, but when Jason said he was willing to pay them himself, if North Atlantic would assign him all rights in the outcome, his complaints soon subsided. After the Midland episode, Pete sensed that Jason had a Midas touch and he might as well hold on for the ride.

Hall's staff did a piece of brilliant research. They developed a well-documented brief along the lines that title to Massachusetts real estate was the direct result of Royal Charters. They then found some of these charters specifically gave over to certain colonists the rights to the sea bottom for one hundred miles from the shore. One young lawyer was dispatched to London to get notarized copies from the Royal Archives. The brief then traced the ownership from the time of the Stuart kings to the beginning of the American Revolution. It pointed out that the laws of the Commonwealth were based on Anglo-Saxon common law, and accordingly, all real things belonged to someone and remained so unless they were either deeded away or seized by force of arms. Hall's argument was capped with the American Revolution bringing title to the citizens of Massachusetts, carefully pointing out that George III made his peace treaty with the several states, not with any central government.

The public was made aware of what North Atlantic was up to in a curious way. After Jason took a Hall-drafted claim with the supporting brief and quietly filed them in the Secretary of State's office, with all the appropriate stamps and filing fees, Hall took the North Atlantic claim and had it probated in the Land Court. One of the court clerks mentioned this odd case to a courthouse reporter, and the North Atlantic Fuel Company claim of the sea bed was a thick headline the next morning.

A bewildered governor was asked of its merits at his morning press conference and he stated that it had substantial merit. He was for anything that would broaden the tax base of the Commonwealth. The bureaucratic machinery took its cue from the governor and closed ranks behind him.

The United States attorney for Massachusetts was thoroughly confused. His eye was on a potential opening in the Congressional ranks. He was loath to move on a hot political issue. When asked by the Associated Press in Washington, the Department of the Interior said they knew nothing of a Charles II grant, that the issue was settled in the United States versus California in 1946, and that the submerged continental shelf was all government property. By then North Atlantic Fuel had a Massachusetts Land Court title that said the soil under the fishing grounds was theirs.

The company's local sales of home heating oil doubled on the North Shore with their notoriety. Jason had the company trucks painted red, white and blue with an outline of the "Spirit of 76" painting sketched on the cabs.

This land coup did not escape the majors. It is seldom that two thousand square miles of high-grade prospects are taken from under their nose with a twenty-dollar filing fee and a few law bills. The phone rang constantly in Pete Pickering's Marblehead office. He directed all calls to Dan Bacon in Houston.

As spring approached, the Department of the Interior had recovered from this boomerang by the long-dead King Charles and filed for a declaratory judgment asserting their authority against Massachusetts in the United States Supreme Court. To everyone's surprise, the Court took the Interior Department's petition under advisement while it read Elliot Hall's brilliant brief. The justices recognized a political issue when they saw one and hastily referred the case to a Special Master in Boston.

By then Dan Bacon's college classmate had risen to exploration chief of the major oil company that farmed out the Midland field. Dan sold one-half of the underwater Massachusetts acreage to the major for a tidy $250,000, win or lose in the Supreme Court.

Jason resigned from the Prescott that summer. His mind was made up long before, but the Prescott was a comfortable job with few demands and a handsome salary for the time required. Getting paid for doing little appealed to Jason. That, combined with his ready access to some of Boston's finer financial minds, held Jason on a half year longer than Janice had ever expected.

Through that winter and spring, Jason had worked but slightly at his marriage. While the Senate was in session, he was seldom home. He had, however, several times talked to Janice about leaving the Prescott. She never argued with him about it, yet each time prudently pointed out that he should be sure of his next move. Now Jason was certain. He wanted the freewheeling world of oil. There were too many restraints and regulations in the money management business. By late spring, his decision was scarcely foolhardy, for with the success of North Atlantic and the crude production in Midland, Jason's income was now above $200,000.

Lawrence Carter returned that August from his month in Maine and was surprised by a luncheon invitation from Jason. They met in the Ritz Café. Jason's resignation from the Prescott came as no great surprise. Lawrence Carter said all the things one should say. Jason was equally polite, but firm in his resolve to try things on his own. It was a very pleasant parting.

When the money came up from Houston on the offshore sale, Jason and Pete had a directors' meeting. It was a civil, restrained meeting with Jason taking the lead throughout. They decided to drill the winter's fuel sales profits with Bacon, take $200,000 of the offshore profits as a down payment for buying a tidewater tanker terminal along the Chelsea Creek in Boston, and declare a $25,000 special dividend apiece. Each went his separate way, contented for the month of August.

Jason took some of his money and, after an exhilarating haggle, was the owner of a silver gull-winged Mercedes. He roared up the drive at Essex that night, contented with the world.

Over cocktails, he persuaded Janice to go off with him that very night on an impromptu trip in his new toy.

10

Janice returned from their whirlwind tour of the Canadian Maritimes with new hope for her marriage. Jason had reverted to the young optimist who had come home from New Orleans. They had done all the silly touristy things of their first years as they drove through the Provinces, poking about shipyards and even a sardine cannery. Jason had given her all his attention and her joyful nature came back in this long absent atmosphere. His optimism and ambition were larger than ever, but he carried a new confidence of having accomplished things on his own. In the lumpy double beds of several Nova Scotia guesthouses, Janice had tried to persuade him to take things easier. But Jason could only see ever widening horizons. It was on this trip that he first broached his thoughts of moving to Houston. Janice held back, yet she knew her man by now. He'd do as he wished.

On their way back through southern New Brunswick, Jason was taking the narrow, twisting shore route full bore when they came over a rise. The sudden hillock opened a breathtaking view of the bay water far below. Janice asked him to stop for a moment, and he turned off into a dusty rutted road that led closer to the sea cliffs.

It was a day after the passage of a summer storm. The riled water danced golden in the high sun as combers rolled onto the cliffs and exploded into frothy silver. The gentle wind carried the heavy tang of salt. Janice was first out of the car; Jason close behind. They clambered down the yellow granite, working closer to the pounding surf, and came upon a sun-drenched niche all of their own. The rocks were warm from the sun. They were quickly in each other's arms. Janice was to always look back to that day as one of the happiest of her marriage.

Later, as the sun moved on, they returned to the Mercedes.

They drove back to the highway intersection and noticed another dusty lane on the other side. Jason spotted a gray, weatherbeaten sign with an arrow pointing inland: "Musquash Minerals." He turned to his wife with a loud guffaw. "Let's look, Jan!" Janice agreed, smiling, for Jason couldn't pass up the remotest scent of a deal. They bumped their way for several miles down the dusty byway, arriving at a dilapidated mine elevator. Since the wheels were turning, somebody or something was on its way up the shaft. Jason took note of several old cars close by, and as he turned back to the shaft head, three thoroughly blackened bodies stepped into the daylight. One of them, his voice carrying the burr of the Highlands, said, "And what may I do for you, sir?"

Jason casually answered, "Oh, my wife and I. we were driving down the highway and we happened on your sign. Do you mind if we look around?"

"Nope, don't mind. Nothin' to see, though. It's all down there."

Jason inquired further and learned that Musquash Minerals had been active for over fifty years; the company worked thin veins of copper, and had four mines in southern New Brunswick. Jason then asked who owned the company. The foreman appraised them both for a long moment before answering. "Well, the best we can figure, it's owned by a bunch of those Toronto brokers. We never see 'em." The man turned back to the shaft as Jason thanked him for his time. They got back in the Mercedes and all the way back to the highway, Jason kept rolling the words "Musquash Minerals" around in his mouth.

11

The career of Jason Steele steadily gained momentum. That October, Jason spent all his time closing out the third annual North Atlantic exploration program. It was to be subscribed at $1,500,000. The first year drilling record had been phenomenal. Twenty successes out of twenty-two, and if current production held up, what looked like a three-year payout on all costs. The coming winter would tell that tale.

The second fund, with Bacon playing less of a stacked deck against nature, had not done as well. Attempting to diversify geographically, he had divided the $900,000 raised in Boston among deeper plays in Louisiana, Texas, and Oklahoma, in partnership with some majors. Out of the ten tries, he got a good gas well in Galveston Bay and one oil well in Oklahoma. The payout on the funds would depend on how well he did with the offsetting acreage in Oklahoma.

The initial partners were still enthused, and between them and their friends, the third annual fund was taken up. Again, to the chagrin of Jason, Lawrence Carter was among the few to decline. He did not know that Pete had gone to his uncle when he was most unhappy with the Midland take-up. Carter adopted neutrality and a wait-and-see policy.

The smoldering truce between Pete Pickering and Jason Steele broke into flame that October. The fight was triggered by an incident far removed from their business partnership. The Pickerings had gone to a Princeton game in Cambridge with two other couples from the North Shore. After the game, they had returned to one of the couples' homes in Manchester for a dinner party that went on and on.

Jason learned of the party from the Monday edition of the *Record American.* "North Shore Socialites in Smash Up." The story went on to tell how Peter Pickering of Marblehead Neck and Deidre Farnsworth of Beverly Farms had missed a turn on the shore road; that Mrs. Farnsworth had undergone facial surgery and was recuperating in the North Shore Hospital; that Pickering had been detained for driving under the influence, and so forth. Jason threw the paper down with a curse. "Jesus H. Christ, just as I'm buttoning up the year-end fund!"

That Pete might have been seriously hurt was one of his later reactions. Jason's first concern was the impression this might create with North Atlantic's more sedate partners. What his associates did in their private lives was up to them as long as it was discreet. What the right people thought was what counted, and Jason expected his associates to honor this code. On second thought, he decided that few of them would ever read the *Record American*. He quickly checked the *Globe* and *Herald* and found no coverage of the accident. This was a break, though Jason was sure it had taken some string-pulling. One of the Standish attorneys must have been brought in early.

In mid-week, Jason met Pete in the Marblehead offices and learned that matters were worse than what he had read in the paper. Susannah Pickering had thrown Pete out of the house and was threatening divorce proceedings on an adultery charge. Jason was furious. For a time, Pete took the berating, but finally, he retorted, "Don't give me any more of this holier-than-thou crap. You're a crook, a plain common crook. Want to know why some of my friends wouldn't drill with us that second time?"

Within the week, Jason and Pete were communicating through their lawyers. This put Standish and Adams in an awkward situation. It had counseled the Pickering family for years and yet it was also corporate counsel to North Atlantic Fuel. The firm solved its dilemma by resigning as corporate counsel, yet keeping young Standish on as corporate clerk. The elder Standish thought this prudent until the dust settled.

Jason fell back on his new-found friendship with Elliot Hall. He was adamant that he would no longer work with Pete. It looked like an unfortunate standoff until Hall came across a forgotten stock option to Daniel Bacon in Houston. It was rather small, representing only 2½ percent of the shares. Jason flew to Houston. He related his version of the fallout to Bacon and won the day with a promise of a further option on another 2½ percent of the stock and a three-year interest-free loan of the needed cash to exercise the first option. The trade also called for Dan to give Jason a two-year proxy to vote the stock as he saw fit.

When Dan Bacon exercised his option on the second day of January, the younger Standish issued the shares and informed his father of this latest turn. The elder Standish advised Pete that a fight was now futile.

Jason next called an annual meeting. It was businesslike and bitter. Young Standish appeared as both the corporate clerk and the bearer of Pete's resignation as chairman and director. Pete and Jason were never again to speak except through counsel.

After the filing of Pickering's resignation, Jason handed Standish his proxy to vote Bacon's newly issued shares. Jason now controlled more than 51 percent of the total outstanding. He proposed a board consisting of Bacon, Hall and himself. There was no opposition. Standish then offered his resignation as clerk. The board accepted with small pretense of warmth.

Through that winter, Jason was more than ever convinced that he had gone as far as he could in a Boston hidebound by breeding and age. He believed Houston and oil were his brightest horizons.

Although Janice had not said no when he first mentioned Houston, Jason knew the comfortable cords that held her to the North Shore. He was determined to sever them, once and for all. He chose subtlety rather than an open ultimatum. He suggested that they go to Aspen for a week of skiing. That was something she couldn't resist. She was unaware that Jason had already lined up real estate agents in the Houston suburbs.

After Aspen, Jason proposed a quick side visit to the Houston office. Dan met them at the airport and took them for a tour of his offices and a look about the city. Houston in February was a far cry from the knifing cold of New England. Janice liked the rising rectangles of glass and the cleanliness of the city. As they wound out through the suburbs, she found the wide flatness of the land both depressing and inspiring. In River Oaks, the shade trees were as high and the homes as stately as those along the Manchester shore. And there was riding the year round.

The Jason Steeles moved to River Oaks that spring. Although there were many loose strings to be tied before the move, one way or another, Jason got to most of them. First, he hired away a passed-over terminal manager from a major oil company and put him in charge of North Atlantic Fuel operations. Then he resigned from the state senate, causing not a ripple in the Republican ranks. They were so much in the minority, one less vote wasn't going to matter. Jason left Beacon Hill armed with appropriate letters of introduction to the higher-ranking Republicans of Texas.

His third and biggest problem was the Essex farm. He would have liked the money, yet he knew Janice had poured a lot of herself into the place. He proposed they should hold on to it and come back to Essex in the summer. With that, Janice agreed to the Houston move.

And lastly, there were his drilling partners. Dan Bacon had continued to find oil, yet even with the tax shelter afforded the income by statutory depletion, some of the largest participants were continually after Jason to find a company to buy out their production. To these people, a capital gain was more attractive than tax-sheltered income. Selling off these fractional interests in scattered wells was not so easy. Jason toyed with the idea of buying a public company and pooling all the partners' interests for stock. He asked an oil analyst friend to look about for him. He was slow to respond, and Jason suddenly remembered Musquash Minerals Company. It turned out to be a Maine corporation, and its shares were occasionally traded on the over-the-counter market in the United States. Jason's parting instructions to Elliot Hall were to look into the legalities of North Atlantic buying control of Musquash Minerals Company.

12

Within the year of starting out in Houston, Jason had his juggernaut up to speed. That his juggernaut was always chugging in a circumspect manner was another matter. There was the embarrassing day that Dan Bacon came into Jason's office all flushed and harried, and announced they had a small gas discovery in West Virginia. Jason was pleased until he learned the full implication of the discovery. Dan had figured there wasn't the remotest chance for hydrocarbons of any sort on the site. The location had come to the company as part of a land package which entailed a work obligation of drilling two wells to earn the acreage. The fund had drilled the first well dry and this condemned the acreage in Dan's mind. He decided to quickly fade his dry hole costs and steal a small profit by selling off eighteen-sixteenths of the second required well. The oversale to investors came as a surprise to Jason, yet he wasn't angry with Dan. His concern was how to deal with the irate investors and yet to hold on to the gas. He quickly came up with a solution that Dan Bacon relayed over the intercom to a trusted yet perplexed engineer. "You get up there right now on a plane. Don't care how you do it, dynamite if necessary, but have that mother plugged and abandoned by tomorrow night, you hear? Never you mind about that little old gas. We'll reclaim the acreage and drill out the plugs when the dust settles later on."

In the second year, North Atlantic completed acquisition of Musquash Minerals and gave shares to all the drilling partners in exchange for their oil production. The surviving corporation was called Steele Minerals Company. The shares were actively traded in the over-the-counter market at around six dollars. The reverse merger into Musquash gave to Jason Steele a net worth of four million dollars in marketable securities.

Jason soon had to sell some of his shares, for he had committed himself to personally develop a South Texas field. With Dan doing a fine job of bringing in the wells, Jason continued to borrow heavily on his Steele Minerals stock with the United of Boston to finance his growth. Six months later, however, the wells lost their natural flow, and an expensive secondary method of recovering the oil was required; Jason's only way out was to sell off a large block of his shares. He vowed never to be caught in that box again.

In July, Jason left Houston to join Janice and the children on the Essex farm. His flight had a stopover in Washington, and Jason, sweltering uncomfortably in the terminal, decided on a beer. He entered the darkened cocktail lounge, and as his eyes adjusted, he made out a familiar figure from his days at the Prescott—Augustus Codman Emery, national sales manager of the Prescott's largest competitor. The Ace remembered Jason, and they soon were sitting together in the first-class cabin of the ongoing section to Boston. Emery was returning from a sales safari along the California coast. When asked why he hadn't taken a direct flight from Los Angeles to Boston, he harumphed for a moment and then replied, "Never, Jason my boy, take a direct flight. They only serve two drinks."

Jason eyed Emery suspiciously for a moment. He would learn with time that this was how the Ace always traveled. Their conversation turned to oil. Emery was intrigued with Jason's ventures in the oil-drilling field, for his own fund sales were on the wane at the moment, and he had an eye out for greener fields. He thought there was a place for the mass marketing technique used by mutual funds in the oil drilling business. Within the week, Jason invited Elliot Hall and Emery to his farm for a conference. From that meeting grew the Steele Drilling Funds.

The two older men did not get on from the outset. Hall was certain that the prospectus for such a fund would be too detailed and cumbersome to ever be successful. He pointed out that Jason, if he were to use public monies and drill them through Steele Minerals, would have many inherent conflicts of interest. At that point in the long afternoon, Jason lost his temper. "Goddam it, Elliot. You tell 'em everything that should be said in that prospectus. Keep my ass out of trouble. Disclose everything. The bastards never read 'em anyway."

Within the month, Augustus Codman Emery was the newly appointed president of the newly created Western Investors Company. It had taken a bit of fancy footwork on Jason's part, for by then Steele Minerals had a nine-man board of directors, some of whom were very distinguished and circumspect. For the most part, they represented the larger blocks of stock held in Boston. Steele Minerals had its own private money-raising arm. Jason's Western Investors mutual fund idea posed potential competition. At the next directors' meeting, Jason did a masterful job of underplaying this latest brain child and he promised that if Western Investors were successful, it would put most of its investments through Steele Minerals. He clouded the picture sufficiently well that he got unanimous approval from his board.

Emery rounded up a group of bright young securities wholesalers throughout the ensuing months. The stock market was in a slump, and Emery overrode all resistance with Jason Steele's cash. These men were to sell a low-risk diversified drilling fund that offered both tax shelter from the drilling and the tax-sheltered compounding effect of the monies being reinvested in additional wells. The goal was an improbable return of twenty-five percent per year. It was improbable, for Western Investors charged about thirty percent of the potential profits for its management fee. If one read the prospectus with care, it was all set forth. Few did. Compounding became Emery's favorite word.

That next March, Jason attended the National Mutual Fund Convention in Palm Beach. Emery had assembled all of his sales force for an ostentatious Lucullian banquet on the eve of the conference. For many of the salesmen, this was their first opportunity to meet Jason Steele. As he came into the decorated ballroom, Emery had his new legion snap to attention and break into sustained applause. Jason waved them down into their seats and gave a short, friendly, welcoming speech. After the fourth wine course, Emery gave a bubbling, rambling speech. "Just go down to your friendly bank. Borrow from them their compound interest tables and direct your attention to the back pages. Don't bother with the dog-eared seven or eight percent pages. Move on, farther back, past the twenty percent pages to the pages unsullied by human hands. Get to the twenty-five percent pages. This is where we can perform. See where you are in several years. Gentlemen, this is what we are selling. Tax-free compounding! Tax free at twenty-five percent per year."

It didn't take many months of these speeches to move Steele Minerals stock over fifty dollars per share.

Book Three

1

To men of less ambition, a twilight ride on a fine spring day along the western shore of Lake Geneva would be an hour to savor in silence. In the lowering light, the valleys had gone to a soft blue and yet, high in the Jura, the snow caps sparkled gold in the sunlight. It was the first week of May, and cowbells could be heard in the lowlands. All of this was lost on Edward Leibowitz and Jason Steele. Their big Mercedes pushed the autobahn limit to Lausanne.

These two men were part of a bloodless world war. The stakes were power and control: control of billions of dollars and an army of twenty thousand salesmen scattered over the globe. It was rather sad that the schemes and battle plans of such a war were made in a place of such tranquility and beauty.

Edward Leibowitz was the operating brain of World Equities. Manny Kellermann was the man the world saw, the flamboyant, hot-blooded bachelor, the incarnate American salesman. Leibowitz was his opposite, and their strength was in their differences. He was a tall thin man, cool, very contained, an excellent listener, ever probing for a flaw. He did nothing without a plan, and nothing happened in Lausanne without

Ted Leibowitz. His facile mind was never at a standstill. He could listen to a proposition and give the proposer three alternatives or variations before the speaker had finished his original pitch.

But now, instead of listening to what Jason was saying, he found his thoughts drifting back over the hectic events of recent weeks. Two weeks before, he had been in Houston on another of his well-known lightning raids. It had started when he got wind through a girl he had planted in Kellermann's office that Kellermann was planning an audit of the World Equities Bank in Liechtenstein. It had to be more than his good Jewish instincts. Someone had tipped Kellermann off. In two years of wandering around the world, Manny Kellermann had not taken the time to read the annual report of the parent company, let alone to start sniffing into the affairs of a relatively small subsidiary bank.

When Ted Leibowitz learned of the audit, he picked up his private line. This one didn't go through the switchboard and it was checked for bugs on a weekly random basis by a security firm that reported only to him. He dialed Arthur Foxx, the man who ran the Steele International Office in Geneva.

"Art, tell Jason I'm leaving Geneva on Swissair 35 at two forty-five this afternoon. It's a direct flight and lands at Kennedy at five o'clock Kennedy time. I must see him. Don't care where, New York or Houston. He can respond through Swissair enroute. Will you get that off on your telex in code please? Thank you."

Five hours, and two-thirds of the Atlantic later, a Swissair stewardess gave Ted Leibowitz a sealed envelope. The cable read: SEE YOU IN HOUSTON FOR DINNER. LEAR JET AWAITING YOU KENNEDY. PILOTS NAME RAY CUTLER . . . STEELE.

When Ted cleared Immigration at Kennedy, Ray Cutler and a Carey limousine were waiting for him. They drove to the Atlantic Aviation Terminal, and fifteen minutes later Ted was squeezed to the back of his seat by the acceleration of the Lear as it clawed for altitude. Four hours later, he was standing in front of the Steele Company hangar in Houston. His wristwatch was still on Geneva time and read one in the morning.

His head and stomach agreed, yet the clock on the face of the hangar read only six in the evening.

Another chauffered Cadillac was waiting at the airport. In less than an hour Ted Leibowitz stood in the reception hall of the Steele mansion in River Oaks and was greeted by an elegant and smiling Janice Steele, who greeted him warmly.

"Ted, we're delighted to see you. What a lovely surprise."

"It did come up rather hurriedly, Janice. Hope you were expecting me?"

"Of course. Beth Wales called a couple of hours ago. We have the green room all ready for you."

"That's fine. I'll just be staying tonight. How are the children?"

"Couldn't be better. Jason just called on the car phone. He'll be here in about twenty minutes. I have to check on something in the kitchen. Can you find your way? Clayton will take your bag up."

After a quick shower and change, he found himself alone in the oak-paneled library. Clayton, the butler, had taken his order for a weak scotch and soda and disappeared. The room amused him. In the world of Jason Steele, everything was for effect, and this room was no exception.

The two long walls held back-lit gun cases heavily done in glass and brass. The far wall was of books, handsomely bound in leather. From the neatness of their ranks, Ted knew they had not been opened since they left the bindery. The last wall was a photo gallery. The President and the Republican national chairman and the Republican senators and governors of the western states were all offering good health or best wishes to Jason Steele.

A new addition caught his eye—a picture of Steele, Kellermann, and himself in straw hats, tanned and grinning, their arms on each other's shoulders with a large sailfish hanging behind them.

"To Jason Steele, the best salesman in the world, from his friend and associate, Manny Kellermann." Ted remembered that afternoon in Acapulco well and he was sure that Jason Steele would never forget it . . .

2

As he awaited a response to his knock on the bungalow door, Jason Steele took the moment to catch his breath and take in his surroundings. In his life aboard jets and limousines, he had lost the habit of walking. The final seventy steps of climbing had taken his wind. Walking was the only way to the high cluster of pink and white bungalows built about a sparkling blue pool on the highest hill above Las Brisas Hotel. The privacy was complete.

The bungalows were carefully hidden among groves of mangoes and palms. The trees swayed in the warm wind from the sea, and their shade brought the temperature down to a lilting eighty-four. This was a far cry from the howling winds and swirling snows of a March "norther" he had left behind in Houston. In the moist tropical air, he sweated from the heaviness of his suit and the climb.

The hills of Las Brisas dominated the sweep of Acapulco Bay to the north and west. As he stood in the sun, he watched, with the practiced eye of a seaman, the long swells of the Pacific crashing and breaking on the high dun bluffs of Roqueta Island in the mouth of the bay. Beach boats with gaily striped sails darted on and off the sands far below him. He became so entranced with the beauty of the bay that he didn't hear the door open behind him. He was startled by a clipped British voice.

"Hallo, and you must be Mr. Jason Steele."

He was further startled when he turned to meet the voice. She was tall, lovely, tanned, and wearing only half a bikini.

"Ah, yes, I am, and who might you be?"

"Cynthia Davies—Cindy to my friends." She extended a long slim hand as she went on.

"Manny said that you might be along about now. Do come in."

"And where is he?"

126

"He's down the hall there in his room. He and Linda have decided it's siesta time. I'm to amuse you until they get up. I've been sunning on the balcony. Will you join me?"

Jason nodded and, wrestling with his tie, he trailed her magnificent lithe figure out into the bright sunlight on the far side of the bungalow. This was the latest twist in a bizarre week.

It had started in Houston three days earlier. Jason took a phone call from a New York broker, Bill Arthur, who had been pushing Steele Minerals stock quite strongly. Jason always took phone calls from brokers when he could.

"Jason," Arthur said, "Ted Leibowitz has asked me if you might join him and Manny Kellermann for a few days of sail-fishing off Acapulco."

Kellermann and his World Equities, Ltd., were reputedly the biggest money-management firm in the world. Jason knew that this could be the chance he had been waiting for, but not wishing to appear overly interested in front of a broker, he stalled for time.

"Well, Bill, I'm not sure. I don't know them at all, and my schedule is pretty well committed."

"Jason, these are people you should know, and they would like to see you this coming Thursday."

"Thursday! You've got to be kidding. Let's see. Thursday I'm due in Tulsa for the Independent Petroleum luncheon. I'm the speaker."

"Jason, have you been watching your stock transfer sheets of late?"

"Yes, although the damn bank transfer agents are always a couple of weeks late in getting them to us."

"Well, it's been active and strong, as we both know. We're involved. I don't think it would be fair of me to say how strong, but I can and will say this, two of Kellermann's funds are very substantial new shareholders of yours, and I think it's time you two got to know each other. In any event, it will show up on your transfer sheets pretty quick."

"Well, it's going to take some juggling but I might be able

to get Bacon to handle that Tulsa lunch. Let me see if it's possible. I'll call you back."

When Jason put down the receiver, he asked Elizabeth Wales to fetch him the latest shareholder list. As he waited, he recalled the whippy and very intense young stock analyst who had come over from Switzerland the previous month. Apparently the fellow had listened well, if what Bill Arthur was saying was true. It pleased Jason that World Equities now owned some Steele Minerals. The performance of the Steele stock had been spectacular in the over-the-counter market in the past six months. Eight or nine of the high performance "Go-go funds" had been very active buyers. But Jason was looking for broader and more substantial support from the big, older funds, the Fidelities and the M.I.T.'s or even his father-in-law's Prescott. They had sent their analysts out, and they had been wined and dined and run through the computerized geology center. But they had not bought in and it was a bitter disappointment to Jason, though one he'd never admit. They seemed hung up on the quality and repeatability of the Steele Company earnings. Jason vowed that he'd show them. If they wanted Standard of Jersey, they could buy Standard of Jersey any day they chose. To him, that was not growth. Steele Minerals would outdrill Jersey in the coming year. And now, the next quarterly report of World Equities would show some Steele Minerals shares. This should broaden the base and the sponsorship of the Steele stock.

Elizabeth Wales entered with the stock transfer sheets. Jason studied them and after he had run the totals, he made some assumptions. If Kellermann had taken down about sixty percent of the transactions reflected on the sheets in brokers' names, he might have close to 360,000 shares. Just a hair under two percent of the outstanding. Unless, he thought, the bastard was into the convertible bonds too. That wouldn't show up. He flicked down a switch on the seventy-button panel. The room came alive to the stereophonic voice of Elizabeth Wales.

"Yes, Mr. Steele?"

"Get me Bacon in here right away."

In a matter of minutes Dan Bacon learned that he was giving a speech in Tulsa Thursday, and the transportation department began checking out the logistics of a flight to Acapulco.

Cindy Davies flopped down on a towel-covered mattress in the center of the sun-drenched balcony. Jason took an aluminum armchair in the shade of the overhang. He watched in amusement and admiration as Cindy reached for a dark tube of Piz Buin and nonchalantly oiled her nipples before she lay back in the full heat of the afternoon sun.

"What do you do for Kellermann, Cindy?"

"I'm rather his girl Friday. I try to keep him close to a schedule and see that he meets all the people that he likes to meet. Where I can, I try to keep him from the press. After that *Time* cover story, it has been rather difficult."

"Then you're sort of his executive secretary?"

"Oh, no, don't be absurd, I can't type a word. There are people in Lausanne for that."

"Oh." Jason thought for a bit and went on.

"Cindy, what's this week look like? I'd like to let my pilots and office know."

Cindy sat up abruptly.

"How terribly rude of me! I should have thought of that. I'll take care of it now. We've chartered a Huckins Sportfisherman. Of course, it's been sitting in the quay for four days. He does plan to fish, though. This is his bungalow, by the way. Ted's is the one on the right as you go out the door. He's over there now with Bronia. You have the one on the left. I don't know how long you're going to be here, but whatever you want, you have only to tell me. For that matter, I don't know why you're here. What do you do, Mr. Steele?"

Jason felt a bit hurt. Although he hadn't been on the cover of *Time, Fortune* recently had given him a quarter-page picture in the "Business Men in the News" section. He replied: "I run a natural resources company out of Houston. We develop minerals and drill oil wells for ourselves and others. And incidentally, call me Jason." A few minutes later, the sound of laughter was heard in the hallway.

A man stepped onto the porch wearing a towel sarong. He

was of medium height, very tan and fit and quite solidly built. Jason guessed that he was in his early forties. As he approached, his level brown eyes and thick lips broke into a slow easy smile. Jason rose as he extended his hand.

"Steele? I'm Manny Kellermann." He was trailed onto the porch by the tallest, most statuesque Swedish blonde that Jason had ever seen outside the pages of *Playboy*. Like Cindy, she too wore only a bikini bottom.

"Mr. Steele, Miss Swensen. Linda Swensen, Jason Steele." Jason shook hands, and they went into the coolness of the living room where an elegant buffet lunch was laid out.

During this first visit with Manny Kellermann, it was the relaxed atmosphere that impressed Jason the most. Here was a man who controlled three billion dollars of other people's monies all over the globe and yet the phone never rang. And his entourage included some of the loveliest girls Jason had ever seen. They all moved about on this private hilltop seemingly without a thought to the world beyond them.

In the afternoon Jason was shown to his bungalow by Cindy. He found his luggage all set out and his swim trunks on the bed. When Cindy saw his surprise, she blithely said, "Oh, yes, I had your things brought up while you and Manny were talking after lunch, and I put your pilots in touch with ours. You might have seen our Falcon at the airport. That way, they'll know when we're going to leave."

She waited outside as Jason changed, and they went to the pool. Shortly, a man came out of the third bungalow. He was about Kellermann's height but far thinner, almost aesthetically thin. He had a long thin nose, intense, appraising eyes, and narrow lips. He dove in straightaway and surfaced close to Jason.

"Hi, I'm Ted Leibowitz." They shook a watery handshake. Bronia, a bosomy German brunette, joined them, and the four cavorted about in the pool like children.

Business? Jason thought that was why he had been asked, but there was no sign of it. In the evening, the three couples shared a candlelit table on Kellermann's porch. The wind had died with the sun, and the waters of the bay had gone to glass. The smoothness reflected the bobbling lights of a cruise ship that had anchored at twilight in the center of the bay. It was one of the least pressured evenings that Jason Steele had spent in a long while.

Over brandy and cigars, it was Ted Leibowitz who opened what business conversation there was.

"Our growth fund manager tells me your drilling monies are running well ahead of last year."

Jason waxed expansive. He was on ground that he knew well, and his instinct to promote was now almost a subconscious reflex.

"That's right. We just closed the first quarter and took in twenty-seven million. That's up from eleven in the same quarter, last year."

"Do you see it going in a linear trend?" Leibowitz's manner was most offhand and casual. Jason knew better as he answered, "I think we'll do better than a linear projection. Of course, that somewhat depends on the economy, but probably more important, what those goddam fools in the Congress are going to do."

"Oh?"

"Well, you read the other day where those Eastern idiots in the Senate want to cut the depletion allowance back to twenty percent."

"How would that affect your operations?"

"Very frankly, it wouldn't. The oil industry will just pass the added cost along to the consumer, but it might have a psychological effect on new investors in oil. That could hurt sales. As I told your analyst, Steele Minerals makes its slice going in."

Manny Kellermann just sat back and listened. He asked no questions. Drawing on his light Havana, he watched Jason Steele through lidded eyes while he stroked Linda's thigh. Finally, after a long yawn, he got to his feet and spoke. "Well, Jason. It looks like our bright boys have finally latched on to a winner. See you in the morning." With that, he retired, taking his Swede with him.

Cindy Davies, who looked stunning in a Chinese sheath of jade-green silk, accompanied Jason to his bungalow. Once inside, she casually slipped out of her clothes and without a word stepped into the shower.

Jason threw a "why not" smirk at himself in the bedroom mirror. He hurried out of his own clothes, thinking admiringly that Kellermann certainly knew how to treat his guests. He quickly joined Cindy. The needling water and the coarseness of the face cloths as they lathered each other soon had them excited to a state that could only be expended in a damp mating on the bathroom carpet.

3

Two days later, they finally used the fishing yacht. Only Bronia, who said she was a bad sailor, stayed ashore. The *Rosalita* was a sleek gray-and-white sixty-footer, a custom-built Huckins, resplendent with white sun awnings. The Mexican skipper ran her the fifteen miles to the edge of the blue water in just under forty minutes. Once there, he worked along the weed-strewn current at slow ahead. Manny Kellermann went into the fighting chair first. When nothing happened, he grew bored and offered the rod to Jason, who declined in favor of Ted. Manny retired to the air-conditioned main cabin with Linda and Cindy.

Ted soon hooked a bonito and boated it in little time. Saying he wanted to quit while he was ahead, he left Jason with the fishing cockpit to himself. Somehow, the skipper recognized that Jason was a man of the sea. He looked down approvingly when Jason took over the chair and they exchanged glances for an instant. The skipper went back to the wheel with a smile.

For an hour nothing happened. Then suddenly there was a twang on the starboard outrigger and Jason found himself in a fight with a fish.

The fish dove, taking almost all of the reel. As he sounded

for the bottom, Jason kept as much drag on as he dared, heaving and swaying on his pole to ensure the set of the hook. From the weight of the rod, Jason knew he had a big one. He kept at it, checking and reeling for every inch the fish grudgingly gave. By now, he had a cheering section. Manny and Ted were shouting and coaching on the upper bridge while Linda and Cindy, down in the cockpit, wiped the sweat from him with towels. The line went weightless. Jason bellowed, "He's on the way!"

Jason and the skipper both knew what to expect. The skipper kicked the Huckins ahead to take up the slack of the line, while Jason reeled in as fast as he could. In another moment, a silver blue sail broke water two hundred yards out on the port quarter and tail danced over a long swell.

"Sail! Sail!" The skipper was as excited as Jason. He expertly wheeled the Huckins into a long starboard turn to keep the line clear.

It went on for an hour and a half. Jason grew exhausted, but he wouldn't give in, and slowly the sailfish weakened. Jason and the skipper were too good a team.

After at least three false starts, they worked the sailfish alongside. They knew the boating had to be quick and quiet, for now was the time of the sharks. The mate had brought out two thirty-thirty rifles. He gave one to Manny Kellermann and climbed high onto the flying bridge tower with the other. Jason had the sail worked within seventy-five yards of the transom, dead astern, when out of the corner of his eye he saw the loping dorsal fin of a shark break water. The cry of "Shark" was just out of his throat when a rifle crack from the bridge and a fountain of water by the fin told him that the mate had also seen it.

The skipper quietly eased the big Huckins down on the fish, keeping it down sun and in low idle so as not to spook him further. The mate gave his rifle to Ted and then went down into the cockpit and picked up a gaff. With the last of his strength, Jason worked the big sail in as close as he could. The mate gave him the gaff, and they had him. The skipper came off the bridge, and they got a loop over his tail just as the dorsal fin of a massive mako shark broke water not ten feet out. The two rifles cracked almost as one. Wounded, the mako broke away. He didn't get far, for soon the waters not fifty yards out erupted into a bloody froth as his fellow sharks ripped him to pieces.

The two Mexicans worked the sail up high on the gin pole, and with a big grin, the skipper hoisted the fish flag to the outrigger peak.

When they got him to the beach, the fish weighed in at a hundred and fifty-five pounds, within five pounds of the Acapulco record. The local newspaper took a picture of the grinning threesome. The photo was picked up by the wire services and run in the next morning's edition of the *Houston Post* as well as the next issue of *Forbes Magazine*, along with a speculative article about what might be forthcoming from the new friendship of money tycoon Kellermann and the mineral entrepreneur Steele.

The night of the big fish, the Kellermann party celebrated by going to La Perla restaurant, where they watched a young Mexican lad dive off a one-hundred-and-twenty-foot cliff with torches in his hands. When they got back to Las Brisas, Manny Kellermann wanted to talk and invited Jason to stay for a nightcap on the porch. The girls disappeared. Manny drew long and hard on his cigar before he spoke.

"I liked what I saw this afternoon. You're a fighter." He eyed Jason impassively in the small light.

"Thank you. I've had to be."

"I know. So have I."

"The magazines say you've done well."

"Not bad for a Jewish boy from Brookline. My father was a cobbler, you know, and Ted now tells me World Equities controls seven percent of the New York Stock Exchange business. Not bad for a cobbler's kid." There was no false modesty in his tone. The words came as a flat statement of fact.

Jason responded with a low whistle as the magnitude of Manny's monetary muscle dawned on him. "And how much of us have you got?"

"I think Ted said five percent, but maybe it's six. I don't know, Ted handles . . ." Manny was very offhand.

134

Steele laughed to himself. That goddam bank and its transfer department, always late. Some day the horse could be out of the barn.

Manny Kellermann went on. "Details are not what I wanted to talk with you about tonight. Are you familiar with the Caribbean?"

"Somewhat," Jason replied. "I've been down to Cape Kennedy a lot with some of the astronauts. They've taken me down the missile range through the Carib."

"Do you know the island of Anguilla?"

"No, I don't think so."

"You probably recall they had a small revolt down there?"

"Oh sure, now it comes back. The Limeys sent in a paratroop battalion and they met them with goats on the air strip. Is that the place?"

"That's it."

"But you're not thinking of a revolution?"

"Not quite. I simply want to buy an island in the Atlantic."

"Well, that shouldn't be very hard. You have enough money to buy every island in the Bahamas if you set your mind to it."

Manny considered Jason's comment for a long moment.

"There's more to it than that. You see, I want to buy an island and start my own country. Flag, stamps, no taxes and all that."

It was Jason's turn to pause.

"That *is* ambitious."

"I want to start my own stock exchange. They tell me your people are quite good with computers and you have a lot of friends who know telecommunications via satellite. I thought a combine of our companies could put it all together and make one hell of a buck while at it: a world stock exchange, all hooked together by Telstar satellite, all the brokers of the world trading all at one place in one time frame. No trading tickets, no stock certificates. All electronic confirmations instantly. No taxes and no snooping federal agencies. Our action. Would you be interested?" It all came out in the same flat tone.

135

Just a simple business proposition to take over the world's money markets.

Jason strongly suspected there was more to Kellermann's wants than the site research for a world stock exchange. It might be his way of feeling out what someone could do for him.

"Yes, I'm interested," he said, deliberately matching Manny's tone of voice. "Fill me in with more details."

4

As they left Acapulco for New York, Manny Kellermann ordered Ted Leibowitz to dig into Steele and his companies. Ted cabled for all of the research files to be sent to New York from Lausanne. The many brokers that fronted for World Equities in New York and along the West Coast were casually requested to update any of their brokerage reports. In certain patches of oil country, around Houston and Tulsa, industry specialists were asked to quietly look into the quality of wells as reported by Steele Minerals. It was done in a routine way. The several funds within the World Equities complex were in and out of so many different oil company stocks in the course of a year that any kind of inquiry such as this one caused no ripples in the investment community.

Because of World Equities' difficulties with the American Securities and Exchange Commission, Ted Leibowitz had worked out a convenient way to run a New York office while technically not having a New York office.

Three years ago, he had discovered William F. Arthur, the floor trading partner of a New York Stock Exchange firm. Arthur was ambitious and his firm was not. He had his exchange membership in his own name, but a major portion of the $250,000 that was tied up in the exchange seat belonged to the partners of Arthur's firm. Leibowitz arranged for a loan to

Arthur from a World Equities bank in Zurich. Arthur bought out his former associates, lock, stock, and staff, and announced the formation of William F. Arthur and Company, members of the New York and American Stock Exchanges. Leibowitz saw to it that Arthur got more than enough of World Equities commission business to furnish his firm with direct cable lines to Lausanne, and apartments and office space for his Swiss visitors in New York. It was thus that Ted Leibowitz provided himself with a sumptuous office near the top of the Seagram's Building on Park Avenue. That his activities in these offices were not subject to the scrutiny of the S.E.C. made them all the more pleasant.

The final report on Steele Minerals Company was compiled and typed in the William F. Arthur and Company offices. The researchers had found industry people with strong and divergent opinions on Jason Steele. One who was interviewed from the uranium business described Jason as "not the first guy I'd give my wallet to if I wanted to go swimming." The industry report was very bullish on the geologic abilities and technical advancements in resource finding techniques that had been developed by Dan Bacon and his staff. The financing seemed sound.

When Ted Leibowitz returned to Lausanne, he and Manny Kellermann spent an hour together. As Ted made his report, Manny paced his study, snapping his crop on his jodhpurs. One of his Swedes had been replaced by a spirited Irish girl who taught riding.

Leibowitz read from the report. "Reliable sources say that several major oil companies are watching the growth of the Steele Funds with active interest. Should the Steele formula prove viable in annual increments over two hundred million, it is reasonable to expect several of the major companies to launch their own programs. The Steele vehicle poses an attractive and inexpensive means of financing an exploratory program off balance sheet. With continued success, Steele and his companies could quickly face major competition."

Manny interrupted impatiently. "That happened yet?"

"Not yet, Manny. He seems to have the field to himself."

Ted set the report aside for a few moments to watch the pacing Manny. They had bigger plans for Steele than just the Fund ownership of his stock. Manny had for the last few years grown frustrated with the erratic performance of his portfolio managers. Clever young men came to Lausanne and did wonders in the stock markets for six or seven months and then, somehow, lost their feel. Manny saw in minerals and petroleum an opportunity that trading in listed stocks did not have. Once proven, natural resources didn't change very much in value. He was fed up with the fluctuating values on the stock exchanges. Fund selling, World Equities had; consistent performance, it did not.

Manny Kellermann then asked. "All right, so much for the technical stuff. What about Steele himself? What do you think?"

Ted took off his reading glasses and considered the question for a moment. "Manny, he could be a real tough cookie for us to handle. They dug into his background pretty thoroughly. He's pretty much made it on his own. Gotten himself overextended here and there, but worked himself out of it. Has a rich wife and that didn't hurt. That's the Prescott money in Boston, but in fairness, he himself has got Steele Minerals to where it is. Runs his shop with an iron hand. Total control. That could be a problem. On the positive side, they've found a lot of minerals more consistently than most of the industry. From what our people learned, his private life somewhat resembles yours, but much quieter. He's got some handpicked dollies on his staff, but from what we could pull together, very few people, even in his own company, seem to know about them."

With that, Manny laughed. "Okay. Let's try the bastard out. We'll feed him ten million out of the Fund of Nations account, this next quarter. Let him gear up. Give him another fifty in the last half of the year if he does good. Let him gear up real big. Have him keep the drillings in the United States. Mostly the Gulf Coast and Oklahoma. American oil properties will look good to the Germans. It would seem that's where Steele Minerals is most competent. If I were you, I'd keep acquiring their convertible bonds rather than the common. We'll get a ride on the stock anyway, and we might as well get paid something while waiting. I really want his geologists, not him, if it comes to that. I'm not saying we grab the company; keep an eye on it though. Is that all?"

Ted laughed. "Yes, Manny. Tally ho and all that crap."

Their meeting was typical of the manner in which investment decisions were made within World Equities. Manny Kellermann was not one to take questions of a policy nature to his board of directors or his operating committee. Once he had given the go-ahead, Steele Minerals became a growing, major factor in the operations of World Equities. As a result, the investment dealings with Jason Steele and his company rested with Ted Leibowitz. Jason Steele and Manny Kellermann began to see more of each other socially. Ted watched from the sidelines with interest as the mutual admiration developed. As Ted came to know Jason Steele better, he concluded that Kellermann and Steele in the same business venture was the equivalent of two wounded mako sharks in the same small swimming pool. Ted was content to take his seat by the pool and watch, as long as the relationship offered no harm to his own interests.

Ted was on a plane to New York the day after his meeting with Manny. He phoned Jason from the airport. He sketched out Kellermann's proposal to drill with him and asked for a meeting in New York to discuss it. Jason could scarcely contain his excitement with the potential of this new account but, as usual, he played it cool. Since Ted was the number two man in World Equities, Jason reasoned that he would send Dan Bacon to New York. To Ted he said that Bacon was the best man for him to sit with, since he was on top of the available drilling projects on a day to day basis. Dan Bacon was on a company plane to New York that night.

The next morning, he joined Ted Leibowitz for breakfast in his suite in the Waldorf Towers. The two men got along well from the beginning. Ted explained that American tax shelter held little attraction for their European investors; they were interested in positive spendable cash. If the Steele Company could produce a twelve percent return on invested capital with a reasonable assurance of reserves in the ground that would throw off over time four times more oil in dollars than the capital placed at risk, then this could be the beginning of a very long and profitable relationship. Dan was certain that this could be accomplished. He started to spread some Gulf Coast Isopach maps across the floor. Ted waved them off.

"Look, Dan, geology isn't my thing. Let's start with your concept, then we'll try arithmetic. If that makes sense, then take me over the maps. Don't bother me with the details. We're only interested in dollar results."

And it was in this manner that Steele Minerals found an additional sixty million of completely discretionary monies to drill that year.

The year passed very quickly, and the monies rolled in from Lausanne with the regularity of a Swiss clock.

The *Wall Street Journal* took note that the Steele Minerals Company was top bidder in the next two Texas offshore drainage sales, beating out Humble in one instance and Conoco in another. The article went on to comment favorably on the meteoric rise of this independent company to the point where it now stood toe to toe and slugged it out with the biggest of the big. The domestic money raising of the Steele Investment Funds under the touting aegis of the Western Investors wholesaling force exceeded the predictions that Jason had made at Acapulco. As Christmas and the close of the tax year approached, Jason and Dan Bacon found themselves counting their many blessings with glee.

The Monday after Christmas, Bacon called a ten A.M. meeting with his treasurer and the Gulf Coast division manager in his glass office atop the newly named Steele Tower. It actually did not get underway until eleven because Dan was late. He was forever coping with domestic crises. He saw his wife little and his children less, and this led to continual problems at home. That he could turn from such a situation to the making of million-dollar decisions so calmly never ceased to amaze his co-workers. He had the nerves of a riverboat gambler and a geniality that kept many people with the company who could never have lasted two days in direct contact with Jason Steele.

People often remarked on the contrast between the two men. Jason Steele was always in a hurry. For him, the concept was what counted; the nuts and bolts were for lesser mortals. He had no patience, even with the fastest stenographer, and therefore seldom wrote letters. The phone was his way. Three teams of two girls each were assigned to handle his calls twenty-four hours a day. If someone he wanted was unavailable, he'd bark through the wires at the helpless girls. Loyal Elizabeth Wales worked hard at keeping the chairman's suite in a semblance of normality, yet even she was often seen coming from his office in tears.

Dan Bacon was just the opposite. He was sympathetic and patient and would listen to anyone with a problem. He and Jason worked towards the same goal but used totally different tactics.

As he arrived that morning, the head of public relations was restlessly waiting to intercept him in the outer reception room. He handed him a clipped and circled copy of the morning *Oil and Gas Journal*. The first article was headlined "Steele Minerals Top North American Driller Last Quarter." As Bacon strode into his office, he was in a jovial frame of mind. He threw the magazine on the desk before the waiting men.

"Read that, you bastards. I told y'all we'd do it."

As they read over each other's shoulders, Dan was on his direct line to his broker.

"Hey, where are we? What? Only up three! Shee-it, that's not enough."

He put down the receiver and turned his attention to the matter at hand.

"All right, gentlemen, let's proceed with our happy task."

For the next two days, they assigned the ownership of wells several months after they had been drilled, wet or dry. On the face of it, it would seem impossible to do. In the way Steele Minerals books were set up, it was really quite easy. There was the big World Equities account into which they could put anything. The people in Lausanne would never know the difference. Then, there were the Steele Investment funds. One was limited to drilling new wells that were immediately adjacent to proven production. The definition of "offset" left plenty of room. The second specialized in wildcatting for new discoveries. Then, there were several smaller private partnerships. These people had been sold into specific projects. In their case it was difficult to adjust the results.

Dan and his crew systematically assembled the year's discoveries and dry holes, took the reserves and cash flows, and divided them up to meet the acceptable requirements of the specific account. The fact that Ted Leibowitz had said he wanted a twelve percent return governed the drilling results of World Equities for the year. This was unfortunate for World Equities. The actual results of the drillings with their fund monies would have thrown off an honest sixteen percent. Bacon was playing Santa Claus for the shareholders of Steele Minerals. In the Christmas shuffle, Leibowitz lost three very good Louisiana gas wells. One went to a wildcat fund that had drilled a string of "dusters." The other two became the property of Steele Minerals Company. Leibowitz wanted twelve percent. Dan Bacon gave him eleven and knew there would be no complaint. Steele Minerals drilled for all these groups as agent and kept title in the company name. The I.R.S. couldn't tell and nobody else was interested. Almost everybody was happy. Only some of the wildcat investors didn't make out too well, but as Dan would often say, "Look at the action they got. Now where else could they get that action? You pay your money and you take your chances."

Steele Minerals Company announced revenues in excess of $260,000,000 and a net profit of $54,000,000. This was better than a clear double on net. The stock broke into new high ground at forty, nearly tripling in price that year after a four for one split.

Ted Leibowitz never did learn of the Christmas shuffle. He might have been upset, but more probably it would have amused him; what World Equities got squeezed out of by Santa Claus, they got back in the rise of the convertible bonds of Steele Minerals.

5

The annual management fee of World Equities, Ltd., was dependent on the growth performance of the Fund of Nations and the several other smaller funds that it managed. Manny Kellermann had used this as one of his big sales points in acquiring control of $2 billion. It was on every piece of sales literature that World Equities put forth. "The Management Company only profits after the investor does." It was a half truth at best, but like many other things, it had been said so often, in so many languages, that most of the world believed it. As chairman of the board and president of W.E.L., Kellermann had an annual salary of $250,000. As executive vice-president, Edward Leibowitz received $200,000. None of the financial reports in the prospectus of the fund mentioned the perquisites and emoluments of these offices—the lake-front office mansion that didn't have a typewriter, the permanent suites in the Waldorf Towers, the Falcon jet, the "Executive staff." The salaries were just the beginning of the day in the life styles of Kellermann and Leibowitz.

There were also stock options to be considered. W.E.L. had one class of common stock and no debt. Kellermann owned twenty-one percent and Leibowitz nine percent. The common stock was traded on several of the Canadian exchanges, and there was a very active over-the-counter market in Europe for two reasons. Many investors in the funds thought it a good idea to own something of the management company, perhaps as a psychological crutch, more than a means to voting power. The second source of activity, and by far the stronger, was the World Equities sales force throughout the world who were all given stock options that were tied to their sales performances. This was true of the entire pyramid from Kellermann all the way down to a typist in the Hong Kong office. The sales force had stock options and faith.

143

When World Equities had first been taken into the public market at $16 a share, many of the sales people had mortgaged their homes or borrowed on their life insurance to buy shares. The price was driven to $28 in two weeks and had crept up from there in the past six months to around $32. Kellermann and Leibowitz were convinced it would go a lot higher if they could keep up a good performance in the Fund of Nations, the largest fund that W.E.L. managed. This meant further wealth for them through the increase in value of their W.E.L. stock options. It should have been academic, for on the initial under-writing, Kellermann and Leibowitz sold off enough shares to put away $25 million and $11 million, respectively, in cash for themselves, irrelevant of the fate of World Equities. It should have been academic, but it was not. Either of them would have started a poker game with the devil, just for the pleasure.

The biggest winner in the Fund of Nations portfolio for the year was Steele Minerals. The stock had tripled in value, and the convertible bonds had done almost as well. The drilling reports on their American oil investments were very satisfactory. The name Steele came up several times in a very favorable light at the January board meeting of World Equities. Manny Kellermann called Jason to tell him of his board's satisfaction.

"Jason, it's wonderful, absolutely wonderful."

"Manny, you old son of a gun, how are you? Yes, we're pretty proud. I told you we could do it."

"Hey, when are you coming over? I've got a place in Kitz-bühel for February. Cindy says to give you her best. Wants to ski with 'the big man from Texas.' "

"Well, Manny, Janice—that's my wife—is coming over with me to London. You know those drilling funds I have. Well, we've had such a good year that I'm calling the next directors' meeting for February at the Connaught in London."

"London, hmm. I have to speak to a rally of our English sales staff on the seventh in London. Any chance we could get together?"

"Sure, great idea. And I know Janice would like to meet you. You've become quite a celebrity in the American press."

"I get the message. No broads, huh?"

"Manny, you're always three steps ahead."

"Okay. Cut the bullshit. See you, say for dinner, London the seventh, the Connaught."

"Right. Look forward to it."

Three weeks later Manny Kellermann was a dinner guest of the Steeles in a private dining room of the Connaught and caused quite a stir on his arrival. The Steeles were giving a cocktail party reception for the twelve drilling fund directors and their wives. These men were for the most part of national repute, such as retired oil company presidents or airline executives. They were there for the weight of names and titles. Their wives were matronly and sedate. Into this gathering Manny Kellermann came dressed in a silver Nehru suit and sporting sideburns. The effect was electric. But while Jason introduced him all around, Kellermann was restrained and reticent. In less than ten minutes, Jason whisked him off to a private dining room. Janice could not break away so abruptly with any degree of grace, so they had a few moments alone. "How you doing on my world stock exchange?" Kellermann asked.

"There's two chances. On the rest, we're kidding ourselves."

"What's the good news?"

"My research people tell me there are two submerged sea mounts off New England that have never been claimed. They're about thirty miles at sea and come right up off the sea bed itself. That's important because of the two-hundred-meter rule."

"What the hell is the two-hundred-meter rule?" Manny asked.

"Last year, the United States became a signatory to the United Nations Convention on the Continental Shelf. Two hundred meters is sort of the rule of thumb in that document. A country can own out to two hundred meters of water. There's some other phrases about commercially exploitable. They won't have any bearing because there's over twelve hundred meters of water in depth between these sea mounts and the American Continental Shelf."

"So?"

"So we build our own island, sort of a Texas Tower deal, in six hundred feet of water. Technically feasible, according to my engineers. Depends how many people you want to put out there."

"Christ almighty, I like it. Jason, ya got big balls. Now what's the second chance?"

"Well, my people have been all through the Caribbean, one way or another. On the islands where a deal might be made, you're sitting on a racial powder keg. Otherwise, there are simply too many mother-country apron strings. Now further up the coast, we may be on to something that could work well. It will depend on your relations with De Gaulle and the French government."

"They might be okay. We've got one of his former premiers on our board, but I still don't see the connection."

"You have to go back into history a bit. Do you remember the peace treaty of the French and Indian Wars in the eighteenth century?"

"Cut the shit, Jason."

"Well, in that peace treaty, so I'm told, France got these two islands just below Newfoundland as a place for their fishing boats to dry their catches and make repairs. France still owns them. They might sell us one or a slice. De Gaulle keeps sticking needles into Britain. He's trying to pull the Canuck element out of Quebec. He's not pleased with the United States. The thought of having the world stock exchange on French territory might just grab him."

"Goddam, you've got some bright people. That's terrific."

At that point, Janice joined them. She had made a special effort this evening. She knew how important Kellermann was to Jason's company and she had read of his free-swinging views on life. The combination was an irresistible challenge. She had spent the morning in a final fitting of her long pale blue Givenchy gown and the afternoon with the hotel hairdresser. Even Jason found himself giving her a second glance.

Manny was charming and drew Janice out in a masterful fashion. He asked where she had been shopping, what she had seen; he had some ideas about places she should visit, and told her the relative merits of obscure mod shops. That he was one of the great salesmen of the world when he wanted to be was apparent this night.

For Janice, Manny Kellermann proved a startling exception to the usual Jason Steele ally. Generally, Jason's business associates were overly deferential in their dealings with her. Their courtier approach and her Yankee upbringing led to unbridgeable gaps. New people flocked about Jason in an endless stream. Fund takeovers, tax loopholes, financing new ventures, Janice had heard them all in her first few years in Houston. It was always the same pattern: Jason Steele, selling, or being sold. She soon lost any enthusiasm for participation in the business affairs of her husband. If the courtiers talked of other subjects unrelated to business, they might meet another Janice. Most often, they were unperceptive, and their patent greed repelled her.

Eventually, with apologies to Janice, Manny brought the conversation back into a business vein. He and his board were delighted, he said, with the magnificent performance of Steele Minerals and he hinted that World Equities would budget and drill $100 million of new monies with the Steele Company in the coming year. He then swung into another topic.

"Jason, I don't know if you're familiar with how our sales force operates in the various countries."

"Only from what I've read, Manny, including publications of your firm."

"In each of these nations that we go into, we try and find a key man, a well-respected native of that country. We bring him to Switzerland and familiarize him with our product and our sales procedures. Then we send him around to other countries where we have offices so that he can learn to cope with operational problems as they arise."

"Yes, I'm familiar with most of that."

"Unfortunately, it has worked too well. We've developed such fine sales forces in some of the smaller countries that now many of the national governments are up tight. They're climbing all over us with restrictions."

147

"Why so?"

"If you were the premier of an emerging African nation, and you saw a bunch of your better educated blacks out beating the drums for investment with World Equities in Lausanne, and you knew bloody well that just about every penny of it would wind up in the American stock market, now what in hell would you do?"

"I'd do everything to stop it, if I could."

Manny nodded. "Precisely."

"So, your success has run into a reverse twist on the balance-of-payments problem?"

"That might be one way of phrasing it, but I think you and your technicians might be able to help us out."

"How's that?"

"Let's take one of these African mini-nations. Our people go to the government and say that we'll leave sixty cents of every dollar that our salesmen raise. We'll leave that sixty cents for the development of that country."

"That's fine, but what happens if there are no stocks in the country that are worth a damn?"

"Forget common stocks; that's where your people come in."

"You mean we come in and drill wells or develop a mine or whatever?"

"Yes. Have you any interest?"

"Of course, we have an interest. Wherever there's a buck, we have an interest, but not as a contractor this time. The way I think that Steele Minerals and World Equities might structure the management company is as a joint venture. We've noticed how well those management fees work for you, year after year." Jason smiled, as he thought, I'll be God damned if I'll be the door opener for Manny Kellermann to take over his own bright world of direct investment in natural resources without a big piece of the action.

Manny Kellermann pursed his lips for a second before he replied in a tentative tone. "There might be room for that. We've never gone into a joint venture with anybody before, but after last year's performance, I think my board might be inclined to accept Steele Minerals as a partner."

Jason's instincts were to close a deal as soon as possible, his way. "Why don't we set up a meeting in Houston?" he suggested. "You send along your sales types who know where you're having your biggest money extrication problems. I'll put them together with our technical types and we'll let them have at it."

"Okay with me. Ted will be over with some of his staff." Manny glanced at his watch. "My God. I hadn't realized we'd talked this long. I'm supposed to be giving the closing address to a sales rally across town in another fifteen minutes. We're launching a new insurance stock plan." He turned to Janice. "Would you like to come along?"

To Jason's surprise, Janice replied for them both. "Yes, Manny, we'd love to."

6

The moment Jason Steele was back in Houston, he set about planning the March meeting of the combined staffs. He was determined to impress the World Equities people, having read of the modernistic splendor of their complex along the banks of Lake Geneva. He first called a strategy session with his two key lieutenants, Dan Bacon, President of Steele Resources, and Arthur Foxx, President of the Steele Company's international operating subsidiary. Jason opened the conference, without even the briefest exchange of greetings, so eager was he to tell them his news.

"Gentlemen, we are about to set up and manage a whole new fund complex. For want of a better title we'll call it Fund of Emerging Nations. World Equities will be our partner. Kellermann's people will do all the money raising. You will see that the money is sensibly invested. The ownership of the management company for these funds will be a fifty-fifty joint venture of Steele Minerals and World Equities."

Foxx and Bacon leaned forward in their chairs.

"This will not be an eleemosynary endeavor. The whole play is outside of the United States. There will be no one to look over our shoulder."

Bacon interrupted. "You mean no one? No S.E.C. or I.R.S. or anything? Not even auditors?"

"Well, there will have to be auditors. Art, you are going to Geneva. You will set up an office and live there. The paperwork of the operation will be in your hands. On the surface, the management company will be taking an organizational fee of ten percent of the monies raised for its efforts in development of investment properties. What kind of commissions Kellermann and Leibowitz pay to their sales people will be their business. That's before the money gets to the Fund. The management company for the Fund will be entitled to our normal twenty-five percent of the net profit to be divided fifty-fifty with W.E.L. I'd like to keep our share outside the United States as far as the tax consequences of Steele Minerals are concerned."

Foxx, who now saw his own place in the sun for the first time, spoke up. "Sounds great, Jason!"

"Now let's play this one right. The shareholders of our company will come out of this just fine. I see no sense in making either Kellermann or Leibowitz any richer, unless we get our share. We want to be smart about it, and if we are, here's the way I see it. Let's assume we're going to drill a well off of one of these little African countries, let's say Ethiopia. Kellermann's sales people get some of the better-heeled Ethiopians to put up some of the dough. Maybe the government comes along for a slice. That cuts out any problems. We put on an internationally recognized set of auditors, as far as the books of the Fund are concerned. Well, we all know we're not going to drill that hole without some kind of rig insurance. For that matter, there's no reason we can't negotiate a per foot rate on the hole with a drilling contractor who needs a special consultant for technical problems. This is where you come in, Art. I see no reason why a bright person cannot set up an independent insurance agency or a small and specialized consulting firm to advise on the hole. Certainly these people are

150

entitled to be paid—preferably cash. Hell, there are plenty of printers that can print invoices. These bills get paid before the auditors ever get to the books and that gives us a cash reserve of our own outside the States. All kosher."

Bacon, with a wide smile, said, "I like it, I like it. No sweat."

Jason went on. "I feel a reasonable division of the venture's revenues might be fifty percent for me and twenty-five percent for each of you. And as to your 'no sweat,' Dan, there might very well be. It will depend on how clever we are in handling it. You're not going to be able to do it like your year-end readjustments. The W.E.L. people are not fools. Only the three of us can know, or we'll be wide open for the biggest blackmail you've ever seen."

Neither Foxx nor Bacon had any qualms about the conspiracy. They both agreed that Jason could rest assured that the matter would be well handled.

As the two were leaving the office, Jason flicked on his intercom. "Elizabeth, will you have Bill Leavitt come up?"

Bill Leavitt, the company's personnel director, was soon waved into a seat at the far end of the massive desk. Jason was in the midst of a call from an investment banker in New York who was telling him all about a small Arizona mineral property he owned under which he was certain there was uranium. Jason finally broke in. "Porter, I'm certain we have an interest. We have a man who is right on top of that whole area who will be very excited to hear about it. I'll switch you to our director of mineral properties, Carl Johansen. Thanks for bringing it to us. Good-bye."

Steele swung his full attention to Bill Leavitt without a pause. "Bill, I have a very special problem for you, and I know you can handle it. Incidentally, that new young receptionist you have out front, Marty Darnley, is very nice indeed. You handled that very well. My present problem is somewhat similar."

After two years of catering to the whims of Jason Steele, Bill Leavitt could expect almost anything. "I'm glad things have worked out well, Mr. Steele. How can I help you today?"

"Bill, I have this group of European businessmen coming

151

in the first week of March. There may be four or five of them, and they may be here for several days. That's a long time to a European man, and these men are very important to the company. I would like their undivided attention while they are here. There should be no need for their having to hunt for themselves."

"I understand, Mr. Steele."

"I thought we'd pick them up in New York with the 707. Fly them into Denver. Give them the land yacht ride up to my ranch if the weather's marginal. Spend the weekend at the ranch. A couple of these people are damn fine skiers, or so they say. If they want to, I'm sure Mrs. Steele will be glad to take them down to Aspen. Now, you understand that Mrs. Steele and the children will be with us for the weekend. Your girls must be discreet."

"Oh, yes, sir, always."

"Now, on Sunday night or Monday morning, depending on weather, we'll fly them on down here and put them up in the V.I.P. suites. You can plan on a minimum of three days and possibly six. That will depend on many things. I want you to coordinate your part with the transportation department. The more attractive and subtle way might be to go at this as sort of a smorgasbord approach. Give them a good spread to choose from. Have the jet staffed with extra stewardesses who just happen to go on up into the mountains on the land yachts too. It would be more tasteful, and I don't think Mrs. Steele would get wind of it. Can you handle it for me, Bill?"

"Certainly, Mr. Steele, be glad to."

7

On the night of the arrival of the World Equities group, the Steeles gave a large Western dinner party at their Colorado ranch. Jason had flown up all of the top operating people of his company and their wives. On the surface, it was a most convivial affair. For entertainment after dinner, a noisy group of Western guitar thumpers had been brought in from nearby Leadville. Ted Leibowitz could still feel the pounding of their super amplifiers across the front of his head. That, and the one or two extra scotches that were in excess of his normal two, left him with the foreboding of a hangover. After the singing, the ranch people had broken into foursomes for several sets of square dancing. Some of the younger W.E.L. people joined in. Ted's dinner partner, Lilly Bacon, was quite insistent that they dance too, so he had given in. Lilly was rather tight, and fortunately she soon excused herself. He took the opportunity to go out on the wide veranda for a moment of night air by himself.

By the sudden loudness of the band inside, he knew someone had come out with the same thought. He was surprised when it proved to be Janice Steele. They talked about the party, the ranch, the pack trips of the summer, and the problems the Steeles were having in completing their all-year-'round heated pool. Ted found Janice quite charming and sensed that she was of a different cut of cloth than most of the other women at the party. After a while, it started to snow, and she shivered and said she had had enough air.

Back inside, Jason joined them at the bar. "Jan, Ted tells me he's quite a skier. He has a lodge at Saint Anton."

"Oh, is that so!" She turned to Ted. "It's a shame, then, that you won't have a chance to try some real Western mountains while you're here."

Ted smiled. "You really don't think you have mountains over here! Have you ever tried the Alps?"

Janice put down her glass and answered forthrightly, "Yes, I've skied the Alps, and we do have some mountains here to match. Would you like to find out?" Ted noticed a definite set to her jaw as she finished.

"I'd love to, but I brought no gear."

"That's no problem. The ranch has a ski room. I think we can fix you up." Janice got up from the bar stool with an air of matronly determination.

In the ski room, Ted found the full equivalent of any first-class ski shop. His foot was narrow, but Janice found boots to fit. She looked up at him from the boot-fitting bench. "So much for the boots. There's a rack of stretch pants over there and a fitting room." Janice indicated the far corner of the shop. "You can handle that?"

"Very impressive," was Ted's comment as he walked over to the corner rack. "And I thought we came to buy oil wells."

The next morning, Ted Leibowitz watched in admiration the ease with which Janice Steele handled the powerful station wagon on the twisting roadway. The sun had not yet broken clear of the eastern peaks into the long valley and the light was flat in the bottomland. There had been a light dusting of powder snow during the night, and it was too early for the ranch hands to have scraped the long road into the Main Lodge.

In less than two hours they had twisted their way through the valleys of the majestic Sawotch Mountains and were at the foot of Ajax Mountain in Aspen. It had been a quiet drive, affording Ted the chance to think and wonder.

Janice Steele was not a beautiful woman. Her features were too strong. But she was attractive and in beautiful shape. The tightness of her Bogner turtleneck reflected a large firm bosom. The glovelike fit of her white stretch pants allowed for no female deceptions. Ted guessed she was about thirty-three, but he underguessed by two years. In his usual speculative way, he tried to conjecture the relationship between Janice and Jason Steele.

It was a perfect, windless day on Ajax Mountain. The sun was high and hot and the chair lift line short. On the long ride up, the stillness of the morning was broken only by the swish of skiers as they traversed beneath the lift or the occasional attempt at a yodel. As they drew close to the unloading station by the summit, Janice turned and said, "We all might have had a bit to drink last night. You have skied some?"

Ted assured her with the same easy smile of the night before. "Oh yes, I've skied some."

At the summit, Janice waited for him to take up a bit of slack on his boot buckles. "Ready?"

"Ready."

Janice pointed down into the toughest expert trail on the mountain and let them run. The trail led off from the smooth open stretches into a gully with an incredible pitch and on through several stands of tall pines. About one-third of the way down the mountain, it broke out onto the manicured openness of the Snow Bowl. Janice went into a long lilting waltz, swinging from one side of the Bowl to the other, waiting for Ted to catch up. On the second swing off the bank, he swept past her in center trail, taking the Bowl flat out in a lovely fluid wedle. "Well, I'll be damned," Janice said as she poled to catch up.

Her eyes were on Ted's supple back as she hunched down for speed. Further down, on a gentle pitch, and with her weight well back, she misjudged a slight hummock. Her tips crossed and in an instant she was a powdered heap.

As Ted heard her startled "Oh!" he deftly checked in a blur. He turned back and his deep laugh rolled up the slope. By the time Janice had disentangled herself and reset her bindings, Ted had "herringboned" up to her. He set in his poles and helped her brush off the snow from her clothes. Her cheeks were burning and for just a moment, he put one hand lightly to her face and brushed back a strand of hair with the other. Their eyes held, then she side-slipped away.

It grew hot enough at noon to take off their parkas and sunbathe in the high light. Janice had suggested having lunch in a private club to which she belonged, but Ted wasn't interested. She was accustomed to Jason's usual friends, and this surprised her. They settled for hot dogs and Cokes in the base cafeteria and went straight back on the hill. On the rides up, the conversation began to come much more freely. Ted found himself telling her of his background: of how he had grown up in the same Brookline, Massachusetts, neighborhood as Manny Kellermann; how he went to law school while Manny went to Europe with the idea of selling mutual funds; how they met one day in Paris, quite by chance. "Manny was in a mess with the S.E.C. and needed a lawyer," Ted said wryly. "I had a brand-new law degree and needed a client. And from that meeting grew World Equities. So, now let's talk about you."

Janice began telling him of her own childhood and of Jason and how they had met; and of their youthful dreams and plans which somehow had gotten out of hand. She hadn't meant to be as frank, to say as much. She stopped in some consternation and changed the subject, wondering what he thought of her. For a reason she couldn't quite understand, his opinion meant a great deal.

She knew what he had told her about himself was only a modest précis of one of the more successful careers in modern finance. She had heard Jason talk of him and Elizabeth Wales told her he was the one who really ran World Equities and was responsible for its fantastic growth. It was said that Kellermann, the salesman, and Leibowitz, the schemer, between them had found a way around or under the security regulations of almost all the developed nations. And that most often, it had been the Leibowitz scheme rather than the Kellermann sales pitch that had won the day.

Throughout the day, Janice became more aware of the bright mind she was dealing with. She found Ted a challenge, and she also found she knew how to talk to this man and hold his interest. This was an exhilarating experience. On the ride back to Leadville, Ted drove and Janice plied him with questions, mostly on the workings of World Equities, which she knew were now closely allied with the Steele interests. From what he told her, she realized that Elizabeth Wales had been correct. For all practical purposes Ted Leibowitz was at the steering wheel of W.E.L. Manny Kellermann had decided he was rich enough and had seen enough of the world. His new interest was to become a self-appointed ambassador of goodwill and peace. He had the idea that in commerce lay the answer to the world's ills.

When Janice asked what Ted thought of the new relationship with Steele Minerals, he quizzically eyed her for a moment, weighing whether or not he was being pumped for the benefit of Jason Steele. He decided to take no chances and answered with enthusiasm that a working combination of Steele Minerals and World Equities could be the biggest factor in world finance. Janice had difficulty in masking her feelings. "Why do you go on?" she asked. "Surely you have what you want?"

"For me it's fun. I'd be bored with anything else. There isn't any bigger crap game and I run a good piece of it." He paused. "But your question wasn't really meant for me, was it?"

"No, damnit, it wasn't," she answered, and lapsed into silence.

Ted sensed the torrent of her thoughts and left her to herself. He lightly threw his arm around her shoulder and gently drew her to him. Janice did not resist. The remainder of the drive was quiet as she sorted out her feelings. She knew there would be friction between the two men, for Jason would never be content sharing his throne. She knew it would be best not to pursue this friendship any further. And yet, of all the trading legionnaires in an endless parade through Houston, Ted Leibowitz was the first she found intriguing.

8

One of the more striking features of the Steele Tower offices was the presentation amphitheater on the thirty-fifth floor. It had been the brain child of Ace Emery and was principally used for sales presentations by his wholesaling force. Here, brokers came to see firsthand the space age wizardry with which the various Steele companies approached the problem of "wresting from Mother Nature her hidden secrets." As a matter of record, those very words were from Emery's preamble to the show he put on three times a week.

The rostrum, through electronic levers, controlled all of the lighting, sound machines, and projectors. The room was even equipped with a direct console tie to the Steele Company computers. It was set up in such a way that if someone had a question on the status of a well, or a mining property, or any other development project, the computer could be queried and the results printed up on a screen on the wall.

It was very effective. If the truth be known, however, one might have reason to doubt its efficiency since no project was assigned an identification number within the computer data bank without the expressed approval of Dan Bacon. He kept the book of numbers on various projects, and the investing public never knew what it owned until after he had assigned the numbers. Once he had decided the ownership, the names of wells and mines would come forth in the quarterly reports or company magazines. At that point, the broker, having read one of these, might ask the status of MacShworley Offset Well Number Three and learn from the silver screen that it made 336 barrels of 44 Gravity oil in the preceding twenty-four hours, incurred $7.35 of expense from a swabber who had gone down to check a pump, and was being allocated $85 of general and administrative overhead for the preceding week. The broker went to the telephone singing the virtues of the Steele system.

Today, there was no need for such window dressing. The amphitheater was being used for a more vital presentation. Dan Bacon had the rostrum, and the World Equities team were comfortably ensconced in the leather chairs. Bacon and Leibowitz were carving up the world; Ace Emery's space age amphitheater was an ideal place for the operation.

Upon his return from London, Jason Steele had had the financial staff identify those emerging nations with the greatest financial squeeze on their balance of payments. The information was easily available from the United Nations and World Bank and certain confidential State Department sources. These nations were overlaid against the list of countries in which World Equities was licensed or was in some way doing business. This cut the possibilities down to fifteen. The fifteen potential candidates were cut down further after the geologic research staff had a chance to go into the possibilities of each region from a depositional or sedimentary view. They high graded the list down to six, and of the six, the Steele Minerals Company had working projects in three.

Jason started the proceedings off this morning with a welcoming speech and a statement that he was turning over the meeting to far more capable hands, and that he would just get out of everybody's way and let them have at it. Since the amphitheater had three concealed television cameras, even if Jason left the room he could, with the flick of a switch, have a grandstand seat from his office three floors above. Dan Bacon took the rostrum, lowered the light level, and put his fifteen-nation slide on the wall.

"Gentlemen, in the interests of time, these are the fifteen nations in which we might find common ground. Have we missed any, Ted?"

Leibowitz turned to one of his assistants, a young German economist. "Gunnar, have you your list?"

Gunnar produced the list from his attaché case and Ted glanced at it. "Right on."

"Very good. Now, for many geologic reasons, any one of which we are willing to discuss, we have reduced this list to six." He went on to his third slide. "Of these six, we can be of some service in the three nations where we have working projects. Specifically, Israel, Mexico, and Rhodesia. Which do you want first?" He paused for effect.

"Israel," said Ted. There was a click, and another slide came on the screen. It was a high level photograph of the eastern Mediterranean from Alexandria to Haifa. Dan continued. "Gentlemen, you are looking at a photograph of the region under discussion taken from one hundred and ten miles above the surface of the earth. As you may be aware, Mr. Steele has many key friends in the space program. Our next speaker is the man who chose the areas to be photographed and can brief you on the technical details of this latest tool of our trade. In its simplest terms, as the space capsule repeatedly tracked over the same points of the Middle East, we had the area photographed at varying altitudes and different angles of the sun. Our photo labs took the negatives and either blew them up or reduced them to a common altitude and created composite photos with these results. In these composites, you will see the most subtle anomalies on the earth's surface come into clear focus and sharp definition. You can understand the competitive advantage this gives us, and we would be appreciative of your discretion as to the existence of these photographs. With that word of caution, I introduce our next speaker, Dr. Andrew Stanley, our director of world geologic research. He will address you on the geologic potential of this area."

Dr. Stanley came down to the podium and picked up a

159

flashlight that cast an arrow on the slide screen. He was a big man, the match or better of Jason Steele in heft. They had little else in common. Stanley's ill-kempt hair was long and gray and quite askew and the leather elbow patches of his tweed jacket were worn. Stanley resented being trotted out from time to time to lay the credentials of academia upon the company sales efforts. He had often been tempted to express this resentment to Bacon, but the Steele Company provided him a way of living far beyond the best endowed university chair and a lavishly financed freedom to pursue his own research. His staff matched in numbers and skill the best of the major oil companies. The pressure on the operating people to place monies in the ground passed around the research geologists much like a mountain stream around large boulders. This was Stanley's solace. He was allowed to run his own show, and for this, he paid the price from time to time.

Dr. Stanley proceeded with a learned lecture, and concluded with an optimistic view that the Suez fault extended sufficiently to the east that a trapping mechanism for hydrocarbons was a very real probability, and that offshore Israel was "A Number One" target in his opinion.

He was followed by Arthur Foxx of Steele International, who, with several of his staff, discussed pricing and marketing of Middle Eastern oil, the effects of the pipeline from Eilat to Haifa, and the position of the Israeli government in granting of exploratory concessions. Just as the session was ending, Leibowitz's German economist asked Foxx, "This is all very well and good, but might you not have difficulty in assuring title to the land for any wells in these areas?"

Foxx appeared flustered for a moment. Dan Bacon rose to field the question with his usual aplomb. "Absolutely not," he said dryly. "We have the best title in that part of the world. The Jewish Army." The group laughed and broke for lunch.

Out of three days of meetings came several agreements. Steele Minerals and World Equities agreed to create a joint venture company to be called World Resources Development Corporation. It would be headquartered in Geneva and Arthur Foxx would be its president. World Resources would launch a small seismic program in Rhodesia and start immediately on a five-well exploratory program in the Mediterranean Sea off Israel. Allowing for intensive seismic work and very expensive labor and insurance rates because of the war zone hazard, a $6 million budget was agreed upon with a $3 million contingency reserve that could be drawn if necessary. The World Equities sales force would sell this venture mostly to their Israeli clients and any others they might find that were interested in the economic development of Israel. It was agreed that interests would not be sold inside the United States as far as Steele Minerals or the Securities and Exchange Commission were concerned.

Ted Leibowitz had no enthusiasm for investment in any Mexican project, for World Equities had few Mexican fund sales. He became more interested when Dr. Stanley showed him the amount of high level magnetic work his staff had accomplished in defining Mexican anomalies with a copper potential. He was fascinated by the way the Steele Company used aircraft and computers in coordination on their basic research. Ted referred to it as "Stanley's flying depth finder," and he came to admire Dr. Stanley the most of the people he met in Houston that week. When he learned the same high level magnetic work had been done in Northern Greenland, he quickly concluded that Greenland was a good speculation with or without balance of payment problems. The Steele Company had already acquired under an exploratory concession from the Danish government of Greenland fifty-two million acres which involved petroleum as well as mineral rights. Ted agreed to pay the Steele Company $2 per acre for one half the play, subject, of course, to the approval of the World Equities board. What convinced him was the geologic presentation put on by Dr. Stanley and the Canadian geologist whom Dan Bacon had brought in. The clincher was a show they gave about ice and its thickness, and how the oil discovered in the eastern Arctic could be easily brought to the American markets with tankers. This was the oldest trick in selling. Excite 'em about one thing and sell 'em another. Even Ted Leibowitz bit.

When the week was all wrapped up and the letter of understanding signed, Jason Steele and Dan Bacon calculated their base costs for the Greenland exploratory permits at fifty cents an acre. The deal with World Equities gave them a profit of very close to $78 million.

Jason was so pleased that he took an extraordinary step. He called all of his officers and key staff and top geologists to a summit meeting in his office. He congratulated them collectively and individually and closed the meeting with: "Gentlemen, this is the year we outdrill Standard of Jersey, worldwide." The enthusiasm rippled through the company and was heard on Wall Street.

9

The optimism of Jason Steele proved almost accurate. The World Equities board of directors approved the purchase of the Greenland acreage. Their approval was conditional to Steele's acceptance of a deferred payment plan spread over four years, or 25 percent of the price per year. This condition was acceptable to Jason since the company was on a method of accounting that enabled him to book the entire profit of $77,-500,000 in the current year, even though 75 percent of the monies were not due from World Equities until the succeeding years. The announcement of this profit caused another jump in the price of Steele Minerals shares. Steele Minerals now met all the requirements, and its shares were accepted for listed trading on the American Stock Exchange. This further broadened the investor interest in the company.

The year was not without problems. The principal problem might have been summed up as too much money, too few places to put it, too few hands, and too little time. Steele Minerals had to develop almost $250 million worth of new wells and mines in the last eight months of the year. No company had ever tried it before. It put an enormous pressure on the geologic and engineering staffs. The number of employees exploded. In many instances, there were simply not the drilling rigs available in the time allotted.

When the financial staff and the operating vice-presidents pointed out the size of their dilemma, Jason waved them out of his office with a smile, remarking that those were "happy problems that they were paid to solve." It soon became apparent that there was another result of the deal with World Equities—Jason Steele's attitude toward the running of his company. Heretofore, his dominance had been total. Dan Bacon was the only other officer with even close to a speaking say. But now, with the World Equities trophy on his wall, he was looking beyond the Steele Tower. This shift in attitude stemmed from his decision that the time had come for him to make his move in the world outside his own business and become the statesman of the resources industries. He had decided that what he really wanted was a Cabinet-level post in the Administration. At the back of his mind, and one of the motivating forces, was the thought that this was something Lawrence Carter had never achieved. Consequently, he spent a good part of his time flying around the country giving speeches to petroleum or investment groups. He spoke so often and on so many subjects that the public relations department took on three additional speech writers.

Dan Bacon tried to hold on to the operational reins, but it soon proved impossible. His standard reply to the operating officers became, "Buy it and get the job done. Don't worry about the cost." As a result, power found its way into unaccustomed hands. Geologists wound up making engineering decisions, engineers were making acreage plays, and the accounting staff lost complete control.

With Jason's withdrawal to an Olympian soap box and Dan's adoption of a laissez-faire attitude toward control of expense, a new and decidedly unhealthy attitude filtered through the company. Not all the new employees were the cream of the industry as to capability or integrity. The need for new people was so intense that the personnel screening people got hopelessly behind on the checking of references. The "head-hunting" firms had a field day, and some of the older and more capable company hands quit in disgust. That left the field wide open for some of the new people to set up business for themselves within the Steele Company. The purchasing department overbought on pipe and pumps and there were all-expenses-paid trips to Hawaii for some of the members of the department. Some of the landmen overpaid on acreage and collected cash payoffs.

Despite its apparent size, the American petroleum industry is a relatively small world. The older supply houses and well service firms soon got wind of what was happening within Steele Minerals. It did not take very long thereafter for the news to reach certain banking and investment circles. The finely tuned antennae of Ted Leibowitz began to pick up the wrong impulses during an August visit to New York. He immediately had the William Arthur staff check out the rumors. When he returned to New York for a long visit in late September, their report was ready. It was carefully couched in words such as "there is no firsthand evidence available," and "it is rumored that," but it did flatly say that previously unimpeachable sources confirmed that in certain district offices of the Steele Company, the land staff were known to be on the take and that the purchasing department had been paying absurd prices without a semblance of competitive bidding.

Ted had over $2 million invested in Steele Minerals bonds for his personal account through several international banks. After reading the Arthur report, he picked up the phone and started to place orders. It took two weeks to sell off the bonds in an orderly fashion and in such a way that no one sensed the magnitude of the selling. He had carefully selected the unregistered bonds, rather than the common stock, to insure that no one could ever trace his holdings. Once he had accomplished the total liquidation of his position at a princely profit, he cabled Lausanne and suggested to his two senior portfolio managers that he was concerned with the economy in general and that it might be a time of prudent profit taking. He noted a small slackening in world fund sales and had one of his inexplicable hunches that it was now a time for cash. He did not specify the Steele Minerals holdings, but by the way he phrased the cable, his men in Lausanne understood.

164

Book Four

1

The world of Edward Leibowitz slipped into a spiraling tailspin upon his return to Lausanne. His instincts were right again. There was a general slackening in the economic pace of the world. It was most dramatically reflected in the daily nose dive of the Dow-Jones averages on the New York Stock Exchange. A drop of fourteen or sixteen points on each day of trading became normal by mid-October. The effect on such a huge mutual fund as the Fund of Nations was disastrous.

The portfolio managers, who had received Leibowitz's cable in September, had liquidated many of Fund of Nations' more questionable holdings before the massive October slide. Among the liquidations was a cut back by one-half of the fund's holding of the Steele Minerals bonds and common stock. This profit-taking in Steele balanced off some substantial losses in other holdings. Strangely enough, after Fund of Nations stopped selling, the Steele stock rallied almost three points and held quite steady through the daily deluge of Wall Street. There were still many believers in the charisma of Jason Steele. Ted and his technicians elected to hold their remaining Steele shares and they looked among their other holdings for cash candidates.

The very size of Fund of Nations was their biggest problem. Before the slide they managed close to $3 billion of assets, and their average holding of almost any security exceeded $25 million. It was not easy to sell $25 million anything in a tailspinning market. The debacle of Wall Street became front-page daily news. This added a tumbling effect to the market slide, for the average holder of Fund of Nations was far from a sophisticated investor, familiar with the tidal ebb and flow of speculation on Wall Street. The drum beaters of Manny Kellermann had preached a gospel of steady growth of assets under professional management. But the most professional manager in the world cannot fight an avalanche.

Many of the fund investors asked for liquidation of their shares. Ted Leibowitz was lucky in a way. His hunch of September had put Fund of Nations in a far better cash position than many other of the large mutual funds of the world. Fund of Nations was able to meet the daily liquidations with ease through all of October and November. By late November, the demise of the Dow-Jones was starting to feed upon itself. Investors read about yesterday's drop and decided it was better to get out with something than be the last and left with nothing. As a result, the markets of early December resembled a stampede more than an orderly retreat. The portfolio managers of the world were forced to sell their finest holdings—American Telephone, Standard of Jersey, and General Motors. Since these were the stocks that made up the backbone of the Dow-Jones, the averages looked worse in the world press on each successive day.

In Lausanne, it came down to a battle of wills between two strong-minded men. Manny Kellermann refused to accept the daily demise of the market as a long-term fact. He claimed that it was nothing more than a readjustment such as they had seen in their earlier days in '62 and '66. Ted did not agree. He and some of his chartists were anticipating a sell-off in the Dow-Jones that could take the averages even lower by as much as another two hundred points. Because of this basic disagreement between the two top men, Fund of Nations did nothing for two crucial weeks, despite the stream of redemption orders from the fund holders. The Fund continued to meet the redemptions but the hiatus in selling of securities caused its cash position to drop to less than $15 million on several days. This was a terribly slim cash reserve for a fund whose assets were still in excess of $2 billion. The situation was sufficiently critical that Ted called for a meeting of the operating committee of World Equities, which reluctantly, Manny agreed to.

World Equities had a thirty-man board of directors. They were men of international renown, former statesmen, or bankers, or men of some economic distinction. They met in Lausanne four times a year and received $4,000 for each meeting, as well as their travel expenses. Their names were impressive on the sales literature. Their effect on the actual operations of World Equities was nil.

Because the board was so scattered throughout the world, the operational decisions were left in the hands of the five-man operating committee, all of whom resided in Lausanne and served in top operating capacities within the World Equities structure. In addition to Kellermann and Leibowitz, the other operating committee members were Louis Epstein, director of sales, Samuel Weiner, director of new project development, and Simon Leeder, Ph.D., who had been with World Equities for just over a year. Dr. Leeder was a former professor of economics at the Sloan School of M.I.T. and now served as director of research.

Before the meeting, Ted assessed his chances of winning a showdown with Manny. He wrote Lou Epstein off as hopeless. Lou had been an encyclopedia salesman until Manny picked him up in the early days. He had grown with the Fund of Nations and took a very limited and Copernican view of the world. Epstein's sun was Manny Kellermann about whom all things revolved.

Weiner could go either way. He spent little time in Lausanne, as his principal activity of late was the development of a casino in Sardinia. He was presently $25,000 overdrawn on his expense accounts owing to certain errors of judgment on a research visit to the Casino at Monte Carlo. Ted had approved and authorized a personal loan for him, secured with less than the normal amount of collateral in the form of World Equities stock which could give him an edge, slim at best. Leeder, the man whose chartists were so certain of a further sharp drop in the Dow-Jones average, was the only one he could be sure of.

On a bitter December night, the four men arrived at the Kellermann mansion at about the same time. Getting into the grounds had become something of a joke in the company. At the front gates, which were electronically controlled, one passed through a televised interrogation by the butler from the main house. The second line of defense consisted of two very ugly Germans, former members of the Foreign Legion. They waited in the glass foyer and scrutinized everyone without the slightest attempt to be civil. All of this was a result of several cover stories in *Time* and *Paris-Match;* ever since, Kellermann had been prey for every wandering panhandler who could find his way.

They were met by the reception committee: Cindy Davies, the social organizer, Linda Swensen, the big Swede, and the two latest additions, the Irish girl, Kathleen O'Brien, and a petite Javanese girl. They were all patiently waiting in the library.

One of the more interesting common characteristics of the World Equities senior officers was that they very seldom drank. Liquor was always close at hand and had been an effective tool in the growth of their funds, yet few of them drank heavily. Tonight, however, Ted was first to the bar and poured himself a stiff scotch. The other three soon joined him.

After fifteen minutes of desultory shop talk, Ted went over to the backgammon table and quietly asked Cindy where Manny was.

"Oh, he's in the sauna. I think he's talking long-distance to New York. Some man who wants him to back a movie, and he seems quite interested. Should be down in a bit."

They had had several drinks before Manny came into the library, an hour late, full of smiles and good cheer for every-one there. Ted was used to this tactic. Conversation, though, was sparse, and gave no hint of the financial crisis that faced

170

them. After a long dinner and two calls to Paris and one to Los Angeles, Ted was finally able to get Manny and the others to sit down in the card room without the girls.

"Manny, we're in real trouble."

"We've been through this before, Ted. Relax, it will all blow over. Give it another month."

"It's not going to blow over, Manny. We can't kid ourselves. Our cash position is tight as a drum, and we either take some drastic steps, or we go in default on some of these redemptions."

The word "redemptions" was anathema to Manny Kellermann. It didn't exist as far as he was concerned. He turned to Lou Epstein, director of sales, who had chewed through two Havanas in the first fifteen minutes of the meeting. "Lou, baby, what's going on? You tell me you've got the finest sales force in the world. You got twenty thousand of these schmucks and you let this guy Leibowitz bug me about redemptions."

Lou said nothing. He studied the green felt on the poker table and let Ted pick up the ball. "It's not Lou's fault. I don't think it's anybody's fault, really. We've been peddling growth throughout the world, and now we're in a time when things have slowed down. We could have a hundred and twenty thousand schmucks beating the drums, and we aren't going to sell a growth fund in a bear market."

"Bullshit. We switch the pitch. We sell dollar-cost averaging! You know damn well things are going to turn. Lou, you get those guys to push more door bells, or I'll push yours." Manny paced the room like a caged tiger.

"Yes, Manny." Epstein's eyes never came up from the green felt.

Ted went right ahead in a calm courtroom manner. "Manny, that's not going to be the answer. We've got to batten down the hatches. If we go into default on redemptions, matters will only snowball."

"I tell you, Ted, the market's going to turn up."

"And I can't agree. Now, Manny, listen to Leeder for a moment. We pay him and his people to get the facts. Just listen for a moment."

171

Dr. Leeder began a discourse about the rediscount rate in the United States, the constricting effects this would have on growth potential in the States, and the octopus effect it would have throughout the world economy. He had spoken for about seven minutes when Manny broke in.

"The hell with all the fancy words. What do you want to do, Ted?"

"In round numbers we have approximately two billion dollars in marketable securities on various exchanges. I would like to liquidate one-third of them into cash in the very near term. I would be willing to put a reasonable percentage of the cash into high quality bonds."

"You have got to be out of your mind. Look, we build almost a three-billion-dollar operation—it's based on one of the hotter growth funds in the world, if not the hottest, year in and year out. Am I right, Lou?"

"Right, Manny."

"And here, this night, near the bottom of a small recession, you want to run for cash. Now, how the hell can our guys sell growth funds with everything in cash? Think of the performance. We're coming up to year end. Now, you tell me, just tell me, how a big glob of cash is going to look in the year-end statement of the biggest growth fund in the world. Why, we could be the laughingstock of the industry!"

"Manny, I can't agree, and I must insist we put it to a vote, just for the record."

"What's this 'for the record' crap? You bringing in all this fancy corporate bullshit? There isn't one of you that would be here if I hadn't been pushing door bells almost alone for ten years."

Under pressure, Manny Kellermann had a tendency to dramatize the early days. Ted could sense the hearts and flowers pitch to Weiner and Epstein and wanted to cut it off. "Manny, I'd like a vote, and what we're voting is a cutback of current fund holdings to one-third cash starting tomorrow."

"And I say you can have your fucking vote, and my vote is no, and Fund of Nations is going to ride it out."

Kellermann won the vote three to two. The relationship

172

between the two men deteriorated steadily thereafter, although it never came to words.

Ted returned that night to his villa high in the vineyards above Lausanne. He tried to sleep, but it was hopeless. After twisting and turning for an hour or so he put on a robe and went down to the living room to stare motionless out at the city that glittered beneath him.

He muttered aloud, "Emotional idiocy, pure emotional idiocy! Why, that little Napoleon wouldn't even listen to the facts!" Ted prided himself on his ability to coldly assess and react to facts. "To hell with Kellermann!" he shouted to the empty room. He began to finely sift through his own alternatives. His personal net worth was mostly made up of stock in World Equities. He was the second largest holder, exceeded only by Kellermann. Ted decided that night to get out, completely out, of his holdings and his position within World Equities. He had given Manny his warning, a full warning within the Leibowitz code. He knew that no one, not even Manny Kellermann, with his billions behind him, could stem the running tide in the Street. Other fools had tried before him.

For Ted Leibowitz, once he had chosen his path, it was never a question of loyalties. He approached any problem of buying or selling with the detachment of a champion backgammon player, assessing the odds of his opponent's next cast of the die. He made his plays in the Street with the same detachment. He gave no thought to the disastrous consequences for others that his actions would mean. This was irrelevant. For him, there was a time to buy and a time to sell. If Manny Kellermann thought he could keep his ship from the reefs with words, that was his choice. Ted Leibowitz would seek his own lifeboat. With that decided, he returned to his room and slept.

2

The fund redemptions continued on a plateau through the middle of the month until the week before Christmas when a burst of tax-pressured selling in New York drove the Dow-Jones down almost twenty points in one day. Several days later, the redemptions of the Fund of Nations hit a peak of $16 million.

It was on that day that Manny Kellermann paid a surprise visit to the Lausanne office of Ted Leibowitz. Ted was unshaven and disheveled. What sleep he had had over the past two days was a fitful series of catnaps in the stray hours between stock market closings or openings in London, New York, San Francisco, or Tokyo. He and the floor brokers working for World Equities on the various exchanges were desperately searching for large block buyers of their finest stocks. The buyers were scarce, and the discounts they demanded on block purchasing further added to the market misery of that Christmas week. The World Equities managers were not alone in this search. There were other funds in Boston and New York and Minneapolis and San Francisco that were in just as desperate a plight. Through luck or wits or arm twisting of the least subtle sort, Ted Leibowitz waged a brilliant delaying action and somehow kept the incoming cash from stock sales just several days ahead of the outgoing checks to the redeeming investors. Onto this gloomy scene breezed a jaunty Manny Kellermann, well groomed, dressed in brightly colored ski clothes. "Ted, I've been thinking about our last meeting."

Ted didn't bother rising from his couch as he watched Kellermann strut around the room. "What have you concluded?"

"I think you're right. One-third cash might look good in the year-end statement. Shit, all the other funds are going to look just as bad. A big chunk of cash might make us look pretty smart. Give the boys in the field some ammunition in stressing professional management. Battening down the hatches ahead of the storm kind of thing."

"Why, you dumb schmuck, that's what I have been trying to get through that bagel brain of yours for weeks, and now you come in here, with less than a week to year-end, and think it's a good idea."

"Okay. So I was wrong. Guy's got a right to change his mind. Now what can we do about it?"

Ted stood up and went over to his desk for the portfolio list. "Come here. You see that block of 800,000 shares of G.M.? Remember that and the big slugs of Polaroid and Xerox? Finest quality, we preached that throughout the world, the people's world of capitalism. I'm trying to cut down on the G.M. The specialist on the New York won't touch over ten thousand shares with a ten-foot pole. The best offer I've got is two bucks under the market from a pension trust for a hundred thou, away from the Exchange. It's that bad, Manny. The day has come when we're giving away G.M.!"

"Jesus! Here, let me see that list. There's got to be some other way."

Manny Kellermann threw off his ski parka and settled down for his first day of serious work in three years. They went down the hall to the telex room, where Manny read the news firsthand. The daily deluge of gloomy cables continued. By midafternoon, as they watched another down side opening in New York, Manny's resilience came to the fore. "Ted, I think I got an idea. Let's get the hell out of here. Take a ride down the lake and talk for a bit."

"The world's falling apart, and you want to take a drive. Okay. I have no better suggestion. Get the car. I'll meet you outside."

Ted went back to his office to get his coat. As he came out of the office building, he found Manny giving a rousing sales pitch to this week's group of Italian sales trainees right in the middle of the parking lot.

The two hopped into the red 4-litre Ferrari, and once on the lake drive, Manny started to pour it on. He put the powerful machine to the floor, savagely gearing down into the tight turns of the lake road and smoothly gearing up close to flat out on the occasional straightaways. Ted sat back, watching the ice-strewn lake whiz by as they tore through the towns of Vevey and Montreux. Neither of them spoke. Finally, almost as if he had drained his frustration with power and squealing wheels, Manny drew into the empty parking lot by the castle of Chillon on the eastern shore of the lake. The puddled ice by the lake edge had piled up, ridge on ridge, about the stone base of the abutments. Only then did Manny speak. "I was watching the lake this morning while I dressed. You see that ice out there? It's been bugging me all day."

Ted acknowledged that he saw the ice. There was little else to see. Manny went on. "Well, I think the ice is our answer. You get the cash out of stocks, and the ice gives us the performance."

"Manny, you've finally flipped out."

"Bullshit, I flipped. We got something going no other fund ever thought of."

"What's that?"

"Jesus, bright boy. What's the single largest investment we got spread through all the funds?"

"I.B.M."

"No, no. I'm not talking stocks. The single largest investment."

"Well . . . the time purchase of those Greenland leases."

"Right. They're my ice."

"Maybe I'm dense, Manny. How's that going to help us?"

"Look, Ted, maybe I was pigheaded about not letting you go for more cash. Now I've changed my mind on that. You take as many bucks out of the market as you think you need to meet our obligations. That way, we look as good or as bad as anybody else in the business, but the ice is our ace. Where is the ice quoted on any exchange? It's worth what we say it's worth. Who else has a spread like that?"

Ted was with him in an instant. "Manny, you prick. It's brilliant. We get our year-end shot in the ass by marking up Greenland. Looks great on the report and slows down the redemptions. Is that what you have in mind?"

"Right on, Teddy baby, right on. And there's no son of a bitch who can argue with us until they drill it."

Manny switched on the Ferrari, and they drove back along the north shore at a sensible pace as they discussed the best tactics for their latest play. It all hinged on Jason Steele.

At Manny's mansion, they had Cindy chase down Jason on the long-distance phone. She reported that he was flying between Houston and Los Angeles, and his switchboard was not able to raise him on the air phone. "Hell, then get Dan Bacon. Ted, you handle the conversation."

Ted was at his most cordial as he congratulated Dan on how well Steele Minerals stock was withstanding the slaughter. He went on. "Dan, Manny and I want to know if you and Jason could meet us in New York tomorrow afternoon, say at two. We've got some new ideas that could be very exciting for us both."

Dan thought they could and said he'd call back if they could not, as soon as he reached Jason. He suggested they meet at Jason's apartment and he wanted to know if there was anything he should be doing, any technical work in anticipation of the meeting. Ted assured him that no homework was necessary, but that he didn't want to go into it because of security reasons.

3

As Jason Steele stepped back from the rostrum of the small amphitheater, the round of applause was thunderous and sustained. The audience was an elite selection of the top producers in two of the East's more august investment banking firms. These people were professional salesmen. They were paying a standing homage to one of the best speeches they'd ever heard.

While he nodded to the several sectors of the room, Jason wore an easy grin, one part modesty for their applause and three parts supreme confidence for what he'd told them. Augustus Codman Emery was close by his elbow. He whispered loudly in his ear. "Superb, Jason, just superb. The best yet."

Jason had to agree. He'd given this kind of speech many times before. The practice had honed him to a forceful smoothness, yet he was far from bored with the repetition. Jason Steele had a winning formula, and he was riding it all the way.

These broker meetings were several months in the making. The first step was usually a visit by either Ace Emery or one of his senior lieutenants to the home office of the brokerage firm, most often high in the canyons of lower Manhattan. The opening pitch to the senior partners was how the sales product of Western Investors, namely the two oil-drilling funds, could create more profitable stock exchange business with a tax shelter umbrella. Managing partners listened attentively to such a preamble. With the debacle in the market, many firms were desperate for new revenues. The managing partner would then usually relegate the signing of an agreement for the distribution of Western Investors Funds to a committee made up of their national fund sales manager and their oil analyst. At this juncture, Ace was home free, nine times out of ten.

Augustus Codman Emery had spent thirty years wining, dining and conventioneering with these sales managers on behalf of two of the most reputable funds in the East. He had a politician's ability to recall names, and in his previous job, had wielded tremendous power in the Street, for he controlled his fund's reciprocity and "give ups." The large funds rewarded a brokerage firm with additional commissions in the form of security transactions. This frosting atop the regular fund sales commission had preconditioned many of the managers to automatically accepting an Emery invitation to lunch at Pavillon or "21."

Convincing oil analysts was an even easier sell. For the most part, their "in-depth knowledge" of actual oil drilling was garnered from *The Oil and Gas Journal* and *Platt's OILGRAM*. Their other sources were the annual reports of the majors. The success or discovery ratio of the several Steele Funds was far better than the national average of the major integrated companies. How this came to be was not disclosed in either the Western Investor's prospectuses or the glossy-magazine-style quarterly reports with pictures. The oil analysts of Wall Street were usually impressed.

Emery had carefully put the Western Investors prospectuses in a parlance that any fund salesman could understand. The product was totally different, but that didn't matter very much. The wrappings were the same, and the old approach of professional management and diversity of risk through size usually worked as well as ever. The money started to roll in ever increasing waves to Houston. "Why send your money to Washington, it's gone forever" was all part of the pitch.

Emery and Steele were among the first to package oil-drilling participations along mutual fund lines. The packaging was ingenious. For many years, oil companies and very wealthy families had drilled wells and deducted the actual cost of drilling as a business expense from their tax returns, perfectly proper under the provisions of the Internal Revenue Code. Where Emery and Steele stole a long march on Wall Street was in their packaging. They created massive limited partnerships, twenty million dollars at a crack and all duly registered with the Securities and Exchange Commission. The Wall Street brokerage firms would then put their highly taxed yet less asset-affluent clients into these partnerships. The tax deductions created thereby offered a shelter from the tax consequences of short-term profit-taking in the securities markets. The limited partnership vehicle allowed the tax deductions of drilling to apply directly to the tax return of the investor. Only in the age of the computer could such an arrangement work, for the accounting was mountainous. The partnership was treated as a single account and a return was filed with the Internal Revenue Service on its activities. The computer would then step in and break out to the tenth decimal point the thirty thousand partners' reports on their percentage of the deductions. These were then used for the individual tax returns. It was all very neat and all very legal provided the input was accurate.

Jason's speech this morning had centered on the growing energy needs of the nation and the idiocy of the Federal Power

179

Commission in keeping a lid on the price for interstate gas transmission. He then expressed his gratitude for the brokers leaving their desks and their families in the busy year-end trading week that followed Christmas and promised that their time in Houston would be profitably spent learning the many uses of the Steele drilling funds.

In reality, any inconvenience for the visiting brokers had been cut to a minimum. After the close of trading the previous night, they had been met by sightseeing buses at their office doors. They were sped to their respective airports in Philadelphia and Richmond and smiled aboard waiting Steele Company jets by a host of pretty stewardesses. The bars were open before the jets cleared the ground and remained so for three painless hours to Houston. The girls were attentive to the slightest whim and were backed by several of Ace's local "wholesaler" staff for the odd broker who wanted to learn along the way.

At Houston, the big jets were wheeled into the Steele Company hangar and disgorged their sotted load into waiting buses fitted out as land yachts, equipped with a second fresh team of smiling girls. And on to the Steele Company apartments, a western banquet, and the next morning, the beginning of a two-day sales seminar. It was all paid for by the investors as a "cost of sale" and the prospectus said so, if one read the very fine print. Few investors ever did.

After the applause subsided, Jason Steele glanced at his wristwatch. This was usually his closing ploy, the harried, hurried executive, and he thereby avoided long question periods.

The brokers could always get answers, but not from Jason. He was too clever to ever be drawn beyond a question of concept. Drilling operations and accounting procedures were not his province and he made no bones about it. He was not above throwing in an oil-field phrase here and there or referring back to his youth as a roughneck on the rigs. But for the details, there were always earnest young technicians close at hand to talk of the "nuts and bolts" of their trade, either landmen or drilling engineers or geologists on top of a particular new development within the fund. Their terminology and their "oily" drawls lent credence to the pitch. They were up to the hour in their particular bailiwick, and their enthusiasm came across. The brokers went away with a feeling of having been included on the inside, which was the intent. To have pieced together the overall picture, the broker would have needed to converse with two hundred such specialists scattered across the oil patches of the globe.

The glance at the watch was not a ploy this morning; Jason was hard pressed for time. He saw Dan Bacon, waving from the back of the amphitheater, and Elizabeth Wales, waiting with his portfolio of papers for the plane. They were due to meet Kellermann and Leibowitz in New York in four hours. It would be tight as usual. Jason was not noted for his promptness. As Emery took over the meeting, he trotted off the dais with a friendly final wave, the very picture of a captain of industry on his hurried rounds.

The company limousine drew up by the whining Jet Star. On the road to Houston Airport, Jason questioned Dan on the sudden urgency of this summit conference, but Dan could tell him nothing. Jason was more amused than concerned by this mystery and wrote it off as another Kellermann eccentricity. He was the last to climb the boarding ramp and had a large smile and a friendly pat on the rump for the stewardess as she trimly waited by the ramp controls.

The jet was taxiing for takeoff as Jason dropped heavily into his extra large seat by the sky phone. He was surprised to find Lilly Bacon waiting on a nearby sofa. They exchanged the politest of nods. Little love was lost between the two. If he had thought about it, he might have expected she would be there. Lilly seldom let the opportunity to shop in New York slide by. Now that Dan drew $160,000 a year and owned several millions of dollars of Steele Company stock, Lilly energetically worked on seeing that it flowed out as fast as it came in. She was redecorating her third house in five years.

Jason had never approved Dan's marriage to Lilly. The sixteen-year gap between their ages was only part of it. The beautiful Lilly was constantly demanding Dan's attention.

Jason was equally demanding and resented with the ire of a feudal monarch any competition, even from a wife. Jason also had heard rumors that Lilly was not the most faithful of wives. When she lost Dan to Jason, as she often did, she had sometimes gone off to some watering spot on her own. Jason wondered if Dan ever heard the gossip about these trips. Lilly was young and impetuous and deeply resented the all-consuming demand the Steele Minerals Company made on her husband. Whatever way she could fight back, she did. Her morality was not Jason's concern. What bothered him was the possibility that one of her whims could become a public scandal.

As the Jet Star lurched forward on its takeoff run, his mind went from Lilly Bacon to the Steele Company and his funds. It had been a good meeting that morning and that pleased him. His company stock was holding its own in a market that had fallen off a cliff. His drilling funds were at an all-time high. Jason mused on these for a while. Several times he had switched position on whether his personally held Western Investors should be a merger candidate with Steele Minerals. As a matter of fact, the merger was scheduled as an agenda topic of the next board meeting of Steele Minerals. However, if things kept going, Western Investors might be far more valuable out on its own in the marketplace. The one drawback was the laundry required for a public registration with the S.E.C. There were many internal conflicts of interest that benefited Jason Steele in the present structure and these would have to be disclosed. Jason had not made up his mind one way or the other, and he intended to preserve all his options to the last moment.

Fitted right over Jason's seat was a small instrument panel that told him instantly direction, altitude and speed over the ground. He studied these for a moment and considered going forward and flying for a stretch. He was a thoroughly trained pilot in his own right and had several thousand hours logged in many of the different company aircraft. An instrument approach into the New York Control Zone was one of his favorite diversions, but he rejected the temptation when he thought of the day ahead. His mind wandered on and he thought about Janice and his own marriage, now in its sixteenth year.

She and the children had gone on vacation to the Acapulco house the day after Christmas. Jason had intended to join them when the Kellermann business came up. There was still a chance he could be in Acapulco in the morning, and he would try, yet he wondered if it was worth the effort. Janice would already be resentful of the delay. Lately, every time they were together, there always seemed to be a quarrel brewing. He couldn't understand her. As he gave her more and more, she seemed to drift farther and farther from him. He knew he was away from home a great deal, but so were scores of other husbands. She had the children and her friends. Her attitude honestly puzzled him. Some day, when he had more time, he thought, he must try to straighten things out.

4

When Manny Kellermann and Ted Leibowitz arrived in the reception hall of Jason's penthouse, Dan Bacon was there to greet them. "Manny, Ted! Good to see you. Come on in. Jason's on the phone. He'll be with us soon."

Jason appeared in a few minutes and waved them into seats. "Well, gentlemen. What's on your minds?"

Manny launched immediately into his plan. "Jason, we're getting the shit kicked out of us on redemptions in the market. That's no big surprise to anybody. All the funds are. Now, what you may or may not be aware of is that World Equities receives a performance bonus at the end of the year that is a percentage of the growth that our management has brought to the several funds. We get ten percent of the growth as a bonus."

Jason intervened for a moment. "We're aware of all that, Manny. We're also aware that you've been a seller of our stock of late."

Ted picked up the gauntlet. "Jason, that was my doing, and for that matter it was done over Manny's best advice. The situation on big block placements has gotten so sticky that we had to let go of some of our highest quality holdings. We found your shares more marketable than our holdings of Xerox and G.M. It was my decision out of sheer necessity. We needed some profits for offsets to the overall picture. I hope that you're aware we maintained better than half our original position."

Jason accepted the flattery with a bland smile and a knowing nod. Manny went on. "Now to get back to why we're here. We got this big chunk of moose pasture up there with you guys, right?"

Bacon protested with a loud guffaw. "Whadaya mean, moose pasture! That's the best drilling prospect in the world right now. Did y'all see the open flow tests on that B.P. well at Prudhoe Bay? Did y'all notice that the Pan Arctic consortium has brought in gas on three out of four of their last pops? Moose pasture!"

That was all Manny needed. He sprang to his feet and faced Dan. "Okay. If it's so goddam great, you can help us. We need a favor, here and now, before year end."

Jason spoke up. "We'll do anything we can, Manny. Now, what do you need?"

"As I understand it, we own one-half of the working interest up in northern Greenland. Is that correct?"

Dan replied. "Correct, subject of course to certain obligations of doing seismic work and drilling some test wells."

"Yeah. Yeah. That's your thing. Now, on these fifty-two million acres, we paid you guys two bucks an acre for a half interest and that's what we hold them at in our funds, right, Ted?"

"Right, Manny."

"Okay. So in round numbers, we got at two bucks an acre one-half of the fifty-two-million-acre spread, or really four bucks for twenty-six million if you broke it down just to our half. That right?"

Jason said, "That's one way of putting it. Go on."

"Well, now, if you guys can do something in the next four days, say like find somebody to buy into a piece of this partnership, say at around eight bucks an acre, then what happens?"

Jason saw what he was getting at immediately. "Then, the

184

whole play takes on a value of fifty-two times eight or $416 million. Your half is worth $208 million. Your cost on the books was $104 million, so you got a paper profit of $104 million, to show in the funds. A ten percent performance bonus is worth $10,400,000 of profit to your operating company." He exclaimed "My God, is that what you're looking for?" as the audacity and magnitude of the swindle dawned on him.

"Yup, you do good arithmetic. Now, can you do it so it looks legit?" Manny's expression was smug.

Jason paused for a few moments. His first instinct was to probe for flaws; to see how he, or his Steele Minerals, could get hurt. He decided if anyone were to be hurt, it would be Kellermann or World Equities. He looked over to Dan, who was smiling broadly. He was an expert in this kind of shuffle, and the very magnitude of the scheme obviously pleased him. Their eyes met for an instant, and then Jason turned back to Kellermann. "Well, Manny, I think we can do it but it will depend on what's in it for us over the long term."

Manny Kellermann was too good a player to let his relief show. With no change of expression, he said, "We'll take care of you. We've been drilling ten million a month with you this year. Things are a bit tough right now, but my chart people are sure we're close to the bottom. We'll raise the ante to fifteen million a month, say by late April. How's that?"

"You've got a deal." Jason paused. "We're going to have to really scramble to line up projects for that kind of money. I think we'd best reduce this to writing pretty quick."

Manny rose and shook hands with Jason and Dan. He picked up his topcoat in the hallway, and turning said, "Okay. I got to see this new filly up town so I'll leave Ted here with you guys to work up the details. Thanks, Jason. Back burner the World Stock Exchange idea for a while, will you? And why don't you come over for some skiing or something?"

After Manny was gone, the three men began to map out the paperwork of the revaluation. Dan was the first to speak. "The way I see it, the big problem will be the auditors. Unfortunately, the Fund of Nations has the same auditors we have. That could be tough, but not impossible."

The legal mind of Ted Leibowitz was in high gear. "I

don't think that's insurmountable. If we could get an established oil company or maybe even a private partnership, yes, I think a private partnership will be even better. We arrange for them to buy, say, ten percent of your half this year. I think it best we do it that way, because then the tax consequences of any paper profit would flow through the books of Steele Minerals. You guys will have tax shelter through intangibles coming out of your ears this year."

"That's all very well and good, Ted," Jason interjected, "but what about the bucks? Our auditors aren't fools. They'll never let us wash a transaction of this size through our books unless some cash changes hands."

"That won't have to be a problem. Whoever we elect to be the lucky purchaser will receive an extremely favorable loan that produces whatever cash you deem necessary. You can count on that through our banks."

"I'm tracking you so far," Jason said, "but I see a few problems with the way you're going at it, Ted. First, we're hot on that acreage and don't want to let go of any of ours."

"That's no problem either. You sell them a slice from your holdings on the last day of this year. If we do it that way, the fund avoids a year-end tax. You don't pay any taxes so that's no sweat. Then, a couple of days into next year, you buy the same percentage of acres back from out of our holdings. So it's really W.E.L. making the sale. We get the year-end performance out of your sale, you get back the land you want. What tax we may have to pay will be next year's problem. Everybody gets what they need."

"I want to run through this once more, Ted, slowly so we all understand," Jason said as he grasped all the possibilities of the opportunity. "Say Dan and myself and maybe Foxx create a Canadian partnership tonight. We do it through a straw or nominee so our board of directors or the auditors or the S.E.C. won't know it's us. We contract on a deferred payment basis to buy two million six acres from the Steele Company for eight bucks, or twenty million eight. You guys lend our partnership ten percent cash for a down payment from your banks. We pay that to Steele Minerals, right?"

186

"That's right, Jason."

"What about the rest of the dough? Will you give us three years on the balance or a put to sell the acres back to you for three years at nine dollars an acre?"

"That would be acceptable to us."

"Then, in the first couple of days of next week, Steele Minerals transfers our purchase to World Equities so it's your acres being peddled and you'll want your cash back?"

"If you like, Steele Minerals can hold the monies as an advance toward our drilling commitment for January."

Jason thought about that for a moment. "No, I think it best we give you most of the money back. We've got another problem we have to talk to you about. Some goddam Arab commandos blew the shit out of one of our drilling platforms off Israel. We're partially insured, but we have some replacement costs, and we have to call on you for the contingency reserve on that play."

"Okay with us, Jason."

"All right, so the two eight goes back onto your books. Everything looks clean. You pay your share on the Israeli play, and our little private partnership owns ten percent of your action in the moose pasture. Is that an accurate summary?"

"That ought to do it, Jason, but the timing is here and now. Your part of the deal has got to be announced in the next couple of days so the auditors will buy it for our year-end statement."

"I agree it's got to be quick. I want it on and off our books damn fast. I don't want any of my directors looking over my shoulder on a conflict of interest bit."

"Jason, you tell me where and into what name you want the two million eight cabled, and I'll have it attended to on the bank opening in the morning."

"All right, it's a deal."

Ted rose to leave and then paused for a moment. "Say, what are you guys doing for dinner tonight?"

Dan replied. "Depending on Jason, I think I'll grab the Jet Star and swing through Toronto and get the paperwork of this new partnership squared away. We don't have a hell of a lot of time. What about you, Jason?"

Jason Steele sensed there was more on Ted Leibowitz's mind. "I'm free. Where do you want to meet?"

"How about '21' about eight-thirty."

"See you then."

5

Since Jason Steele first entered the promotional end of the oil business, he had carefully cultivated the maître d' on duty at the lower stairway of "21." Now, after almost ten years and countless ten-dollar bills discreetly changing hands, they all knew him. They greeted him with a booming camaraderie, were ever solicitous of his coat and his well being, and when they could, gave him his choice of the house.

The night of his dinner with Ted Leibowitz was no different. When Jason asked if Mr. Leibowitz had arrived, he was promptly led to a corner table on the lower floor. He could tell from the location that Ted was also known there. His host rose as Jason drew near and extended his hand.

After the maître d' left with Jason's order for a Jack Daniels and water, Ted said, "Jason, I want to thank you for your help this afternoon. If Manny had listened to what he was told several months ago, our visit might not have been necessary."

"Oh, how's that?"

"Well, our economic staff, and God knows, we got enough of them, called this market downturn quite early. Manny wouldn't believe them, and we fought. I wanted a very high cash reserve. It came to a vote and I lost. Manny couldn't see a growth fund in cash. It got pretty tight for a while."

"How does it look now?" Jason asked.

"Well, he finally saw reason and we've built up a pretty good cash reserve. Redemptions were damn strong for a bit, but they've tapered off this week."

A waiter arrived with Jason's drink. He studied it for a moment and then took a good taste before he went on. "So, you think you've turned the corner?"

"Yes, I do. I'm sure there may be more selling pressure, but Christ, there are some mighty big bargains kicking around. It's been a long time since we could buy Telephone close to a seven percent yield. How are things going with the Steele Company?"

Jason toyed with his glass and then replied in a tone of considered confidence. "Well, I gave you the bad news about those goddam Arabs this afternoon. Foxx tells me he can get that rig patched in a Greek shipyard. I'm a bit skeptical of that. I can't imagine a Greek yard working on a Jewish rig. Those Arabs blacklist tankers and crews at the drop of a hat. The shipyard could kiss their tanker business good-bye. We'll see. Other than that, the domestic drilling funds are doing damn well. They're running about fifteen percent behind what we raised last year, but I think that's commendable when you consider the economic state of affairs."

"Do you see a turn in the economy?"

"The best pulse I can get out of Washington is that the President is going to loosen up," Jason replied. "Of course, we don't know when. He ran on a platform plank of curbing inflation. He's finding that isn't as easy as he thought, and he faces Congressional elections come November. So all in all, I see him easing up pretty quick."

Ted saw his opening: "I'm glad to hear that, because it bears on the real topic that I wanted to discuss—you and Manny and World Equities."

Jason hesitated for a moment, as much for dramatic effect as anything else. Then he said, "Ted, I think that's such a fascinating topic that we had best get our dinner on the fire or I'll starve to death."

Jason waved over the head waiter, who was alongside in a moment. Perhaps one of the reasons that Jason was so popular at "21" was that he took on their menu as a challenge. He selected a light dinner this night—oysters Rockefeller, beef Wellington, potatoes Duchesse, watercress and endive salad. Ted, on the other hand, settled for filet mignon and a hearts of lettuce salad. They shared a bottle of Bordeaux. Once these decisions had been made, Jason brought the conversation back to the topic Ted had broached. "Now, what's this about Kellermann and me?"

"Jason, the time is right. I think Manny has got to go. He's lost most of his board support. He's never in the shop and it shows." Ted let this sink in for a moment and then went on. "If it's done right, the whole matter can be accomplished with a minimum of blood."

Jason's response was a long "Hmm." Kellermann had just given him the drilling monies commitment of all time and he wasn't about to risk it lightly.

Now Ted toyed with his glass. His tone was very controlled and cool as he spoke. "Jason, I think you're the man to replace Kellermann."

"You want me to take control of World Equities?"

"Yes."

Jason gave his attention to three oysters before he said anything further. He went on cautiously. "Let us suppose, and I stress 'suppose,' that I was interested in the control of World Equities. How would you suggest that I would set about it?"

"I'm constantly aware of blocks of the management company stock that might be purchased. Let's not kid ourselves. Some of Manny's crew from the old days are very large holders. A lot of them have been living pretty high on the hog since we went public last year. Paper millionaires if you will."

"Yes, I know most of this."

"Well, whether Manny likes it or not, we're having a recession. Our fund sales have slowed up and as we told you, we're running into redemptions. Now mind you, I don't want you to get the impression that this is serious for the long term."

"I understand, go on."

"Let's put it this way. If a discreet basket could be placed under these shares as they come loose, it might not take very long to assemble a sizable speaking voice in the affairs of World Equities, and it could be done in such a way that Manny need never know until it was too late."

Jason thought this over for a long time. If Ted was right, and if this coup could be pulled off, he, Jason Steele, could become the single most potent factor in the financial markets of the world. This was heady stuff, even for the ego of Jason Steele, but he was no fool. As he sliced away at his beef Wellington, Jason considered the alternative risks. If he made a pass at Manny Kellermann's throne and did not kill the king in the first swipe, what might be the retribution?

If the drilling support of the Fund of Nations were withdrawn, Steele Minerals Company could lose almost one-half its business. It might have a disastrous effect on the price of the stock. Much of his stock was pledged as collateral with banks all over the world to support his personal ventures. He had used the borrowed cash as the financial backbone for getting Steele Investment Funds and the Western Investors Company off the ground. If he lost, it could be his head in the basket too. And yet it was Edward Leibowitz, the President of World Equities Limited, making the proposal. It had to be considered. What was that Shakespearean quote Ace was fond of using, something about a tide in the affairs of men? Jason Steele wondered if this were his tide. But there was something he couldn't fathom and he finally asked, "Why don't you take the shot yourself, Ted?"

Ted Leibowitz, before opening the conversation with Jason, had carefully weighed the risks. He was convinced from what he could see of world sales and the decimated ranks of the sales force that World Equities had seen its high water mark. Manny Kellermann had his fortune conservatively stashed away, independent of W.E.L., with a major part in quality bonds and real estate. He himself was well fixed for the rest of his days if he never turned another dime. But it wasn't just a matter of being well fixed for him; there was a play to be made and he was a player, a born player, and the international money marts of the world were his stadium. He would never retire willingly. The play now was how to personally get out of World Equities with one massive sale. To do it, he had to find an ego even bigger than Manny Kellermann's. He had no qualms as to personal ethics. He had told Manny throughout the fall what he thought of the situation. And he had given Jason a reasonably accurate picture of the current situation at World Equities. The scene was blacker than painted, but then, Jason Steele was a big boy.

He looked up and answered Jason evenly. "I gave it a lot of thought. As you've guessed, I wanted to. I finally concluded I'd have as big a credibility problem as Kellermann; that the outside board would best buy a successful outsider; that led me to you and with you I figure I can get back on the field when matters settle out."

His reply, a masterpiece of selected facts, seemed satisfactory to Jason.

"All right, Ted, let's assume I have an interest. What's next?"

"Well, as we both know, the management company common is the key. It elects the board and has until recently been in secure hands. It is a fact that some of the big holders are overextended, and some of the banks, especially the German and French banks, are putting on the squeeze. They have no love for W.E.L. It's a buyers' market."

"Okay. What next?"

"Let's say you were to set up a smoke screen through a friendly bank, and certainly not a bank where World Equities has any obvious leverage. Let's say that the word got out to these European banks that there was a market for the collateral on these overextended loans. That's when we start to nibble."

At this point Jason decided he wanted dessert. Not until the waiters had cleared the table did Ted continue. "Manny still has twenty-one percent of the company stock. I have nine percent, so just to match him in a proxy fight before the annual meeting, we would need another twelve percent. Even that won't be enough to get the job done, though."

"What magnitude of monies do you think will be required to get the job done?" Jason asked.

Ted took out a thin diary and a gold pencil. "Let's run through the arithmetic. There are ten million shares of common. The common has been trading lately around eleven and twelve. I think if we could go into this with, say, thirty percent and then it was announced that it was Jason Steele who sought

192

control of World Equities, let's see, I think we can put it together for somewhere between thirty-eight and forty-five million dollars. If the German and English sales people vote with us early as I will tell them to, then it might be done for less."

"That's a lot of cash in this money market, Ted." Jason mentally considered the possibilities of assembling forty millions of cash in one of the world's tightest money markets. It would be no easy task. And then, if Kellermann blocked him, and if the forty was lost, it could trigger a domino reaction that could put him right back on the beach where he had started. The thought was acutely discomforting. But then he thought of the opportunities that opened up if he had control of the World Equities monies and sales force. He would have a willing army in the field, an army to move any new project that he could dream of. Kellermann had already set a precedent by having the fund make investments in resources projects. His mind raced on to three or four billions in his projects. He turned back to Ted. "Now, what about this smoke screen of yours?"

"As the operating officer of the company you're buying, I can't come out in the open on this play until the home stretch or maybe never. I can be far more help inside. I can steer a lot of that loose stock and certainly arrange some friendly loans based on blocks of our own common with some of the World Equities banks. So perhaps the easiest way is to set up something that looks innocent and reasonable just on the chance our cover is broken. Something like a trust fund, maybe for your children. Certainly Manny is well aware that your kids have a few bucks. So your children are buying in trust some shares of W.E.L.—that's perfectly natural. You could even tell him it's an expression of your faith in his masterful management or some crap like that."

"Okay. So far, so good. Then what?"

"We play a bit for luck. This playboy image of Manny's isn't helping him any with the more conservative elements of the W.E.L. board in this bear market."

"Do you mean the board could be turned against him?"

"That's very possible, and you know, they were terribly impressed with the performance of Steele Minerals proprietary investments last year. If we link that with this Greenland re-evaluation, you could be their golden boy."

Jason wiped his lips with great deliberation. Behind the deliberation were other thoughts, remote from, yet related to this present deal. The previous week back in Houston, he and Janice had had the sharpest fight of their marriage. For the first time, Janice had openly accused him of being unfaithful and had made barbed comments about his relations with some of the girls on his staff. She had hinted at this before, but had never come out and said it. She had been as angry as he had ever seen her and he thought about how attractive she still was. Perhaps now was the time to work out some sort of peace treaty with her and get back into his own bed for a while. If he embarked on this new play, he would be able to spend even less time with her, and his time away from the family had long been their chief bone of contention. Yes, before taking on anything else, he had better do some quick spade work to improve relations at home. It would even be rather nice to have her support in what could be the biggest play of his life. He was torn between the time it would take to marshal the money for the Leibowitz play and his promise to join Janice in Acapulco.

He gave the waiting Leibowitz one of his widest smiles. "Are you going to be in town for a couple of days, Ted?"

"Yes, I am. I've got to wrap up the Greenland paperwork."

"Very good. I'll give you my final decision within the next two days." Jason insisted on picking up the check.

6

Ted was awakened at seven A.M. by the insistent ringing of the bedside phone. He quickly shook off his drowsiness and groped about for a light in the heavily curtained Waldorf suite.

"Ted, sorry to get you up so early." It was Jason Steele. "It's going to be a busy day. I've given considerable thought to our discussion of the other evening, and I have made up my mind. I would rather not discuss my decision on the phone. Could you come over in say an hour and a half?"

"Sure, I can be there."

Jason went on. "On that other matter up North, Bacon has sent a telex draft to our downtown office of his thoughts for a public relations announcement. It's coming up here by cab, and I wanted your concurrence on what is said. Our P.R. man is coming over at eleven. It might be best that you approve this and leave before he arrives. I'd like to have it on the broad tape before the close of trading today. It's the next to last trading day of the year, and I think it would look far better as a release today than tomorrow."

Within the hour, Ted was in the private elevator leading to Jason Steele's New York penthouse. He was greeted in the reception foyer by a smiling Elizabeth Wales, who led him to a comfortable chaise longue in the grandiose bedroom.

As he took his seat, the words "Good morning, Ted" boomed forth from the open door of the tiled bath. "Be with you in a minute. Now, Elizabeth, where were we on that letter?"

Ted was amused by the composure of the woman as she studied the shorthand pad and replied, "Mr. Steele, you have just told the Secretary that any Administration support of the Kennedy and Bayh attack on the intangible drilling deduction will incur your extreme displeasure and would be a disaster for any party money raising efforts this fall."

"Ah yes, well, that pretty much finishes it up. Invite him, and oh yes, his wife, can't remember her name, but I'm sure you have it in the file—tell him that Janice and I would be delighted to see them at the ranch in July, and we have set aside two cabins so that he can bring his children along. Close it with kind personal regards and have it ready for my signature this afternoon. That will be all, Elizabeth."

"Yes, Mr. Steele." She picked up her pad, nodded to Ted and left the room.

195

From the bathroom came a resounding flush, and in a few more moments, Jason entered the room and shook Ted's hand. "Good morning again, I find this my best part of the day. Seem to do my best thinking. Come on, let's get some coffee."

Ted trailed Jason down the long hall to the living room where a silver service was set up on the sideboard. Jason was the personification of a gracious host as he poured the coffee. Ted knew this studied casualness was all part of the Jason Steele legend as directed by Steele, and he was sure he knew what Jason was going to say. He was sure his fish had bitten.

"Now about the matter we were discussing the other night," Jason began. "I would like to go ahead with it but I'm going to need some help the way this money market is. You indicated that forty-five million would get the job done?"

"That's correct, Jason. In round numbers, forty-five million should safely do it." Ted found the masking of his own elation a difficult task. Luckily, Jason was too caught up in the mechanics of the play to notice anything.

"All right, now from the outset, this arrangement is between you and me, no one else. It isn't a move by Steele Minerals Company. It must be a private play until I say otherwise. In no way are Bacon or Foxx or any of my people to be let in on what is going on until I say so. Is that understood?"

"Understood."

"If there are to be any communications, they are to be between us directly. I don't know how secure your telephones are, but we've found several bugs planted about the Steele Tower in the past two years. Matter of fact, Ted, I don't know how far the Europeans go in this area, but you might have your own switchboard checked from time to time. Avoid telephoning me, whenever possible."

"The Europeans are quite good at espionage, Jason. I will have it looked into."

"Very well. Now, the other night, we discussed a smoke screen. Why don't you take me over that ground again so we are both clear."

Ted set forth his thoughts in orderly fashion. He suggested that Jason set up some form of family trust in an offshore bank,

196

perhaps the Seaman's and Merchants Bank of Curaçao, an independent correspondent of all the World Equities banks. He said he had used the Seaman's with very satisfactory results in several of his private transactions and knew they were discreet.

He then quickly sketched out some of the details of the family trust. He suggested Jason select a trustee with care so as to maintain a controlling interest in the trust, and that he should reasonably fund the trust from the beginning—five million should be more than adequate to establish credibility in the bank. And it was very important that he choose a sensible name for the trust that would not readily be associated with himself by any of the middle management in W.E.L.

The trust would become the basket that he'd spoken of earlier. Now when he received inquiries from European banks as to the sale of blocks of W.E.L. common stock they held as collateral, he could suggest to them that they make their offerings to the trust either to the Trust Department of the Seaman's or occasionally to a nominee account in the Trust Department of the World Equities bank in Liechtenstein.

Ted explained. "Then a steady accumulation in one place won't become obvious if the offerings are alternated. When the initial funds of the trust are expended on the stock purchases, I'll arrange for the trust to borrow monies from W.E.L. banks all over the world, with the shares as collateral. If it's done properly, control of W.E.L. operations can for the most part be acquired with W.E.L. money. What could be sweeter than that?"

"I agree," Jason said. "If it works, it's a sweet deal. And you seem to have covered all the bases. As I see it, the market should turn up in January or February and there'll be a bottoming of selling pressure. What do you think W.E.L. will do?"

Ted replied. "I think W.E.L. common will rise and that will give your trust further borrowing leverage."

There was only one remaining detail—the matter of Ted's cut. It was agreed that he would have a thirty-three percent interest in the net profits of the play and would be retained as the chief operating officer later on after the demise of Kellermann.

The trust was funded with $4 million Jason raised by pledging some of his Steele Minerals stock with the Boston bank as collateral for a loan. As he was the largest shareholder of Steele Minerals and the chairman of the board, he was restricted by regulations of the S.E.C. as to what he could sell without a formal registration.

There was another complication. Some of his shares were bought under a stock option plan whose terms called for them not to be sold for three years without an "investment letter" opinion from appropriate counsel, as to their being free to sell. However, Jason's certificates were not marked with these restrictions. The Boston bank asked no questions, and Jason Steele volunteered no answers.

It was just eleven o'clock. The house phone rang announcing the expected P.R. man from the company with Bacon's press release on the Greenland sale. Jason left the living room and returned with an envelope. He began rummaging about in the desk for a letter opener.

"Say, Ted, do you know anything about salting?"

Ted considered the question for a moment, knowing there had to be a twist, and decided to play along. "Do you mean salting food or something like that?"

Jason laughed. "No, no, not that kind of salting. Salting a mine. Doc Stanley, our director of geology, called yesterday. He was all hot to buy a bunch of these abandoned silver mines up in the Rockies. Claim's there's going to be a rise in the price of silver, and reworking some of these abandoned mines could become quite profitable. I told him to go ahead. Later, when I thought about it, it reminded me about salting. In the old days, the miners would sprinkle a bit of gold dust around in an old hole, and then have someone come across it and get quite a ride on the shares. This envelope here could contain the biggest salt job in history. Manny Kellermann needs year-end performance, so Dan Bacon salts the Greenland ice."

The next morning's edition of the *Wall Street Journal* carried the following article:

"Houston, Dec. 29. Steele Minerals Company today announced sale of 10% of the company's interest in a 52,000,000 acre tract of Northern Greenland exploratory permits. In making this announcement, Daniel Bacon, President of the Houston based natural resources development firm, stated that the purchaser was a Canadian mining partnership. The sale price was $20,800,000 or $8.00 per net acre. Terms of the purchase from Steele Minerals were 10% cash with signing and five equal annual payments in the succeeding years. The Canadian partnership is to assume its share of the work commitment burdens necessary to hold the exploratory permits.

"Bacon further stated that under the terms of the purchase and sale agreement he was not at liberty to disclose the identity of the purchaser. Sale of this acreage in the Greenland region served to heighten speculative interest in the high Northern wastes. With recent discoveries on the Alaskan North Slope, and several gas finds in the Canadian Arctic islands by the Pan Arctic consortium . . ."

The article continued down the entire left column of the front page.

With a few variations, the Leibowitz smoke screen was to be put into effect in the weeks that followed. Jason sent his trusted Boston attorney, Elliot N. Hall, to Curaçao to set up the Haskett Children's Trust with the Seaman's and Merchants Bank. When he had phoned Hall with initial instructions, the lawyer immediately had a series of questions. Jason tried to cut the conversation short. "Elliot, just get the job done. I trust you on the details." But Hall was not to be so quickly set aside. He said to do a good job, he needed more information as to the purpose and intent. There were also certain tax questions that would have to be faced, such as foreign direct investment restrictions and taxes thereon. Controlling his impatience, Jason told Hall that he had it straight from Kellermann that W.E.L. common had turned the corner and was now a real bargain. It seemed like the perfect opportunity to put to rest any future obligations to his children. On this hint of the familial ambivalence that the old lawyer had sensed was never far beneath the surface of his client, Elliot Hall set about drafting the trusts and was flattered by Jason's suggestion that he be the trustee. At the outset, he had no idea of the size of the burden intended for this trust vehicle. After making the arrangements in Curaçao, Hall flew on to Europe and made arrangements with the W.E.L. bank in Liechtenstein for an identical subsidiary trust. The trust instruments referred to a senior or controlling trust instrument in a Boston bank but the foreign banks were not given a copy of this so they could not know the true owners of the controlling trust. They were instructed to clear all transactions through Hall's law firm.

Jason directed Arthur Foxx in Geneva by coded company telex to invest all the profits from the private partnership that they had with Dan Bacon in the common stock of World Equities Management Company, commenting that he thought W.E.L. common looked like an exceptional buy at these levels. Foxx, who was certain that Steele knew something that he did not, also took the opportunity to pledge some of his own "investment letter" Steele Minerals stock with a German bank and buy $250,000 of W.E.L. common for his own account.

7

In mid-March the *Wall Street Journal* carried the following article:

CONFIDENCE CRISIS AT W.E.L.
DISSIDENTS OF BOARD SEEK OUSTER OF
KELLERMANN AND LEIBOWITZ

"Lausanne. March 15. The midnight oil burns in the Board Room of the World Equities Building in this tranquil Swiss city. The principals of this fight within the world's largest money management firm cannot be reached for comment. They can be seen entering the building from chauffered limousines at early hours and their marathon meetings go on to well after midnight. Uniformed guards keep members of the press at a considerable distance.

"Few facts can be established. Each morning the mini-skirted public relations staff of the massive money manager smilingly promise that a press statement will be forthcoming that day. Each night, they solemnly promise that a statement will be released the next morning. The press of the world wait in the bistros scattered about the sprawling W.E.L. complex."

The *Journal* article continued on and filled two columns in the center section. The reporter had tried to sift through the fact, fiction, and fantasy of the story. He wrote that the thirty members of World Equities board of directors were in Lausanne; that they were apparently evenly divided between those who sought the heads of Kellermann and Leibowitz and those who backed them; that to further complicate a complex situation, it was also rumored that the dissident board members had offers of financial aid and advice from an unnamed French banking group.

Since the turn of the year, the Dow-Jones average on the New York Exchange had tumbled one hundred and fifty points. W.E.L. had faced the unrelenting pressure of investment redemptions from all quarters of the world. The situation was not as bad as it had been at the turn of the year, but the daily outgo was now running close to three million dollars. Monies from new sales were at a virtual standstill. Of the twenty-thousand-man sales staff, eight thousand had left the company. The greatest defections were in the British, Italian, and German selling groups.

The most clearly identifiable fact that the press corps could establish from sources independent of W.E.L. was that many of the selling staff had overcommitted in either direct purchase of W.E.L. common stock for their own accounts or in exercising sales bonus stock options with borrowed monies. Many banks that held large blocks of the stock had literally thrown the pledged collateral on the open market. The price per share at year end had been driven from $12 to a mid-April low of $4. One of the principal contributors to this lack of support on the open markets was the delay in the publication of the annual report. Management was claiming a substantial gain in the year-end performance of the Fund of Nations based on a rise in values of the Fund land holdings in Greenland. It was rumored that the auditors refused to sign the statement of audit without certain supporting evidence.

Surprising as it might seem, the rumors of the bistros of Lausanne were extremely accurate. To Ted Leibowitz, as he sat back in his tall chair at the head of the huge table, there was a delicious irony in the division of leadership on the board. At that moment, Lord George Gordon-Gorham was speaking. Kellermann had brought Lord Gordon-Graham onto the board as a sonorous name in aiding fund sales throughout Her Majesty's former empire. His Lordship was not expected to go forth and sell the funds. His name was all that Kellermann needed or expected. Lord Gordon-Gorham had risen to the post of Home Secretary and had served as a governor of the Bank of England. He was of less than middling height, bald as a billiard ball and as he stood in Parliamentary stance, with his thumbs jutting into his pockets, his substantial pot belly became more pronounced. He glared across the huge table, through his half-rimmed spectacles, at a slumped and sullen Manny Kellermann. His words flowed forth in the most measured Oxonian tones as he stated in no uncertain terms that Kellermann and Leibowitz and their Greenland transaction were the lowest form of common flim-flammery and that if World Equities were to weather this crisis and go forward, and sensibly protect the monies of a trusting world citizenry, this could only best be accomplished without the presence of these gentlemen. In his way, Lord Gordon-Gorham had a tremendous amount of courage, for after his civil service retirement, a substantial amount of his life style was dependent upon his directorship fees from World Equities.

As he sat back and listened, Ted Leibowitz appeared to be the most calm and contained man in the room. In his own objective way, Ted had to agree with Lord Gordon-Gorham, even though it was partly his own hide that was being flayed off. Stranger still, he found it entertaining. The obsequious mouse was roaring like a lion at mighty Manny.

However much Ted agreed with or admired Lord Gordon-Gorham, he certainly did not vote with him. The timing was wrong. If the redemptions kept on for another month at the current rate, and if the continental banks kept pounding away, hitting all available bids for the common stock of W.E.L., and if the auditors kept their noses out of the subsidiary banks for just a bit longer, and if Jason Steele kept open the mouth of his basket to catch the falling stock, then, and only then, would Lord Gordon-Gorham be stunned by a switch of board voting that he never suspected.

As matters stood in the room that night, Manny Kellermann had been able to maintain his "fuck all" attitude by a vote of sixteen to fourteen. He refused to accept the debacle in the morale of his sales force. He himself was a salesman and he had built his empire out of the back of a third-hand Volkswagen. And he had no intention of stepping down, just because these carefully tailored latter day saints were telling him he had to. It was they who would go, but it couldn't happen right now or the whole house that he'd built might come tumbling down. Manny understood timing to a degree, and Ted understood Manny. They sat and waited the dissidents out. Ted did it with politeness and finesse. Manny did it his own way.

When Lord Gordon-Gorham had finished, he was greeted with murmurs of approval from his side of the polished mahogany table and with stony silence from the Kellermann faction. Although Manny by rights should have chaired the meeting from a seat at the long end next to Ted, he preferred a middle seat with Lou Epstein and Sam Weiner on either flank. He cared so little for proper procedures that Ted Leibowitz was the de facto chairman of the board for most of the midnight marathons.

Erich von Falkenheim, the managing director of Fund of Germany, and another ardent supporter of the dismiss-Kellermann faction, next indicated that he wished to speak. Ted assented with a nod, and Von Falkenheim got to his feet.

"Gentlemen, this is the tenth night we have gone beyond midnight, and there is still no solution. I cannot stress strongly enough what damage we do ourselves. My sales force has disintegrated. Just this morning in the Hamburg papers, there are two full-page advertisements for my salesmen to come over to other funds and to bring their account books with them. This is foolishness. If it keeps up much longer, there will be no more World Equities. We will be fighting over a dead horse. I propose a compromise. We say nothing to the world and they will believe the worst. The redemptions and the sales force are in a deplorable state, but so are those of other funds. It is this aura of the unknown that we must defeat. I propose that we adjourn for two weeks. I propose that we announce that the board, after ten days of thorough study, has examined the internal affairs of the company and considering the current state of the world economy, is unanimously of the view that the present management should continue; that we have streamlined the supervision of the board and are creating a five-man executive committee, two to be named by Lord Gordon-Gorham and three by Mr. Kellermann, and that this executive committee will oversee all of the operations of the management company through this time of financial crisis. Mr. Kellermann remains chairman of the board, Lord Gordon-Gorham to chair the executive committee. The announcement should also state that the company is sufficiently liquid to meet all of our obligations. That is what we should say to the world.

"Now, what we say to each other is another matter. I still think there should be a change in the leadership. Mr. Kellermann says not. There is an annual meeting this July, and perhaps the shareholders will say something entirely different, who can tell. In between, for the good of the public, I think the new executive committee should be empowered, subject of course to the final approval of this board at its next meeting, to seek out an advisory group of the finest financial minds in the world to aid us in this time of trouble. The new executive committee should also sort out these many offers of so-called help. I see no other solution with the present makeup of this board. I don't want the company to fall."

Ted saw his chance. On behalf of the Kellermann faction, he congratulated Von Falkenheim on his statesmanlike view of an extremely difficult situation and expressed the hope that if Lord Gordon-Gorham and Von Falkenheim might stay behind a few moments longer, he would draft a release for a press conference the next morning. Manny shrugged his acquiescence and walked out of the room without a word.

A massive press conference was held in the sales training hall the next morning. Manny Kellerman, with Lord Gordon-Gorham on his right and Von Falkenheim on his left, read the release. Afterward, Lord Gordon-Gorham and Ted deftly fielded all questions. W.E.L. stock rose two points that day.

It was one night later that Ted learned that Manny was planning to seek a spot audit of the World Equities bank in Liechtenstein. He learned of it in the bed of the British girl whom he had placed as Manny's receptionist. The next night, Ted was in Houston.

8

In the Steele library, Ted Leibowitz was studying a gold inlaid elephant gun when Janice entered. As he turned from the glass cases to join her, he commented, "That's some collection."

"Yes, Jason's quite a collector. You've seen the cases in his office, of course?"

"Yes."

"And the hunting paintings and the horns?"

"I've seen it all."

"Well, aren't you impressed? You're supposed to be."

"No. I'm not."

"Neither am I." The mask of gaiety left her, and her features came into a set hardness as she reached for the buzzer by her elbow. "And with that, it's time for a drink."

Clayton came quietly into the library and took her order for a bourbon. As the butler left, Ted took the armchair close by Janice and studied her for a long moment. Then he put his hand on her arm and said softly, "Hasn't gotten any better?"

"No. Worse if anything. The man is insatiable. He has everything, and goes for more. He spends no time at home—and everyone knows about that entourage of girls that he drags about on the planes." She shook her head. "And currently, the Sunday supplement of the local paper is running a three-part series. They call it 'Jason Steele, Billionaire.' You can imagine what effect that has on the children. Our oldest boy, Jamie, do you know what he does first thing in the morning?"

Ted could see that Janice was on the edge of tears.

"What's that?" he said sympathetically. She paused while Clayton unobtrusively served her bourbon, and then she went on.

"Jamie is twelve. The first thing he does at the breakfast table is reach for the paper and turn to the financial section to see yesterday's results on Steele Minerals Company. Jason one time told him that he had 200,000 shares in his own name in a trust, and this little twelve-year-old figures out his net worth each morning over his orange juice."

Ted covered her hand with his. "I'm sorry things are so difficult," he said.

"You're almost as bad, Ted, but at least you seem to be able to see your greed for what it is—a game that you can laugh at. And you have no family strings across your path. Jason now dresses in the most psalm-singing robes of hypocrisy you could ever imagine. He has become a senior spokesman for the independent petroleum industry, an adviser to the Republican party, and a messiah of tax shelter for the masses. His latest pitch is, or it is probably Ace Emery through Jason, but either way, his latest pitch is that you, his investor, can have the same thing going for you as the Rockefellers and the Mellons."

"Have you made up your mind what you're going to do?" Ted asked.

Janice turned and looked levelly at him for a long time. Then she replied, "Yes, I have. The only question is when. There is nothing more between us, and I have no delusions. I am just another prop on the stage of Jason Steele, producer, director, and principal lead. The whole damn thing is a charade, and I am sick of it. If it weren't for the kids, the when would have been long, long ago."

"Does he know?"

"No, he doesn't know. The ego of that man is . . ." There was a bustle in the reception hall and a booming "Good evening, Clayton" heralded the arrival of Jason Steele. He strode into the library, gave Janice a dutiful kiss on the cheek, and offered his hand in greeting to Ted.

"Well, well, the lion of Lausanne himself. Nice to have you here, Ted. The arrangements at Kennedy all right?"

"Just fine, Jason."

Jason eased his bulk down on the deep couch beside Janice and devoted his attention to a tray of cheese and crackers, as Clayton came in with his drink. "And how is our friend Mr. Kellermann?" he asked.

"A bit harassed."

"I would imagine. You've been getting your fair share of the press in New York."

"It's been unbelievable. But I think we bought a bit of time with that press conference the other day."

Janice rose. "I can see you two have many things to discuss. I'll say good night to the children and see that dinner is ready. Another half hour be all right?"

Jason kept his eyes on the cheese tray as he answered "Fine, fine, dear. Now, Ted, tell me what is really going on?"

Ted launched into a detailed briefing of the recent events within World Equities. He told Jason the background of the split on the board, how the sides were drawn, and of Manny's determination. Jason listened attentively, eating and sipping as he did so. "And the time is now, Jason," he concluded, "in the next couple of weeks. Lord George and the Germans are desperately casting about for a change of leadership. They keep dragging in this French bank. They don't know about you yet, but I am certain you would be the most acceptable alternative."

"Good. Well, I've got matters pretty well lined up on this end."

Clayton came in. "Mrs. Steele asked me to inform you gentlemen that dinner is served."

207

Dinner in the heavy opulence of the dining room was strained and mercifully brief. Janice made a feeble effort to keep the conversation flowing, but Jason was uncommunicative, being far more interested in eating quickly and getting back to the library. Ted tried to give moral support to Janice, but his efforts weren't very successful and he was glad when the meal was over.

Janice excused herself and as soon as Clayton had closed the library doors, Jason picked up the conversation. "All right. So the time is the next couple of weeks, and you think the Lord George side will buy me as an acceptable replacement for Kellermann?"

"That's right, Jason, but there are some problems that must be addressed before you come over."

"What problems?"

"Well, I think Manny has gotten wind of your activities through the W.E.L. bank in Liechtenstein."

"Are you certain?"

"I have it from a very reliable source. Just to play it safe, I planted someone in his office. He dictated a query to the auditing people two days ago, asking why the cash reserves seemed so low. The way things work in W.E.L., the query will take four layers of administration before anyone goes there and really starts to dig. That gives us enough time."

"What really has to be accomplished?"

"Your trust in the W.E.L. bank in Liechtenstein has a four-million-dollar loan backed with common. Until the market break last month and our confidence crisis in the press, everything looked kosher, but now, to be frank, that loan is almost two million under water on a market value to money loaned basis. The manager called me, and I told him I'd handle it."

Jason studied Ted for several moments before he replied in a very flat tone.

"You and your chart people weren't so damn smart on calling this market. That stock has been dropping like a rock."

Ted returned his stare with a look that was a mixture of hurt and sincerity. "Yes, that's true, we weren't so smart, but

208

we're not the only ones. Take a look at the performance of some of the old Boston funds."

"Screw the Boston funds. My play, or should I say our play, is in Lausanne."

"We're going to win it, Jason. Have patience. In the meantime, I think you should plan to come and address the board in Lausanne. But before that, and damn quick, get the trust loan out of the bank in Liechtenstein and into the Seaman's with the rest."

"Christ, Ted, that's going to take another chunk of cash. You know our stock isn't exactly at its high-water mark."

"It's got to be done, or Manny might blow us both out of the water before the board."

Jason gave him an appraising look. "You still think we're going to pull it off?"

"I do, but there is one other matter."

"What else?"

"You know this French banking group that Lord George keeps dragging out as financial advisers, the de Fondervilles. He claims that if they step in as advisers, they will offer a cash infusion into the Management Company of another eight or ten million."

"What the hell does W.E.L. Management Company need any more money for? You told me they had all they needed."

"The Management Company is not hurting, but Lord George's pitch is that it would look far better if, with a change of leadership, the new management has enough confidence to infuse a meaningful amount of cash. So I think you might also consider bringing in some old financial firms to offset the French."

Jason exploded angrily. "Leibowitz, you're incredible! First you tell me we can make this play for not over forty-five million. I'm in for that plus five already, and now, you've got the balls to come here tonight and tell me I've got to drop another two into Liechtenstein to free up the trust, and if we want to come to your Lausanne tea party, be prepared to tote along another ten million of chips, just for openers."

Ted, feeling the vitriol in Jason's complaint, said sooth-

209

ingly, "I know, Jason, but times have changed. And remember what you have to win. You will have control of billions of dollars."

Jason rose and paced the library for a few minutes. "Yeah, I know, but it's taking one hell of a lot of my own scratch to get there. Okay. I'll see what I can do."

Book Five

1

The cortège of Mercedeses turned off the Lausanne autobahn and into the narrow streets that twisted down to the lake shore below the city. The vesper light had faded into darkness when the black cars drew up before the nineteenth-century splendor of the Beau Rivage Hotel.

Jason Steele stepped out of the lead car as the doorman ceremoniously opened the door. "All right, Ted, thank you. I'll expect your car in an hour. There'll be three of us, Emery and Hall and myself." Jason went into the hotel as Ted's limousine drove off. He was met by a cluster of newsmen but brushed right through them.

An hour later the car was back, and the Steele party were driven to the Leibowitz house far up in the vineyards above Lausanne. The heavy stone shell of an eighteenth-century farmhouse had been gutted and an architect had started from there. The living room was two stories high, with a huge glass window that overlooked the city. Dark beams stood in stark contrast to the rough, whitened plaster. The furniture was heavy Spanish antique. Ted, resplendent in a maroon smoking jacket, greeted them.

When they had settled down and the houseman had left

213

to get drinks, Jason opened the conversation. "Ted, I know you and I had a chance to go over this on the drive out here, but for the benefit of Elliot and Ace, I'd appreciate your going over this French pitch once more."

Ted nodded. He directed his remarks to Elliot Hall, with an occasional deferential turn to Emery. "Well, as you gentlemen are probably aware, over the years, our management sales force have been granted stock options in the common of W.E.L. These options have been tied to their efforts in selling the funds. Up until three years ago, when a salesman left us or was in need of cash, there was an in-house market for his shares. After a while, this got to be big and burdensome. We finally came to the conclusion that a public market in the shares would relieve this pressure. The W.E.L. underwriting was handled by a huge international syndicate, made up of brokerage houses and private banks around the world, most of whom we did business with. Our underwriter in Paris was the House of de Fonderville. They were an established firm before the Napoleonic wars. Well, when the current crisis of confidence occurred, the House of de Fonderville had many accounts that were sizable holders of W.E.L. common shares. The Baron de Fonderville has been a close friend of Lord George Gordon-Gorham for years, and, as you might guess, detests Kellermann. There is a tinge of ethnic distaste, but mostly it's business. When the crisis came, Lord George went to the Baron and asked his advice. From that meeting came today's confrontation of the W.E.L. Board with the senior partners of the House of de Fonderville.

"The Baron was quite magnificent this morning. He barely recognized Kellermann and made all of his points with Gordon-Gorham's side. What he had to say could be boiled down to this: that Kellermann and I have to go, and that if the reputation of World Equities is ever to be restored, it has to be with a more sensible and sane approach to money management. He said the stock of W.E.L. would be worth nothing unless there were immediate drastic changes in the makeup of the board. He was really something to see. In the midst of his diatribe, the Baron glared at Manny and said that he would not consider entering the picture unless Kellermann sold him

214

all of his shares at the present price for the common, namely, $4.oo, and left the scene completely. If this were accomplished, then the House of de Fonderville would lend the management company $8,ooo,ooo for three years at the present bank rate in Zurich and in turn would expect an option on two million shares at a price of $2.oo. Oh yes, and one more thing, one of the contingencies of his loan was that all of the directors' shares, other than those that Kellermann must sell, are to be placed in a voting trust for the period of the loan and the House of de Fonderville is to name the voting trustees."

Ace Emery interrupted. "Well, how did Kellermann take this?"

"He almost had apoplexy, but he did listen. Remember, Manny's not a fool. He's as jumpy as a cornered coyote, but he wasn't about to tell the Baron de Fonderville to go to hell. Well, gentlemen, that's the competition."

"It certainly doesn't sound like any big problem to me," Ace said. "The Baron might make good wine, but he knows nothing of mass marketing of funds."

"Augustus," said Jason, "shut your ass. What do you think, Elliot?"

"I think we have room, Jason, although I must say the eight million loan and the reputation of the House of de Fonderville are formidable opposition. As I see it, we can match or exceed the openers, on good faith money, if you will. I would be doing you a disfavor if I were to say that the name of Jason Steele is at present a match for that of the Baron de Fonderville. Much of this fund money is European. The key to the play could be the ego of Kellermann. You might play to that for the time being. Your alternative is to demand a stockholders' meeting in light of the so-called crisis. How many shares do you now control?"

Jason replied, "Elizabeth gave me a report on it this afternoon. I now have a shade over twenty-three percent of the common and one way or another, I may speak for another eight or nine. You put my twenty-three with Ted's nine of the common and you've got close to thirty-one percent of the say."

Elliot went on. "Then if the Von Falkenheim crew came with you, you could throw Kellermann out. Now mind you,

I am not advocating such a drastic step, yet. I had some of my people look into Canadian law. Remember, the management company is domiciled in Toronto. Well, if you dismiss Kellermann and he still has twenty-one percent of the voting common, he could make life awfully damn miserable for us in a proxy fight. This gets me back to where I said there was room. It seems to me that your long suit consists of technologic ability, sizable cash reserves, and a reputable American group of financial institutions as your partners in this endeavor. Your shortest suit is the continental repute of the House of de Fonderville. If you can get the first three points across to Lord George's people and if you don't push severing Kellermann's ties totally, then you could pick up a coalition within the board that Ted describes without pulling the muscle of your present holdings. I would try this approach first."

Ellot paused for a long pull on his drink. "Remember, Jason," he continued, "some of these Kellermann people have been around since day one. It could be terribly difficult reconstructing their knowledge, and it's far easier to get this firm back on its feet with them on our side. I advocate the middle ground inside the Baron."

Jason considered the advice for a few moments while he stared out of the window. Then, without turning, he said, "Ted, what are your thoughts?"

"Well, I have to agree with your learned counsel," he replied. "There is no sense in fighting until we have to. The Baron backed Manny into a corner. No one likes corners, least of all Manny Kellermann. No, I agree with Elliot. There is no need to show the exact magnitude of your strength until it comes to a showdown on control. We can win that one when we have to, but for openers, I think the reasoned, sensible approach has the best chance of drawing the two factions to a new common cause. I'd try it."

The houseman announced dinner. All through the meal, the conversation mined the same vein. The four men were totally immersed in the vortex of W.E.L. and its problems. There was nothing else.

There was another dinner meeting near Lausanne that night. Manny Kellermann was host in his mansion by the lake shore. The atmosphere was less gracious and far more electric than the Leibowitz dinner up in the hills. Kellerman was pacing up and down the room while Lou Epstein summarized the findings of an investigation he'd made.

"The loan was covered late last week. Bell, the manager of our bank, said that a young lawyer was in with a cashier's check for $2,100,000 drawn on a Boston bank. That brought the loan up above water. The lawyer had written instructions from the trustee, Elliot N. Hall, the same guy we see tomorrow with Steele, to transfer the stock with the remaining balance of the loan to the Seaman's and Merchants Bank in Curaçao. We delivered the stock on Friday and got a $4,000,000 payment from the Seaman's. That cleared it up as far as our bank was concerned. Now if you add that up with what Benny has just told you"—Epstein indicated Benny Freidman, the comptroller of W.E.L. who nodded agreement at the end of the table—"you come to 2,300,000 shares of common. The Seaman's is sitting on twenty-three percent of the vote."

Kellermann stopped his pacing and exploded. "That two-timing son of a bitch Leibowitz. And he's done it right under my nose with my own bucks."

Epstein confirmed that it was Leibowitz who had instructed Bell on the loans.

Kellermann went on, "So now we deal with Jason Steele. It could be his father-in-law, but I don't think so. At least it's a new player. I'm damn sick of Lord George Gordon-Gorham and his Baron friend."

2

Jason Steele tied his robe as he came into the plush splendor of his drawing room atop the Beau Rivage. He was disheveled and damp from a long steamy bath which had soaked out the tiring tension. A glance at the gilt clock on the mantel told him that it was twelve-thirty in Lausanne. Doing some quick subtraction, he figured he could still catch Dan Bacon by phone before he left the office. He absently studied the distant lights of the French shore across the lake as he awaited the operator's response.

"Yes, operator, this is Mr. Steele in the penthouse. I have two calls for you to place. I would like to speak as soon as possible with Mr. Daniel Bacon in Houston, Texas, U.S.A." Steele gave her the details. While she was placing the first call, he asked for Marty Darnley's room. A sleepy voice responded on the first ring.

"Hello."

"Marty, I've got some phoning to do. It might take thirty or forty minutes. Could you plan to come up then?"

"Sure."

As Jason replaced the receiver, he reflected for a time on the lightning chain of events of the recent weeks. His immediate concern was whether Dan and John Palmer, the Steele Minerals treasurer, had been able to raise the $10,000,000 in cash that he was planning to offer the World Equities board in the morning. But there were other important concerns.

Late the night before, when they were still in Washington, he had a long talk with Elliot Hall. Elliot wore three hats. He served Steele Minerals as both general counsel and as a member of the board of directors, and at the same time he was Jason's personal attorney. This had posed an occasional conflict in times past, but nothing of such magnitude that Jason, with his unique ability to tell his board no more than necessary, had not been able to cope with.

In the early days, Elliot and his staff had questions on questions when they were putting together an annual report or prospectus. Over the years, however, a mutual faith had grown between the two men. Elliot no longer dug in like he used to, and the size of his annual retainer kept Jason reasonably sure that he would not push too deep into details.

During their conversation, he had for the first time given Elliot an idea of the immensity of his deep commitment in the move to control World Equities. Elliot had been fully aware of the common shares that had been purchased in Curaçao; he had not been aware that the monies to balance the loans there

218

had come right out of the Steele Minerals treasury. Jason realized this put him in an extremely awkward professional position.

Elliot had instantly recognized the problems that Jason's use of company monies might pose and he took a firm, yet fatherly position with him. He had insisted that Jason at least inform the executive committee members of his board that he was planning to make this move against W.E.L. with Steele Minerals money. Jason was extremely reluctant to do so.

"Shit, Elliot, if I start taking this move up with the executive committee, we'll be forever and a day getting a decision. The game's moving too fast. This could be the biggest financial coup of all time. The board knows damn well that World Equities made up forty percent of our gross business last year. If I let them go down the drain, or into unfriendly hands, the net effect to our shareholders is going to be a disaster. Just look at the inventory of projects that we've built up and are holding for World Equities this year. If they back away, we're dead as a smelt."

"Look, Jason, we've been through a lot, and you pay me well to give you the best of legal advice. Steele Minerals is now a publicly held company. You saw this afternoon, right here in Washington, the mentality of the watchdogs that guard the public interests. Now just think for a moment. You've got a huge stake by any standards going into World Equities for your own account. Now, I'm also certain if questions arise that we can make a fine face as to how you made this move for the benefit of the Steele Company shareholders for reasons of camouflage and speed and not for yourself. That is what I assume." He eyed Jason quizzically for an instant. "But just imagine what that bulldog down at the S.E.C. could do to you if the slightest thing went wrong. I think this play has to be brought to the board, or barring that, to the executive committee."

"Goddamit, Elliot," Jason snapped. "I've already talked with Dan. He knows what's going on. That leaves the three outsiders on that damn committee. We both know that Jim Riley's off on a cruise in the Greek Islands, and Creighton's off looking at some tin mine in Australia. That leaves Higby.

Shit, if I have to ask that guy's permission, we'll never get anywhere. He asks more questions than the entire board put together."

Elliot replied in as conciliatory a tone as he could muster.

"I'm up here tonight because you have sought my advice. You simply must touch the bases. If you don't, and if anything goes wrong, the stockholders could have you for breakfast."

"To hell with the stockholders. They're having the ride of a lifetime. That fucking Higby, though. Having to ask him anything just galls me. I don't know why I ever asked the bastard on the board."

"We both know why you asked him on the board. His chain of TV stations is a pretty big voice in the oil patch."

"With Dan on my side and the other two in the boondocks, I have Higby outvoted two to one, no matter what he says."

"Jason, when will you learn that you're a public figure, and that you run a very sizable publicly held company. You just can't continue to do things the old way. You'll get shot out of the saddle. Now, pick up the phone and touch base."

Jason fumed for an hour. In the end, he had the Washington operator connect him with the Steele Company switchboard and gave orders to find Henry Higby. Fifteen minutes later Jason was conducting a light and casual conversation with him.

"Henry, Jason Steele."

"How you been, Jason?"

"Fine, Henry. Say, Janice and I were terribly sorry we couldn't get to that station opening down in Corpus."

"We sure missed you, Jason, it was a mighty fine party."

"Well, we're sorry. I also had another thing on my mind. You been following Kellermann's problems over there in Lausanne?"

"Sure have, Jason. Don't look good either."

"I'm not certain that it's as bad as the press makes out. But as you know, they're a pretty good customer of ours. I've been asked to go over there and see if I can make peace on their board. We might have a shot at taking control."

There was a long silence on the line, and finally Higby replied, "That's a mighty big play, Jason. What exactly do you have in mind?"

"Well, I thought I'd fly over and see what was going on. Ted Leibowitz has asked me to address their board the day after tomorrow on what we're doing. There might be a big chunk of their voting common come loose, and if it does, I just thought we might grab it."

"You thinking about it for the Steele Company?"

"Yes, it certainly would be for the Steele Company. Thought it might be an opportunity and wanted to touch base with you before I went over."

"Jesus, Jason, it could be a big one, but, goddam, I'm not sure I trust those Europeans. You're never sure what you're buying."

"Well, I'm just going to have a look around and I'll let you know what I find out."

"It's one hell of a big play, Jason. It could be good, then again, it could be bad. I don't think we should make any move though, unless we talk with the whole board. That guy Kellermann sure has been getting bad press."

"That's true, Henry, but you know me. I'm always willing to look. I'll keep you informed. Now I better get some sleep."

"You do that. Best to your missus. I'll be hearing from you. Bye now."

"Good night, Henry."

As Jason Steele replaced the receiver, he smiled at Elliot. "That wasn't as bad as I expected."

"What did he say?"

"He said it was one hell of a big play and could be a good one."

"You didn't tell him about the money."

"Hell, Elliot, that's a detail. He thought it could be a good play and said to get on with it. I've touched base just like you said, right?"

Elliot frowned. "Well, I suppose you have, but you might have said a little more, though."

"You told me to talk with the man and I did."

Elliot knew the futility of pushing the issue any further.

The French phone by Jason's elbow rang and brought him abruptly back to Lausanne and his immediate concerns. He picked it up and learned that Bacon was on the line. At the same instant the door buzzer announced the arrival of Marty Darnley.

Jason shouted into the receiver. "Dan, be right with you. Got to open the door."

He hastily opened the door for Marty with a finger to his lips. He then went back to the phone while she ambled into the bedroom.

"Okay, Dan, one of my midnight snacks. Now, did you get the dough lined up?"

"Well, Jason, I've got six in hand. It isn't comin' easy. You told me not to go near the banks. I should have the balance by tomorrow afternoon. I'm selling a couple of production payments on the offshore Louisiana gas. Got a pension fund in Pittsburgh that says they'll take it. The terms are stiff. They want a four-year payout and eleven percent on their money.

"Take it. It'll be chicken feed if we glue this one together."

"It isn't that simple, Jason. John Palmer is giving me a lot of static about the indenture terms on our bonds. He's saying this little carve-out loan puts us in violation of the bond indenture agreement."

"Who the hell's he working for?" Jason shouted angrily. "He's not the bondholders' policeman! Have him figure out a way around it."

"I'm on top of it. Now relax."

"How the hell can I relax! I go before these people in another ten hours and I've got to be sure the cash is in the till or we blow the biggest scene ever."

"I'll handle it. Relax."

"Dan, you have to handle it. That dough's got to be here. Any more negatives out of Palmer and he's on the street, you hear?"

"Jason, it will get done."

"It has to! I don't give a damn what you do, what you

222

sell. I want to be certain I can cable that money tomorrow night if I have to."

It was Bacon's turn to get angry.

"Tomorrow night! You're out of your mind. For four million bucks, these pension fund people are going to check title and all that crap. I'm going to need at least four or five days. Incidentally, there's a bag man in this one. The mother wants five percent."

"I don't care. Pay it if you have to, but just get the job done. I'll give you seventy-two hours, absolutely no more."

Jason slammed down the receiver and went to the bedroom. Marty Darnley lay in bed idly thumbing through the Paris edition of *Vogue*. With a smile, Jason said, "And now to more serious matters."

3

The long Mercedes limousine drew up before the World Equities Building at the exact stroke of ten. Two hundred yards away on the gardened grounds, restrained by a rope barrier and a cordon of firm W.E.L. security police, a large knot of photographers recorded the entrance of Jason Steele and Elliot Hall with long lenses.

Inside the heavy bronze doors, the same lovely French girl they had seen at the airport awaited them.

"Good morning, Monsieur Steele. Good morning, Monsieur Hall. Monsieur Kellermann has asked me to bring you. Could you follow me, please?"

Jason exchanged glances with Elliot as they followed her into the silent elevator for the ride to the top floor. The girl's emphasis on "Monsieur Kellermann" had not escaped either of them.

She ushered them to stiff leather seats in a Spartan reception hall, and said quietly, "I will tell Monsieur Kellermann that you have arrived. He will be with you presently." She went to the far end of the hall and unobtrusively slid through the wide-paneled doors. In a few moments, Manny Kellermann emerged. He was dressed uncharacteristically in a somber brown business suit, but managed to look extremely jaunty. He vigorously shook Jason's hand. "It was very good of you to come over, Jason. It sure is nice to have a real friend in times like this."

Jason, equally affable, introduced Elliot. "Come on," Manny said as he led them toward the wide doors. "They're all here waiting for you."

As Jason entered, the board members stood up. Manny indicated two empty chairs at one end of the long table and then, passing behind the standing members, waved a surprised Ted Leibowitz from his chair at the other end. Manny put no dramatic emphasis into his taking the chair. He was all business this morning.

"Gentlemen, of the several offers of assistance that our newly formed executive committee has been able to screen in the past two weeks, certainly one of the most sensible, and most deserving of your serious consideration, is that of our next speaker, Mr. Jason Steele, Chairman of the Board of Steele Minerals Company of Houston, Texas. I need not remind you of the many successes that Mr. Steele's company has had in the development of natural resources. We of World Equities have been fortunate to participate in several of them.

"You will all have the opportunity to meet Mr. Steele and his attorney, Mr. Hall." Manny gestured toward Elliot Hall. "You can discuss views on a personal level over the next few days. Now, let's get down to brass tacks. Mr. Jason Steele."

Jason rose to his feet. He was the epitome of self-confidence. His dark blue business suit and silk brocade tie had been selected to connote substance and conservatism. He appeared tanned and relaxed, in marked contrast with several of the haggard countenances on the men who were now studying him. He paused for a few moments, looking from one side of the table to the other.

"Gentlemen, I am grateful for the opportunity to . talk

with you in this time of trouble. We are great admirers of the company that you have built. As a token of my faith, where I could set aside a little money from my own commitments, I have been buying some of your shares throughout this difficult period. I have done this because I am convinced that you will weather these squalls and get World Equities back on the road to prosperity. I would like to be of some help in that endeavor, if I can." His mention of the shares was a last-second reassessment. His instincts told him that all was not right between Kellermann and Leibowitz and he had too much at stake not to cover his bets.

He spoke without notes, and as he went on he caught and held the gaze of each board member as his eyes moved over the room. This was something that he had learned from his earlier days of sales meetings and fund sessions in the building of Western Investors. It worked well. He continued.

"Now, we all know that an expert is a guy from out of town. I would not be so presumptuous today to come here and tell you that I can put your company back on the road with the waving of a magic wand. After all, you gentlemen built this company. What I might be able to do is furnish a new and different view. I am the first to admit that I have a vested interest in World Equities. You are Steele Minerals' largest and most valued customer. I certainly want that relationship to continue, provided, of course, that we continue to do a good job with your investors' monies.

"It seems to me that your trouble centers in the mind rather than on a profit and loss statement. There are very large funds in the United States that have turned in far less creditable performances in this late market recession than your Fund of Nations. I think your portfolio people are to be commended for their foresight in having so large a cash reserve set aside before the storm hit.

"I return to my comment about the mind. There are two minds that World Equities must dominate: That of your investor and that of your salesman. I have had some experience with both. I will start with the latter, for I confess that I am inherently a salesman, a promoter, for that matter, if you will,

225

but I am also quick to point out that all of us in modern business are promoters of one sort or another. There is nothing new in this world that is brought from the drawing board to operational status without promotion. If you don't believe me, just watch the tender loving care that my friends at NASA give to their relations with the press and public back in the States. Why? Because they are promoting dollars out of the Congress, and to accomplish that end, they must dominate the minds of the American taxpaying public. We all know which drum our Congress marches to.

"The ego of a salesman is probably the most delicately balanced mechanism on the face of the earth. It is either on top of the mountain or on the bottom of the ocean. There is never any middle ground. It has to be nurtured like a hot-house plant, and yet, despite all of this attention, that ego will slip away. I have yet to discover a means of maintaining a hundred percent enthusiasm one hundred percent of the time. Once I convinced myself that peak enthusiasm all of the time was a physical impossibility, I developed a theory of front and back burners, if you will. In America, we speak of putting things on the front or back burner of a stove. The ones on the front burner are attended to immediately and the ones on the back burner are given less attention. To make the meal come out right in the end, they all have to be rotated in their time. Well, I have found this same thing applies to a sales force, especially a sales force as scattered as yours. I am convinced that I, and some of my sales people can be of some help to you in maintaining or rebuilding sales enthusiasm.

"The other mind that I mentioned is that of the investor. Now we, within our several drilling funds, have many investors; though of course, nowhere near the numbers that you have. Maybe twenty-five thousand or more. They are by no means fools; they are sophisticated. If they were not, they would not be seeking the tax shelter that we provide."

Jason paused and deliberately poured himself a glass of water from the crystal carafe before him. As he did so, he measured the effect of his words on the board. There was little question that he had their attention. He was sure that his "all

226

work together, I'm not a known-it-all or a dictator" pitch was taking hold. After a second sip, he went on.

"Now as to the investor, it might appear on the surface that our client is a different breed of cat from the average W.E.L. client, but I don't really think so. Our client expects growth in just the same way yours does. As a matter of fact, I think he's more greedy than yours, since he is willing to put his monies under the risks inherent in direct investment in natural resources. Looking for the rewards that he does, he must accept the bitter with the sweet. We drill dry holes just like anybody else. Our point is that we drill so many wells for the investor that the odds of technological skill come to work for him. This is no different than the doctrine of large port-folios of securities that your people sell. Where I think there is a big difference in our approaches is that we regularly tell them the news, good or bad, every three months. You people let the newspapers do that for you, and in my opinion, that is asinine. The investors are your clients, not the newspapers of the world, and to let those irresponsible idiots spook your hard-found clients in the interests of peddling newsprint is just plain silly. I think we can be of some assistance in reopening the doors of communication with your clients.

"Now this sounds like one hell of a lot of words, but I thought it best we establish common ground of mutual ex-pertise from the outset. I am certain that a working partner-ship of my interests and those of World Equities can be that much the stronger if we are frank and open with each other from the outset.

"I had thought to come in here today and say what I thought was all wrong about your operations and tell you how I could straighten it out and what I would ask in return. That approach was very much in my mind as I flew over here yester-day. I have reconsidered, for I think there is far too much talent among you for a stranger to come in here today and tell you how to run your business.

"I will say what we can and cannot do. I have brought with me the man who has built our nationwide wholesaling sales force. He is a man with better than thirty years of wholesaling experience with the most reputable funds in Boston. His name is Augustus Codman Emery, and if you think he can be of help, I would make him available for a conference with your top sales people to see if he has any new ideas on how to approach the restoration of sales morale.

"I have also brought over Mr. William Leavitt, who is our personnel director at Steele Minerals. Mr. Leavitt has an extensive background in analyzing and coping with people problems. Perhaps he might be of some help.

"It occurred to me that if there is one area that we can point with pride to as having a worldwide established area of competence, it is in the use of computers to lighten the load of paper. With the thought that we might be able to help in the cutting of your overhead, I have brought along two of our top computer people.

"Now, gentlemen, in conclusion, I want to stress one thing. We have not come here to tell you how to do things. We have come to help, for we consider World Equities a very valuable customer. If you are convinced that your problems can be better solved, please don't hesitate to tell us. And in one last area, should you believe that there is a need of financial assistance, we are prepared to help. Gentlemen, I await your questions."

Jason's frank, open approach so disarmed the board of World Equities that there was a long moment of stunned silence as he retook his chair. Lord George Gordon-Gorham was the first to break the silence as he got to his feet and started to clap and shout "Hear, Hear!" The entire board soon joined, and the ovation lasted several minutes. Jason had caught them completely off guard, and he knew it. He beamed and nodded to the applause.

When quiet came back to the room, Lord Gordon-Gorham was the spokesman.

"Mr. Steele, we thank you. I must confess that you are a genuine surprise to many of us. I had had visions of ten-gallon hats and boots and that sort of thing, which we over here rather assume goes with a Western oil man. From the people along my side of this table, we would welcome a series of meetings with your assembled experts and are very grateful that you were so thoughtful to bring them." He looked away from Jason to the far end of the table where Manny Kellermann also stood. "Mr. Kellermann?"

"For the first time in several weeks, I agree with Lord George Gordon-Gorham." The board dissolved into laughter. When it subsided, Manny went on. "Now I suggest we break for some morning coffee. That will give you a chance to meet Mr. Steele and Mr. Hall. Reassemble in fifteen minutes."

The board adjourned to the outer reception hall where a long coffee sideboard had been set up, attended by white-jacketed waiters. With Manny and Ted at each elbow, Jason circulated among the group, exchanging pleasantries with the board members.

When the morning meeting resumed, the atmosphere was for the most part cordial, although there was an awkward question from Von Falkenheim concerning the sale of World Equities' holding of petroleum permits in northern Greenland.

Jason decided to meet that issue square on as he answered, "As you may or may not know, Steele Minerals acted as your agent in that transaction. I think it is an excellent example of how you have let your relations with your investors fall into the hands of the press. I think that Mr. Kellermann demonstrated remarkable leadership in obtaining some cash from that sale in an extremely difficult time. I was sorry from my own profession's view that he felt it necessary to let go of some of that acreage when he did, but then again, Mr. Kellermann knew the needs of your organization far better than I. As an oil man, I tell you that those holdings are the hottest patch of promise now available to the industry. You saw how quickly those Canadians snapped up that acreage when it became available. Lastly, I hope that your auditors have told you that World Equities has received the cash from the first of that transaction?"

Von Falkenheim seemed mollified for the moment. "Yes, they have certified that the money is here."

The meeting went on until one, when lunch was announced. There was no question that many on the board thought they had found in Jason Steele a viable solution to their problems. Lord Gordon-Gorham tried to sound him out on the terms of his aid, even before luncheon, but Jason deftly ducked the issue by saying that he wasn't really prepared to put a price to his help until his people had the opportunity to dig into the present state of affairs and report to him on possible solutions. Lord Gordon-Gorham agreed that was prudent.

As they went down to the dining room, Manny Kellermann took Jason by the elbow and whispered, "Jason baby, you were beautiful, just beautiful."

4

After a long luncheon the two factions of the World Equities board went their separate ways for a stroll in the manicured gardens. The sun was high and hot and many took off their jackets in the new warmth of spring. Manny told Jason and Elliot of the genuine interest of the board, and said the proposal would come up for formal consideration at the afternoon session. After their walk, he showed them to their limousine and in parting, asked Jason to come by for dinner that night.

On the lake side of the gardens, Lord Gordon-Gorham and Von Falkenheim had detached themselves from their followers and were seated in a hedged arbor earnestly arguing. Jason's casual announcement that he had been an active buyer of W.E.L. stock had not passed them by. Uncertain as to how much he might own, Von Falkenheim sent one of the younger board members off to see what he could learn at the treasurer's office. He firmly believed that Jason Steele was cut from the same cloth as Manny Kellermann. Lord Gordon-Gorham, on the other hand, was willing to give Steele the benefit of the doubt. He advised letting the Steele party have a look inside W.E.L. and waiting to see if they could be of help.

Lord Gordon-Gorham won the day. At the afternoon board meeting, it was unanimously agreed to let the Steele men talk with their opposite numbers within W.E.L. Steele would then be given time to sort out what his men learned and, in four days, he would meet with the W.E.L. executive committee. If he was then prepared to make a tangible offer, the entire board could be reconvened at Lausanne in a week.

Lord Gordon-Gorham pointed out to Von Falkenheim that they could always fall back on the de Fonderville offer if they had to. Since that offer entailed an obvious blood bath of a shareholders' proxy fight, it had to be regarded as a last resort. He was sure that de Fonderville hands at the W.E.L. helm would only be over Kellermann's dead body. Although Von Falkenheim thought the latter a delightful idea, he conceded that it might be a bit premature.

Late that afternoon Lord Gordon-Gorham phoned Jason Steele to extend their invitation to look inside World Equities' internal affairs.

5

On their way down from the afternoon board meeting, Manny Kellermann casually asked Ted Leibowitz to stop by his place in an hour.

When Ted arrived at the lake mansion at the appointed time, he was surprised to find Manny already waiting for him in the front hall, dressed in his business suit, but with a riding crop under his arm like a field marshal's baton.

"Come on, let's take a walk," he said. "I got a lot a things to say, and this isn't the place to say 'em. Too goddam many ears."

Manny led the way down through the gardens. He seemed to be studying the gravel of the pathway as he flicked the riding crop into the palm of his hand. Ted, watching a fleet of becalmed sailboats edge their way back to the moorings off Le

Cercle de la Voile de Lausanne, waited for him to break the silence of the deepening twilight. A showdown had been inevitable for months. Finally Manny snapped his crop with added emphasis and turned to face him.

"Teddy, baby, I've been fucked in just about every way by the best in the world, but you take the cake. You slipped it to me, and I never even felt the novocain. Now, I don't mind a good fucking, and I've even paid for my share, but you, you prick, you didn't even kiss me. Not even one word of warning. What have you got to say?"

"Manny, what are you talking about?" Ted decided he might as well play it to the end.

"You're beautiful. You stand there with those big eyes and ask me what I'm talking about. You know damn well what I'm talking about. Your setup with Steele."

"My setup with Steele? Manny, we've been looking for help. He's got the cash and some very capable people. He's certainly more palatable than the de Fondervilles."

Manny grew visibly angry, "Cut the shit. I'm talking about the stock. The stock you sold to Steele."

"Oh that."

"Yeah, that. Did you sell him all of yours?"

"Yes."

"Does the poor bastard know it was your stock?"

"No. By the way, how'd you learn?"

"You dumb schmuck. That little English broad in my office. You're not the only one with a prick."

Manny turned back on the pathway and they walked on for several moments. The only sound was the crunch of their feet on the gravel. "So the poor bastard has got himself twenty-three percent of the voting common and thinks he's got another nine of yours as a kicker in the hole. Is that right?"

"That's right, Manny."

Manny let go a long low whistle. "Wowee, you're beautiful, Teddy, just beautiful. What a setup! Wish I'd been in on it, just for the fun." And then he said in an almost plaintive voice, "But why, Teddy, why? Why would you fuck your friend Manny?"

232

"I didn't fuck you, Manny," Ted said, barely controlling his anger. "You fucked yourself. I look on it as a straight business deal. I've been your prat boy holding your pants while you screw everything in sight. You leave me to tend the store. Well, I don't mind that. But when I come to you and say we're running low on inventory, namely cash in a bear market, you say, 'Shit, no, it can't happen to Manny Kellermann's fund.' Well it has and it did. I come to you and say that Epstein and Weiner need a kick in their non-selling asses, and what do you say? 'No, no. They're my boys. The best in the business.' Well, that's so much horseshit. Those guys caught the top of the fund-selling tide over here in Europe, but now that the big banks are moving in, they got some selling competition. Manny, we've been over this before. It was a business decision. I think W.E.L. has had it. I've acted accordingly."

Manny studied him. "The Toronto people tell me you went short a big block of W.E.L. too."

"That's correct."

"So you sell this sucker Steele your common off the top, take the cash and short the stock, and you've made a buck all the way down this slide?"

Ted smiled, "Manny, it doesn't matter to me. As long as there's a game and a winner and a loser. I play them either way. Up or down."

Manny whirled and strode away in the dark. He shouted over his shoulder. "We'll see about that. The game might not be over."

6

An hour later, a confident Jason Steele arrived at the Kellermann mansion. He had just broken away from a staff meeting at the hotel, where he issued marching orders to his employees on what was to be accomplished over the next three days. He was feeling on top of the world and in fine fettle for a celebration of some sort. He had come to the right house.

In the entrance hall, Cindy Davies met him and whisked him past the German guards and into the library.

Manny rose from his backgammon game and greeted him warmly as did the other three members of his entourage— Linda Swensen, the pretty Swede; a demure little Javanese, Suke; and Kathleen O'Brien, who was patiently waiting at the gammons table.

"She's whipping my ass," Manny said. "Maybe it's time we had a little chouette to get me off the hook. Do you play?"

"Very seldom." Jason smiled. "And besides, I know when I'm out of my class."

"That's so much bullshit." Manny laughed toward Kathleen. "You should have seen this guy today. What a show! He had those stuffy bastards eating out of his hand."

Kathleen rewarded Jason with a vacant smile and idly shook her dice cup. Manny was playing host tonight and he personally took Jason's request for a Jack Daniels and went to the bar. When he returned, he asked Kathleen. "Whose roll?"

"Yours, Manny."

He apologized to Jason. "She's got me by the balls. It'll be over in a minute. Do you mind?"

Jason shook his head. He moved closer to the board as Manny cast a deuce and a four to close off a point on his inner board.

Kathleen's long slim hand reached for the doubling cube and slowly turned it from sixty-four to two. She purred, "You won't mind a double now, will you, Manny?"

"Screw you, my dear. One hundred and twenty-eight bucks! No dice. What's your tab?"

Kathleen consulted a pad of numbers and with pencil in hand slowly did her addition. "Let me see. That's another sixty-four. That comes to the grand total of $532 for the evening." She came up from the paper with an ingenuous, little-girl smile.

Manny didn't bat an eyelash.

"Okay. I'll get it for you when we go upstairs. Now, Jason,

234

you've had too good a day to get bogged down all night in business."

Jason agreed that matters had gone well, but, he said, "There's a lot of staff work to be done before any final offer can be made." Manny nodded.

"That's what I kind of figured. So we got three days while the gnomes go to it. Not much we can do about it till after the spade work, right?"

"That's true," Jason answered. "What do you have in mind?"

"Well, it's springtime, when a young man's fancy and all that bullshit. I have a yacht chartered down in Portofino for the month of May. Haven't had a chance to use it. How about going down there and we'll take a run over to Corsica? Or we could go over to Monte Carlo if you like."

"No, Manny. I'm not much on gambling. Corsica sounds like fun to me."

They debated how best to get down to Portofino.

"I'll drive you and the girls to Geneva and we can take my plane to Genoa," Jason suggested.

"That's no good," Manny said. "There's too goddam much paperwork to getting a private plane clearance into Italy on such short notice. But I've got an idea. We'll take the two Ferraris and we can have a little sporting bet on the first to Portofino."

When Jason protested that he was unfamiliar with the roads, the girls eagerly produced road maps and a course was agreed on. They planned their start for first light of dawn with a breakfast pit stop in Montreux. The morning's course twisted up through the Alps, working east toward the Simplon Pass, and luncheon was set for the small Alpine village of Domodossola. Then a long afternoon flat out across the Lombardy Plain, down around Genoa and on into Portofino. With good fortune, they would have dinner on the yacht.

Throughout dinner that night, Jason, trading hard for a handicap, continued to protest that he was at a considerable disadvantage not knowing the locale. At first Manny said he didn't have to worry because he'd have Cindy with him and she had a competition license from the Sports Car Club of Britain. Eventually, however, he gave in and gave Jason a fifteen-minute handicap to be subtracted from his arrival time at Portofino. And so, their private Grand Prix was arranged with a sporting stake of one thousand dollars.

The evening was very gay and it passed quickly. After dinner, Jason phoned Elizabeth Wales at the Beau Rivage to have a bag of sports clothes sent over and he told her that he was going off with Kellermann for a private conference and would be gone at least two days and possibly three. Elizabeth reported than Dan Bacon had called and left word that everything was taken care of at his end. This conversation brought a certain sobriety to Jason's mood, for he remembered that he had planned a full day of meetings with his staff, and here he was, going off with Manny and the girls. When he mentioned this to Manny, he agreed to modify their plan and have his Falcon jet pick them all up in Corsica, which would give Jason the time he needed.

Later that night, after Cindy had showed him to his room, Jason tried Ted's private number and learned from the house man that Monsieur Leibowitz had left for Paris and would be unavailable for a day or two. At that moment, he was aware of Cindy unbuckling his belt. Then he felt the touch of her fingers and then her tongue. He put down the receiver and lay back into the nestled pillows.

"That's enough business," Cindy murmured as she twisted about and nibbled at his ear. Jason agreed. He slowly and firmly drew her to him, his hand coming up her side to cup her breast, leaving a path of anxious goose bumps. The tightness had come into his throat and thighs and all thought of business was gone from him for the night.

They slept well and were up before the light of day, rested and ready.

7

The first fingers of gray light were reaching up over the eastern peaks as Cindy and Jason walked down the pathway to the Kellermann garage. Manny, Kathleen, and Linda were already there. The two girls were turned out in sporty fashion with matching white hip huggers and tight blue windbreakers. Manny wore white driving coveralls. He was flipping a silver franc back and forth in his gloved hands.

"Heads, the convertible. Tails, the sedan. Your call." The silver coin spun up in the air.

"Heads," Jason called.

"Heads it is. I get first out of the garage."

"Okay with me." Jason went to the convertible, laid their bags in the luggage compartment, and carefully strapped them down.

Under the harsh light of the huge garage, the powerful machine glowed a fiery red. Jason set about systematically checking all of the gear. Manny, who was settling his passengers into the matching red sedan, shouted over to him.

"Hey, that's cheating. Don't you trust me?"

Jason smiled as he replaced the dipstick and started to twist the wooden wheel while watching the reaction of the tires. Once satisfied, he slipped onto the leather seat. He slid it as far back as possible to give him a straight-armed grip of the wheel. Cindy was quietly watching the entire proceeding. As he finished adjusting his shoulder strap and reached for the ignition key, she spoke.

"You've done this before."

"Ayup, quite a bit when I was a kid. I also happen to have a car like this." Jason laughed as the mighty engine whined into life and matched Manny's roar in the confines of the stone garage.

Jason let the engine settle down as he slip-sticked through

all the gears. When the temperature and oil pressure were to his liking, he took a pair of large-lensed shooting glasses from his pocket, put them on, and gave a thumbs up sign to Manny. He wound her up and was off on the instant with Jason right behind him. The guards had been told to leave the gate barrier open. Manny went into a screeching skid as he slid onto the main road without the slightest thought to oncoming traffic.

He ignored completely the occasional lorries heading for markets along the lake road, passing them on the flats or on the inside of curves. Jason held on. They did the serpentine eighteen miles to Montreux in just a shade over fifteen minutes.

Manny pulled up by a small café and they all went inside for steaming mugs of coffee.

"Say, sport," Manny said. "You told us yesterday you were some kind of businessman. Boy, if your stockholders could see you now!"

"The aftermath of a misspent youth." Jason laughed. "Used to do some drag racing out on the beach flats when I was a kid."

All agreed that it was a dead tie to Montreux. Manny tried a bit of the needle.

"Now look, Jason, fun's fun, but I don't want to be the guy to call Janice. When we start hitting those twists beyond Visp, up in the Simplon Pass, I want you to use your head."

"Just relax, Manny. I'll take care of myself. I've got you to watch."

"It's up to you, but I warned you. Now, after we lose you, the place for lunch is this little trattoria right on the left of the main road just as you're coming out of Domodossola. It's called Pierro's. Got it?"

Cindy paid the bill, and they were off.

They now had the full light of morning As they left the lake and twisted into the Rhone Valley beyond Monthey, the road hugged the northern bank of the river. There was a morning mist still on the water and in the occasional dips of the road. The red machines tore through the blinding fog without a thought of braking. In the long, tortuous valley, the highway grew more crowded as the day's traffic appeared on the road. There were now many lorries and double camions. Just before Sierre, Manny slid by a bus on the inside of a turn. Jason had to brake. There was no room for him. When he finally hit the next straight, Manny had opened a half mile. Jason settled down to work, and as they roared up on the village of Visp, he had cut back the lead by half. Cindy had been carefully checking off the map. Just after the turn at Visp, she leaned into his ear and shouted.

"You've got a very tight turn to the right in this next town, called Brig. And then comes the hard part. We head south up over the Alps. You drive beautifully, my dear."

Jason grinned his acknowledgment and kept his mind on the road. The red Ferraris were racing through the most spectacular scenery in the world. On their long run by the Rhone, they had passed to the north of the snow-capped Matterhorn and south of the Jungfrau. The valleys were lush with the new green of spring.

As they screamed up into the high country south of Brig, they left all of this lushness behind. The road now flaked back and forth through solid snow fields. The turns were extremely tight and very demanding. A gorge of several thousand feet waited patiently at their shoulder. In many places, the melted snow had drained across the road and frozen during the night. In the shadowy places, the sun had not yet come back to work. On one such patch, Manny almost lost his rear end. Jason judged that he came within half a tire width of oblivion in the gorge. Before Manny had again settled down, Jason had cut his lead to three hundred yards.

Jason was thoroughly enjoying his morning. Driving a powerful car was one of his pleasures and he did it well. He was very smooth through the gears and had an excellent eye for the fall line of a curve. The red machine stayed right on the edge. He was just a fraction of a second quicker than Manny and by the time they had breasted the crest of the Simplon Pass and were twisting their way down the Italian flank of the Alps, he had again drawn into Manny's slipstream. The cars were even at the customs gate.

At Pierro's, they all agreed that it was still a tie. The girls

239

celebrated with a bottle of Chianti. Jason, watching Manny's expression, offered the wheel to Cindy for the long flat across the Lombardy Plain and over the Po River.

Manny rose to the bait. "Jesus Christ, you're not going to try and beat me with my own broad."

"There's nothing in the rules that says I can't," said Jason. "You told me she's a good driver and I came to relax."

Then he drove in the final nail. "And besides, she's got fifteen minutes to burn."

They fueled up and again started off. Cindy was not quite Manny's match, but close to it. To the south, there were another twenty-five miles of serpentine road before they hit the flat lands of Lombardy. On that stretch, Manny opened three-quarters of a mile. It was obvious that he did not intend to have any broad of his hold him. Just as he started to draw away, Kathleen O'Brien waved a white handkerchief through the rear window. "Shit" said Cindy and stuck out her tongue in frustration. Jason roared with laughter.

Over the flatlands there was no change. The cars were beautifully matched and both drivers had their feet to the floor. The speedometers clung to a steady 125. After they crossed the Po River and started to work into the foothills of the Apennines to the north of Genoa, Manny's superior skill through the turns again paid off and by midafternoon Jason had lost sight of him.

They skirted Genoa and picked up the new super highway down to Rapallo. The road was cluttered with after-work traffic, and as hard as she tried, Cindy found it impossible to make good time. They drew up by the outdoor café of the Hotel Splendido to find Manny and his crew studying his wrist chronometer at a glass-laden table. They knew the glasses were a ploy. The village church bell was just finishing the stroke of five. Jason was first out of the car, with a shout, "Okay, Kathleen, when?"

Manny looked hurt. "What's the matter, Jason, don't you trust me?"

"Oh yes, Manny, I trust you." Jason laughed. "I just wanted to get the time from your official scorer."

"Much as I hate to say it," answered Kathleen, "you won by four minutes with the handicap."

Jason gave Cindy a kiss and ordered a round of drinks.

"You sure can handle that thing, Manny," he said diplomatically. "In the middle of the pass there, I thought you'd bought the farm."

Manny acknowledged that it had been one hell of a ride and if he was disgruntled about losing, he didn't show it as he handed over a thousand-dollar traveler's check.

The *Istalena* was 125 feet of floating splendor. Her very bulk dominated the harbor and took most of the quay beneath Castello Brown, the old villa castle that guarded the western bank. The captain, a tall thin Italian, was waiting by the gangway. He informed them that the forecast was good and the night's run across to Ajaccio would take about eleven hours. Manny went forward with him to the navigation cabin while a ubiquitous little Genoese steward showed Jason and the girls to their quarters. There were two sumptuous master staterooms and, farther forward, two double staterooms, the equal of any on a North Atlantic liner. The steward looked perplexed when Linda and Kathleen asked that their bags be put in one of the master staterooms, but he did as he was told.

8

A change in the low throb of the engines woke Jason. After a moment to get his bearings, he arose and slid back the curtain over the portlight. They were anchored in a spectacular harbor surrounded by high mountains. Jason closed the curtain again and headed for the bathroom. When he came back into the big cabin, Cindy was stretched out full length, naked, with arms extended and yawning into wakefulness. Jason studied the firm fullness of her beautiful body before sliding back into the bed. "Good morning, Miss Davies."

"What do you have in mind, Mr. Steele?"

"A bit more of last night."

"Good lord, you're insatiable." She flopped over onto her front, propping herself up on her elbows to kiss him. "Hmm, toothpaste," was her comment. Steele worked his arms around her and started to stroke her round buttocks. His fingers passed over her vaccination mark, and he disentangled himself to take a look.

"What's this?" he asked.

From the end of the bed came a giggle, "Oh that, that's where they blow me up in the morning."

Breakfast was served on the open fantail. Because of her size, there had been no room at the quay for *Istalena*. The captain had dropped anchor several hundred yards off the shore. It was a tranquil morning, the quiet broken only by the chug of the fishing boats on their way into the gulf. A cloudless sky and a white sun gave promise of a perfect day. Manny had finished eating when Jason joined him.

"Well, the Stirling Moss of Houston himself. Have a good sleep?"

Jason tasted his croissant. "Yes, never slept better. What's up for the day?"

"Napoleon's birthplace is just over that hill. We could walk up there and then find a cove for a swim and a picnic. The Falcon will be in Ajaccio first thing tomorrow. If we leave around eight, we should have you at the Beau Rivage around ten-thirty. Sound okay?"

"Just fine." Jason poured a second cup of chocolate and picked up another croissant.

Throughout the carefree day, Jason sensed something was weighing on Manny. He seemed to be overdoing his bonhomie, and occasionally Jason caught him studying him with what seemed to be a cold and calculating look in his eyes. This puzzled him, but the three girls and the idyllic setting prevented him from spending much time in serious speculation. After the *Istalena* weighed anchor for Ajaccio, Jason came up from the stateroom to find Manny in the saloon, sprawled on a wicker settee with a gin in his hand. As the steward took Jason's order, Manny motioned for Kathleen to leave the room.

It was then his mask of cordiality dropped away from his face. In a steely voice, he said, "So you think you got me by the balls!"

The switch in his attitude was so abrupt, it caught Jason unawares. He looked up in feigned surprise, uncertain as to how much he really knew. "What are you talking about?"

Manny leapt to his feet and glared down at Jason. "Cut the crap. What do you take me for! I know what you've been doing in the common. If we're going to work together, it's going to be on my terms, not yours."

The color rose in Jason's cheeks. So Manny knew the play! He testily retorted, "We'll see about that." And as he had second thoughts on the possible price of his anger, he went on more temperately. "Now I don't want it to come to a fight . . ."

"You 'don't want!' " Manny snarled. "Let's cut the cat and mouse. It's a standoff, and you, you big dumb bastard, you don't know it!"

Jason made an effort to remain calm. "What kind of a standoff?"

"You, Mr. Cat, think you're holding all the aces; you think you control the common. Well, that isn't so. Leibowitz fucked both of us."

Jason's face went chalky white. He rose slowly to his feet. "What do you mean?"

Manny laughed a long sardonic laugh, then turned on his heel and left the saloon. Jason followed him hurriedly, repeating, "What do you mean?" His voice was strident now with tension.

Manny was leaning on the rail of the fantail. "Boy, you've been fucked by the best and you don't even know it. That stock you bought, a lot of it was Leibowitz's. You don't have his nine percent as your ace in the hole."

"That son of a bitch!" Jason stared down into the water. He felt sick.

"So you see, it's a standoff. You haven't got much more stock than I do. If we don't vote together, the whole goddam thing goes up in smoke. It's us versus the world, Jason baby, or else."

Jason turned and went slowly back into the saloon. He

needed time to pull himself together—time to think about what happened now. His hopes for a lightning victory were gone. Elliot had warned him that a proxy fight could be long and bloody and expensive. The siege he faced would be all of these. He had not come prepared for a siege. He had neither a battle plan nor the logistical support lined up. He was in Europe with borrowed ammunition and each day the bloodletting of interest alone might draw him down. There was nothing he could do but see what Manny had in mind. What other choice was there? He returned to the fantail. The fishing boats were returning; the sun was a fiery ball dropping into the western sea, but Jason saw none of these. His tone was controlled as he spoke. "You said 'or else'?"

"Yup."

"What did you mean?" Jason shifted about uncomfortably.

Manny, his back to the rail, answered with an edge of irony, "We're going to find out if you're well named, Steele. You could be one of the greatest bullshit artists of all time. Who knows? But you're in so deep, you've got to buy the last card. That's some position for a guy who doesn't gamble." As he paused for a sip of his gin, Linda Swensen came through the glass doors of the saloon. He rudely waved her inside and went on. "I tell you what. The girls are·all in there waiting for dinner. Let's get that over with and then I'll tell you where we make a deal."

Dinner was a disaster in spite of all the efforts of the three girls. As the steward started to clear for dessert, Manny abruptly went below to his cabin for his cigars. Jason went back out on the fantail, and when Manny reappeared, he started right in.

"Okay. Now as to my terms. I have enough bread even if World Equities winds up on the shit heap. But I also have pride. Manny Kellermann built World Equities Limited. Okay? Leibowitz says it's all washed up." Jason was grateful that the darkness made it impossible for Manny to see his face. Manny continued. "Well, I don't agree with Leibowitz. So Gordon-Gorham and Von Falkenheim and their crew are all uptight. Hell, we've been in some tight ones before. And now you come along, Leibowitz's perfect patsy, and he blows the

244

scene. Well, that's his way, but I plan to prove the prick wrong. You may or may not be the right guy to pull this thing out. I vote with you if you do the following, and if you don't, well then . . ." His voice trailed off into the night. Jason waited.

". . . I'll make this a sporting proposition. If you meant what you said the other day to the board, then there won't be any problems. We'll be working for the same thing. If it turns out to be a ration of crap, that's another thing. There's too many saviors beating about us already. So, I go with you if you agree to a performance trust. I put my stock in it. You put yours. You do the performing, I watch. I go along with Gordon-Gorham's window dressing idea, so in the next two weeks you put together a first-class consortium of new financial advisers. I'll listen to your ideas on that. I know most of it's going to be name-dropping B.S. anyway. The French have offered eight mill in trade for my stock and my head. Well, fuck them. The cash will look good, though I'm not sure it's necessary. So, within the terms of the performance trust, you put ten mill into W.E.L. Management Company capital. Any problems with the American government are your own. You came to this tea party on your own, you get home on your own. I've had it with those meddlesome S.E.C. bastards. I don't think you're going to have any sweats on the first part of this. Once you get your mitts on W.E.L., you've got to stabilize the sales force and the redemptions for the next three months. After that, you've got to move the assets back up fifteen percent in the next three months. You can do that with either the dough now in the till or raise new dough. You agree to all this, we let Gordon-Gorham be the chairman while you're doing it, you get the job done, you can buy my stock at five bucks. Sound fair?"

Jason protested that the sales force and fund stabilization were dependent on factors beyond his control to a degree. To this, Manny replied, "Tough ass. You took this shot at me on your own. I didn't ask you in, and you can walk out tonight if you can afford to. These are my terms. You do them and you've got my shares and clear control. Oh, yeah, and one other thing. I want Leibowitz's ass at the next meeting."

Jason clenched his teeth. His stomach churned, a bitter

cauldron of lead and bile. His dream of world domination had become a nightmarish fight for his own survival. He was no longer the dictator. Manny was dictating to him. This abrupt switch in roles he found almost impossible to absorb. His mind raced for alternatives to the Kellermann ultimatum, but he could find none. He sulked off to his cabin.

Cindy, who was waiting for him, tried to pry from him what had gone wrong. When she got nowhere, she tried another tack. As Jason lay staring silently at the cabin ceiling, she tried gently massaging him, but there was no response.

9

When the Falcon jet landed at Geneva, Elliot Hall, Ace Emery, and Bill Leavitt were all waiting. Manny and the girls went off in a limousine. Jason returned to Lausanne with his staff.

His briefing started during the drive. The usually effervescent Ace Emery reported first, and his words brought no joy. He had spent the past two days with Lou Epstein, world director of sales for W.E.L. The once vaunted twenty-thousand-man sales legion was now down to ten thousand, and of these, it was Ace's opinion that many were part-timers who moonlighted on nights and weekends. In the current week, the redemptions of the fund were running a bit over two million a day, while new sales were holding at a fairly steady six hundred thousand, almost all from monthly investment plans. The most professional block of salesmen, those centered in Britain and Germany, had been decimated by raids from rival funds. He felt that nothing short of a major restaffing from the ground floor would get W.E.L. back into action. Jason glumly asked, "How much will it take and how long?"

Ace pulled some notes from his pocket. "If you say we need another seven thousand more in the field, and allow for a

246

head hunting and training cost of two thousand per man, it will knock the hell out of fourteen million. That's not allowing anything for new managers either, and that's where the big morale problem rests."

Bill Leavitt took up after Ace. The clerical staff of three thousand in Lausanne was down by a third, he said, and the remainder spent a good portion of their days seeking new employment. It was going to take quite a shot of pep pills to get them moving again.

In his suite at the Beau Rivage, Jason learned from his computer people that the W.E.L. data-processing system was right up to date, and there was little saving that could be brought about in that area.

The way Jason felt, it was difficult to put on any kind of a front, but he began to realize the effect his glumness and preoccupation was having on his staff and the pall that he was casting. He knew it was essential to get back into the spirit of the Jason Steele who first flew to Geneva. With an optimism he didn't feel, he told them everything was going to work out and dismissed all but Elliot Hall from his suite. When the door closed, his true feelings became apparent. "Jesus, Elliot, what am I going to do? I'm into this mess so goddam deep, I've got to go on with it."

Elliot pondered his chief's dejection a minute and then concluded that the gravity of the moment warranted a martini. From the sideboard he asked, "Just how deep are you into it, Jason?"

Jason was very slow to answer. He wondered just how candid he could be, even with his oldest business friend. He decided to make a clean breast of it, hoping that another mind might show him some daylight.

"Elliot, it's hard to believe the extent of the mess we're in." The plural ending did not escape his lawyer. "I've got fifty million tied up in those trusts at present market value; right now they're under water by fifteen million. I had to borrow fifteen million from the company before I came over, to clear up one loan in the W.E.L. bank. So that makes fifty-four out of pocket, and we still haven't got the golden goose."

Elliot stirred his mixer deliberately as he considered his next questions. "May I ask how you raised that amount?"

"I hocked my Steele Company stock," Jason answered in a low voice.

"You're aware, Jason, that most of your holdings are not registered—they're either control or investment letter stock. You can only sell one percent in any year under government regulation. That's the bank's problem too—of course, you might consider a full registration."

"Of course I'm aware." Jason's answer was edged with exasperation. "We've been over that ground many times, and there's no goddam time for any registrations."

"Have you thought of what might happen if the banks ever start to pull the plug on you?"

"Shit, Elliot, it's too big for them to pull it. If they take me down, they go with me. You know the old story about always owe the banks so goddam much that they got to help you out."

"Which bank are you into the deepest?" Elliot took an armchair beside Jason.

"The United of Boston."

"Your father-in-law's bank!"

"The very same." Jason sighed and went on. "And to make matters worse, I'm not pulling together the financial backing as fast as I'd hoped. I just don't think they realize what complete control of World Equities could mean." He looked rather wistfully at Elliot. "We just might be going into this thing by ourselves."

Elliot answered slowly, sympathy in his voice. "Well, Jason, you can always go to Lawrence Carter and have the Prescott Company join in."

"Yes, I could do that," Jason replied, and his hand went quickly into his pocket to touch a telegram Elizabeth had handed him that morning. It was from the investment chairman of the Prescott, politely declining any participation in the takeover of World Equities.

"This might be a time to swallow your pride, Jason." Elliot put down his drink, removed his glasses, and started to

248

rub the bridge of his nose. "What about some others for your consortium?"

"I haven't really paid it much attention up to today. Sort of looked at it as just the frosting on the cake as far as the investing public is concerned. I've got to knuckle down and get at it, right now."

"It's about time," the lawyer said drily.

"Yeah, I guess so. I've been dumber on this play than on any other. Kellermann's got me by the short ones." With that Jason poured forth all the recent revelations beginning with the defection of Leibowitz and concluding with the performance demands of Kellermann. It came forth in a torrent until Elliot at last had full comprehension of the web they were caught in. His comment was, "You've sure built some box, Jason!"

"Christ, that kind of remark doesn't help any," Jason said sourly. "I'm looking for some positive thinking. Anybody can tell me I've been a bad boy."

"I agree that you're in so deep that turning back would be very difficult," Elliot temporized. "And you're sure that Kellermann is adamant on the performance agreement with him—the ten million and the consortium?"

"Oh yeah, the bastard even went so far as to call me the greatest bullshit artist of all time. How do you like that?"

"Now mind you, what I am to say is neither as legal counsel nor as a director of the Steele Company, but it sounds to me as though your only hope is to bootstrap yourself out with the Steele Company and hope some others tag along for the consortium requirement. It's going to take a tremendous amount of quick cash. You could withdraw the merger of your Western Investors into the Steele Company and sell its own shares to the public. There's another way. You know, Jason, many of these insurance companies are looking to diversify and take on other selling products. With the right buyer, that might be the quickest."

"I've thought of those. Clayman tells me it would take at least a hundred and twenty days to get a registration through the S.E.C. I haven't got that much time. Besides, all those bas-

249

tards will ask too many questions. No, I'm afraid you're right about the Steele Company being the only way."

"You must also consider the reaction of the outside directors on your own board."

"To hell with them. I built that goddam company. If I start to let those mealy-mouthed bastards start running things, we're all dead." There was an echo in the room.

The rest of the afternoon. Elliot and Jason worked out a plan whereby Steele Minerals would take over the holdings of the Haskett Children's Trusts. This would require a public relations story to the effect that Jason's moves were necessary and sensible in clearing the way for assuming control of a very valuable customer. They both felt the board would have to go along. Because of the high inventory of projects that the Steele Company was holding for W.E.L., there was little choice but to try and save their major buyer. Elliot Hall knew the professional risks he was taking with his collusion on this scheme, and his mind was a maelstrom of loyalties and a lack of alternatives. In spite of occasional carping comments from his partners, Elliot's firm had never had such a client as Jason Steele. The Steele Company was by far its largest account. Elliot Hall took pride in his own judgment, yet he had no delusions that Jason's latest venture could be accomplished without scars. This was not the time, however, to withdraw.

He told Jason he thought he should personally indemnify Steele Minerals against any losses that might occur on the W.E.L. holdings by the Children's Trust. If they were to be transferred to the Steele Company name it would take even more cash to free up the shares with the banks and there would be an obvious paper, if not actual, loss. He argued that an indemnification would make things look much better, especially with the outside board members. Jason agreed to think about it.

Later that day, Jason got a bewildered Dan Bacon on the line and ordered him to raise another ten million at any and all costs. He would not say over the phone what it was for. And in his next phone call, Jason stiffly accepted Manny Kellermann's terms for acquisition of control of World Equities.

That night Manny joined Elliot and Jason for dinner,

and they worked on a written outline of the terms of the performance trust agreement. Then they worked on their strategy for the morning meeting with Lord George Gordon-Gorham. Manny left the Beau Rivage in a very pleased frame of mind. If he was skeptical as to the ultimate results, he did not say so.

At nine the next morning, Jason and Elliot met with the executive committee of W.E.L., chaired by Lord Gordon-Gorham. The meeting got off to a confused start when the chairman asked as to the whereabouts of Leibowitz. Manny Kellermann didn't answer. He simply slid a piece of paper down the polished mahogany. There, on W.E.L. stationery, was Leibowitz's neatly typed resignation as both an officer and director. Manny had found it, much to his irritation, on his desk that morning. It denied him the satisfaction of firing Leibowitz before the executive committee.

If previous votes ran to form, the Leibowitz letter changed the balance. There was now an even split. Von Falkenheim and Gordon-Gorham on one side and Kellermann and Epstein on the other. Manny Kellermann asked to speak.

"Lord Gordon-Gorham, as you will recall, at the board meeting three days ago, this committee was empowered to negotiate with Mr. Jason Steele on the terms of a rescue endeavor on his part. We were to afford his staff the opportunity to look into the affairs of the company. Mr. Steele has had this opportunity, and I have had a chance to negotiate with him over the past several days. I think, under the circumstances, Mr. Steele is prepared to make an extraordinarily generous offer of aid, and I strongly recommend it to this committee. Would you now call on Mr. Steele?"

Lord Gordon-Gorham nodded to Jason. For the next half hour, Jason read the draft of agreement that he, Manny and Elliot had worked out. His voice was flat and dry. Steele Minerals Company, he said, was prepared to offer sales and financial assistance under the following terms: The Steele Company would put ten million into working capital and would structure a consortium of international monetary repute that would serve as financial advisers to World Equities. The consortium would consist of a major European bank, a major American bank, a top-drawer American investment banking firm, and a top-rated American insurance company. The members of this consortium must be announced to the W.E.L. board within two weeks.

Manny then read his understanding of the obligations of World Equities. W.E.L. would continue to invest in natural resources with the Steele Company at the same rate as the preceding six months and would honor all commitments now in existence. Also, the Steele Company was to get five seats on the W.E.L. board during the intervening months to the conclusion of this agreement. Lastly, the Steele Company would put their twenty-three percent of the voting common that it now controlled into a voting trust with Kellermann's holdings. If the Steele Company performed as agreed within the trust terms, it had the right to buy all of Kellermann's holdings at five dollars a share. If it did not perform, then Kellermann had the same right to buy the Steele holdings. During the interim period, Kellermann would give up the board chairmanship to Lord George Gordon-Gorham but would retain his board membership.

As all of the terms Manny had forced on Jason in Corsica were spelled out, Gordon-Gorham, Von Falkenheim and Epstein became more and more astonished. Such terms seemed incomprehensible. Lord Gordon-Gorham had several pointed questions, which Jason or Elliot was able to answer to his satisfaction. At that point, he then said that in his opinion it was indeed a generous offer and he would commend its acceptance to an emergency meeting of the full board in four days time.

As they left the board room, Manny put his arm around Jason and laughed. "See, pal, it wasn't as bad as all that, now was it?"

Jason made no attempt to reply. All he could manage was a wan attempt at a smile.

The World Equities board met on the fourth day and after much deliberation, accepted the Steele Company offer. When several of the British members wanted assurance as to the quality of the consortium that Jason would assemble, he assured them that the names would be before them within the two weeks agreed upon. And when one of the younger Germans wanted to know if Jason might expect any difficulty with the American Securities and Exchange Commission in light of Manny's celebrated feud with them, he answered that he was certain he had enough powerful friends in Washington to adequately meet any contingency.

The agreement was signed, and Jason had Dan Bacon cable the ten million to Lausanne. He declined the opportunity to participate with Lord Gordon-Gorham and Manny in a conference with the omnipresent horde of newsmen, saying he would leave that in their experienced hands, but he would hold a briefing for the American financial press when he got to New York. After smiles and handshakes all around, Jason was escorted to his limousine by a phalanx of W.E.L. directors. Everyone looked confident and happy. The long lenses of the news photographers recorded the event, and the photos were transmitted by cable to the New York press even before Jason arrived at the airport in Geneva.

10

The next morning at La Guardia Airport in New York, as the Steele Company 707 whined onto the concrete by Butler Aviation, smiles were conspicuously missing. A harried and rumpled Dan Bacon gnawed at his fingernails while waiting for the boarding ramp. He was the first up the ramp as one of the pretty company stewardesses swung open the door and greeted him with a cheery "Good morning, Mr. Bacon."

Dan merely grunted and pushed aft to Jason's private cabin where he found him having a massive breakfast. Unceremoniously, Dan signaled all of the aides out of the room. Their greetings were brief as the cabin cleared. With the departure of the last assistant, Dan shoved the door shut and growled,

"Have any of those high-priced idiots told you what's been going on in the American press?" He slammed his attaché case onto the table, scattering several coffee cups as he did so.

Jason's face registered surprise. "No, they haven't. What's up?"

"Well, we've been getting killed in this press. Just plain murdered. Heah, you wanna see some of it?"

He dropped a fistful of news clippings on the table. The general tenor was that Steele Minerals had successfully completed its negotiations for acquisition of control of World Equities, and that several spokesmen for the S.E.C. refused to make any comment.

Dan paced about the close confines of the cabin. "And to top it off, I've had calls from half our board asking me what the hell's goin' on. Well, I couldn't play Denny the Dunce with them, now could I? I think I put them off by saying there'd be a special meeting of the board as soon as you got back. I hope that's all right with you?"

"That's just fine, Dan," Jason said. "Now calm down and pour yourself a cup of coffee. I think we've pulled off the biggest financial coup of all time. I've got an agreement that gives us effective control of World Equities."

"We meaning who?"

"Why, Steele Minerals, of course. Who else do we work for?"

"Steele Minerals!" Dan exploded. "Jesus, Jason, we haven't even gone to the board, and you've taken control of World Equities? Good God."

"Now you just relax, I've made us one hell of a deal. The board will be no problem. We've simply got a few chores to accomplish. No big sweat."

Ever since that shattering night on the Corsican coast, Jason had exerted all his efforts to pulling himself back together. Within, he was still a frightened man. He would often break out in cold sweats during the day and at night he prowled his hotel room, most often seeking sleep with tumblers of brandy. He realized he'd brought his empire to the edge of a total collapse, and he wondered where he had gone wrong. That bastard Leibowitz—any thought of him brought a curse to his lips, but was there more? Was it in ignoring the corporate rules of the game and blatantly making up his own as he went along? Was it in trying to reach too far too fast and therefore doing it clumsily? Whatever the answer, the web he was caught in was one of his own spinning, and only he could cut his way free. He realized a good front was a necessity, for his gloom could infect his people. A confident air and a smiling face were his first defense. Jason intended to play the deck out to the last card. It was this Jason who treated Dan's concern with such casualness.

"What kind of chores?" said Dan. "What's gotta be accomplished?" There was uncertainty and suspicion in his voice.

"I'll fill you in on the way to the apartment. You got a car here?"

"Yes, I had a Carey limo come right out to the ramp. It's there now."

Jason stood up, stretched and yawned, and then called to Elizabeth Wales for his jacket. "Okay. Let's go. We've got a day's work ahead of us."

At the foot of the ramp were two reporters and a news photographer. Jason was affable but firm. "Sorry, boys, can't make any comment at this time. We'll have a full-scale briefing at the Plaza in a day or so. Give your names to my secretary up there and she'll make sure you get a call as to time and place. Grab some coffee while you're there. Her name's Mrs. Wales." Jason brushed by them and into the limousine.

By the time the black car drew up in Sutton Place South, Dan Bacon's face was ashen, and he was smoking his cigarettes down to a pinched nub. He had learned all the terms of the performance agreement. Once inside the penthouse, Jason turned to Dan and put a hand on his shoulder.

"You see, Dan, there really isn't very much choice. We all either hang together or we hang separately. It's that simple."

Dan moved over to the wide picture window overlooking the river and jammed his hands into his hip pockets. "Jesus, Jason, the company takes over those stock loans on the trusts. That's fifteen mill. And now the ten we just sent to Lausanne. Twenty-five million smackers, and you say the board won't give us any grief?"

Jason joined him by the window. "No, I'm certain they won't if the paper work is done right and everything is presented in a reasoned light. We've saved our best customer and got our hands on billions of bucks. How can they bitch?"

He went over to the phone. "And now, let's get hold of our P.R. people and set things up at the Plaza."

11

On the other side of the Atlantic, there were other people equally interested in the affairs of World Equities. About the time the 707 touched down at La Guardia, Edward Leibowitz was ushered into the stately office of Baron Louis de Fonderville in Paris.

The old gentleman rose from behind his massive desk and extended his hand.

"*Bonjour,* Edward." They shook hands vigorously, and the Baron indicated a tall armchair close by his own.

"Good afternoon, sir."

"It would appear things do not go well for our interests in Lausanne, Edward. Is that so?"

"Not at all, sir, I think they could not go better."

"How is that? From the press this morning, I learn that the board has made an arrangement with this man Jason Steele and his company. Is that not true?"

"Oh yes, that's true."

"Well then, that closes out our little game, does it not?"

Ted smiled in a very self-assured way. "Oh no, sir, I think the Steele thing simply extends the game longer and brings in a new and even more profitable activity for us."

"Oh." The Baron leaned back in his chair and touched his slender finger tips together. "How is that?"

"I happen to know that Jason Steele is terribly overextended in his attempt to take control of World Equities. To raise the capital for this activity, he has heavily pledged many

256

of his shares in the Steele Minerals Company with several American banks."

The Baron arched his fingers into a narrow cathedral as he leaned back in his tall chair. "Ah, now I see. So if we attack the shares of the Steele Company, we take away his foundation and he falls, and W.E.L. is left at the altar. *N'est-ce pas?*"

"Precisely, sir."

"And how do we attack, Edward?"

"Well, sir, Steele Minerals is traded on the American Stock Exchange. We go short those shares. We sell shares we don't have at this high price, we arrange for some bad news, and after the price drops, we buy the shares that we have sold at a far lower price and cover our shorts by delivering these later shares."

The Baron grew impatient. "Yes, yes. I understand the procedure. How do we arrange for the bad news?"

"You said you have read the release of Lord Gordon-Gorham and Kellermann in this morning's papers?" The Baron nodded. "Then you noticed that Steele is obligated to produce a first-class consortium of advisers in another two weeks?"

"Yes, I have read all of that. And yet, I wondered if there was not more to the story?"

"You can be very sure that Manny drove a tougher bargain than the paper tells."

The Baron mused in a soft tone. "Yes, perhaps Lord Gordon-Gorham will tell me."

"If not, I can find out. But the key thing, sir, is for you to arrange that none of the reputable European banks join Steele's venture."

"That is very possible."

"Then, that makes things rather easy on the American side. Steele has not yet made his peace with the S.E.C. on the legality of this move in the States. He has said that will be no problem because of his friends in the government. Now if the names of the several institutions that he claims will join him just happened to appear in the financial journals before Steele gets his clearance in Washington, it is my opinion that the embarrassment will cause his consortium to disappear."

The older man was closely watching Ted as he spoke.

Ted was smiling, but he had a strange air of detachment. De Fonderville studied his hands and there was a long pause in the conversation. Then he again looked at Ted and said, "I think all of this is possible, and now, for what do you do this?"

Ted responded in a very level tone. "I would expect one-half of your profits on the short position in the Steele Minerals stock."

"That is too high," de Fonderville huffily retorted. "You take none of the risk, yet you expect one-half of the profit. That is not good business."

Ted's detachment vanished as he reached into his breast pocket. "Ah, but Monsieur le Baron, there is no risk. I have brought with me a list of Mr. Steele's consortium friends."

12

"Christ! That really does it!" Jason Steele slammed the phone down and glared at Dan Bacon.

"Another one?"

"Yeah, the Provident in Miami." Jason sighed and slumped into a sofa. "They are terribly sorry, but until the S.E.C. thing is cleared they can't come out in the open. They're going to issue a press release this afternoon stating that they are not a member of the consortium and denying the story in the morning *Times*."

"Well, that takes care of the big three right good," Dan said glumly.

"It looks that way, and it isn't over yet. You know it has to be Leibowitz. No one else could have put the pieces together this quick. What's our stock doing this morning?"

"Off two at the opening, seemed to be holding around twenty-six at noon," Ace Emery answered from the far corner of the room.

The sun was pouring through the penthouse glass, and a

wide shaft caught Jason full face as he turned toward Emery. "Hey, Ace, get that curtain for me, will you?" The curtain was drawn, and Jason returned to face Dan and a silent Elliot Hall in the center of the large living room.

"Twenty-six—that's off seven points in the last two days. Someone's really clobbering us. Any ideas?"

"I talked with our brokers this morning," Dan answered. "They had their floor man visit with the specialist. Seems to be coming from all over. Not big blocks, but steady. And then, there's a good mixture of selling on the short side. Every time there's a repeat or an uptick in the price, the specialist has been slugged with a five-hundred-share short sale. They said he was getting gun-shy of making any support until after our press conference this afternoon."

"That's typical." Jason glowered. "I thought those bastards got paid to stabilize things."

Elliot Hall finally spoke. "Well, Jason, now that Dan has mentioned it, just what are we going to say this afternoon?"

Jason got up and started to pace the long room. "I had hoped that we could announce the key members of the consortium, but that's obviously out. By the way, are we set up in Washington in the morning?"

"Yes, Jason. We have an appointment with the Secretary at ten in his apartment in the Waterview. We're due with Bernstein at the S.E.C. at eleven-fifteen. We have one of the Lears at La Guardia at eight, and ground transportation is all set in Washington."

"At least something still goes right," Jason said wryly. "Well, I think we can say that everything is in good shape. All of the pieces are falling into place. We're scheduled before the S.E.C. in the morning. What the hell else can we say?" There was no response from the other three, so he went on. "We'll just have to play it by ear."

Elliot spoke up. "Jason, I wonder if it might not be best to postpone this press conference until after our visit to Washington. Certainly there will be something more substantial to say then."

"Christ, Elliot! We're getting killed in the market. If

259

we don't say something, our stock will be at twenty before sundown."

"That's something to consider, but on the other hand, what will be Bernstein's reaction if he reads that you talked to the press before you went to the commission?"

"Screw Bernstein." Jason's face had taken on a deep shade of plum. "I grow sick and tired of these goddam federal busybodies. Do you think I'm going to let some twenty-five thousand a year kike lawyer tell me how to run the Steele Company? You can bet your sweet ass I'm not."

Elliot rose and went over to Jason. "I simply think it will look better, Jason. The etiquette of officialdom if you will."

Jason had regained his composure, and he put his arm around Elliot's shoulders. "Elliot, old man, under any other circumstances, I would agree with you. Neither of us had any idea that matters had snowballed this badly in the press over here. Well, they have, and that's that. Now we either do something about it or we're all going to be broke. A nice tea party with your friend Commissioner Bernstein isn't going to get the job done with our stockholders. Agreed?"

"Perhaps you're right."

"Now come on, you guys. It's not a funeral." Jason had put on his suit coat. He straightened his tie and smiled. "We got the biggest thing going in the business. Steele Minerals is front-page news. With a little balls, we can turn it into something really positive. Let's go. We're due at the Plaza in twenty minutes."

13

The celebrated ballroom of the Plaza Hotel is the historic site of the New York Debutante Cotillion. This particular afternoon's activity was a far cry from the Cotillion. As Jason Steele marched down the center aisle for his debut with the world press, he was beaming and nodding to all, radiating confidence. About sixty men and women were scattered about on folding chairs set up in rows on the parquet floors. There were no television cameras. There was, however, a solid squad of still photographers flashing away as Steele made his entrance. The bursts of strobe light glimmered in the crystal chandeliers.

The press corps studied the burly Houston financier with professional curiosity as he climbed to the platform. The assembly was a mixture of the world wire service men, city side regulars, and financial journalists. Between them, they had seen it all. There was a breeze of skepticism blowing through the ballroom.

As Jason strode to the draped table, he was closely trailed by Dan, Elliot, and Terrence Sweeney, the Steele Company's public relations counselor in New York. He took his seat and at the exact stroke of three o'clock, he stood to introduce himself and his companions. He then launched into a long preamble about press speculation on his recent activities in Lausanne. He said he hoped to dispel such speculation that afternoon. He would tell all that he could as frankly as he could, and the terms of his transaction with World Equities would be distributed. He neglected to say that the more onerous Kellermann terms of the agreement had been carefully edited out.

The first harpoon was thrown by a rather buxom, middle-aged lady on the center aisle. It came wrapped in a languorous Southern drawl. "Mistuh Steele, with an eye to the Administration's strong dedication to evening out the balance of payments abroad, do you expect Administration support on this move of yours to put thirty million American dollars into a Swiss mutual fund company, and if so, why, suh?"

Jason imperceivably blanched as he took a deep breath. "Well, ma'am, that's a good question. I want to stress from the outset that the moves and the monies of the Steele Minerals Company and its associates are not, and should not be, a matter of national policy, except within very broad guidelines. It is a corporate activity with the avowed intent of making

261

money for our shareholders, most of whom are American. I would like to point out that most of the money managed by World Equities is invested right here in New York in the securities of American companies listed on the New York Exchanges. Secondly, in my own personal, reactionary way, I don't think this investment should become a matter of national policy. Our economy, as you all are aware, is in a sizable recession. Anything that can be done to help that situation should receive the Administration's blessings. Either way, there is the confidence of the small investor all over the world to be considered. The little people who have put an awful lot of money into World Equities and thereby into the capital of American companies, these people have been badly shaken. Now, if this confidence can be restored with some administrative realignments in Lausanne, and thereby bring relief for the selling pressure on W.E.L., then that should help matters right here in New York. Does that answer your question, ma'am?"

The buxom lady again rose to her feet. "No, suh, it really doesn't. The S.E.C. has not yet spoken on whether Steele Minerals can or cannot take over W.E.L. Now, I don't think you'd have gone this far unless you talked with those people down there in Washington, so you must have received some kind of administrative approval. I just want to know why they're letting you put thirty million American dollars into a Swiss mutual fund when they're cracking down on everybody else?"

Jason replied rather testily. "There is no question about our needing the approval of the S.E.C., and I think I've already treated on the other part. It is my opinion that it's not a matter of national policy, and it could be a damn good thing for the American economy. Yes, sir?" Jason redirected his gaze to another raised hand in the front row.

A slender young man with a very clipped British accent rose. "Mr. Steele, yesterday morning's *Times* carried a rewrite of an article in the *Daily Mail* on the makeup of your consortium. If you have seen the article, might you comment upon its accuracy?"

"Yes, I have seen the article. I think the release was unfortunate and, in my opinion, deliberate on some person's part. There is no question that I have been in touch with several of the institutions that were listed. There is also no question that this consortium cannot take final form until after our visit to Washington."

The young man rose again. "You mentioned deliberate action on some person's part. Might you identify that person?"

"No, I will not at this time."

The young reporter persisted. "The article mentioned the Prescott Management in Boston. Is that still a possibility?"

"Yes," Jason answered. "Yes, a real possibility. And you, sir?" Jason nodded to another raised hand.

An older, rather stout man got to his feet. His accent was difficult to identify, either Swiss or German. Terrence Sweeney, the P.R. specialist, whispered into Jason's ear, "Watch out for this one. It's Beister from *Der Spiegel*, pal of Von Falkenheim's from way back."

"Herr Steele, you have mentioned administrative realignments to restore investor confidence. Do you mean by that, firings, and if so, how many, and what are your comments on the replacement of Kellermann by Lord George Gordon-Gorham?"

"Well, sir, I'd like to try those one at a time." Jason wore an uncertain smile. "I did mention administrative realignments. I meant that there are people on their staff in Lausanne that are either disaffected or have gotten plain lazy. Now, under our operations, they are either going to learn to work in the heat of the kitchen or they're going to be let go. How many, I can't say, but I would expect quite a few. You can start at the top or the bottom, I don't care. Good money management is plain hard work. Now about Mr. Kellermann's retirement. I am afraid it was a regrettable but necessary step. Mr. Kellermann, through many years of long work, built quite an industry. He has been a leader in bringing capitalism to the small people. This was and is a very positive contribution to the economy of the world. Unfortunately, Mr. Kellermann had turned the reins into other hands in recent years and devoted his attentions to other areas."

263

There was a knowing snicker through the audience. Steele recognized it. "No, I have an idea what some of you are thinking. Mr. Kellermann's ideas on world peace through industry and capitalism are not to be overlooked. In all events, we are delighted that it is his intent to stay with us on the board and I am certain that he can make a very positive contribution in the area of sales. For the interim, the chairmanship of Lord Gordon-Gorham and the sales direction of Herr von Falkenheim should have a very stabilizing influence, and we are impressed with their leadership."

From the left center came an unidentified questioner with the nasal twang of Brooklyn. "What's happening to your stock?"

"That's an operational question that I think Mr. Bacon here is far more capable of answering." Steele took his seat and nodded to Dan.

Dan got to his feet in reply. "Well, suh, as far as I know, there might seem to be more sellers than buyers. It's been off in the past few days. Perhaps people were a bit uncertain just what was going on over there in Lausanne. The company's operations have never been in better shape. I am certain that we will easily exceed our net for last year. Now with this deal that Mr. Steele has made in Switzerland, which I, incidentally, think is one hell of a good deal for the Steele Company, who can tell? We get those people back on the track, who can tell what we'll earn next year? I'm very optimistic."

The heat did not let up. Jason and Dan, and occasionally Elliot, worked at it hard, but they were not able to dispel the skepticism nor answer the key questions: the who's and why's of the consortium and would there be a peace treaty with the S.E.C.

Perhaps the unkindest cut of all came toward the end of the conference from the same slender young man with the British accent. "Mr. Steele, there was a quote in yesterday's *Times* from an unidentified Parisian banker which I wonder if you might comment on. The quote ran, 'There seems to be some question of who is rescuing whom.' "

264

Book Six

1

The glaring headline in the Houston *Morning Post* was no surprise to Jason Steele. He had known the outcome of his battle with the Securities and Exchange Commission for three days. But the thick black letters in front of him on his desk was one of the few tangible realities in a nightmarish two weeks of groping for every string. Jason Steele had failed, and as he brooded in the lonely splendor of his tower office, his eyes kept returning to the newsprint.

"S.E.C. BLOCKS STEELE BID FOR W.E.L."

"(Washington, June 4.) The Securities and Exchange Commission today stated that the takeover of World Equities Limited of Lausanne, Switzerland, by Mr. Jason Steele, Chairman of the Board of Houston-based Steele Minerals Company, would be in violation of the Commission's American sales ban of two years ago. This ban was the bitter culmination of a longtime feud between Mr. Emanuel Kellermann, the colorful and controversial former chief executive of the mammoth mutual fund company, and the American Commission. The Commission's ban stated at that time that World Equities and any of its associated entities were banned from selling their funds in the United States and its possessions. Where Jason Steele and his plans for rescuing the troubled W.E.L. fell afoul of this decree was within the phrasing 'and associated entities.' The Commission has ruled that Steele Minerals would, if it assumes control of W.E.L., be considered as an associated entity and thus be forbidden from doing business in the United States.

"A spokesman for Steele Minerals Company said that Mr. Steele and company attorneys were studying the Commission's ruling and would make a public statement after proper appraisal . . ."

A soft buzz called Jason's attention to the gleaming telephone console beside him. He punched a button and shouted into the emptiness of the vast room. "Jesus Christ, Elizabeth, I told you to hold all calls."

The very walls replied in the composed and stereophonic tones of Elizabeth Wales. "Yes, sir, I know, sir, but it is Mr. Bacon, and he insists that he speak with you."

"Goddam it, I need time to think. I'll call him back."

"Yes, sir." There was a pronounced click and the walls went quiet.

Jason got out of his chair and nervously started to pace the long room.

The first hint that the winds of Washington were not at his back had come when he had visited his hunting crony, the Secretary, at the Waterview on the day after the New York press conference. As he came down to his limousine, Jason had a gnawing doubt. Elliot Hall and Sol Clayman were waiting for him.

"Well, how did it go?" Elliot asked.

"Oh, it went just fine. They're coming out to the ranch for the middle two weeks of July. He'll do everything he can to help. He hasn't heard any rumbles out of the White House, so he assumes no news is good news." Jason was staring vacantly out the window at the mid-morning traffic. His reverie was

268

broken by a question from Sol Clayman, who was perched rather tensely on the jump seat of the big limousine.

"Had the Secretary read that woman's column on the balance of payments question?"

Jason's eyes coolly appraised him. "Apparently not, and I certainly didn't bring it up."

Suddenly it dawned on him that the things that had gone unsaid at his morning coffee at the Waterview were the things that bothered him the most. The Secretary had been too hearty. He had wanted to talk of a Carolina duckshoot and the party prospects for the fall. Several times, Jason had to bring the conversation back to Lausanne and his need for help. He left the Waterview with nothing but a promise of help where possible, and there had been emphasis on the word "possible."

The black car drew up by the granite steps of the Securities and Exchange Commission Building. Commissioner Lester Bernstein and four of his young lawyers were waiting about a long table in the austere hearing room. Jason tried the big man entrance. Wearing a confident smile, he went to the far end of the table to shake the commissioner's hand. "Well, well, Mr. Commissioner, nice to see you again. I've been busy since we last met."

The commissioner was a small, spare man in a shiny, rumpled blue suit. His balding gray hair was a wind-tossed wreath, and his eyes were flat blue buttons. He looked up over his steel-rimmed glasses directly at Jason, with the trace of a polite smile. "Yes, Mr. Steele. So we have read."

The hearing room did not get any warmer. Jason, Elliot, and Sol Clayman ranged along one side of the bare table and the S.E.C. people along the other. Commissioner Bernstein opened the meeting. "As you are aware, but just so the record will reflect it," Bernstein nodded toward a stenotypist quietly pecking away in the far corner, "we are having this meeting at your request. We might assume that the subject matter will be your recent activities in Lausanne, but just so the record will be complete, I'd be appreciative if you, or perhaps one of your attorneys, will state exactly what you are here to discuss with the commission this morning."

269

Jason turned to Elliot to indicate that he start things off.

Elliot N. Hall was the very picture of a distinguished Boston corporate attorney. He was dressed in a well-tailored pin-striped suit and vest across which stretched a hefty gold chain with a dangling Phi Beta key and a Porcellian Club pig. He chose his words with care as he began to speak about the proposed assumption of World Equities control by Steele Minerals Company. Hall was not two minutes into his talk when Commissioner Bernstein interrupted.

"Mr. Hall, my apologies, but I must interrupt. You have just mentioned the selling ban between this commission and World Equities. Quite frankly, that matter is between that corporation and this commission. Now, despite what I have read in the papers, I cannot legally discuss the matter with you until we are assured that you gentlemen legally represent the board of World Equities before the commission. Have you an appropriate resolution?"

Elliot Hall was red-faced with embarrassment. "Mr. Commissioner, no sir, we don't. We have the letter of understanding on the terms of the acquisition of control." He passed over the letter and Bernstein glanced through it.

"I am sorry, Mr. Hall." The commissioner stood up as he spoke. "But I cannot discuss that consent decree with you at an official meeting until we are certain you are the properly authorized people. Your letter of intent does not give you that authority. Until you have such authority, the affairs of World Equities and any modification of the decree cannot be discussed. I am sorry, but as an attorney, I am sure you will understand." He quietly walked out of the room, closely trailed by his squad of young men.

Jason Steele swore all the way back to the limousine.

Sol Clayman and Elliot Hall talked briefly with the waiting reporters and told them that the meeting had been adjourned for a week to wait on the arrival of some papers from Lausanne.

After countless transatlantic phone calls, the appropriate authorization was drafted and passed by the W.E.L. executive committee. Fortunately, Lord Gordon-Gorham was understanding and willingly extended the deadline on the formation of the consortium to allow for this unforeseen difficulty.

In the interim, Jason made the Washington office of the Steele Company a command post and spent all his time on the telephone. He talked with every senator and representative who would listen, and gave select dinner parties each night at the Shoreham. He twisted and tugged on every arm that was available to him as a result of his many years with the party. He found leverage on the commission a scarce commodity and yet he almost succeeded.

On his second visit to the Securities and Exchange Building, Bernstein was not the presiding officer. Jason had created sufficient warmth on Capitol Hill that the two senior commissioners decided they had best attend. The chief commissioner, Louis Blair, a recent Republican appointee, presided. Bernstein sat to his left and the second commissioner to his right. The meeting opened with an air of cordiality. Elliot Hall again launched into his preamble of the previous meeting after submitting the appropriate authorization. He argued that the World Equities sales ban should be lifted because circumstances had changed; W.E.L. was coming into more responsible hands. The commissioners listened attentively. They asked questions, but were noncommittal. The Steele party left the hearing without a hint as to the outcome.

Reporters were again waiting in the hallways, but there was little to say. Jason answered what questions he could and was far more gracious than he had been after the first meeting. The press interpreted that as a clue that matters were going his way.

Since his return from Lausanne, the pressure of the press had been unrelenting. Elizabeth Wales had been besieged with requests for interviews. None had been granted, for Jason was far too busy with his politicking. This left the press to its own resources. Reporters had gone back into their files and dredged forth clippings of Jason's activities in the Massachusetts legislature and of his Cinderella marriage into the powerful Carter family. Several papers ran a series of articles on the rise of Jason Steele to wealth and power. The general theme of these

271

articles was the man of power behind the party. Ironically, Jason Steele was now front-page news, something he had always aspired to, but he did not realize the full impact this publicity was having on his cause before the commission.

Two days after the second meeting, Jason took a call from his friend the Secretary. He had just talked with Commissioner Blair, he said, and things did not look good. The White House would not intervene; the press had made too much of the balance of payments issue. Besides, any intervention would not set well what with Jason's known party connections. Bernstein had told his fellow commissioners that if there was any lifting of the ban to favor Steele, he would resign his unexpended term and make the whole matter a political issue. The Secretary was terribly sorry. The potential embarrassment was not worth the candle with the fall elections drawing close. Jason asked him if he could go to the White House. The next day, the Secretary called back to say that it would be unwise with such a sharp press corps always waiting at the door.

Jason Steele gathered up the pieces and flew home to Houston. A day later, one of the S.E.C. attorneys called Elliot Hall and read the text of the commission's decision that was being mailed that day. In substance, the letter stated that the commission did not have before it sufficient reason to lift any of the terms of the previous ban. It went on to say that if Mr. Steele went ahead and took control of World Equities, it was the consensus of the commission that he would be subject to the decree. What went unsaid was that neither Steele Minerals nor Steele's own Western Investors Company had any choice, and if they went ahead with the W.E.L. takeover, they would be barred from doing business in the United States where any public offerings through S.E.C. registration were concerned.

That had been three days ago. Now the decision was public knowledge. And still Jason had not made up his mind on the next move. His pacing was again interrupted by the soft buzzing of the intercom. He went back to the phone console and the thick black headlines.

"It is Mr. Bacon again, Mr. Steele, and he will not be put off."

2

Elliot Hall and Dan Bacon entered Jason's office. Their dejection was apparent as they slumped into chairs on either flank of the huge desk. "Where's our stock this morning, Dan?" Jason asked.

Dan replied in the most despondent of drawls. "Shit, Jason, it broke four points on the opening. It was holding 'round fourteen just after lunch." He pointed to the newspaper on Steele's desk. " 'Course that didn't help any."

"No, it sure didn't. But that's spilt milk. On the brighter side, I think I made some progress with Lord George on converting that ten million from working capital to a loan. He'll go with me if I stretch the term out to two years. He's being very reasonable under the circumstances."

"Did you discuss the performance trust and whether Kellermann would let you off the hook in placing all of our shares in his trust?" Elliot's tone was measured and meticulous.

"Yes, I did, and Lord George was afraid that Kellermann would be sticky on that. He felt that was a matter for me and Manny. Let's look at it another way, though, Elliot. That stock is still in Curaçao and free of a W.E.L. bank, thank God. There must be some sort of technicality we can find that will let us get out of sending it over to Switzerland. At the very worst, Manny would have to sue me for nonperformance."

Dan's voice carried a new edge of skepticism, "What about the ten million they already have?"

"That would be a matter for their whole board, and it is Lord George's view that the board will be reasonable—that it has the feeling that we gave it a good try, albeit foolish."

The phone console buzzed and Jason flicked it on. A banker from Boston wanted very much to talk with him, Elizabeth said, but Jason told her he'd have to call back later.

Dan started to laugh. "What's so funny?" Jason growled.

"So they're starting to catch up with *you* too! Man, when

that stock broke twenty-two, I had calls from all over from my friendly bankers. Very polite, all of 'em. They just needed a bit more collateral to keep a couple of my little ole loans in balance. Shit, I've had writer's cramp for a day now from signing stock powers. The old lock box is getting right close to the bottom."

Jason rose in exasperation. "Come on, you guys, let's get the hell out of here. Order a plane and we'll fly up to the ranch. I need some fresh air and time to think."

Elliot and Dan looked at each other and silently agreed that it would be better to reason with Jason in a place with a minimum of phones. Elizabeth called the company hangar and the three set off for the airport. They would be at the ranch in two hours.

The day was perfect for a flight over Oklahoma to the high ridge of the Rockies. The tawny bottomlands of Colorado had all been tilled into marshaled rows for the spring crop. The air was smooth and the cabin was lulled by the high whine of the twin engines. The noise left each man to his own thoughts. The pilot expertly wended through the craggy ravines; the snow-capped crests whisked by high above the small plane. Summer had come to the high country, and the snow fields ran off into shimmering streams in the heat of the sun.

The pilot threw the plane into a tight bank and soon let down over the tall pines onto the long narrow strip of the Steele Ranch. As they got out, Jason proposed a skeet match. He directed them to a waiting jeep, then slid behind the wheel. The other two had been through this before. Even though the empire was on the edge, they knew the game had to be played out, Jason's way.

The kick and thud of the gun and the powdering of a hundred pigeons finally had the needed cathartic effect. Jason took a seat in the spectator cabin that had been built beside the skeet range on the highest ridge over the ranch, and looked at Dan. "All right, now that I've got that out of my system, what's on your mind?"

Dan was ready. "Well, Jason. There are two things most pressing. We've got to make some sort of announcement about whether we're going to fight the S.E.C. in the courts or not.

And we've got to sit down with our own board of directors and tell them what the hell's gone on."

Jason sighed, a long dejected sigh. "Yeah, I guess you're right." He looked over to Elliot who was just coming into the cabin. "Counselor, what's your opinion of our chances with a suit against the decision by the S.E.C.?"

Elliot propped his gun up in a rack while he considered the question. "I think that we can overturn the decision in the courts, but there is the element of time. Such a litigation, what with depositions and study of the evidence to support the original decree, might take as long as a year. Maybe a year and a half. Either way, it will be appealed."

Jason turned to Dan with arched eyebrows and a semblance of a smile. "Well, my boy, that takes care of question number one. We can't be out of business for a year."

"Okay, Jason, so when do we make an announcement about it? It seems to me we had better button up the details on the ten million with Lord George, and how we're going to get the money back. But what in hell are we going to say to our directors about the fifteen million of stock we have hocked in Curaçao. Those guys will be some pissed."

"We tell them the truth. Dan, you make million-dollar decisions every day of the week on either land or wells. What's the difference? It was my decision to make the play for control of W.E.L. So it's turned out dry. That's something that can happen in our business."

"Yeah, Jason, what you say is so, but what I do comes under normal operations and there are board guidelines on how far I can or can't go. You know—authorizations for expense and that kind of crap. But we're talking about twenty-five million bucks out of the till. Maybe more to free up what's still hocked. Lending money to W.E.L. or buying out your kids' holdings in W.E.L. doesn't exactly fall within board guidelines." Dan was gaining both heat and momentum.

Elliot nodded in agreement. Jason's cheeks took on color and he went over to take his shotgun from the rack. "Yeah, perhaps so. I've been thinking about that too. I'm going to hit a few more birds, and then I'll tell you how we play it."

Jason powdered twenty birds straight without a miss, then

put away his gun, and all three started walking toward the jeep.

"Dan, both you and Elliot know that I did talk with Higby before I went to Lausanne, right?"

"I think that's correct," Elliot answered. "I was there when you placed the call, and I heard your side of the conversation."

Pointedly ignoring Elliot's reservation, Jason went on, "And it's a matter of record that neither Riley nor Creighton were available. That leaves three men on the executive committee. Me, you Dan, and Higby. I told Higby what I was doing, so all three of us knew. I don't see that we got any sweat with our own board. Hell, that's what we set up that executive committee for in the first place, for this kind of emergency." His face was the picture of righteousness.

"That's just nifty, Jason," Dan coolly replied. "But we might have a hard time explaining twenty-five million already gone, and fifteen of it into a trust for your own kids. That's a pretty big emergency. And to make matters worse, you should hear John Palmer on our current cash position. He claims we cleaned the cupboard."

"You know," Jason retorted in a liverish tone, "that goddam Palmer is forever bitching. He's nothing but a penny-grubbing old lady, and I think you better get rid of him, Dan, I really do. He's never taken a positive view of things since the day he walked in the door."

"That may be, and I'll allow he's a bit of an old lady, but remember, Jason, it was our friends at the bank, your big bank, the United of Boston, that suggested Palmer for us."

"Yeah, but that was when we had troubles."

"Jesus, Jason!" Dan's exasperation and frustration finally broke into the open. "If we had troubles then, what the hell have we got now? When are you going to face up to it?"

"Look, Dan," Jason said calmly. "I am facing it. I know things look bad and we have a lot of problems, but I also know we won't lick them by running scared. We've got to put on a good face. If we let ourselves get depressed or overwhelmed or panicky, it'll have a snowball effect and we can't let that happen. I don't really think things are as bad as they seem. We

276

can cut down here and there. We have that block of W.E.L. stock, and I'm sure W.E.L. will pay us back the ten million. Cash really isn't their big problem."

"It might not be a problem for them, but it sure made one for us in one hell of a hurry."

But at this point, Jason ended the conversation. "Come on, I've got to get going. Let's grab the plane back to the city." Halfway down the hill, Jason asked Elliot who rode beside him, "What really is Dan so uptight about? I touched base with the executive committee like you said. Just what in hell can the board do to me?"

"Jason, I'd rather not think about that, if I don't have to. I know you're on safe ground with your executive committee approval, but it might be best to get a formal resolve by the full board as soon as possible so we'll have everything buttoned down correctly."

Dan, who was leaning forward from the back seat, butted in. "Right. I told most of those guys we'd have a meeting as soon as you got back, Jason. That was three weeks ago. Now when are we going to do it?"

As he pulled the jeep up beside the plane, Jason answered, "How about next Tuesday? A special meeting. I'll get Janice to give a sit-down dinner out at the house. Send a couple of the jets around to fetch them all. Make them feel it's real important. Let's do it up right, while we're at it."

3

On the following Monday afternoon, Jason, Elliot and Dan were in Jason's office working on the final draft of the company news release. Despite the despondency around him, Jason continued to plunge ahead with much of his usual arrogant buoyancy. He attended to the selection of each word of the release as though it were the triumphal announcement of the greatest discovery Steele Minerals Company had ever made. The final product was a masterpiece of fact and regret, a broadside against the unimaginative obstinacy of the S.E.C. and a prophecy of the bright future of both World Equities and Steele Minerals Company.

Elizabeth Wales deposited copies of the final draft before each man. Dan, in an effort to get Jason back on the track of normal corporate relations, said, "Reads real fine. What do you think of holding it until after the board has had a chance to see it in the morning?"

"I think you're out of your cotton-picking mind," Jason exploded. "That's what I think. After this is released, there's damn little they can do about it."

"Yeah, but this bit in here about converting that ten million bucks into a two-year loan, how's that going to set? I can hear a couple of 'em now carping on the fact we're not a lending institution."

"Look, Dan, the deal's done." Jason subsided as quickly as he'd blown up. "So it didn't turn out to the best of our expectations. On the other hand, we've helped to save our biggest account. This is an operational matter, not something for those guys to pick over."

Everything considered, Jason had been extremely lucky with the developments in Lausanne the previous week. Lord George Gordon-Gorham, acting according to expectations, had agreed that the hard position of the S.E.C. was a factor on which they had not counted. He understood why the government would not intervene on Jason's behalf, and he successfully overrode Manny Kellermann's objections to the loan conversion by the board of W.E.L. He had pointed out to the board that Steele had been apparently sincere and had backed his sincerity with ten millions of cash. The board concluded that if Kellermann desired to press further on the specific performance provisions of his private agreement with Steele, that would be his own decision. They had enough troubles of their own, without getting into an international hassle with Jason Steele.

The release as approved went out before the board meeting. It said: "(Houston, June 11.) Jason Steele, Chairman of the Board, Steele Minerals Company, today issued the following statement:

" 'In compliance with last week's letter from the United States Securities and Exchange Commission, Steele Minerals has elected to convert the $10,000,000 presently advanced to World Equities Limited of Lausanne, Switzerland, into a two-year loan of working capital funds, bearing 7½ percent interest. We have reached this decision with extreme reluctance and announce with regret that Steele Minerals must withdraw any further operational or financial assistance that would come within the scope of the W.E.L. sales ban. This decision has been forced upon us by an unimaginative interpretation of an outdated consent decree on the part of the American Commission. We do not think the Commission has realistically assessed the World Equities fund's effect on the American securities markets, nor the benefit to be derived from having this company in responsible American hands. We have had ample and detailed opportunity to examine closely the affairs of World Equities and are firmly convinced that the Company is in a far better financial position than many comparable funds of its size. Under the leadership of Messrs. Kellermann, Von Falkenheim, and Lord Gordon-Gorham, they have imaginatively anticipated this time of trouble in the marketplace and we are certain will promptly restore W.E.L. on the road toward prosperity. Because of our optimism, we are delighted that our loan carries with it the privilege to convert into shares of W.E.L. Management Company Common.

" 'In the area of developing resources for emerging nations, the partnership of Steele Minerals and World Equities will go forward. . .' "

4

As Jason and Dan were putting the final strokes to their press release on the W.E.L. withdrawal, a fleet of private jets was on its way to bring the "outside" directors of Steele Minerals to the special meeting.

279

The Steele Minerals board comprised six outsiders, all of them captains of industry in their own right. They had been invited on the board by Jason Steele with an eye for what they could do for him. Jason took great pride in his control of the board. Before any important meeting, he would be on the phone to insure that "all his ducks were in line" before a matter went to a vote. He could go into a meeting on any given day with five sure votes, those of the "insiders," the men who worked directly for the company. Besides Jason himself, they were Bacon, Palmer, Hall and Foxx. It never had to be stated, yet all these men clearly understood that the bread on their table and their manner of living were totally dependent on their fealty to Jason Steele.

Late that afternoon, as Jason was driven to his mansion, he was thinking about the next day's meeting. He was not nearly as confident as he would have his colleagues believe. He had an uneasy feeling, a feeling that was impossible to drive from his mind, that his control of the board might not be as firm this time. But he was determined not to let anyone suspect he was anything other than completely confident.

Janice had refused to hostess a full-scale sit-down dinner for the directors. The matter had been resolved in favor of a catered Hawaiian luau on the back patio and all of the attendant details had been placed in the hands of Elizabeth Wales. That relieved Janice of any burden, save dressing for her own dinner party. Jason's thoughts turned to his relations with Janice as the black limousine whisked through the outer suburbs. When he had returned from Lausanne, she had greeted him as coolly as if he had come back from a weekend of play at Palm Springs. The very next night, however, her greeting was far from cool. She was waiting for him in the front hall. There was no pretense of pleasantries. The instant the butler disappeared with Jason's topcoat, she tore into him. "Jason, did you tell a press conference in New York that the Prescott is going to join your group?"

Jason considered the fire in his wife's eye as he answered, "I said that it was possible. I never said it was a fact."

Janice was blazing. "I had a call from Father this afternoon. He said his people sent you a very clear telegram in Lausanne. That they—"

"What telegram?" His indignation was superb. "I've been wondering when those stuffy bastards would do me the courtesy of an answer."

She considered that for a moment and looked squarely at him as she spoke. "Then you never got a telegram. . . ?" She turned back into the hallway before he could answer.

"No, damn it," he bellowed after her.

The Lausanne trip brought their deteriorating relations to a head. Janice was neither interested nor sympathetic to his troubles; she was weary to death of his business and said so. After that, they made pretense of a successful marriage only in public or in front of the children. They had long ago moved into separate bedrooms.

Although Jason realized this armed truce could not go on forever, he wanted at all costs to avoid any adverse publicity of the kind a divorce would be sure to bring. He anticipated that Janice might ask for one eventually, but he doubted that it would be soon. He counted on the fact that divorce would go against the grain for the former Janice Carter and that she would consider very carefully the effect on the children. In his present circumstance, he was acutely aware of timing, and his strategy was to keep things on an outward even keel as long as possible. He'd let Janice make the next move, yet he idly wondered if there was another man in the picture. There had certainly been no affair that he could detect and although he was away a good part of the time, he knew he had employees who would delight in reporting gossip to him if there was any. No, he concluded that Janice was not the type—she was of too fine a breed to ever take a chance on causing public embarrassment.

Jason's son Jamie greeted him in the hallway and quietly followed him up to his room. He watched from the bed as his father donned his custom western garb, including hand-tooled boots with the rolling "S" embossed in gold. Jamie, a tow-haired lad of twelve, seemed to be groping for words as he fidgeted about the room. Finally, Jason asked, "Something bothering you, son?"

281

Jamie looked at his father, his cheeks flushed pink with embarrassment. "Yeah, Dad, there is. The kids at school say we're going broke."

Jason tugged at his boots with a grunt. "And how do the kids at your school know?"

"Oh, they read the papers, Dad. You know. This W.E.L. thing. Our stock is down to fourteen."

"Yes, son, I'm well aware." Jason could not hold back a smile. "But what those friends of yours don't know is that at fourteen, that stock is the best buy on the board. Come on, let's go down. People will be coming, but just get this clear. We're in good shape. So we drilled a dry hole. You have to drill them every now and then. You just don't worry about it. You can't worry about dry holes or you never get anything done."

His father's words brightened Jamie considerably and he led the way down the stairs. They were identically dressed in bright cowboy shirts with silver-tipped string ties, custom twill riding pants and monogramed boots. Jason headed for the patio to inspect the arrangements. As he passed through the leaded glass doors, he could hear the gravelly crunch of an arriving car.

At the far end of the flagstoned patio, there stood a squad of black waiters. Behind them, in a huge stone barbecue pit, a massive pig turned slowly over the glowing coals while a white-hatted chef was basting the crackling skin. Bars were set up in each corner. The overhanging tree limbs held bright lanterns against the coming darkness.

Jason looked about him and had just turned to Elizabeth Wales with a soft "Very good" when a bustle at the glass doors announced the arrival of Augustus Codman Emery and his new bride. Jason had a respect for the new Mrs. Emery that he held for few women. She certainly was nothing to look at, even though she made every effort. Perhaps what attracted him was that she had run her own fund-selling force in New York and run it well. She had sobered the Ace considerably and that was a positive step, Jason thought, as he went forward to greet them. "Welcome, Judith. Evening to you, Ace. Janice should be down in a moment." A waiter was at their elbow in the instant. Mrs. Emery was expressing her admiration of the Hawaiian motif, when a pretty girl in a sarong appeared with a plate of hors d'oeuvres. Both men's eyes tracked her as she left them, something that did not escape the new Mrs. Emery. "Down boys, it's early." Jason smiled and Ace asked, "Anybody or anything you want me to concentrate on tonight?"

"The merger's still in the wind. I sure want to get that accomplished as soon as possible. With the current state of the Steele stock, the sooner we get Western Investors turned into marketable stock, the better I'll like it." With the fall of his Steele Minerals stock, Jason was in serious jeopardy of having his loans summarily called by several banks. He had run out of liquid assets to put up against these calls. His one hope was his ownership of Western Investors, which was still free and clear and of considerable value. Since there was no trading market for these shares, a merger of Western Investors into Steele Minerals was the quickest and cleanest route for him to obtain desperately needed liquidity. Although he had his doubts that the outsiders on the Steele Company board would go along with this shotgun marriage, he had to try. He had no other choice.

Ace reached down for his deepest Bostonian tone. "You're not expecting any problems on that, are you, Jason?"

Not wanting to discourage him, Jason replied confidentally, "No Ace, I'm not expecting any, but you asked what might be accomplished. You circulate with your usual enthusiasm and get across what a bargain the Steele Company is getting. You should get to know these guys anyway. After the merger, it's my hope you will come on the Steele Company board."

"That's very kind of you, Jason, and needless to say, I'd be delighted."

Janice stepped onto the patio, and Jason left Ace to join her. She looked about at the decorations and said without much enthusiasm, "Very nice, I'll have to congratulate Elizabeth."

"And you look very lovely, my dear," Jason replied in a missed attempt at gallantry. "Why, thank you, dear, I'm glad you noticed." Her tone was the same but with a bit more bite.

Then Dan and Lilly Bacon and Michael Collins appeared. Jason was pleased with Collins' early arrival. He was the newest member of the Steele board, having been elected a little over a year before, and he was the one Jason knew the least. After a civil exchange with Dan's wife, whom he detested, Jason took Collins by the elbow to a corner bar. "Michael, my boy, we're delighted to have you out here."

Collins, a handsome, deeply tanned man in his mid-forties, ran the largest real estate firm in New York. He had fought his way up from the bottom with a broad good humor and a fast mind with figures. There was little that got by his shrewd eyes. On any winter trip to Houston, he could be counted on for a side swing through Vail or Aspen for skiing. He had spent several days at the Steele Ranch in the Rockies and become a good friend of Janice and her sister, Jean. He gave back Jason's bonhomie in spades.

"Jason, it's a pleasure to be here." With his drink now in hand he went on. "I see by the papers you've been busy."

The edge of irony escaped Jason. He reached for a note of sincerity as he answered. "That is the understatement of the week."

"It looks like they gave you a pretty good workout."

"You know, all in all, I think we came out of it pretty well. Sure would have liked to get our hands on those billions of bucks, but then, who could tell the S.E.C. would be so goddam obstinate?" Collins, who came from a city where, to survive in the real estate game one had to be a Democrat, simply couldn't let the opportunity slide by.

"What happened to your Republican pals?"

The entrance of some new guests gave Jason an excuse to break away. He did so with a parting shot. "Your Democrat friends weren't much help either. But it's a long story. I'll be back in a few minutes."

Three more directors had arrived. Stanton Harris, the president of a huge midwestern chain of drugstores, was the first to shake Jason's hand. He had come down from Chicago with David Coons, the rough diamond of the Steele board. Coons, a handsome and outspoken man, had built a comet of a company in the air freight trade. His specialty was the flying of oil-drilling equipment up to the North Slope of Alaska, and Jason had worked out some aircraft leases with him. In Coons's shadow waited Henry Higby of Dallas. Jason thought he seemed a bit standoffish as he greeted him. Once again, Jason sensed that the morning meeting could become a donnybrook, despite his pocket borough of votes.

Jason caught Dan's eye and motioned him over to a corner of the patio. "Dan, make sure that our people circulate. The more we keep the others moving about, the less chance of any cliques forming between now and morning."

Dan agreed, and they went their separate ways. Their tactics, however, were not a total success. By mid-evening, Collins and Higby found themselves sharing a wrought-iron love seat as they concentrated on plates of savory pork.

"Henry, where they got you set up for the night?" asked Collins.

The question caught Higby with a mouthful of pork. He held up his hand. "My envelope says I'm preregistered into the new wing of the International. What about you?"

"Same place." Collins smiled. "What's the chances we get out of here early tonight and have a drink in my room?"

"Right good as far as I'm concerned. What's on your mind?"

"I don't know exactly. But I'm sure of one thing; this isn't the place."

Higby rose to again fill his plate. "Give me the word when you're ready to move." Collins watched the small man disappear in the crowd about the barbecue pit. His seat was soon taken by Janice's younger sister, Jean Patterson.

Jean was pert, petite, and eye-catching. Her white pants suit did her full justice. Like Janice, she was fond of outdoor life and was an expert skier. Collins thought of her as a happy person, less serious than her sister. She was in Houston regaining her confidence having just obtained a Mexican divorce, which the Carter family attorneys decided was more expedient and acceptable than a public laundering of Carter linen in a Massachusetts court.

The whiskey and the night air had washed any restraint from the Steele patio. Collins, now well into his fourth bourbon, bawled over the party din, "Jeannie, baby, now just how the hell are ya and how's your love life?"

"Pretty poor pickings tonight, Mike," Jean pouted. "All

you people ever talk about is money. There are other things."

"Yeah, like what?"

"Oh, girls, and traveling and skiing. Now take Jason, he goes all over the world, and never sees it."

"A busy man."

"That's one way of putting it. There are others, and less polite."

"Don't think I better get into that. Things are looking up for you though. Your pal Coons has arrived."

"Mike, stop it! David Coons is just another business friend of Jason's, like you."

"That's not what I hear. Come on, let's get with some more food. I'm still hungry." Close to eleven, Collins went up to Henry Higby. "Henry, I think it's time an eastern boy got to bed."

5

There was no banter as the Steele Board members took their seats about the large table. Perhaps it was circumstance that found the six "outsiders" ranged down one side of the table. Crawford Creighton and Stanton Harris were the closest to the Chair. Higby, Collins and Jim Riley made up the side, leaving the last into the room, David Coons, the far end seat, squarely facing the chairman.

Jason Steele was brusque and business-like as he brought the board meeting to order. As he rose to speak, several members reached for the pads of yellow paper and sharp pencils that were the sole burden of the long table. "Gentlemen, we thank you for interrupting your busy schedules to be with us today. There is much ground to cover, so we might as well have at it. The first topic on the agenda has been hanging fire from the last two meetings; it is the terms of the merging of Western Investors and the Fund Companies into Steele Minerals.

Michael Collins requested an independent appraisal of the properties within the funds at the last meeting. As this is an operational matter, and as I have a vested interest, either way, go or no go, it might be appropriate that I excuse myself while this matter is taken up. Dan, will you take over the chair?"

Jason left the room and Dan rose. "Well now, I think a lot that Mike asked for has been accomplished. We've had a firm in Tulsa go through what those funds have. They've got some right fine production as you will see." As he said this, he pushed a button underneath the table. Elizabeth Wales and two pretty secretaries entered and distributed bound volumes of the report.

Much of the report was in a language that few of the outside members understood. Dan let them read on for a few minutes. Then Henry Higby asked, "Say, Dan, just what are these fellas saying when they talk of proven probable and proven possible reserves? Seems to me you either got it down there or you don't."

Dan began a very long technical explanation of the several kinds of ways to assess the value of production in the ground. When he'd finished, Stanton Harris spoke up. "Dan, these appraisers are giving a present dollar worth to this proven possible category of just over seven million dollars, is that correct?"

After referring to the report for a moment, Dan agreed that the value was correct. Harris continued. "Now, I know there are obvious differences, but, when I send our accountants out for a check, inventory isn't a major problem. I think what causes me concern is the possible criticism if we were to vote on this merger and were to give Jason Steele seven million dollars of Steele Minerals stock on this one category alone. I realize it's a small portion of the total fifty that may be involved, but I'm not sure it will look right unless there's more supporting evidence."

Michael Collins took up where Harris left off. "Stan, you think that's bad? Take a look at page four. The good will and the sales expertise of Western Investors is listed as worth a nice round ten million dollars. Now, for other reasons, I happened to be in the building in downtown New York where

287

this man Emery has his Eastern divisional headquarters. It's a mighty fancy place, incidentally. We're the rental agent for the insurance company that owns it. Well, anyway, I just thought I'd poke my head in the door and say hello. I see a good-looking receptionist, doing her nails at the front desk. That wasn't so bad, but she was dressed in tennis clothes. When I introduced myself, she told me the boss is off in a golf tournament up in Westchester, the second in command has just resigned to go with another fund, and the third salesman is home with a cold. And this Tulsa appraisal firm is telling us the good will is worth ten million."

As the board broke into laughter, Dan quickly tried to bring order back to the table. "Yes, but don't forget, Western Investors salesmen raised one hundred and fifty million dollars of drilling money last year."

"That's true," agreed Arthur Foxx, "one hundred and fifty million."

"This is all very interesting," said Henry Higby, "but how are they doing this year? We're into June. There must be some sort of figures."

Neither Dan nor John Palmer had these figures and the latter left the room to get them. In the meantime, the board broke for coffee. When Palmer returned, he reported that Western Investors had raised twenty-six million for the first five months as compared to sixty-three for the same term last year. Coons spoke up. "There sure has been a recession, but I'm not sure it's been that bad."

Collins didn't let up. "What about the sales force, Dan? Seems to me that the whole thing with this fund-selling business is having troops out pushing doorbells. What's the present status of their wholesale force? Hey, how about getting Emery over here?" Dan glanced at his watch. He knew what Ace could be like, unprepared. Reluctantly, he picked up the phone and asked Elizabeth Wales to find him.

Ace was not located until after lunch, and he was a disaster. He tried to bluff it through, but the third martini and the surprise of the call took their toll. He was not on top of the situation.

288

Dan was growing desperate. There was a whole new tone to the board, and he was being caught in the cross fire. He excused himself for a moment and rushed down the hall to Jason's office.

"Jason, we're getting the shit kicked out of us. If it keeps up, we'll never get that merger through."

Jason assessed the information with apparent calm. "Who's doing the kicking?"

"It's all of them as far as I can figure. No one man."

"You mean our own people too?" Jason's voice rose sharply.

"No, not them. It's the outsiders. They seem very suspicious and they're asking a lot of questions today. And some of them aren't easy to answer. They may be annoyed about Western Investors being the first item on the agenda."

"Well, they've had their chance to chew. Put it to a vote. You can count on Coons and I think Creighton. Let's get on with it."

Dan went back to the meeting, and another round of discussion ensued. Finally, he brought matters to a head. "Gentlemen, there's obviously a difference of opinion at this table, and that makes for healthy companies. Now, you all remember that Jason told us at the last meeting that he doesn't care one way or the other. He's fully prepared to take Western Investors public on its own, but he doesn't want anybody criticizing him later, so he's brought this offer to us first. In my opinion, he's got himself one hell of a going Jessie in that company, and I think it will fit right into our operations. We've been working with his people for the last couple of years, and we get on real fine. May I take a vote. The vote is whether we accept Jason Steele's offer to merge Western Investors at the appraised value of fifty million. The fifty million to be a tax-free exchange into the current market value of Steele Minerals stock. Do I hear a second?" Foxx seconded the motion.

The motion did not carry by a vote of five to four. To Dan's astonishment, David Coons disqualified himself, stating that his company was leasing several aircraft through a subsidiary of Western Investors, and he felt it best under those circumstances that he not vote. Creighton went with the Higby and Collins bloc. Jason had excused himself for obvious conflict of interest reasons.

Dan went to Jason with the bad news.

"Jesus Christ," Jason said angrily. "I turn the meeting over to you on a perfectly routine matter and you blow it. Have you any idea what that vote does to my personal position? Why in hell do you think I've been ducking all those bankers' calls for the past few days? Those goddam idiots are going to put me to the wall."

Dan argued that he had done his best. "All the regulars played the game, Jason, but it was your own Ace who really blew the merger clear out of the water."

It took some time for Jason to regain his composure sufficiently to go back to the board room. Once there, he retook the chair and with an unruffled smile said, "Well, now that we have that small matter settled, we come to the main reason that I asked you gentlemen out here today. I think it might be best to begin at the beginning of our recent activities. You will recall that Messrs. Kellermann and Leibowitz told us to gear up for a considerable amount of new investment in natural resources. This was at the end of last year. Well, in mid-April, Leibowitz, their operating vice-president, came here and laid the true state of affairs in Lausanne before Bacon and myself. Without going into all of the details, Leibowitz invited me to go to Lausanne to see if we could be of assistance in getting World Equities back into a positive operational status. Now, as many of you are aware, I have personally been a long-time admirer of Manny Kellermann and over the past few years have one way or another built up a reasonable holding in the stock of W.E.L. for myself and my children." Jason then sketched out the details of his negotiations with Lord George Gordon-Gorham, his renegotiation of the investment of ten million into a two-year convertible loan, and his recent troubles with the Securities and Exchange Commission. He pointed out that the S.E.C. position left the company with no alternative but to drop the takeover. Otherwise, the government agency might have shut down all the company's American fund-raising activities overnight. His speech was a masterpiece of obvious fact

290

and artful avoidance of uncomfortable detail. He strongly emphasized the size of W.E.L. as a Steele Company customer and completely avoided any details of the performance trust. As he told it, the fifteen million that he had put into his Curaçao Trust was an utter necessity on his part in order to avoid any conflict of interest with his role in the Steele Company. He made it all sound extremely circumspect and virtuous.

When he finally paused for a glass of water, there was an uncomfortable silence in the room. The outside members were staring at Jason, and the company men were studying their note pads. At last, Stanton Harris cleared his throat. "And what would you like us to do now, Jason?"

Jason didn't miss the ironic emphasis on the "us." For a few seconds he toyed with the glass. "Well, Stan, I thought the board should be informed."

Harris shoved back his chair and rose to his feet. He was a small rotund man, and very set in his ways. He went about things with the precision of the prescriptionist that he had once been. "Informed," he roared. "Why, dammit man, you have not told us one thing that we have not read in the *Wall Street Journal* in the past month."

"Oh yes, he has." Jim Riley was now on his feet. "I've never heard anything about the family trust until today."

Jason turned to face this opposition from a new quarter. "Jim, there was no other way. You certainly wouldn't have me go make a play for W.E.L. and have all that stock for my own account at the same time. That wouldn't have been ethical."

Collins swung into the action. "Hey, wait a minute, one thing at a time. Stan has asked what Jason wants us to do, and I've got another question. How have you done this, Jason?"

Jason's face had now become chalk-white. "Well, in the absence of the board and because of the emergency nature of the proposition by Leibowitz, I went to the executive committee. Obviously I thought the proposition was a sound one. Bacon agreed. Jim Riley was off cruising in Greece." Riley nodded that that was so. "Creighton was out of pocket in Australia, but I discussed it with Henry."

Henry Higby, at the very opposite end of the table, jumped

to his feet. "Jason, that's a goddam lie. You told me you were going over there to look things over. You didn't say anything about giving or loaning those people ten million dollars. I told you to be very careful in dealing with those foreigners. There was no mention of your borrowing fifteen million for any stock for your children. You did mention there might be a block of common kicking about, but goddam it, man, you never said it was yours, and I told you anything like buying their common should go to the board."

"Apparently there's a misunderstanding, Henry," Jason answered very coolly.

"A misunderstanding. I guess there sure as hell is!"

"Gentlemen, gentlemen," Collins said. "There's no sense in losing our tempers. That's reserved for us Irish. What do you want us to do, Jason?"

Elliot Hall now spoke up. "I think I can help out here. Jason and I have worked out a loan agreement with the board of World Equities for this ten million. I think it would be most appropriate to have ratification by the board, even though Jason already has a majority of the executive committee approval, for it now appears that Henry did not agree." He was interrupted by Higby who was still standing.

"I sure as hell did not," he shouted.

Elliot ignored the interruption and continued on in his best courtroom manner. Privately, he was appalled by Higby's protest. He had been about board rooms a long time and could not countenance such behavior. Besides, his oldest allegiance was to Jason. "Even though there is this disagreement, the fact remains that a majority of those available on the executive committee did approve, and in all events, it might look best if, by routine resolution, the board approves the loan." He was again interrupted, this time by the still irate Stanton Harris.

"What about the fifteen million to his family trust, Mr. Hall?"

"I think it best we make that a matter for a second resolution by the board."

"Now, how in hell are you going to do that?" Collins demanded. "There's twenty-five million out of the till. It's all this company's dough, and it's all tied up in World Equities.

Right? Right. It's all one deal, yet you want to make it into two. That makes no sense."

Elliot had difficulty holding back his temper. "Look, Collins, this company pays me to be general counsel, and I'm telling you that as far as the corporate records are concerned, these are two separate and distinct transactions."

Collins snarled back. "And I'm saying to you, Mr. Counselor, that's a bunch of bullshit. The same people are involved in both moves, and the bucks are out of the same company and have gone to the same place."

"Gentlemen," Stanton Harris said, "may I suggest we have a fifteen-minute adjournment? And may I also suggest that we reconvene with Mr. Steele excused, as it would appear that it is a matter relating to him that is now before this board." The others grudgingly agreed.

Collins went down the hall and took possession of an empty office. He was closely followed by Higby.

"I told you the son of a bitch might try that, Mike. I just knew it in my bones."

Collins took a long drag of a cheroot. "Henry, you called it right, but that doesn't help matters very much, does it?"

"No, it doesn't," Higby allowed, "but goddam, I never told Jason he could do that. I never thought he'd go voting loans to his own kids."

When the rest of the outside faction had joined them, a strategy was decided upon; they agreed that nothing would be passed that day, allowing both Higby and Collins to seek outside counsel as to legal exposure on any move by the board. Collins reminded them of their responsibility to the company and told them they could be personally sued by any of the bond or shareholders for innumerable reasons. He stressed the importance of their retaining outside and more objective legal counsel.

A similar strategy was evolving in a smaller caucus in Jason Steele's office. Both Dan and Elliot were advising Jason to postpone the vote. "If we put this thing to a vote now, we're dead," Dan said.

"Okay, then, we'll play for a little time. That will let us get all the trust paperwork in order and will give me a chance to do a little politicking. I suppose if we go to a vote today and Coons stays out, it'll be another five to four, is that right?"

Dan nodded.

"Okay, so we have to swing two votes. I can handle that, if I get a little time."

Jason kicked his large swivel chair around and stared stonily out at the skyline. His action indicated that the meeting was at an end.

When the board reconvened, Jason was absent. Elliot Hall went into a detailed briefing on the conversion privileges within the ten-million-dollar loan. The board listened awhile but Collins soon lost patience and interrupted him. He demanded to see the documentation of the fifteen million that had been put into the Curaçao Trust. In answer, Elliot rather officiously stated that the papers were in his files in Boston, and not immediately available. There was an exchange of glances about the table.

In exasperation, Collins then proposed that the meeting adjourn for two weeks so all the papers could be brought together. A motion was passed to reconvene the meeting in New York two weeks hence.

6

Jason Steele spun around to his phone console, and after a quick glance at the company directory, savagely punched out a number. "Is Mr. Barreault there? . . . Yes, Mr. Steele. . . . Jacques? . . . Did you get the job done? . . . Good. . . . Could you come up right away? Thank you, that's fine . . ."

Jason flicked a second switch.

"Yes, Mr. Steele?"

"Jacques Barreault of the photography department will be up in a few minutes. Send him right in. And, Elizabeth, keep your eye on that meeting; let me know when it breaks."

"Yes, Mr. Steele."

Five minutes later, the buzzer announced the arrival of Jacques Barreault. Barreault was a swarthy young man, with long black hair. He wore flare pants and a brass-buttoned blue blazer. He was uncomfortable in the Tower and did not take the chair Jason offered him.

"So, it went all right, Jacques?"

"Ah, yes and no, sir. They turned out the lights at an unfortunate time to get the whole job—it wasn't an infrared scene —but I think I have enough." Barreault inclined his head toward a manila envelope tucked under his elbow.

"Prints?" Jason's hand reached across the desk, and the man hurriedly handed him the envelope.

"Yes, the prints and the negatives. I developed them myself."

"That was smart." Jason ripped open the envelope and studied the glossies. After a careful thumbing, he looked up with a curious smile. "You did well, very well." He stacked the prints and stood up, reaching into his pocket. "Let me see, our deal was a thousand dollars, that right?"

"That's right."

Jason drew forth a thick roll and peeled off ten one-hundred-dollar bills. He handed them to Barreault. "And it is clearly understood that only you and I are to ever know of this?"

"Oh, yes, sir, that's right, sir."

As Barreault left the room, Jason turned his attention to the pictures. They were photographs of his sister-in-law, Jean Patterson, and David Coons and had been taken the previous night in the Steele Company guest apartments. Jason had ordered a one-way mirrored wall built in the master bedroom the day before. He had thought it wise to have a little insurance in case his control over the board weakened, and when he learned that Jean would be on hand for the party, he thought it probable David Coons would oblige him and provide that insurance.

There was no question as to the identity of the lovers. Several were of Jean undressing before the mirror with a naked

Coons waiting on the bed. Jason compared Jean with Janice. She was fuller-breasted and wider through the hips and, from what the pictures showed, far less inhibited.

Jason shoved the prints back in the envelope and went to a large hunting painting on the wall behind his desk. He lifted it aside and pressed a knot in the paneling. The entire panel swung open to reveal a small safe. He placed the envelope inside and hurriedly closed it as his buzzer began to ring. The directors' meeting was breaking up. He grabbed his jacket and hurried out.

Although Jason was affable as he thanked everyone for coming, the strained relations were apparent. Stanton Harris and Henry Higby were barely civil. As Michael Collins strode by him with a very offhand good-bye, Jason said, "Mike, I'll look forward to seeing you in New York in a couple of weeks."

"Prepare yourself, Jason. It gets hot in New York in June," was Collins' laconic reply.

David Coons was among the last to leave. "When you heading back for Chicago, Dave?" Jason asked.

"Oh, I thought I might grab the first Braniff flight in the morning. I understand Stan's planning on taking the Lear right now. I don't want to hold him up."

Jason was all smiles. "Hell, Dave, we'll rustle up a plane for you first thing. I wonder if we might get together for a drink later on?"

"That would be fine with me, Jason. You name it."

A half hour later, Jason entered David Coons' suite in the guest apartments. He went behind the bar and poured a couple of stiff Jack Daniels. David was going to need it, he thought grimly. Once seated, Jason placed his glass on the cocktail table and emitted a deep sigh. "Well, David. It looks like I've got myself a tight one."

"You aren't kidding, Jason. Talk about a rock and a hard place, why, man, there was a time there, this afternoon, I thought they were going to order up a rope."

"Yeah, well, if I'd pulled it off, they'd all be around for the bows. How far do you think they're going to push me?"

"I really don't know, Jason. You forget where you heard this, but Higby and Collins are getting some outside legal advice. They don't trust Hall. To put it mildly, that board's scared shitless."

Jason coolly appraised David as he asked, "What about you?"

David returned his stare with unblinking eyes. "Jason, I'll help you where I can, but I don't know how far this directors' liability thing that Collins and Higby were mouthing off about goes, I really don't."

"Can I count on you in a showdown?"

"Jesus, Jason, it's going to have to depend on what the showdown's all about. No sweat on the ten million for W.E.L. I go along with that because you made the move for the company. But this fifteen for your children—I don't know. As Higby said, how the hell can I vote on that?"

Jason stood up and moved behind his armchair, leaning on it as he spoke. "Look, Dave, we're two guys who've built something from nothing. Now maybe I haven't learned yet all the right ways of running one of these publicly owned companies, and maybe, though I'm not admitting it, my play for W.E.L. was a mistake. But hell, man, it wasn't many years ago, you were running that bush operation and you came to me for bucks for equipment. Now I need a friend."

David had also risen to his feet. "Jason, I agree with everything you've said. I'm grateful for the lease of those planes. But because of the planes, I felt I shouldn't vote for that merger on Western Investors today. Perhaps the best solution would be for me to pay you out, and pick up the present residual on those planes. That way I won't be in a box the next time."

"Shit, Dave. I need help, right here and now coming up in New York."

"I know that, Jason, but what you can't get through that thick head of yours is that there's this liability thing. You left those guys reading about themselves in the *Wall Street Journal* for a month. They had no idea what you were up to, and this Children's Trust for the fifteen, that's a real tough one. This liability business has got them all bugged, and frankly, it worries me, too."

Jason drained his glass loudly and smacked it on the table. It was time to play his trump.

"Dave, you're voting and you're voting with me and I'll tell you why. You've been fucking around out here with my sister-in-law, and now you think you can just grab a plane and go back home. Well, that isn't the way it's going to be. You either play it my way, or some photographs of you and Jean wind up in Minnesota . . ."

7

A growing company is a delicate and precisely balanced gyro. With the failure at Lausanne, the whirling wheel of Steele Minerals slipped into the erratic and teetering winddown of a child's toy. The juggernaut of Jason Steele was no longer the darling of Wall Street. A man could make mistakes, and he had. The brokers who loved him the most left him first.

In the week after the announced withdrawal from W.E.L., the Steele Minerals stock was pounded down to nine dollars a share. This stock was the centerpole of Jason's tent. As it came down, Elizabeth Wales could no longer fend off the calls from his bankers.

Jason's bland, smooth exterior had vanished. He no longer made any pretense of being in complete control. Since his week in Washington, he had lost twenty pounds. His pants hung in folds from the belt loops and his custom shirts were slack at the neck. He was haggard and irritable. Elizabeth caught the full brunt of this irritability and averaged three crying sessions a day in the middle office.

Now her voice filled his office. "Mr. Steele, it's Mr. Oglethorpe again. This is his second call this morning, and there was one late yesterday."

Jason answered the walls with an audible sigh. "Yes, I know. I guess I better take it this time."

Harvey Oglethorpe was the executive vice-president of the

United Bank of Boston. He was the man above the vice-president who regularly handled his account. Jason had avoided the regular man for the past two weeks. Oglethorpe was not to be avoided so easily. He picked up the receiver.

"Hello, Harvey."

"Good morning, Jason, we've been trying to reach you for some time."

"Yes, I know, Harvey, I've just been flat out."

"Well, I can understand that. Jason, what concerns us is your note coming due on the first of July. You may recall that at the end of April, you borrowed three million. We rolled that in with your old loan for the million and a half for a sixty-day renewal."

"Yes, I remember."

"Well, Jason, that note is coming up in another week, and I've been trying to do some planning for the third quarter. In late April, we were holding eleven million dollars' worth of Steele Minerals stock."

"Yes, I know all that."

"The collateral people have just brought to my attention that the value of that holding is just a shade under three million, using yesterday's close."

"Yes, Harvey, I know."

"Jason, as you are aware, we normally like to maintain a two-to-one ratio or better. You can never tell when the bank examiners might walk in. Now, we're aware of your problems, but we're going to need at least another six million of collateral or it will be necessary to cut down substantially on that loan. We would prefer the latter."

"I understand. Let me talk with my staff and we'll see what we can do."

"Then I'll hear from you on what you're going to do in the next few days?"

"Yes."

"That would be fine, Jason. It is quite urgent. Oh, and one last thing, could you have your treasurer check to see that the stock we hold is registered?"

Steele now knew that selling his collateral had been discussed at the top in the United of Boston. He grimaced for an

299

instant and then there was the semblance of a smile as he thought to himself, I wonder what those bastards will do when they find they're holding unmarketable stock.

In the next week, there were several other calls of the same tenor. The Steele stock hovered between eight and ten. All of the top company executives had incentive stock options in the high twenties. Many had put up stock for loans to buy new homes and cars and the other material benefits that trail in the wake of a corporate comet. They, too, were getting phone calls. The numbers were smaller, but the pressure was the same. All of this worked like a fine hard dust in the wheels of the Steele machine. The irritability and uncertainty filtered downward. Soon, even the telephone operators' normally cheery greetings took on a note of near-desperation.

One morning Jason took an unexpected call from Bill Leavitt, the director of personnel. "Mr. Steele, Mr. Bacon thought it best that I bring this matter to your attention."

"What's on your mind?" His tone should have warned Leavitt that Jason needed no more problems.

"Well, sir, it's hard to exactly put into words. All of this attention in the newspapers of late has caused quite a stir among the employees. It's doing me no good in holding some of our good young people, and in fact, everyone seems to be getting so jumpy that the work just isn't getting out."

Jason Steele lost his temper. He held the receiver away from his mouth and shouted, "Then can the bastards."

Leavitt persisted in a conciliatory tone. "Sir, I normally would, but it's not that simple. There's been a marked slackening in new applications. Replacements could be a problem."

"Jesus, Bill, people are your problem, not mine."

"I recognize the responsibility, sir, but just a few words from you, the board chairman and chief operating officer, will do far more than a lot of head chopping. If we chop heads, I think it'll only make things worse."

Despite his anger, Jason saw the logic in this. "Well, what the hell do you want me to do?"

"If I set up a meeting of the top operating personnel, and you gave a small talk, I'm sure things will quiet down real quick."

"All right, when and where?"

"What about tomorrow afternoon in the officers' dining room, say four o'clock? That'll only cost us a half hour till quitting time."

As he marched into the huge room the next afternoon, Jason made every effort to be the Jason of old. Smiling confidently as he was greeted by the upper echelon of the Steele Company, he went directly to the microphone which had been set up.

"Gentlemen, the news of our funeral is a bit premature. At the outset, I want to dispel any and all rumors that there are going to be firings or salary cutbacks. We're going right ahead with business as usual.

"I would be less than candid if I did not tell you there are some areas where it might be best we tighten our belt. We have been described in the press as a flamboyant go-go company. This has hurt and I'd like to correct it. They talk a lot about our planes and offices. Sure, we are a big aircraft user. Our people cover that much more ground in any day. However, to bring our true image back into focus, it might be best to double up on some of these trips, where we can.

"As to our offices, they stay as they are. I am certain there are other economies in small areas that can be effected. In the executive dining room, we will start paying for our own lunches. I would be very grateful if you will get across to your staff that the phones on their desks are there for company business. It comes down to leadership, men, and I'm counting on you to set the proper example. Where we can save money sensibly, we should. I will be personally grateful for any and all assistance in this area. We've got a healthy, growing company, and if we pull together, it's going to stay that way. I confidently expect we'll easily exceed our performance of last year." Jason paused for a round of applause. "The company is in no way busted as some prophets of doom have been saying. We are going to be in a tight cash position for a time but we've been in those before.

"Now, with twenty-twenty hindsight, anyone can say the move for World Equities was a mistake. I went into it with my eyes wide open to protect our best customer. If it was a mistake, it was made with the best of intentions. That's behind us, now. For the future, we've never had more hot projects. We're getting a rig into Greenland this fall . . ." Gone from Jason's mind were the nagging phone calls. He was the Jason of old, the messiah of tax shelter for the masses, hitting his stride.

The meeting ended with a thunderous roar of applause. The next day, the Steele Company stock rose a full point.

8

In the Steele Tower, the new optimism was by no means universal. Despite his pep talk, Jason continued to vent his frustration all the next day on his immediate staff. The smallest annoyance would trigger an explosion. By the end of the day, when he slammed out of the office saying he was going to Los Angeles for an unexpected conference, Elizabeth Wales was again on the verge of tears. She was still not quite composed when she called the Steele home to relay the information about Jason.

That Jason would not be home that night didn't concern Janice in the least. Indeed, she was glad of a respite from keeping up the pretense. Jason had done little traveling over the past weeks. But Janice sensed Elizabeth's distress and was concerned. Within Jason's business circle, Janice was fondest of Elizabeth. She knew Elizabeth had always been a stabilizing influence on Jason and she admired her for her ability to stay calm under the most adverse circumstances. That she was now losing control indicated that things were very bad indeed inside the Steele Tower.

"Elizabeth, what's going to happen?" Janice asked.

"I don't know, but I'm very worried," Elizabeth replied. As Jason's personal assistant, she had always felt it necessary to be very circumspect in her relations with Jason's wife. But she was almost past the point of caring. She had taken the job with Jason against the advice of many of her more conservative friends. Divorced and childless, she felt she wanted a more exciting working milieu than that provided by a bank or brokerage house. She had not regretted her choice until recently. There had been times in the past when she had doubts—doubts about the manner in which Jason was conducting his business or was handling people. But although she was his personal assistant, there were many facets of the business she knew nothing—and preferred to know nothing—about. Jason was careful to keep it that way, for he knew Elizabeth was a strong asset to his personal staff and he wanted to preserve her loyalty. Consequently, Elizabeth had no particular reason to be concerned until Jason's involvement with World Equities. She had watched him become progressively more tense, more irascible, at times almost irrational in his behavior. Now, her loyalty to Jason was being put to the test. She knew he needed her but she wasn't at all sure how long she would take the pressure and unpleasantness.

When Janice suggested she join her for a swim and dinner, she decided to accept, although she had the feeling there would be only one topic of conversation. Surprisingly, however, Janice laid down some ground rules as soon as she had arrived. They could talk about anything but what went on inside the Steele Minerals Company. For a while the rules were observed. Janice talked about the children and about their summer plans. Elizabeth discussed her last trip to Europe. But several cocktails and after-dinner brandies later, Janice suddenly asked, "Well, which of them did he take with him tonight?"

Elizabeth's discomfort was obvious in her slowness to respond.

"Elizabeth," Janice continued, "I've known about them for some time. Now, who was it?"

"Betsey Brine was the stewardess on the plane." Her answer came from deep in her throat.

"So it's the blonde tonight, is it?" Janice took another gulp of brandy. "I'm sorry, Elizabeth. I've broken my own rules."

"It's time I went home, anyway. Thank you for letting me unwind. It was just what I needed." As Janice walked her to her car, she asked in an offhand way, "Elizabeth, why didn't

Jason answer the Prescott Company telegram in Lausanne?"

"Why, Janice," Elizabeth answered in surprise, "it didn't call for any answer. They said they had no interest. Why, you know I'd have him answer if . . ."

Janice broke in with, "Oh yes, I know." She was abrupt in her farewell and she turned back hurriedly to the lit doorway. Her hurry was to hide her tears.

Her unhappiness had turned to anger by morning. She packed an overnight bag and caught an early Braniff jet to New York. As the plane leveled off at altitude, Janice studied the fleeting fleece of cumulus beneath her. She knew she had to get out of Houston, to get away and think, do anything and nothing, yet get away from Houston and Jason.

Janice fell from cloud-gazing into a light sleep. As the aircraft touched down at La Guardia, the thump of the wheels brought her awake. She collected her small bag from beneath her seat and was the first off the flight to the taxi line. When she got out of the taxi at the Sutton Place apartment, she was assisted by a new doorman. He was polite and apologetic, but he made her identify herself before he let her in. Once inside the penthouse, she went directly to the phone, dialed the William Arthur and Company offices and asked for Mr. Leibowitz.

The telephone operator pondered this request for a moment. "I'm sorry, madam. Mr. Leibowitz is no longer here. Ah—one moment, I'll connect you with someone who may be able to help." There was an annoying click-clack and then a soft voice. "Sharon Cohen speaking."

Janice had to think for a moment. "Oh yes, Miss Cohen. I wonder if you might help me. I'm a friend of Ted Leibowitz and happened to be passing through New York. I wanted to say hello."

"Well, Miss, ah . . ." There was a pause.

"Carter, Janice Carter."

"Yes, Miss Carter. I guess you didn't know Mr. Leibowitz had left World Equities."

"Oh, I read something about that. I just had the off hunch

he might be in New York." Janice's dejection carried through the wire.

Miss Cohen became sympathetic. "Hold on, I'll see if the bossman has any ideas." The line went silent. Janice was thankful she had been quick-witted enough to use her maiden name.

Miss Cohen was quickly back. "You might be in luck. Mr. Arthur thinks Mr. Leibowitz is due into the Carlyle later today."

Janice left word with the Carlyle desk. She then called her father to arrange a meeting in Boston the following day.

In the afternoon Ted Leibowitz returned her call. When she said she was only staying over one night, and was he by any chance free, he quickly lied and said he was, and he'd be delighted to take her to dinner. A pretty Swissair stewardess lost out that night.

At eight o'clock, Janice welcomed him at the penthouse door. He had never seen her look prettier. She was tanned a golden brown from her spring tennis and swimming. He opened his arms and she came into them very naturally and they kissed. "Stand back, let me look at you," was his greeting.

She stepped back in the hallway and did a gay pirouette as Ted closed the door. "Did anyone ever tell you you're beautiful?"

"Why, thank you, kind sir." Her brown hair was combed out straight, long and light, and her green eyes had a sparkle that he had not seen since their afternoon skiing. From her clothes, Ted guessed she had no thought of their dining out. She wore perfectly fitting bright green and white pants, and a casual silk shirt. "I see you're dressed for dinner," he teased. "Will it be Pavillon or 21 tonight?"

"I thought we might have a drink and then decide."

"Agreed. Let me be bartender. What would you like?" Ted went to the bar to find everything set out and ready.

"There's a bottle of sparkling burgundy in the icebox underneath. I thought I might have some of that." Ted set the bottle and glasses on a tray and carried them over to her on the long couch by the picture window. He went through an exaggerated ritual of uncorking the wine and pouring Janice a sample taste. "To your satisfaction, Madame, or shall we send it back?"

"It's perfect. Pour yourself some and come sit beside me."

Ted did as he was told. "Here's to the ski slopes." Janice laughed. He drew her close and gave her a long kiss. She suddenly twisted out of his arms, hurriedly lit a cigarette, and after a deep draw, began to pace up and down the large room. Finally she stopped directly in front of him. "I'm leaving Jason."

Her announcement didn't surprise Ted. He felt sure she would not have called him had she not reached this decision. He let her continue without interrupting.

"I've held on just as long as I could. Probably longer. I'd even hoped to stick it out through his present mess." Janice paused for another puff. She seemed to have thought it all out and was now very calm. "Well, I can't. It's not worth fighting for. Soon there'd be nothing left of either of us." After a few paces, she turned and looked levelly at Ted. "You know, it's not this World Equities mess, either. I don't know who's really responsible for that, although I know who Jason thinks is. What I do care about is saving something of me, for myself and my children. Maybe even starting something new." She made an attempt at a smile, but her eyes were misty. "Our life has been a lie for a long long time. When I learned about his girls, I was terribly hurt, but I didn't want to face up to it. I kept thinking he'd get tired of that sort of thing and would come back to me after a while. He used to need me, I think. I kept hoping maybe he would again and maybe we could save something. But it got worse, not better. And I didn't even hope any more. You talked him into that World Equities and now he's in trouble up to his neck and I don't give a damn. How's that for a loyal wife? Right now he's off in Los Angeles, probably trying to borrow money and being comforted by one of his stewardess whores. And his wife? Why, she's necking in their New York penthouse with the man probably responsible for his downfall. Now, isn't that a happy scene. Just shows what money can do for you." Janice's monologue wound to a close. She snubbed out her cigarette and stood by the sofa.

306

Ted got up and put his arms around her. He spoke softly. "You're doing the right thing and we've both known it was going to happen. It was just a question of when."

Janice drew back. "As for you, Ted Leibowitz, you're not much different than Jason and his greedy flock. At first I thought you were just another of the same breed. I've met so many of them. All they ever talk of is a new way to make money or a new tax dodge or a new way to take the public. But what fascinates me about you is that you at least seem to treat it as a game. And you're subtle about it. Everyone always has to know what Jason's done and how much he's made. It's as if he always had to be impressing someone. You don't seem to care about that, and that makes you different. I think you could laugh if you lost." Her voice trailed off. "Jason can't."

Ted poured another glass of burgundy. "I hope what you say, Jan, is true—that I could laugh. I hope so; but don't ever forget, I like to win and I play to win. It is sort of a game, but it's a very expensive game. Other people set the rules and I play around them. That's my way of operating. As for Jason, I've always had the feeling that he was out to prove something to someone, or out to beat somebody. You said it yourself—he always has to be impressing someone. I never worried about it much in our business dealings, because I figured as long as we owned his stock, and he was a winner, then it was a great piggyback ride for the share-holders of World Equities. And it worked okay for us, but as to what Jason was trying to prove, I'm not sure that it wasn't all mixed up with you and your marriage."

"What do you mean?"

"Well, the more obvious explanation of his drive is that he was determined to supplant Manny Kellermann as the big-gest international wheeler-dealer of all time. Less obvious, but I think closer to the truth, is that he wanted to beat your father —and always has."

"Come on. What you're saying is Jason's got an in-law Oedipus complex."

"Something like that. You asked me and that's my opin-ion. Now come here. To hell with Jason Steele."

307

He pulled her down to him and into a long embrace. As he started to unbutton her shirt she murmured in his ear, "Agreed. Screw the whole world of Jason Steele."

"My, my, they never taught you that at Radcliffe."

"There are other things they never taught me."

Janice sat up and with a shrug of her shoulders, she tossed aside the shirt and reached behind to free her lush breasts of their lace bra.

His lips closed on her breast, his tongue teasing her nipple. Lightly he walked his index finger down her firm belly. He could feel her flesh rise with pleasure. He traced several idle circles about her navel and ran his fingers quickly up and down her thigh. Janice suddenly raised her buttocks up off the couch so he could pull off her slacks and panties. She let her thighs part and his fingers found her soft and expectant.

By now, Janice was pulsing with anticipation. As she reached toward his trousers, he sat up and hurried out of his clothes. He entered her, thrusting in and up with such force that she cried out. She reached up and wrapped her arms around him, and as she pulled him down hard on top of her, they both gasped with the intensity of the act.

9

On the morning of the special meeting of the Steele Company's board of directors, the traffic of Park Avenue already shimmered and danced crazily in the heavy heat. Traffic sputtered, horns blared, cab drivers sweated and snarled, and tempers flared.

Matters were not very different in the air-conditioned suite at the Waldorf Towers. The big living room crackled with tension. The members of the board were sprawled about in shirtsleeves as Jason Steele brought the meeting to order. His opening announcement set the tone of the chaos that would follow. Two days ago, he said, he had received the following letter of resignation from the board from David Coons. What Jason did not say was that in the same letter, he had also received an exercise of the purchase option of the lease aircraft and a certified check for the outstanding balance. His night of the mirrors had shattered in his own face, and he was left without even an ear in the enemy camp. The board was now balanced five to five, provided he himself could vote, and that was highly unlikely, under the circumstances.

During his two weeks of grace, Jason had carefully re-examined his relations and dealings with each of the six outsiders, probing for weak spots where he could bring leverage to his side of the table. He had found only two. Michael Collins' real estate firm was on a retainer to advise a Western Investors subsidiary on a garden house condominium development in La Jolla. The fee was $50,000. Jason had considered going to work on Collins and concluded that the man would just laugh in his face and tear up the contract. The second possibility was a joint venture in potash in Saskatchewan with Crawford Creighton's company. When Jason went to his Canadian vice-president to find out the status of that project, he learned that Creighton had an iron-clad operating agreement and that the Steele Company was two months behind on its payments under the work commitment. His options had just about run out.

When he finished reading Coons' letter of resignation, the first question came from Stanton Harris. "Jason, do you have any idea what precipitated David's resignation?"

Jason had settled himself on the sofa behind a coffee table littered with papers. He stroked his chin before he replied. "Yes, Stan, I think I do. I think our leasing him some aircraft caused him some personal embarrassment at the last meeting. As you know, we've been using a lot of his equipment and people to fly seismic crews into Greenland. His business is really booming."

"And that's all you know?" Harris asked.

"Yes." Jason answered, very coolly.

Michael Collins boomed out, "Well, let's get back to where we left off in the last meeting."

Jason replied. "Mike, as you know, I was out of the room

309

and Dan had the chair, so it might be appropriate for him to take over. Would you like me to leave?"

"That's not necessary," Collins said. "You might as well be heard and hear what goes on firsthand." The other members indicated their agreement.

Dan Bacon took the lead. "When we adjourned, Elliot Hall was saying the board should consider the activities in Lausanne as two separate and distinct transactions, and had proposed that the board ratify the loan of ten million dollars to World Equities for two years at . . ."

The battle lines were clearly reestablished when Collins butted in. "Let's cut the bullshit, Dan. We went through that before, and I said they had to be looked at together, since the money went the same way."

Dan became edgy and loosened his tie. "Yes, well, that's where we were, Elliot, would you like to continue?"

Elliot Hall got to his feet and read a lengthy draft of a proposed motion to ratify the loan in Lausanne. As he sat down, the murmured seconding motions of Foxx and Palmer were simultaneous.

Dan then asked whether there was any comment prior to a vote. Collins answered, "Dan, you can't go at this piecemeal. This board hasn't enough facts to make an intelligent vote. I want the minutes to record my objection."

Collins had raised a touchy subject. Elliot Hall was usually responsible for the taking of minutes but over the years this formality had been handled in an increasingly offhand fashion. He always kept quite accurate notes, but the final written record that was put into the corporate minutes book was subject to the editorializing of Jason Steele. Elliot's notes and the final minutes didn't always agree.

Dan looked uncomfortable; Jason carefully studied the toes of his polished shoes; Elliot rustled about among his papers. It was clear no one really wanted to test Collins. Dan considered his alternatives and concluded that if the pattern of the last meeting was any indication, a vote would be futile. So he turned to Collins and said, "All right, Michael, what specifically would you all like to know in order to be sure of an intelligent vote?" There was the slightest attempt at irony in his question.

"Hall said that he had the paperwork on the Curaçao Trust in his files in Boston. I think we ought to see that and the records of the purchases for openers. In other words, I would like to see exactly what we're getting for the shareholders' money."

The lid of the box was lifted. Each question led to more questions rather than answers. When the purchase records were shown, they revealed that the fifteen million was better than twice the present market value of the trust holdings in World Equities stock.

John Palmer was asked about the pension fund borrowings in Pittsburgh and the resultant status of working capital within the company. His answers were truthful and the desperate financial straits of the company became apparent. He was asked about receivables, and this brought out the large debits on behalf of World Equities and Western Investors. The W.E.L. debit led into the Greenland transaction. Palmer was asked the makeup and financial strength of the Canadian partnership that had bought into the play. As he didn't know anything about it, he referred the question to Dan Bacon. Dan's answer was vague; he merely spoke of a law firm in Toronto. The room became fraught with uncertainty.

Henry Higby kept glancing at his watch. His wife had booked them for the afternoon sailing of the *Queen Elizabeth,* despite the troubles of Steele Minerals. One o'clock came, and the meeting continued without lunch. At one-thirty Higby left.

Jason started to count noses. The import of Higby's departure had not escaped the others. There were several uneasy looks about the suite as the door closed.

By two o'clock, Jason sensed that both Collins and Creighton were anxious to get away. Both had said at the opening that they were due at other meetings that afternoon. He put a gentle elbow into Dan's ribs and indicated a note pad he held on his knees. The pad read, "Put it to a vote on the ten."

Dan broke into a detailed discussion of debit aging between John Palmer and Stanton Harris. "Gentlemen, it's get-

311

ting well along, and we still have this motion by Elliot Hall that has been properly seconded. I suggest we get on with the meeting and put it to a vote."

The resolution to approve the ten-million-dollar loan was approved, five to four, Jason casting the winning vote. Michael Collins jumped to his feet. "Jason, I don't think it proper that you vote on this matter, and I want my objection to this vote so recorded. You're the guy that made this play, and I don't think you should be voting on such a close issue to approve your own actions. For that matter, I'm not sure Hall or Bacon should be voting." There were shouts of agreement from the others.

Jason lost his temper for the first time that day. "Christ, Michael. It was a routine operational loan to save our best customer. No different than drilling a hole or anything else. Perfectly routine, and I see no reason why I shouldn't vote."

"Well, dammit, I do," Collins heatedly answered. "When are you going to learn that this company belongs to the stockholders, not you? We've got them and the government breathing down our necks. We could get our asses sued from here till hell freezes over. Both collectively and as individuals."

"I still think the ten million loan was a routine operation." Jason had regained his composure.

"Counselor." Collins was now glaring at Elliot Hall. "Will you tell the chairman about shareholder class action suits? Christ, if this comes out, they can eat us alive and they will."

Elliot started to get to his feet, but Jason waved him down. "Look, I've voted and that's that."

"The hell it is, and I suppose you're planning to vote on the fifteen for your Children's Trust too?"

"No, I don't think that would be right." Jason returned Collins' glare and the telltale color was now high in his cheeks.

"Neither do I, and if your vote stands, then I hereby move that this board instruct the general counsel to institute all necessary proceedings to get back the fifteen million that's gone to Curaçao." What Collins was saying in no uncertain terms was that Jason would never get board approval for his loan to his Children's Trust, and once that was voted down, the majority of the board would demand that Elliot Hall bring theft proceedings against him. There was nothing that the insiders could do to stop it.

Dan leapt up. "Now, Michael, one thing at a time."

"No dice, Dan. If you guys think you can stack the deck the way you're doing, I want no part of it."

"Well, why don't we break for lunch and come back at it in an hour."

Collins glanced at his watch and then at Creighton, who was quietly stuffing his attaché case. "No, let's get this settled, once and for all. I said I had an appointment two weeks ago. My motion stands, unless the last vote is rescinded."

Dan conferred with Jason and Elliot. "The last vote is rescinded," he said. "Now what?"

"Look, Dan," Collins explained. "We all know this is one hell of a tight corner. Now we think there's a way out. There is room for unanimous approval of the World Equities loan, provided we do something about cleaning up this fifteen million in the Steele Children's Trust. We propose that Jason put up with the company marketable securities at 125 percent of that loan as a cushion; that he agree to pay back the company any losses that ultimately come out of that transaction, and that he write an agreement to hold the board harmless from anything that arises from the Children's Trust. He is to put the trust holdings in Houston with the company. If he does that, then we'll unanimously approve the first ten million to W.E.L. Let Hall put it in legalese, subject to final board approval, of course."

Dan leaned toward Jason. "I don't see any other way. He's got us by the balls."

Jason again studied his toes while his mind raced about like a cornered rat. If he didn't go along, they would hit him for theft. If he did go along, how could he ever come up with that kind of collateral? His one glimmer of hope was Janice's personal holdings. There wasn't much more he could lose, but he was determined not to let the others know just how far down they had him. He stood up. "Goddam it," he said. "I know you have every reason to conclude what you have, but you're wrong. I made this play for the company. You're holding my feet to the fire because it didn't work. I just wonder what you would be saying if things had gone the other way. I don't agree that it should be a personal responsibility, but okay, damn it, I'll do what you want."

10

There was a decision made in Houston that same morning which was also vital to the way of life of Jason Steele. The week before the New York board meeting, Janice had returned to Houston. She had come back full of parental and legal advice, and she meant to have it out with Jason, and to tell him of her decision. She was willing to stay for a limited time but on her own terms. But she hadn't seen Jason at all. He had not been home in over a week.

That morning, the sky was cloudless and a warm wind from the south rustled the lush greenery by the Steele swimming pool. Janice found it a perfect day for sun-bathing; the tranquillity and warmth soon lulled her into a light sleep.

Her nap was broken by the scrape of an aluminum deck chair on the flagstones. Janice removed her sunshades with a sigh to find her sister sitting close by.

"Hi, Jeannie. Put on your swimsuit. The water's beautiful."

"No. I didn't come for a swim." Jean Patterson's eyes were full of fire and there was an uncharacteristic stiffness in her bearing.

Janice had risen to tuck her hair beneath her swim cap. "Hey, what is it?"

"It's Dave Coons and me and Jason."

"What have you got to do with David Coons and Jason?"

Jean blurted out the whole story of her relations with Coons, and the consequences. Janice was faint with shock. She couldn't believe her husband would use her own sister for blackmail, and yet she knew Jean would have no reason to lie. She suddenly felt she couldn't stay in the house another day.

When the children came home from school that afternoon, they were hustled into fresh clothes and into the packed
station wagon. Their questions were not answered. Janice
drove to the airport herself, leaving no word with Clayton or
the other servants as to where she was going. Clayton saw the
set of her jaw and the hurried ferocity of her packing and
knew it was not his place to ask.

At the airport, Janice called her father and made arrangements to be met. They arrived at the Carter home just after
midnight.

The contrails of their paths might have passed that night,
for a weary Jason was heading west. He reached home at three
A.M. and learned that his home was empty.

11

As Jason slowly came down the stairs, his thoughts
wholly revolved around his tribulations as he saw them, a
matins litany of rogues and mishaps. Leibowitz, the double-
crosser, the back-lashing Kellermann, Bernstein from the
S.E.C., obstinate and self-righteous, Higby and the other old
ladies on his board, Collins and the others, all running for
cover. Then he looked at the empty chair at the dining room
table, and came full circle back to Janice; Janice, who held the
life ring in his last chance for survival. And not only the life
ring, but also the raft from which he could rebuild his empire.
And she was gone.

Jason left his breakfast untouched. He went out to the
patio and slumped in a dew-laden chair. There could be countless reasons why Janice had gone, he thought, but only one
place she could be just now. She had gone back to the world
of the Carters. In all the years of their marriage, he had never
completely seduced her away from the forms and values she
was born into. And, in spite of his success, and although at one
point he could have bought them all out, he had never meas-

ured up in her eyes to the solidity of the Carter system. Whatever he tried to do for Janice, whàtever he had given her was always accepted with graciousness, but never, except in the early days, with much enthusiasm.

He recognized that he had always resented the Carter power. That was why he'd broken with Boston. And Janice had come with him willingly then, he thought. He remembered their first days in Houston and the big parties they'd thrown, parties that were important to him so he could become known. Janice had been rather uncomfortable with many of the people, but he had written it off as shyness. He had never for a moment suspected that what he ascribed to shyness might be embarrassment at his obvious drive to be somebody in Houston. He had to admit Janice had been a good sport then. She never let her own feelings come out.

Later, when Steele Minerals started to move, he had insisted she travel with him, and they'd gone all over the world. He had supposed that she liked that sort of life, but the truth was she wanted to stay close to her own nest. That hadn't been the case in their first years in Essex when she resented being tied down. He knew now that Janice had changed but he had been too busy or too insensitive then to realize it.

Still, he thought, it had only been in the last few years that their marriage had started to come apart in every way, even in bed. He had had no qualms about playing around. That was all an accepted part of the world he moved in. Rarely did Janice say anything about it. Perhaps if she had, it might have been better.

So much for the past, Jason thought. What am I going to do now that she's gone? For tax and estate reasons over the years, many of their holdings were in joint name, including 150,000 shares of Prescott Company stock. He'd bought that block for Janice four years ago, hoping to impress his father-in-law. Typically, Lawrence Carter had never commented, although Jason was sure that he knew. At $54 a share, the Prescott shares were worth over eight million. There was also her own family trust. The last time he had looked at the portfolio several years ago, the market value of her share was $35 million. With Boston prudence, it had probably grown from there.

This fifty untapped millions of borrowing power was what he had counted on when he had said "Yes" to Michael Collins.

Jason left the patio and went upstairs to her room. As far as he could see, she had taken very little. In the wall safe behind the long mirror in her closet, every piece of jewelry he had ever given her was still in its place. Only the children's pictures and a few other items were missing from the makeup table. Little else.

If there was hope for the continued existence of the legend of Jason Steele, Janice had to come back. The Carter wealth had been the grease for the launching of his ship, and now held the last line that might hold her off the rocks. Jason went to his library and punched out the Carter number.

A maid informed him that Janice was out with her mother and the children were having swimming lessons at the yacht club. That was typical of Janice, Jason thought. Never waste a moment. He asked the maid to tell Janice that he had called and to say he would appreciate it if she returned the call.

Jason left the empty mansion and drove his Cadillac downtown. The Cadillac was part of the economy move. The big limousines had been placed on blocks in the company hangar, and the purchasing department had replaced them with new Coupe de Villes for Jason and Dan. His drive into the city was a welcome distraction, and on the way he talked himself out of his depression as he'd done so many times lately. He resolved that he would let nothing shake him further; he would put up a good fight to the very end.

He strode through the office reception area, whistling and with a chipper hello for all the pretty faces. His mood did not escape Elizabeth Wales or Marty Darnley. They exchanged arched eyebrows as he disappeared through the door to his inner office.

Elizabeth followed him in with his morning mail and the message that John Palmer wanted to see him as soon as possible. "What's on Palmer's mind?" Jason asked.

"I don't know."

"Then have him come up right away," he replied, as he leafed through the mail. The first thing he saw was the final demand notice on his loan from the United Bank of Boston.

He knew that he should never have let Oglethorpe's call go unattended, but he had had no alternative.

Palmer came in and stood nervously by the corner of the long desk, shifting his weight from foot to foot like a little boy. Jason's eyes finally came up from the correspondence. "John, my boy, what's on your mind?" The heartiness of his chief caught Palmer off balance. "Here, have a seat. Have you had your morning coffee? I haven't." He pushed a button and ordered the coffee before Palmer could speak.

Leaning forward and nervously clearing his throat, Palmer said, "Jason, we've gotten a bitch of a letter from the S.E.C. It's their deficiency letter regarding our proxy statement. Their interrogatory is longer than the material we sent them."

"Jesus, will they ever let up!" For a moment, Jason almost lost his temper but he remembered his resolve. "Well, what do they want?"

"They've asked for a mountain of work. I could take a couple of months to assemble the documentation they're asking for. And of course, you realize we can't have an annual meeting for the stockholders until they approve the proxy material."

"Well, that might be a blessing in disguise." The last thing he wanted to face was a gaggle of querulous stockholders. Jason eyed Palmer, who was more nervous than ever. "Might as well have your people get at it, but don't push 'em too hard. We could use some time. What are the big questions?"

"They want the supporting agreements on the Greenland sale for W.E.L. and . . ."

"That's none of their damn business! It was a transaction outside their jurisdiction. There's no law that says we have to disclose our customers to those goddam bureaucrats."

"That might be, Jason, but without their approval, we'll never get the proxy approved." Palmer's tone was apologetic and temporizing.

"What else?" Jason glowered as Marty Darnley brought in their coffee. "What else do the bastards want?"

"They want audited financials, at least through the first quarter, the paperwork on the loans to W.E.L., and the minutes of the directors' meetings, to name a few . . ."

318

"Send that letter off to Elliot Hall, p.d.q. We'll see what he has to say," Jason interrupted.

"What really causes a problem, Jason, is they want all of the details of our big loan from the Pittsburgh pension fund."

"Why is that any big problem?"

"Well, as I told Dan at the time, it's my opinion that loan is in violation of our bond indenture. Frankly, Jason, I can't sign any statements that would support that loan. I simply can't." Beads of perspiration stood out on Palmer's brow.

Jason watched his wilting treasurer with a cool detachment. "John, if that's what's causing you heartburn, Dan or I will handle it."

Palmer groped for words. "I thank you for that, Jason, but there's more to it. I've been worried sick for weeks, and now with this interrogatory, frankly, I'm not up to the job any more. My nerves are shot. It's best for me to resign." As he said it, he drew forth a letter.

Jason decided to play it out in a friendly fashion despite his exasperation and his premonition that Palmer's resignation was only the beginning. "I'm really sorry you've made this decision, John, but I guess you know best. It's sure not the easiest time to make a change, though. Have you any recommendation for your successor?"

"My personal choice would be Vern Francis. As comptroller, he's completely familiar with our computer setup."

Jason knew there was little more to be gained. "Okay. John, I'd be appreciative if you go have a visit with Dan, and you can count on me for the highest recommendation on whatever you try." Jason knew his words were less than the truth, but this was the way the game was played.

Jason's day got no better. He called Oglethorpe and tried for another week on his loan. He explained that he had been away for several days at a directors' meeting in New York. Oglethorpe was very cool. He said he could make no promises, it was now an executive committee matter in the bank.

Dan called to say that he had met with Palmer and agreed that Vernon Francis was the only logical choice, unless they wanted to start all over.

319

Jason phoned his home and learned from Clayton that there had been no calls from Mrs. Steele.

The Steele Company stock got hammered with a late flurry of selling and closed at 7½. This loss of a point and a half on Jason's five million shares cost him another $7,500,000 in net worth for the day.

12

Jason seldom got drunk, and he always confined his philandering to places other than Houston. But when he learned how the stock had closed, he thought, any man who loses $138 million of net worth in less than two months has a right to get drunk, throw a party, do anything he damn pleases, wherever he pleases. He reached for his private phone and set up a small party with Marty Darnley and Betsey Brine in his personal suite in the guest apartments.

He poured down two double sour mashes, and was contemplating the amber warmth of an undiluted third when the hall buzzer called him to the door. He opened it for Betsey Brine, a beautiful blonde of twenty, with sloppy bangs and long smooth hair that flowed down her back. Her smile was half little girl and half lusty nymph. She stepped into the hallway and greeted Jason with a daughterly peck on the cheek as she laughed. "Well, well, the bossman himself. It's been a long, long time." She breezed on ahead of him into the vast living room and plopped her shoulder bag onto the marble mirror stand.

"Pour yourself a drink," Jason suggested.

As she worked about the bar and the icebox beneath, Jason glassily ogled her long brown legs that the purple miniskirt she was wearing set off to perfection. Jason had first seen her waiting on tables at Janice's ski club in Aspen. She was a free spirit who skied the winters in Colorado and sunned away the summers in the surf of California. They had swapped banter after Janice had gone back to the slopes. Later that week, Jason had Bill Leavitt arrange for Betsey Brine to see the world as second stewardess on his jet.

Having made herself a frosty screwdriver, she flopped down in the deep sofa beside him and lightly dropped her hand to his thigh. With her usual air of impertinence, she said, "What's up, boss?"

Jason groaned. "Betsey, my girl, I am depressed, with a capital D. I need some cheering up, real bad, and hoped that you and Marty could do it."

She smiled at him brightly, threw her arms about his neck and gave him a soothing kiss on the cheek with an air of mock sympathy. She purred, "You poor dear." She quickly broke away. "I guess you do need something. I've never heard anyone chew out anybody like you did to poor Mrs. Wales on the phone the other night."

Jason had a dim recollection of a long conversation over the sky phone about a missing deposit slip. He had started his defense with, "Yeah, I had one hell of a day—" when he was interrupted by a second buzzer. He got up with a grunt and went to let in Marty Darnley, bolting and chaining the door behind her.

Marty had come from a long day of stalling off creditors in the reception room of the Steele Tower. She kicked off her shoes with a grateful sigh, and stretched out full length on the sofa opposite Betsey. Jason poured her a brown bomb of bourbon and set it beside her. She took a long sip from her glass, and as she put it back on the coffee table, she said, "Boy, I sure hope those guys of yours get some money together quick. I've never met such unpleasant people."

Jason didn't want to hear about them and said so. He sat down again next to Betsey and cupped her breast in his huge hand. He felt her nipple rise through the thin fabric.

"No, Miss Darnley, our creditors are not my favorite topic of conversation tonight. As a matter of fact, they can all go fuck themselves."

Marty giggled. "Can I tell them that tomorrow? I'm sorry, sir, but Mr. Steele has specifically instructed me to inform you that you are to go fuck yourself."

Jason roared a deep belly laugh, his first in several weeks.

321

He leaned back against the cushions, pulling Betsey toward him. She dropped her head to his lap and started to open his fly.

Jason began to paw her clumsily, trying to loosen her bra. "Here, lover," she said. "You better let me do that." She pushed his hands away and sat up far enough to get out of her blouse and bra. Jason shoved her head downward again. "Keep at your work," he said.

Marty had been eyeing them both for a time with a feigned air of detachment. Then she got up, poured herself a second stiff bourbon and sank down on the other side of Jason. She took his head in her hands and kissed him, a long kiss with her tongue. Jason's response was sluggish.

Marty drew back on her haunches and looked into his eyes, her own face now a mixture of sympathy and sadness. She sighed. "You poor dear, they're really making things tough for you. Do you want to talk about it?" Jason slowly nodded his head. He did want to talk. He wanted very much to talk. He wanted to tell her of his dream of controlling the biggest money empire in the world, and of the people who turned against him. But when he tried to find the words he could not. "I'm too tired," was all he could manage. "Get me another drink."

Betsey, who was getting nowhere, raised her head. "I don't think the boss has it tonight," she murmured to Marty. "I need another drink too." She picked up Jason's empty glass and went to the bar. Coming back to the couch, she too eased out of her blouse and slipped off her skirt, leaving but the briefest of black sheer panties. "Well, we'll give it another try. But time out, you two. This damn couch is too small. Let's go to the bedroom." Marty agreed and got to her feet.

The two girls each took an arm, pulled Jason up and carefully steered him to the supersized bed in the far room. Marty pulled off his shoes and stockings and pants, while Betsey worked off his shirt. Jason's will was with them in their work, but his flesh was not. The bankers and his worries and his wife were in his head and in the room, and, try as the girls did, they could not drive them away. Jason had been economically castrated, and two of the world's beauties could not heal the wound. His fifth drink was his undoing. He slipped off into a sodden slumber.

Betsey was the first to break away from the snores. "It's hopeless," she said with a wry smile. "Forget it, doll, he's long gone."

Marty sighed in agreement as she rose from the bed. "And so much for Jason Steele."

13

Jason woke to a pulsing head and an empty room. The night was a blur. The pent-up ache of his loins was the worst of his woes. He shuffled heavily down the hall to the shattering bright light of the living room, high above the city. He drew the curtains with a groan.

His luck did not improve in the next two weeks. His stock was driven to five dollars, mostly by the sale of his own shares. The United Bank of Boston gave him one more warning on his loan and then unceremoniously sold him out. The forced swallowing of 300,000 shares caused market constipation for several days. Yet surprisingly, brokers still found believers in the stock at the price level of between 4½ and 6.

Although he tried countless times, Jason never could get by the maid in the Carter household. He considered a call to his father-in-law at his office and then thought better of it. Finally, on a Friday afternoon, he ordered his jet into readiness and flew to Boston. A waiting limousine quickly took him to the Carter home where he learned from the startled butler that the Carters, Janice and the children had gone off on a month's cruise to Nova Scotia. He considered following but on more sober thought, gave the idea up. He knew he could spend a year in that country and never find the Carter sloop.

Another blow fell on Monday. Ace Emery was pacing

about in the reception room when Jason arrived. The heap of cigarette butts in the ash tray indicated that he had been waiting for some time.

Jason motioned him into his office. Ace was spluttering, and although it was early in the day, Jason knew he was well into his sauce.

"Those bastards, those lousy bastards!" was Ace's reply in greeting.

"Who and what now?" Jason slumped into his chair.

"The bastards have withdrawn our registration statement."

"Goddam it, Ace! Make sense!"

Ace tried to pull himself together and finally poured out a semicoherent tale of how Western Investors had sent to the S.E.C. a perfectly routine quarterly report that would keep the current prospectus legal for the sale of funds by the company. The S.E.C. had replied with a detailed interrogatory that had arrived that morning, and had withdrawn the effectiveness of the current prospectus until their interrogatory was answered. What it meant was that the selling legions of the Ace were brought to a screeching halt, and Jason's last free property of any consequence was virtually valueless until this ban was lifted.

As with an hourglass drawing down to the precious few, the sands of Jason's were running out faster and faster. The payment of current bills and payroll drew drumhead tight. Irate creditors invaded the company offices although few ever got through the outer office janissaries. It was impossible now for Jason to adjust to the reality of his position. Abetted by Ace Emery, he spent his time dreaming up new funds so that a harried Dan Bacon had to step into the breech. Dan began to sell off the empire's best producing properties. Their values under pressured sale shrank.

Despite a paucity of cash purchasers, Dan proved a master in adversity. He faced daily threats of bankruptcy without batting an eye and he soon had the creditors working for him. He drew up a plan of the company's producing wells, how the monies would be allocated amongst the pressing debts, and what would be sold. Once he got the major creditors to agree to his plan, the smaller people saw that a forced bankruptcy was to their disadvantage as long as a breath of life remained in the corporate shell. No one could really believe that such a colossus had been brought to such a humbling halt in such a short time, and many convinced themselves that the cash drain was only temporary; that Steele Minerals would soon be up on the top again.

Permission of the board of directors was needed before Dan could put his creditors' battle plan into effect but Jason refused to call them together. He said he didn't want to see them so soon again. The first serious fight the two men had had in eight years was the result. Dan, disgusted with Jason's refusal to face the facts, finally sent telegrams in Jason's name calling for a meeting of the board.

On the eve of the emergency meeting of the board, the most formidable opponent of them all had come onto the field against Jason. Before, the Securities and Exchange Commission had slapped a selling ban on his fund companies, and had followed it up immediately with a cease-and-desist action in the federal courts. Jason had quickly counterattacked with a platoon of his own lawyers. The day before the emergency meeting, a phalanx of investigators from the Internal Revenue Service had marched into the fund management offices and asked for the books as they had a perfect right to ask. The management company was the general partner for thousands of investors throughout the nation who had sought tax shelter in oil. An empire based on tax shelter for the masses was bound to suffer the slings and arrows of bureaucratic retribution. No government can survive if the tax avoidance of the few is packaged and brought to the many. Jason had counted on the sinew of his strings in Washington but his failure before the Securities and Exchange Commission showed the flaw in his defense. The bureaucrats of the Tax Service with their instinct for survival came marching through the same gap.

When Dan casually suggested they have dinner that night with Michael Collins and Stanton Harris, Jason did not immediately respond. He said he'd let Dan know by mid-afternoon. Jason had no great desire to join Collins and Harris in a social setting. The morrow's meeting would be awkward enough. But the investigation by the special agents of the I.R.S. had shaken him more than he let on—that and his new loneliness. With no further thought, he flicked on the intercom and accepted.

Jason had no reason to suspect Dan's motives. For more than eight years, he and Dan had been the top team in natural resources. Jason as the field marshal and Bacon as the front-line commander had offset each other in their strengths and their weaknesses. Their success had been the talk of Wall Street. In all those years, Dan had never questioned his field marshal and as far as Jason was concerned, nothing had occurred that could change that relationship.

Dan had always been comfortable in his position, content to leave the limelight to Jason. But Jason's frantic phone calls from Lausanne had sown the first seeds of doubts. He had protested and pointed out what the loans could do to the company, yet he eventually did as he was told. Jason owned the golden handcuffs about his wrists, handcuffs that had been forged from smaller threads over a long time: Cash loans to meet Lilly's extravagant whims; aircraft leases to avoid taxation, leases for which he put up no cash because Jason had arranged the financing; stock options that would please a prince. The threads grew thicker when luncheon clubs, country clubs, personal planes and other whims were added. By the time he was forty, Dan Bacon was living the life of a president in any of the Standard Oil companies, something he could not have hoped to achieve at another company for another twenty years.

Dan, for his part, had been torn in his loyalties since he had taken Collins' call earlier that week. The imperious phone calls from Lausanne still stung. Still, he knew his own success had hinged on Jason. And in the middle of his mind was the sure knowledge that something drastic must be done to restore Steele Minerals confidence in the street. Despite his certainty, Dan could not bring himself to strike the first blow.

Jason arrived at the restaurant fifteen minutes after the appointed time. Collins had engaged a private dining room and he, Dan and Stanton Harris were waiting. Their greetings were restrained and after Jason had ordered a drink, Collins came right to the point.

"Jason, we'd like a report on how you are doing on putting up the collateral on the fifteen million." Collins, who already

326

knew from Dan that Jason had done nothing since the last meeting, eyed him steadily while he waited for an answer.

"I'm working on it, Mike," Jason replied. "I never had so many things go so wrong all at once. Janice is off with the kids cruising with her family. When she gets back, we'll put up some marketable securities and get it taken care of. Frankly, I need her signature on some of the stock powers."

Stanton Harris, looking very prim and proper, peered over his half-rimmed glasses. "Jason, this is a very serious matter and can't wait on your wife's whims to go cruising. This company belongs to the shareholders, not the needs and personal desires of any one man. I have gone over this activity of yours with my own attorneys and I'm informed that as the director of a publicly owned company, I can be held individually and personally liable for that money. There is a definite obligation to see to the stockholders' interests. Now this is going to be met by tomorrow or I simply must resign from your board, and I will not hesitate to publicly state my reasons for the resignation."

"And I will do the same," Collins said.

Looking for moral support, Jason turned to Dan, but none was forthcoming. Dan's eyes were riveted to the tablecloth. Jason turned back to face the other two. "Damn it! I need more time. Janice will be back in another week."

"That's a risk I cannot afford to take," Harris said glacially.

Jason pushed back his chair and jumped to his feet. "Just what in hell do you want me to do? I've said that I'd guarantee that loan, even though I don't think I should."

"But you haven't and that was seven weeks ago," was Collins' retort.

"The company faces an intolerable cash crisis, as far as I can learn," Harris added.

Jason leaned on Dan's chair. "And what do you have to say about this, Dan?"

Dan did not look up as he answered. "I'll do whatever you and the board want me to."

Jason's head swiveled back to face Collins. "And what does the board want?"

327

Collins looked him straight in the eye. "Your resignation as chairman and chief operating officer."

"And I'll see you in hell," Jason shouted, and he slammed out of the room.

Later that night, Jason called Dan at home. Without the slightest note of humility or repentance in his voice, he asked, "Just what does Collins think he's doing?"

"Jason, you heard him. They want the collateral or your head."

There was a moment's pause and then Jason said, "My resigning won't accomplish anything. The way I got it figured, with Higby still abroad, Coons out, and Palmer replaced by Vern Francis, we're one vote up on them."

"If you're going to play it hard ball, that's true, Jason. But I can't seem to get across to you just what a crack we're in. We're desperate for cash. The only way I've kept these creditor vultures off our back so far is with this payment plan of selling off our assets in an orderly fashion. But we need the board. Otherwise, it's Chapter Eleven in the bankruptcy court. You must see this."

"I don't see what that has to do with my resignation. We can vote the authority for sale with or without those outside bastards. What's the difference?"

"It's going to look one hell of a lot better if the whole board goes along on this selling."

"Hell, Dan, this 'looks' thing isn't worth chasing any more. Of course, I know we're in a crack. But if they force me off the board, it's not going to get any better. All I need is time and a base to get things turned around. So we sell off some things for some cash."

"What about Higby, though? The board has made their approval conditional on your collateral. If he doesn't go along with us on that executive committee vote, now where the hell are we?"

"I'll straighten out Higby one way or another. Which way you are going to play it is more important."

"Jesus, Jason, you just haven't been listening to me," Dan said with anguish. "Unless we have cash now, we'll be in the bankruptcy court."

328

"Look, my friend," Jason replied icily, "I'm not going to fuck around with those guys any further. I'm not resigning and I'll get to that collateral thing when I can. My back's to the wall and we both know it. But you and Foxx are going to be with me all the way. Otherwise, the board will become aware of some of our little partnerships. You get the word to Foxx." The line went dead.

The board of directors of Steele Minerals never did take up the matter that prompted the meeting. As soon as Jason called the session to order, Michael Collins asked if the collateral guarantees had been accomplished. Dan said they had not been. Stanton Harris then demanded to know when they would be. Jason's answer was vague—he needed his wife's signature on some stock powers and she was still away on a cruise.

Collins then abruptly proposed that Jason resign as both board chairman and chief operating officer. The motion was seconded by Stanton Harris. It was defeated five to four with Jason casting the winning vote.

Harris thereupon rose to his feet. He said he would no longer serve on the board and he handed Elliot Hall a written resignation. Michael Collins was less polite. The Lausanne affair amounted to out and out theft, he said, and if the board would not take the proper steps to protect the interests of the shareholders, they could all go to jail. As he spoke, he glared at Dan, who had called him that morning to tell him he had to stick with Jason. He had offered no explanation. Collins had known then the outcome of the meeting. He concluded his remarks with the statement that he was going to notify the appropriate federal authorities immediately. With that, the four outside directors left the room.

As the door closed, the eyes of the assembled Steele Company officers turned for reassurance to their chairman. But Jason, toying with a pencil and a pad of paper, offered none. Excusing himself, he said he would try and talk sense to those that had left. After he had gone, there was dead silence. Finally, Dan turned to Elliot Hall and said, "Well, Elliot. Are we still a board?"

329

"Yes, Dan, you're still a board. The majority of those that are left have every right to replace those that have resigned until the next stockholders' meeting."

"Then I can get some authorizations to sell off some of our stuff and it'll stand up as far as the buyer is concerned?"

"That's right, Dan." His words were more a sigh than a statement. In his thirty-five-year practice of corporate law, Elliot Hall had never encountered such a morning. Father and mentor that he had been to Jason Steele, Elliot knew that the four who left the room were powerful men. They would be heard from.

Dan then got the meeting down to business as if nothing had happened. "All right," he said. "The general counsel says we are legit. I need a motion to enter a sales assignment plan with our creditors to keep them off our back. I also need authority to sell off some fifteen million of our properties at my discretion. Here's a list of what I'm thinking of putting up. The best thing we have going is that Greenland play, so I guess I'll be selling that first."

Vernon Francis, the new treasurer, unwisely interrupted. "Dan, what was Mr. Collins saying about collateral and jail? I don't think I really . . ."

"Forget about that. What is important now is to give me some sales authority. If we don't get going, somebody is going to take us to bankruptcy court, whether we like it or not. Do you like your job, Vern?"

The new Steele Minerals board gave Daniel Bacon all the authority he needed and the selling of the Steele empire swung into high gear.

14

"Mr. Steele, Mr. Lawrence Carter's on the line." The voice of Elizabeth Wales broke in on a conference between Jason and Elliot Hall. Elliot rose to leave, knowing full well

that a call from Lawrence Carter was not an everyday occurrence, but Jason indicated he should stay. With a flick of the
switch, he told Elizabeth to transfer the call to a smaller office
close by.

As he picked up the phone, the nasal Yankee tones were
unmistakable.

"Jason, we've just come back from down East. Janice is
well aware of your phone calls."

"Well I'm glad you're back, Mr. Carter. I want to straighten
things out."

"I don't normally get involved in the affairs of my children. They are old enough to stand on their own. In this
instance, though, I felt it right that someone speak with you.
I hate to be the bearer of bad tidings, but Janice has no intention of returning your calls."

"Mr. Carter, if I could talk to her, just once . . ." The
plaintive note in his voice did not escape Lawrence Carter.

"I'm afraid it is too late for that, Jason. Janice has asked
me to tell you that any and all future communication must
come through Standish and Adams, our family lawyers."

There was a long moment of silence that said everything.
Lawrence Carter continued. "I'm sure you know Charlie Standish. Getting in touch with him should be no problem."

"I wish there were some other way."

"Well, I'm certain she's made up her mind. I am truly
sorry for your troubles. Good-bye, Jason."

"Good-bye, Mr. Carter."

15

In the succeeding three months, the storm swirling
about the Steele Tower gained strength each day. The pressure
continued on the stock, driving it down below five on several
days. In August, Jason and Dan issued an extremely optimistic
quarterly report which stated that Steele Minerals would exceed

the earnings of the previous year. That same week, Jason and Elliot received copies of a letter from Michael Collins to the Securities and Exchange Commission setting forth in detail the background that prompted his resignation from the board.

None of this came as a surprise to Jason, for he had been well briefed by Elliot on the legal actions that he might expect. There was no way that he could defend himself on the monies he'd ordered into the trusts unless he made some step toward collateralizing the company. Finally, one morning Jason went to the family safe in his home and withdrew the stock certificates that he held in joint name with Janice. At her writing desk, and with three of her cancelled personal checks before him, he practiced her signature for over an hour. He then executed the necessary stock powers. The next day he delivered the Prescott Company and Western Investors shares to the Steele Company treasurer as his first step in making up the collateral required by the previous board. He also sold some Steele Mineral shares through a broker who asked few questions. He now had sufficient cash to meet his most pressing personal obligations.

Next, he called another board meeting which he attended but did not conduct. Dan assumed the chair and made a motion to amend the resolution of the previous board which had required of Jason over eighteen million dollars of free and marketable securities as collateral for the loans to the Children's Trust. These securities could be legally sold at any time within governmental regulations. Instead, the board was asked to accept eight million dollars of Prescott stock and eight hundred thousand shares of Western Investors stock as full and adequate collateral within the intent of the previous board. The eight million dollars' worth of Prescott stock were free and marketable. The eight hundred thousand shares of Western Investors were not. Not only were they not marketable and highly suspect as to value as long as the S.E.C. selling ban stood, but further, they only represented twenty-five percent of the outstanding shares of the company. Jason had persuaded Dan that he needed reserve ammunition in the event of further attacks. Dan's motion to the new board gave a theoretical forty-million-dollar value to Western Investors as a whole. At this bold-faced contradiction of the resolves of the previous board, there were murmurs of dissent from Vernon Francis and the operating vice-president who ran the Pacific division of Steele Minerals. The latter, an elderly man with forty years around the rigs, went so far as to comment on the offered eight hundred thousand shares of Western Investors. "Why hell, Dan. They've got about the value of eight hundred thousand used Bull Durham wrappers." Nevertheless, the motion was carried, after Dan spoke again about bankruptcy court, by a vote of five to one. It now looked on the records as if Jason Steele had gone to Lausanne for the benefit of the Steele Minerals shareholders. Any correspondence that could prove awkward was adjusted or rewritten to reflect that the transactions had been made in the Steele Company name.

There still remained one flaw in Jason's defenses. He knew that no matter how well he covered his tracks through votes of this board, there remained Henry Higby. If it came to litigations, he knew Higby would testify that as a member of the executive committee, he never gave Jason permission to make the World Equities move. In that event, the legitimacy of Jason's move was conditional upon his compliance with the Collins resolution concerning his resignation, made at the New York meeting. With Janice's trust fund now out of reach, there was no way he could fully meet the terms imposed by the board. Jason toyed with the idea of arranging for Higby's disappearance on his return voyage from Europe. From his old days on Beacon Hill, Jason still had the connections for letting such a "contract." He turned this over in his mind for several weeks, but all the while he really knew he couldn't take such a step, even to save his empire and himself.

16

In early October, Dan brought Steele Minerals through the eye of the financial hurricane. He successfully sold the Greenland exploratory permits to a French oil company which took over all of the operation, including the rigs. The board of World Equities decided to hold their remaining acres and to drill their committed wells in partnership with the French. The Greenland sale produced fourteen millions of cash, almost enough to hold the trade creditors and banks and the bondholders and the pension funds at bay, at least for a time.

While Jason was occupied with the internal affairs of Western Investors, Dan took full command of the Steele Company. He tried his best to trim sail for the second half of the storm he knew must come. For a company so big and so committed, this was not easy. Despite Jason's promises to the contrary, over one thousand employees were laid off that summer. Marty Darnley and Betsey Brine were among the first to go.

The sumptuous penthouse in New York had been repossessed for nonpayment in September, and when the company fell behind on the lease payments of its aircraft fleet, the banks holding the paper now took no chances. As each plane fell in arrears, the fleet was steadily reduced until only one small Lear jet was left for Jason's use.

Jason's house and ranch were now attached by an Oklahoma bank that had lent him money on W.E.L. stock. This didn't worry him, for this property was in joint name with Janice, and the bank would be a long time getting it. He had no sympathy for his creditors. They were in the money business and risk was a commodity of their trade.

It was from the bank quadrant that the storm next hit. With little warning, the Securities and Exchange Commission launched a suit in the federal court in Houston, accusing Dan and Jason of selling unregistered stock. Through Elliot Hall, they argued back that it was the banks that had sold the stock, not they. By selling out their holdings, they said, the banks had taken a beneficial interest in the stock. The court, however, did not accept this theory and granted the S.E.C.'s motion for a thorough investigation of Steele Minerals. A squad of investigators and accountants occupied the Steele Minerals offices that very afternoon.

Elliot Hall was not so certain that the government wouldn't break through Jason's cover-up of his Lausanne ne-

334

gotiations. He had brought a squad of attorneys to Houston in an effort to cover all the flanks where Jason might be vulnerable. The most obvious flank was Western Investors, where several irate limited partners in the funds whose investments were no longer redeemable were already starting "class action" suits. Several banks who had lent money for well-completion equipment stepped in with liens, asserting their loans had precedence over the production runs of the investor partners. The adverse interests in this litigation were so numerous that the litigation would be in the courts for years.

Elliot worked hardest on trying to lift the government's selling ban on the funds of Western Investors. If these could be freed up, then the "class action" suits might fade away, and Jason might be able to turn the inherent value on that company's net profits interest in the two hundred millions drilled by the public into cash. This could just save him. Elliot was convinced that the ban would never hold up in the courts. The Houston newspapers and the national financial journals had a field day. Stories of the jets, the apartments, and the New York penthouse that cost the company $120,000 per year, and Jason's habit of paying more than $20,000 a month of various traveling expenses in cash and never filing very elaborate records with the company appeared regularly. As a result, a full-scale investigation of Jason Steele and Steele Minerals by the special agents of the Internal Revenue Service was launched.

In early November, after a particularly grueling session with the investigation team, Jason said goodnight to Elliot Hall and got off his private elevator at the garage level of the Steele Towers. He was tired and he wanted to go home. Only Clayton was left at the mansion, for the S.E.C. investigators had learned that the rest of the household staff were on the company payroll. As he came up to his Cadillac and slid the key in the door, someone quietly tapped him on the shoulder. Jason whirled around to confront a stranger.

"Mr. Steele, United States marshal." The man deftly flipped open a set of credentials. Jason paid them scant attention. When his throat loosened, he asked, "What do you want?"

"I want you to come with me. You're under arrest." The man nodded toward a waiting black sedan and another marshal.

335

"Arrest! For what? Do you know who I am?"

"Oh, yes, Mr. Steele, I know. The warrant reads grand larceny, using the mails to defraud, embezzlement from an employee benefit plan and plain embezzlement." The marshal handed the warrant to Jason. As he held it high in the dim light to make out the words, the marshal slapped handcuffs on him. "You'll have plenty of time to read. Are you coming peacefully?" And he steered Jason toward the sedan before he could answer.

Two hours later, Jason, accompanied by Elliot Hall, was brought before the United States commissioner. Livid, Jason bellowed that he was not guilty. The commissioner glanced over his steel-rimmed glasses for an appraising moment, and then coolly went back to his papers. Bail was set at $50,000. As the banks were close, it took Elliot an hour to arrange for a bail bond.

Jason spent that hour in the detention section of the courthouse cellar. The clang of the cell doors ringing through the tiled corridors was a reality that Jason Steele had never faced. He felt that he had met the ultimate in ignominy when two unwashed draft evaders with love beads and beards were unceremoniously dumped on the bench beside him.

But he had not yet met the ultimate. After the proper surety had been delivered to the clerk, the arresting marshal again tapped him on the shoulder.

"Mr. Steele, one more formality." He indicated a door in the far corner of the clerk's office. Jason trailed him to a brightly lit room, where he was hustled before a huge camera and a numbered placard was placed in his hands.

Afterward, the cameraman took Jason to a nearby counter and deftly rolled out a set of fingerprints on a blocked-off form. As Jason was rubbing away the oily ink with paper towels, the camera equipment groaned and clunked. The cameraman came back and he held up a colored mug shot with the ominous numbers across the bottom. As he did, he laughed.

"A mighty fine likeness, Mr. Steele, don't you think?"

Jason Steele retched, a long splattering retch, all over the waxed tiles.

336

Epilogue

The bright glare of the March morning hit him as he stepped from his hotel and brought a sharp pain between his eyes. Jason hurriedly put on his sunglasses. It was a beautiful day, the kind of weather that had been the joy of his youth. Winter was not yet off the field, for there were still sullen gray heaps of snow in the deep shadows of the buildings, and an occasional blast of cold from the north cut through his light topcoat. But it was a day that spoke of spring, with an occasional puff of the south wind. It took Jason back to the days of fishing with his father.

When Jason's trial had been moved to Portland, Maine, Benjamin Steele had been the only person to appear and offer him moral support. Their meeting had been awkward, for there had been little to say. His father was now in his mid-sixties. He still worked his seines each day, though he now had two young helpers. As often as he could, he made the long drive from Manchester to sit in the crowded court room and listen to things he did not understand.

As Jason set off on the ten-minute walk to the federal courthouse, his stride was no longer that of the jaunty mineral entrepreneur. Although the case for the defense might open that

339

day, he had little reason to hurry. For the past fifteen days, as the government prosecuted its case, he had walked this route. Often he idly window shopped along the way and observed the people around him and he sometimes found himself wondering if these Maine people, with their conspicuously slower way of doing things, didn't have the right answer after all. Maybe in his drive for the world's financial fleece, he had been chasing something that could never be his.

Still, even now, he had no regrets although his empire was in smoldering ruins. The government attorneys and the bank trustees for the bondholders had forced involuntary bankruptcy on Steele Minerals and his other companies. But Jason's fortune had been made in wildcatting and promotion. He understood risk, and he had arrogantly played on his luck. He still considered his play for World Equities his guttsiest play. In the last analysis, the loss was unimportant. That he had made the try was all that mattered, and he could accept his financial failure.

What was far more difficult to accept, however, was prosecution as a common criminal. Even after his indictment for embezzlement of company funds and the indictment of Dan Bacon that followed, he couldn't really comprehend what was happening to him. In his wildest battle defenses, he had never expected criminal complaints.

The initial trial had been brought in the United States District Court in Houston. As an opening ploy and with little hope of success, Steele and Bacon's lawyers had brought a motion for a change of venue, claiming that media publicity had been so intense and adverse to the interests of their clients that there was little hope of a fair trial in Houston. To everyone's surprise, the judge granted the motion and the trial was moved to Maine, the corporate home of Steele Minerals. The Maine federal court had the shortest docket in the nation. As a result, the Steele-Bacon trial had begun right on schedule in mid-February. The federal prosecution rested heavily on the testimony of Henry Higby, who was adamant that he had never approved the World Equities loan nor the Children's Trust purchases. Jason had hoped to rebut this with Elliot Hall's

340

testimony but this hope was short-lived. On the third day of trial, with Higby still on the stand, Elliot pitched forward at the defense desk and slumped to the floor. He died that night in the Maine Medical Center of a cerebral hemorrhage. The trial was postponed for four days.

When Higby retook the stand, his testimony was deadly. He was a faithful diary keeper, so Jason's phone call from Washington and his own dated comments were a matter of record in a small leather-bound volume. The government next placed expert accountants on the stand. They traced the flow of $400,000 of the employee pension fund monies through the Steele Company books directly into the Children's Trust in Curaçao. The ledger books, the cables, and the calendar backed this up. At this point, Dan Bacon switched his plea to guilty. His testimony was now expected to close the government's case.

Elliot's death and Dan's decision had been terrible blows to Jason. He was left with no choice but to face what had actually been apparent for some time: His days in the sunlight were numbered. For a man who had always had the freedom to indulge his every will and whim, the thought was intolerable.

The ultimate irony was that while the weeks dragged on and Jason, immobilized by the charges hanging over him, awaited his fate, developments in the financial world of which he had been such a part were moving rapidly. But this time Jason had no piece of the action. He could do nothing but stand on the sidelines and watch.

In late January, the French company which had taken over the Steele Minerals leases in Greenland announced a fifteen-hundred-barrel a day discovery on the very first hole. On this news, the stock of World Equities soared back through fifteen dollars a share. Jason learned that Lord Gordon-Gorham had come to terms with the House of de Fonderville, which had assumed total control of the management company for the funds; Lord Gordon-Gorham had been retained as board chairman, the Baron de Fonderville became chairman of the executive committee, and most galling of all, Edward Leibowitz was elected president and chief operating officer. Manny Kellermann had finally been forced to resign. The tide of fund redemptions had been stemmed. With the Greenland discovery, the sales of World Equities regained some of their former momentum. This was no help to Jason or his companies. The trustee in bankruptcy had sold off the W.E.L. shares that had come out of the trust. But the Greenland discovery pleased Jason nonetheless. It proved he had been right. There was oil under Manny's "moose pasture."

Not very long afterward, Jason read in the paper that Manny Kellermann had formed a new company to develop condominiums in Majorca. This news triggered the Jason of old. If Kellermann could come back, why couldn't he? And for a while, Jason's evenings were spent in a burst of feverish activity. He contentedly scribbled outlines for new funds. If he could make the right deal with one of these Maine paper companies, why, with their land and his selling, he knew he could build the megalopolis right on up to the Canadian border. A leveraged land would be his return.

As Jason turned that morning on to the broad pavestoned pavilion that led up to the solid granite steps of the old federal courthouse, the usual host of reporters and television crews were waiting. *The United States vs. Steele* was the biggest case that Maine had ever seen. Jason hunched forward in his top-coat, leaning into imagined winds as he went up the steps. Suddenly someone tapped him on the shoulder. He spun angrily, expecting another persistent reporter, to meet a uniformed Cumberland County sheriff, a gaunt man with a face of flint. "Mr. Steele, Sheriff Hiram Stoddard. I must serve you these papers." The man slapped an envelope in Jason's hands and turned down the steps. The cameras whirred.

Without looking at the papers, Jason went on into the courthouse. From his lawyer, he learned that the switch by Bacon was expected to cause a day or two of pleadings on admissible evidence and motions for a mistrial. Jason asked if he would be needed that day and was told he would not.

As he walked down the steps, the sun was bright. The reporters eyed him with professional detachment but they had long ago given up any attempts at interviews. Jason was too well counseled.

342

He went across to an empty bench in the park opposite where he opened the envelope. The last thread snapped. *Steele vs. Steele,* it said. Janice was claiming residence at the family summer home in North Haven and was suing for divorce. It would be far quicker for the Carters than any action in Texas or Massachusetts.

Jason shrugged, shoved the papers into his pocket and looked across at the solid granite mass of the courthouse. He knew he would soon face another granite mass—with bars. It was only a matter of time. Then, with something of the purposeful Jason of old, he returned to his hotel. He took his rental car and headed north along the winding shore route.

Jason pushed the Chevrolet to its limit and drew up to the Rockland ferry with half an hour until the noon boat. He remembered a small hunting store a block away. He strode up the hill and entered the store. As the tinkling bell on the door subsided, Jason, for the first time, considered the slim state of his wallet. There were only seven tens in it. The proprietor, a shriveled old man in a red checkered shirt, came from the back room. "Ayup?"

Jason affected a casual, offhand manner. Slowly he looked about the glass cases. "Thought I might do some target shootin'." He paused by a case full of pistols and revolvers. "You got maybe a long-barreled .38?"

"Ayah." The old man moved to a case and unlocked it. He drew out a blue-black revolver. "Here's what'cha lookin' for. Brand new Smith and Wesson. Eighty-four dollahs plus tax."

Jason hefted the weapon for a moment. "Nice feel. Weren't thinkin' of going that deep though. Maybe you have something secondhand. Down round thirty dollars."

"Not long-barreled .38, I don't." The man put it back with a put-upon sigh. He shuffled to another case in the bar corner of the store. "Got heah an old 'Detective Special.'" He appraised Steele coldly. "Three-inch barrel though. Won't be much good for target shootin'. Twenty-nine, ninety-five plus tax, of course."

Jason snapped open the chamber and sited the bore. "Oh,

343

I don't know," he said. "Might have some fun with this. And a box of shells." As Jason reached for his wallet, he had a second thought. "You take credit cards?"

"Nope. Just cash."

Jason passed over four tens. The man eyed him for another moment and then turned toward the cash register.

Jason was one of three persons on the ferry. The warm wind of Portland had not come up to Penobscot Bay. A chilled nor'wester rolled across the blue-green waters snapping the crests into crisp white caps. Jason huddled from the wind in the sunny lee of the upper deckhouse. As the ferry cleared the Rockland breakwater, she overtook close aboard a rusty coastal dragger. The fishing boat turned into the ferry's wake to avoid the long bobble of the quarter wave and then chugged on at her own measured pace. Clear of the point at Owl's Head, the vessels parted, the dragger turning south to the open sea. Jason watched the fishing boat till she was a black speck on the southern horizon. He thought of his father and of his own boyhood, the orderly world of work and reward and cash on the barrelhead. With a wry shrug, he turned to look at the blue hills of Camden as the ferry made the sweeping turn into the thoroughfare that split North Haven Island. There were a few people down to meet the boat. Jason knew no one.

He set off down the west road, a road he knew well from the early summers of his marriage. The last of winter was still on the island. His shined shoes were soon sodden with mud and slush. In less than an hour, he came to the Carter summer house. For a long time, he sat on the porch stairs in the warm sunlight and watched the gulls wheel about in the wind. As he studied their effortless soarings, his thoughts returned to reality. The whirling freedom of the gulls could be his, should be his. He put the pistol back in his pocket, left the box of shells on the steps, and headed toward the ferry landing.

When he got back to Portland, he phoned his lawyer and learned that the judge had called another day's recess to further study pleadings. Jason's second call was to the Portland Air Charter Company. After many rings, he got an answer.

"Ayup, Portland Air."

"Good evening," Jason said. "I'd like to charter an Aero Commander for a trip to Halifax in the morning."

"Ain't got one."

"Have you got any other light twin? Over-water equipped."

"Ayup. Got a twin Beech. We ain't got a pilot free, though."

"Oh, that's okay. I've got my license and my logs with me. Must have close to five hundred hours in the Beech . . ."

Two mornings later, Janice Steele, at her farm in Essex, met the following thick headline on her breakfast table.

"MINERALS MAGNATE MISSING

"(A.P.) Halifax, Nova Scotia. The wreckage of a small twin-engined aircraft, chartered and flown by Jason Steele, embattled chairman of Steele Minerals Company, was discovered yesterday afternoon in the surf off Cape Sable by the Canadian Air Sea Rescue Service. The aircraft was on a flight plan to Halifax yesterday morning and was declared missing by Canadian authorities after failing to make a routine report at the intersection of the coast. Investigators of the Canadian Service reached the scene by late afternoon and at low tide found neither Steele's body nor the craft's survival equipment in the wreckage . . ."